EXILES

EXILES

THREE SHORT NOVELS

PHILIP CAPUTO

Alfred A. Knopf   New York   1997

THIS IS A BORZOI BOOK
PUBLISHED BY ALFRED A. KNOPF, INC.

http://www.randomhouse.com/

Library of Congress Cataloging-in-Publication Data
Caputo, Philip.
Exiles : three short novels / by Philip Caputo. — 1st ed.
p   cm.
ISBN 0-679-45038-6 (hardcover : alk. paper)
I. Title.
PS3553.A625E9   1997
813'.54—dc21   96-44459
CIP

Manufactured in the United States of America
First Edition

For Patty and Harold

And with thanks to John Ware,
who left the barbershop one day
with a tale to tell

CONTENTS

STANDING IN

I

THAT NIGHT, somewhere in Georgia or South Carolina, he became a boy again and went to confession in the parish church where he'd been baptized. He was waiting in line with other sinners, young and old, while high on the wall above the side door, sunlight bright as hope itself fell in multicolored dowels through a round window with stained-glass panels arranged like spokes in a wheel. Vigil candles sputtered near the altar in ruby-red mantles. Otherwise, the church was dark. The church usually spooked Dante when its lights were off, its shadowy alcoves suggesting occult mysteries and secret condemnations, but this time he found the dimness restful. It was good to be in a familiar place among familiar faces; he was filled with a sense of belonging as serene and solid as the soaring stone pillars and the thick granite walls across which, in marble friezes, Christ walked the stations of his passion. One by one, the people in front of Dante entered the confessional, then knelt in the pews to say their penances, foreheads pressed to folded hands. Finally, his turn came. He stepped into the box, its air stale and dull, as if it held a memory of the dull sins confessed within it over and over, the stale absolutions granted. He could not see anything except the translucent screen that framed Father Talley's silhouette. Crossing himself, Dante went to his knees and caught the scent of Father Talley's aftershave—English

Leather. "Bless me, Father, for I have sinned," he said, and suddenly everything went out from under him—the kneeler, the floor, the earth itself. He was plunging down a bottomless pit, faster and faster, his happiness sucked out of him instantly, replaced by a vertiginous terror as he plummeted, the wind of his passage roaring in his ears.

He woke dangling upside down, like a sleeping bat, in an enclosure as dark and almost as small as the confessional. He heard a drawn-out screech; a foul smell rose into his nostrils. Then, the fog of sleep lifting from his brain, he realized that the screeching was the Silver Meteor's wheels, shrilling on the rails as the train came to a sudden stop in the middle of the night. The violence of the deceleration had almost thrown him out of his upper berth; his legs and feet were tangled in the bedsheets, which were all that had stopped him from falling headfirst into the toilet. Twisting sideways, he reached up with one hand, grasped the sideboard of the berth, and pulled himself back into bed. He lay breathless for a few moments. The terror soon passed, and grief came in its place—the same grief that had ridden with him to the train station, that had sat beside him at dinner in the dining car and finally crawled into bed with him, clutching him as he'd fallen asleep. It had let him go while he dreamed and, like a lover sure of its claim on his heart, waited as he flirted with rival emotions, patiently waited for the dalliances to end and the chance to embrace him again.

Voices began speaking: a man and a woman. They sounded as if they were talking to a conductor. Had there been an accident? the woman asked. And then the man: Should they get dressed in case they had to evacuate? Dante swung out of bed, switched on the light, and raised the window to look up and down the tracks. All he saw were the lights from other windows planing across the gravel roadbed. A woods lay beyond, the trees ranked so thick in the blackness that he would have thought the train was stuck in a tunnel if it weren't for the scent of wet earth and pine and flowering dogwood. All right, they were in the middle of a woods, but where? The Silver Meteor had pulled out of Miami at a little past two in the afternoon, and it was now half past twelve in the morning. Ten hours at an average speed of, say, sixty miles an hour would put it in Georgia for sure, maybe in South Carolina.

He got into his jeans and stepped barefoot into the aisle, where he saw that the man and the woman were questioning not a conductor but themselves. The aisle was crowded with a dozen other passengers, milling in confusion. Dante grew worried: the train was scheduled to pull into Penn Station at four this afternoon. He would then have to take a subway to Grand Central, then Metro North to Norwalk. If the train was stalled here for only an hour, he would be late.

Looking for a porter or conductor, he went into the car ahead, a deluxe sleeper, with recessed lights glowing softly on walls covered in a grainy beige upholstery. It didn't have the glamour of the bygone passenger trains he had seen on the American Movie Classics channel, speeding in black and white across his grandfather's America, but it made his car seem as shabby and harshly lit as a midnight subway car. The passengers were awake—he could hear them speaking quietly behind their closed compartment doors—but they hadn't come out to stand around, nervous and flustered, or to go hunting for a conductor. Maybe they who could afford deluxe tickets expected someone to come to them and explain what was going on. Maybe they thought nothing bad could happen to them. Dante hoped that was true, because then nothing bad would happen to the rest of the train they were connected to, and the Silver Meteor would get moving again and bring him home on time. He walked down the deserted aisle almost with an intruder's wary tread, half expecting someone to tell him, shirtless and shoeless as he was, to get back where he belonged. He felt a hundred old resentments, imagining that his grief would not clutch him so ferociously if he were in these accommodations; like most people without money, Dante suspected that it *did* buy happiness, or at least the tools to blunt life's sharper edges.

In the dark passageway between the sleeper and the dining car, a woman stood at the bottom of the boarding stairs, smoking. Dante would not have noticed her there, three feet below, if he hadn't caught the quick furtive movement of her hand as she hid the cigarette behind her back, like a schoolgirl caught sneaking a drag in the hall.

"Oh, you're one of *us*," she said, in an accent that sounded almost British. She gave a short, husky laugh and brought the cigarette to her lips.

"Us who?" Dante, holding the handle of the dining car door, looked down. The woman's hair cascaded over her shoulders in pale waves, but he couldn't tell its color. She was in a bathrobe, tightly cinched around a waist slender as a young woman's. But her voice wasn't young.

"One of us passengers as opposed to crew," she answered. "An authority figure. An enforcer of rules. They don't allow smoking even on Amtrak anymore. So now the only good thing about riding these trains is gone, thanks to the health Nazis."

"Yeah, guess so. I don't smoke."

"Good for you," she said approvingly, yet with a seasoning of sarcasm, and then she inhaled, the ash's flare revealing a square chin and a wide, slender mouth with two deep lines at each corner, like parentheses. His mother's age, Dante guessed, still unable to think of his mother in the past tense. "If you're looking for someone to tell you why we're sitting here in the middle of nowhere, don't bother."

"Nobody knows?"

"Some fellow in a blue uniform told me something about a malfunctioning blocking signal, whatever that means."

"A blocking signal is like a traffic light. Like a traffic signal for trains."

"Are you a train buff? Or are you just afraid of planes?"

"No. I—"

"I'm old enough to remember when train travel had some style, when the trains had the stuff to go with their grand names," the woman interrupted, drawing on the cigarette again. She smoked like the actresses on the AMC movies, her wrist cocked, her chin tilted haughtily. "Now they've only got the names and none of the stuff. Riding Amtrak is like riding those Soviet trains or, worse yet, the Long Island Rail Road. Dreary, dreary. I wish my husband would see a shrink."

Dante said nothing. He'd begun to wonder if she'd been drinking as well as smoking. There was something boozily compulsive about the way she was speaking, compulsive but also compelling. Her voice, mellow and deep, arrested him, its patrician tone commanding him to stay and listen, though the steel platform plates were cold against his feet, though the night air filtering through the crack between the plates gave him goose bumps.

"I mean that he ought to see someone about his fear of flying," she explained. "This is a deep-sea fisherman who thinks nothing of going way out into the ocean in a small boat, but let him just see an airplane and he breaks into sweats, his heart rate hits triple digits. So we take trains or ships when we go anywhere. They practically know us on the *QE 2*."

"The ocean liner? The big British one?"

"Why, yes, dear. What did you think I meant?"

The way she put the question made Dante feel stupid and awkward. "I meant to ask if you're British," he said. "You sound like it, kind of."

"Must be those fancy schools my parents wasted their money on. No, I'm as Yankee Doodle as Indian pudding. I guess you don't travel much. . . ." She hesitated and leaned against the stairwell, looking outside. "Forgive me. Sometimes it seems that traveling is all my husband and I have done the last five years," the woman went on, now with a distance in her voice. "Cruises. Tours. As soon as we come back from someplace, we start planning where we'll go next. Travel is a kind of drug, a way of not facing things, I suppose. There is a forgetfulness that comes with motion, don't you think, Mr. . . . May I ask your name? Striking up temporary friendships is an old tradition on trains."

"Dante. Dante Panetta."

"Dante. I like that. *Dante.* Fitting too. Because here you are, in a dark wood. But then, aren't we all?"

He had no idea what she was talking about.

"Greer Rhodes," she said, and she took a last drag, opened the door, and with a mannish snap of her forefinger launched the cigarette into a long arc over the embankment, its glowing ash vanishing before it struck the ground. "Well, Dante, I wonder how long it'll be before someone tells us how long we'll be stuck here. How far are you going?"

"Penn Station. Then I've got to get up to Norwalk. That's in Connecticut."

"I know. You're from Norwalk?"

"Yeah, but I—"

"We're neighbors," she interrupted. "Fair Harbor."

Although Fair Harbor hardly made them neighbors, except geographically, meeting someone from his home state and county brought a warmth to Dante's breast that recalled, faintly, the moment in the dream—that too brief moment of happiness when he stood in the church he knew, among people he knew. It came to him, with the chagrin and pleasure of discovering the obvious, that loneliness was the power holding him here in conversation, not some magical quality in Greer Rhodes' voice.

"I was going to say that I moved from Norwalk a couple of years ago. To Miami."

"Miami? That's an awful—" She stopped herself. "Forgive me a second time. I tend to be too blunt sometimes. You probably like Miami. The Beach. The Art Deco district. Nubiles in thong bikinis."

Though he wasn't sure she could see the gesture, Dante shook his head.

"Friends of ours live there. Coral Gables," Greer Rhodes continued. "We were just sailing with them in the Bahamas. Should say I was. My husband was bonefishing. Anyway, they love the place. I don't see the attraction. Something about living in a hurricane zone that makes life too unstable. People too."

"I moved there before the last big one. Andrew. The mall where I work—Dadeland? A mess. Like if the wind blew a little harder, the whole thing would've been a parking lot."

"What do you do in a mall?"

"Cut hair. I'm a barber. My boss likes me to say 'hair stylist' because most of our customers are women, but I'm a barber. My day job."

"And what do you do at night?"

Had this been asked with less of her Yankee Doodle directness, it would have sounded flirtatious.

"Play electric bass when we've got a gig. Hector Baroso's Latin Jazz Band."

"A Renaissance man."

She started up the stairs. Just then, with a crashing of couplers all along its length, the train jerked forward, backward, then forward again, knocking her off balance. She grabbed the handrail, spinning around and falling. Dante lunged, caught her under the arms before she struck the edge of the top step, and lifted her up to the platform.

"You okay?"

"Sure. Sure." She rubbed her upper arm. "Just twisted it a little. Thanks for sparing me and Amtrak the trouble of a lawsuit."

They stood facing each other for a second, Greer a head shorter than Dante's six-one. She gave off, through the stale tobacco odor, a scent of cologne and soap that reminded him of his mother when she came out of the shower.

The train was rolling steadily now, gathering speed.

"Well, we finally appear to be unblocked," she said. "Time I got back to Julian and our healthy, smoke-free compartment. Maybe we'll see you at breakfast. That should be in Virginia."

"Any idea where we are now?"

"In a dark wood, dear," she said, with another of her curt, throaty laughs, and pushed against the door to the sleeper. Dante, reaching over her head, held it open for her, then followed her down the aisle. In the light, he saw that she was older than his mother. Mid-fifties maybe. Her skin looked good, but her hair was a dim and lifeless gray that covered her head like a shawl of cold ashes. She would look younger if it were shorter, he thought, and was mentally trimming and shaping it when she stopped at her compartment and, turning toward him, started to say good night.

She didn't finish, wincing and making a sound too loud to be a breath, too soft to be a gasp.

"Something wrong?"

She said nothing, staring into his face with such intensity in her close-set eyes that he could not return her gaze. He looked instead at the elaborate monogram embroidered on the pocket of her robe.

"Mrs. Rhodes . . . Are you okay?"

First she nodded, then she shook her head, then she nodded once more and murmured, "Oh, my God."

She was so changed from the brusque, jaunty woman he'd spoken to only moments before as to seem a different person altogether. What if she was unbalanced? What if she screamed? He pictured porters and conductors rushing in to find him, half naked, with a hysterical woman in a bathrobe.

He took a step to move past her, but stopped when she held up her palm and whispered, "No . . . Wait . . . Wait." Her eyes had moistened, the pupils moving back and forth like blue ceramic disks sliding under the thinnest film of water.

"How old are you, Dante?"

"Old? What's that got to—?"

"Please."

"Twenty-four."

Her lips pursed as she raised toward his face a trembling hand through which the first blue veins of age had begun to show. Her fingers reached for his cheek; then she folded them, lowered her hand, and vanished behind her compartment door so swiftly he almost didn't see it open and close. She seemed to have dissolved, like an apparition.

THE NEXT MORNING, Dante sat alone at a dining car table, poking indifferently at his scrambled eggs while he watched the countryside reel past. He did not see Greer Rhodes and was surprised to find himself disappointed. He would have thought he'd be relieved by her absence, but he craved company, craved distraction from the dread and sadness deepening in him with each mile. He had hardly slept, and had crawled out of his berth an hour earlier with a feeling of inner collapse that was almost physical; it was as though his bones were losing their rigidity. He was shrouded in a fear that he would not be able to get through the next two days, and disgusted himself when he began hoping for a serious illness to strike him, or for the train to break down after all and give him an acceptable excuse for not appearing at the wake and the funeral.

He could not imagine her coffined and lifeless, not that tall, broad-boned woman. Ever since his father walked out, twelve years before, she had been both mother and father to him, as he had been son and man of the house, mowing the small lawn, raking the leaves, and, when he was old enough to play bar gigs, turning his meager earnings over to her to help pay the bills. He shouldn't have left her. He kept thinking he could have saved her if he'd been there, leaped somehow into the path of the oncoming stroke and pushed her out of its way.

A steward with a coffeepot and a trained smile asked if he wanted a refill. Dante nodded. Then, gesturing at the trees draped in light, spring leaves and at the rolling pastures where horses grazed, he asked if they were in Virginia.

"Sure are," the steward answered, carefully positioning the spout as the car rocked gently. "We'll be comin' onto Richmond shortly."

"How late are we going to be getting into New York?"

"Ten, fifteen minutes only. We highballed last night to make up the time. Hit one fifteen one stretch. Said to my buddy, 'We go any faster, we'll have to tell folks to fly the friendly skies of Amtrak.' You have a good day."

As the steward walked away, Dante noticed a man four or five tables down quickly turn his head aside, the way people do when they've been staring at someone and don't want to be discovered. Dante pretended to look outside. In his peripheral vision, he saw, or imagined, the man again fix him with a penetrating gaze. When he switched his glance from the window, the man's eyes darted away, then fell to the newspaper on his table. There was nothing familiar about him and, except for the ponderous eyelids that made him look sleepy, nothing remarkable. Wispy brown hair. Heavy, flushed jowls, a polo shirt bearing a designer's logo or the logo of a golf club, like all the middle-aged guys Dante had seen striding across south Florida fairways or waiting under hotel marquees beside impatient wives for an airport limo.

The man suddenly looked up from the newspaper, and now it was he who caught Dante staring at him.

Screwing up his nerve, Dante called out across the empty tables between them.

"Do we know each other?"

"What? *What?*"

The flush in the man's cheeks darkened.

"Do we know each other? You've been staring at me for the past five minutes."

"Oh, for . . . This is . . . Excuse me," the man stammered, then pushed back his chair and stood. He was big, a little taller than Dante, and heavyset in the way of an ex–football player long out of condition.

"Hey," Dante said. "Sorry. I thought you were staring. No big deal."

The man gave him a parting glance, then turned and fled from the dining car, showing a bald spot on the back of his head, as round and bright as a planet.

Dante shook his head and wondered if he was going a little crazy. No, dammit, the guy had been looking him over. This led him to wonder further if he was involved in a case of mistaken identity, an intrigue, maybe a murder mystery. He didn't entertain this notion seriously; he was common clay, and uncommon things never happened to him.

He was finishing his third cup of coffee when the tall man came back, with Greer Rhodes walking reluctantly behind him. A big leather purse hung from her shoulder, and she was wearing pleated khaki trousers and a snug white turtleneck that showed a body a thirty-year-old would envy. She had pinned up her hair and combed it back in front, revealing a high, lined forehead.

Dante greeted her with a small wave, which she returned with an economical nod. She was scrutinizing him from a distance, frowning like a gallery patron puzzled by a complicated painting.

Then her husband—Dante presumed that's who the man was—came over and planted himself in the aisle beside his table.

"Well, it seems . . . Greer and I, we . . . It's remarkable, all right, uncanny's I guess the word for it, so the way Greer reacted, last night, the way she reacted then . . . So," he said, punctuating the shards of his sentences with coughs and snorts. "We owe you . . . You were right about me . . . I was . . ."

Greer let out a sigh that seemed to express impatience with not only her husband's stumbling speech but all the exasperations of a long marriage. Not that Dante knew much about marriages, long or otherwise.

"Julian is trying to tell you that we owe you an apology," she said, moving closer. "I for acting the way I did last night. It must've made you wonder if I'm a little batty."

He shook his head.

"You don't have to be polite. Would've thought the same thing my-self if I'd been in your moccasins. I asked Julian to—I don't know how to put this—to check you out if he saw you and tell me if I was imagin-ing things. He *was* staring at you, and we apologize for that too. It was rude, but we hope you'll understand when we explain."

Silent for a moment, Greer began to examine him from up close. He was unsettled by her stare as it moved across his brow and down his nose and along the line of his jaw with a concentration he could feel physi-cally, as if his features were being caressed by a blind woman trying to identify him by touch.

"What's this about, Mrs. Rhodes—?"

She raised two fingers. "Greer. Please. May we join you?"

Dante shrugged, mostly out of confusion, but the Rhodeses took this gesture to mean yes and sat down across from him. They no sooner had than the steward appeared to tell them that breakfast was over and the dining car closed until lunch.

"Then I guess we'll have to adjourn. How about the observation car?" Julian rumbled, lowering his voice an octave on the last two words, drawing them out and rounding his *r*'s in a down-easter drawl.

"If you want to," Greer said to Dante. "We'd like to explain."

He stood and followed Julian, who moved from car to car with the aging athlete's fading grace, the memory in his joints of injuries suffered long ago grown sharper with the years than the memory in his muscles of passes caught and races won. He climbed stiffly to the upper deck of the observation car, his bulk filling the cramped stairwell.

"Greer tells me that you . . . in one of those malls, a salon thing . . . that you cut women's hair. A hairdresser."

"Hairstylist," Dante corrected amiably. He was used to the reaction his profession typically provoked in men. "And I cut men's hair too."

"How do you like that? I mean to say, what's it like?" asked Julian as they passed under a long glass dome ribbed like a ship's hull turned bot-tom side up.

"Pays the rent."

They all three sat down, away from the other passengers.

"It's his day job, dear," Greer explained protectively. "Dante's a mu-sician. Latin jazz."

"Latino, hey? Cha-cha." Julian shook his shoulders in an imitation of a merengue that was as clumsy as his mimic of a Latin accent had been crude. "But this styling thing . . . you must work with a lot of women, I imagine. I know that nowadays, feminism and all, a lot of men have to . . . I know that, but I wonder if it's . . . how you . . ."

Looking up at armadas of clouds sailing through a sky darkened by the dome's tint, Dante smiled bitterly to himself. He ought to have told Greer he was a barber and left it at that.

"There's six women stylists, and my boss is a woman. Cuban lady. She's got six women, three men. Two of the guys are and one isn't, and I'm the one who isn't, all right?"

"I don't understand. Not one what?"

"You understand perfectly well," Greer said tightly, and exchanged a fleeting, sidelong glance with her husband before she turned back to Dante.

"I'm sorry," she said.

"Y'know, you keep apologizing for one thing and another, and I still don't know what in the hell is going on. What is it you were going to tell me?"

She laid the purse on her lap. A veil of sadness fell swiftly over her candid face, then as swiftly lifted, her expression changing to one of resolve. She opened the purse and withdrew a photograph, which she passed to Dante facedown.

He turned it over and blinked.

"Remarkable, isn't it? Uncanny, like I said?" asked Julian.

Dante did not respond, entranced by the image of himself in a military uniform. He squinted at the photo of his double from up close and examined it at arm's length, looking for differences. The soldier's hair, what little of it showed from beneath his army cap, was slightly darker, his lips were slightly thinner; and his chin was straight and square, a bit like Greer's, while Dante's was cleft (though the indentation was cosmetic, the result of a bad spill he'd taken in a hockey game years before). Every other feature was the same: the Roman nose, the small ears, the deep-set copper-brown eyes, and the left eyebrow that arced higher than the right, creating an expression of perpetual skepticism. That last detail astonished Dante the most. His eyebrows were a family trademark. He'd inherited them from his mother, as she had inherited hers from her father, and to see the trait replicated now in a stranger was more than remarkable; it was spooky.

He handed the photograph back to Greer. As she replaced it in her purse, she bit down on her lips, the way women did when they wanted to spread their lipstick evenly, and the lines bracketing her mouth deepened. The light from the observation dome seemed then to fall upon her mercilessly, whitening her hair, accentuating the parchment whiteness of her skin. She looked suddenly very old.

"Clayton. Our son, as I suppose you've guessed."

Folding her pale hands over her purse, drawing her knees tightly together, cocking her chin ever so slightly, she struck a pose of pride and steely self-containment.

"Well, yeah, I did. But . . ." He paused, turning with a bemused expression from Greer to Julian and then back again.

"Adopted," said Julian, answering the unspoken question. "That's why there isn't much resemblance, except for the chin. He's got Greer's chin."

Dante felt a light tremor in his chest. "Adopted?"

"Greer and I couldn't have any of our own, so we adopted Clay."

Dante asked when that was, and Julian told him it was in 1966.

"Where? Connecticut?"

Julian shook his head. "Portland. Where I'm from, in case you couldn't tell by . . . Maine . . . In case you couldn't tell by the accent, Maine is where I'm from. Portland. There was a home there for unwed mothers. Still had those back then, and that's where we adopted Clay."

"Just a tiny baby," said Greer. "Three months old."

Dante leaned his head against the back of the seat and watched one cloud after another hastened into and then out of sight by the speeding train.

"Do you know who his birth parents were?" he asked.

"Oh, no. They never tell you that," Greer replied. "It's the law."

Looking outside, at passing tableaux of black children playing in the yards of brick and shingle cottages crowded below the roadbed, Dante did a quick subtraction. His mother would have been nineteen in 1966. A nineteen-year-old Irish Catholic girl, especially in those days . . . In an instant, an entire melodrama unfolded in his mind. The discovery that she is pregnant . . . Her lover refuses to marry her, leaves . . . The panic and shame she would have felt, then the mental strain of keeping the truth from her parents for as long as she can . . . Then the flight, when she begins to show, to a home in a distant city. What reason for leaving would she have invented? And what would have drawn her to Maine? The whole scenario seemed fantastic, and yet the trembling persisted in

Dante's chest. That his mother might have borne an illegitimate child didn't bother him as much as the thought that she would have kept it secret from him. There would have been a hint at least. He would have preferred to speculate about his father, but Dad had been overseas in 1966. And then there was that trait, so peculiar to his mother's side.

He took out his wallet, opened it to her photo, and showed it to Greer without a word. She looked at it carefully, then at him.

"Your mother?"

He nodded.

"May I ask her name?"

"Margaret. Everybody called her Meg. Meg Dougherty was her maiden name."

"She must have had you when she was quite young. She doesn't look a day over forty."

"Forty-one in the picture. It's seven years old. She gave it to me when I got out of high school. It's the eyebrows. The way the left one goes way up, higher than the right. Y'know, like she's raising it? Like you've said something she doesn't believe?"

"It was the first thing I noticed about you." Greer pointed at him and traced an outline of his brow in the air, an affectionate smile on her face. "They're Clay's all over again. And your eyes as well. That light, light brown, and the pupils like two tiny ancient creatures preserved in amber."

The tenderness with which she gave this unusual description made Dante blush, for he, and not her son, seemed the object of it.

Julian patted him once on the knee. The touch was meant to be re-assuring, but it was delivered hard and awkwardly and came off as a blunt attempt to gain his attention.

"Now, we can guess what you might've thought, might be thinking right now," Julian said. "Greer, last night, she thought about it too, and we talked it over this morning, and . . . Well, I'll try to put this delicately as I can. . . . We think the chances that your mother or father was one of Clayton's parents are pretty remote. Even if they *both*, ah, got together five years before you were born, the chances that they would've had your identical twin are astronomical. In so many words, just in case you've been wondering, in case you've had any doubts, we don't think you need to." He paused. "Unless, of course, you might have heard something, un-less you might know something we don't."

"No. I don't," Dante said curtly. "It'd be news to me."

"Excuse me for bringing that up, but you'll understand that we're curious."

"So am I."

"Right. Right. That settles that, I guess."

"Then how do you explain this? It's really weird."

"Can't. There's that theory. Everybody is supposed to have a double somewhere."

Dante said that he had never believed it. If it were true, then half the people in the country would look like the other half, and it was clear that they didn't.

"Of course, dear." Greer's voice had assumed its customary forthright tone. "We have to think that this is some incredible accident of genetics."

Dante wished for a more solid assurance. "Incredible accident" didn't quite do as an answer, didn't completely allay the disquieting suspicion that his mother possessed a covert history she had seen fit not to share with him. If only he could ask her! It seemed cruel for this mystery to come upon him now. He wanted no doubts to trouble him when he saw her tonight, wanted no unanswerable questions to blemish her memory.

"Why, Dante, we've upset you," Greer said.

"What?"

"You look upset."

"I do?"

His hand rose and roved over his cheeks and mouth, as if he needed to feel his expression to know what it was.

"Oh, I was worried we would. I told Julian not to say anything about the adoption, that it would be bound to raise questions."

"It's not that. That's only part of it. I'm going up to Norwalk to—"

"Norwalk. Right. Greer mentioned you're from there," Julian blundered in.

"My mother died yesterday. I'm heading home for her funeral."

"Oh, my, I'm so . . . Oh, my," Greer said, and an uncomfortable silence fell. Julian cleared his throat and appeared for the moment unsure about what to do with his hands. He scowled and uttered a low groan that plainly was not an expression of sympathy. It seemed to say: Now, why did you have to bring that up? Clearing his throat again, Julian began to cast erratic looks around the car. Greer gave him an out, asking if he would go to the café car for coffee.

"Sure, glad to." He stood, grateful and relieved. "How do you like yours, Dante?"

He motioned that he did not want any.

"You mustn't mind him," said Greer after her husband left. "Julian has a difficult time with emotional situations."

"If you say so. He made me feel like I said something wrong."

"Please, please don't. Julian dislikes hearing about tragedies. Sometimes I think he resents it because it puts him in a position of having to respond, and I'm afraid Julian's repertoire of responses is rather limited."

Dante resisted the temptation to say: That's his problem.

"You'd never know, listening to him, that he graduated magna cum from Dartmouth, would you?"

"I went to barber college; I wouldn't know nothing about Dartmouth, Mrs. Rhodes," he said, and saw her flinch.

The Silver Meteor had slowed in its northward career, and as it ran sedately past warehouses and under viaducts upon whose sooty walls graffiti taggers had left their marks, Greer said:

"Oh, Dante. Here we are, virtual strangers, and yet I feel that I know you so well. I do know your grief, yes, believe me I do, and your bitterness. Forty . . . She would have been only forty-eight?"

Dante nodded. He could tell that she wanted to know how a woman that young had died, but was too well bred to ask.

"It was a cerebral hemorrhage," he volunteered, and then told her that it had happened at eight-thirty in the morning, outside the office where his mother was a receptionist. She had just left her car and was walking across the parking lot to begin work when she dropped as if she had been shot through the brain. She was pronounced dead on arrival at Norwalk General, and someone from the hospital found Dante's number in her purse and phoned him at the NuWave salon two hours later. He remembered laying down his electric clippers after he hung up and holding on to the counter cluttered with hairbrushes and shampoo bottles, because the floor seemed to be heaving under his feet. He remembered seeing the reflection of Consuela Balbotin behind his own in the mirror, she frowning and gesturing at him to attend to his customer, until he turned and told her what had happened and asked for a week off.

"Consuela's got a lot of heart. She called the airlines for me, got me on a flight to La Guardia, even drove me to the airport," Dante went on, in a voice steadier than he thought he would be capable of. Talking about it was doing him good, made him feel that he was describing a tragedy that had happened to someone else. "The plane had some mechanical trouble, flight was canceled, and they're trying to get me on another one, but all I was thinking about was to get going, get moving, so I called Amtrak, and here I am. Probably would've been home quicker if I'd thought straight and just waited for another flight."

The train was idling through a switchyard, between a long, motionless line of boxcars and another of silver passenger cars gleaming in the April sunlight. A voice crackled over the speakers: "Richmond. This is Richmond. All passengers for Richmond, be sure to clear your luggage and belongings from your compartments or the overhead racks. Richmond is the next."

"Dante, Dante," said Greer, and, taking his hand in hers, declared that she felt awful for him and ashamed of herself for sending her husband to spy on him, for troubling him at a time like this . . .

He did not want to hear any more apologies and made a gesture of dismissal.

"It's okay. Last thing I want is to be by myself."

"I can imagine. That emptiness . . ." She hesitated, and it appeared that she had to make an effort to maintain her composure. "That emptiness that comes over you when you're alone. Like the you that makes you you has disappeared from inside and all you are is a body that looks alive but isn't. Yes, I can imagine."

It was exactly like that, he thought, and it could not be imagined by anyone who had not known it. Possibly Clayton Rhodes had been away from home a long time, stationed in some foreign country, and Greer had begun to cry last night because she missed him.

The train stopped with a bump. Laughing redcaps waited beside empty baggage carts on the platform below.

"Where's your son stationed?" Dante asked.

The abrupt change of subject seemed to catch her off guard.

"He's in the army, isn't he? Or was that picture taken a while back?"

"Yes, a while ago," she answered quietly. "You've not been in the service, Dante?"

He shook his head.

"That's a navy uniform Clayton's wearing," she informed him, then added with a peculiar, brittle formality: "It is the uniform of a naval aviation cadet. It was taken when Clayton was a year younger than you are now. When he was in training at Pensacola. To fly fighter planes from an aircraft carrier."

"He's on a ship, then?" Dante persisted; he wanted to know.

"No. He was once," Greer said, and he could see, in the hurt in her eyes and in the set of her jaw, as he heard in the breath that whispered through her trembling lips, a profound sorrow at war with the will to master it.

"He was on a ship in the Persian Gulf—I should say during the Persian Gulf war. His carrier had orders to go to the gulf. It was based in Naples, which is supposed to be such a lovely place, but I don't think so. The ship had put to sea, the Mediterranean, and Clay's squadron was practicing bombing runs, strafing, all that dreadful stuff. Clay flew an F-16, and something went wrong. No one will ever know what. A flameout, a mechanical failure. He crashed into the sea. He was twenty-four. All the years Julian and I devoted to him, cared for him, worried about him when he got sick, educated him—all of it gone in an instant and nothing left of it but some wreckage and an oil slick on the water. I don't know if the pain would have been less if he had died in combat, or worse, or the same. The same, I suppose. One moment he was there, like an eagle in the sky, and the next moment gone. You know, sometimes I see it happening as if I'd been there. I see his plane, with the fire glowing from its tailpipe, crashing into the blue, blue sea. The sea the Greeks and Romans sailed, my Clay sailed and died in. He was a warrior who fell from the sky into the sea of the Greeks and Romans. I suppose that's my strange way of coping with it—to make something mythic and grand out of what amounted to a mechanical failure."

Her recounting of the disaster caused her face to lose its clear, frank look; the expressions that played across it were too vague and fleeting to read. Even her features seemed to relinquish some of their definition; it was as though Dante were looking at her through a slightly foggy glass.

"And travel," she went on. "Travel helps us cope. We drink the drug of motion. New faces, new landscapes, new customs—anything to fill up that hollow, although, of course, nothing can. I don't wish to minimize your loss, Dante, but you're young, you'll marry someday, have a family, build a life. But Clay was all we had, all we ever could have. And when I saw you last night, in the light, it was—my God—like a resurrection, or a reincarnation, but I knew it couldn't be, and so the sight of you brought it all back, as though it happened only that day and not five years ago."

Dante almost felt guilty about this. He followed her gaze as it drifted outside, to the platform where the redcaps were now filling the baggage carts and new passengers were boarding, while those detraining shook welcoming hands, fell into welcoming embraces. The sight of the happy homecomings brought to his chest the hollowness Greer had spoken of, and a weariness overcame him. He wished he could lay his head on her lap and rest in the comfort of her arms, like a small boy, while the man in him wanted to hold and comfort her. He had the impression that she felt the same opposing urges to give and receive solace. For what seemed a long time, but could not have been more than a few seconds, they sat silently in a capsule of shared sorrow, hers old, his new. Then, turning, he noticed Julian standing in the aisle with two coffee cups in a cardboard tray. He felt so close to Greer at that moment that her husband's return came as an intrusion.

"Oh, there you are, dear. What took so long?" she asked.

Julian sat down and, with the tray on his lap, pulled the tabs off the covers on the paper cups.

"A line. Everybody decided to take a coffee break at the same time," he said. "Here's yours. A little skim, one packet of Equal."

"Thanks." Greer took the cup as she might a cocktail glass. She was becoming herself again, although Dante didn't know her well enough to say who that self was. "God, I'm dying for a cigarette with this."

"That's the word for it," said Julian with a caustic curl of his full lips. "Dying."

"My very own in-house surgeon general, issuing warnings."

"If the fit's that bad, you could go outside. We've got a few minutes before the train pulls out. Either that or wait for the bar car to open."

"The bar car sounds better. I told Dante about Clay."

Julian's hooded eyes slanted toward her, and the two again exchanged a quick, sideways glance. Dante, like his mother, had a sensitive antenna for the things that were said with gestures and looks, so he trusted his perception that something more than a glance had just passed between the Rhodeses: a message encrypted in the private code of a couple who had lived together a long time.

"Was he . . . did they find him?" Dante asked, mostly because he felt compelled to say something.

"So she told you about the accident, the crash."

"Well, yeah . . ."

Julian became suddenly agitated, his cheeks taking on the color of a bruise. "Ah . . . Ah . . . ," he grumbled, swatting at the air with one of his big hands. "She didn't have to. . . . You didn't have to tell him, Greer. Ah . . ." He rose partway from his seat, and a look of alarm spread across Greer's face. She practically lunged to clutch his arm.

"Julian. Please."

He settled into his seat again, the spell of temper passing as swiftly as it had come on. Greer relaxed and, with a faintly embarrassed smile, said that Julian had to watch his blood pressure. Dante was perplexed. Why should his learning about the accident affect Julian's blood pressure?

The Silver Meteor was in motion again, creeping through Richmond's heart. A few minutes later, it rattled past the older suburbs, where pink and white blossoms flocked cherry and dogwood trees, and then, gathering speed, past the sparsely foliated reaches of new developments and shopping malls. Greer, staring at Dante again, shook her head and said she couldn't get over it, just couldn't get over it. There had to be some plausible accounting for the astonishing resemblance. Oh, Dante's voice and mannerisms were different. The way he shyly turned his head aside while speaking—Clay never did that. He looked straight at you, she said, and yet somehow past you, as if his thoughts were wandering far away. Dante squirmed, feeling like a captive specimen under study, and was grateful when Julian, who was also shifting about uncomfortably, abruptly changed the subject. He declared that the Civil War was his hobby and spoke for a time about General Grant's bombardment of Richmond. Dante pretended to be interested. He didn't know how a war could be a hobby, and, history having been his worst subject in school, he knew next to nothing about the Civil War. The only war that held any significance for him was Vietnam, and that only because his father had been wounded there and so acquired a convenient exoneration for the mess he would have made of his life even if he hadn't gone to war. Well, he'd had his good moments. The times when he took Dante fishing on Long Island Sound had been the best. Fighting big fish on big water seemed to quiet his devils, but otherwise it had been a succession of lost jobs, drinking binges, and violent rages; and Dante had to admit that on the day his mother told him that the old man had walked out, he felt joyous. It was odd how his memories of the old man had blurred.

In fact, whenever he thought of his father now, he pictured him not in human form but as a storm that had whirled through his and his mother's lives, frightening them, smashing things up, and then whirled out and left them to clean up the debris.

"How is your father taking this? It must have been a terrible blow for him," Greer asked out of nowhere.

Startled, Dante drew his head back. It was as if she had been reading his mind. He answered with a harsh little laugh, which she responded to with a puzzled frown.

"I don't know where he is. Last time I saw him, I was twelve. Haven't even heard from him since."

The Rhodeses looked at him. Dante then noticed something about Julian. The sleepy appearance created by his drooping lids was deceptive, for the gray eyes beneath were alert and hard and calculating.

"You can't really mean that," he rumbled. "Not seen him even once? Or at least heard about him? What about your grandparents?"

"They split up when my dad was a kid. My grandmother left Norwalk after she got remarried. That was before I was born. She lives in California, I think. I saw her only a few times when I was kid. And my grandfather . . ." Dante shrugged.

"I always thought Italian . . . You're Italian on that side, aren't you?"
Dante nodded.

"Well, I always thought they were close-knit. Italian families, I mean."

"I guess mine wasn't."

Greer's frown deepened, and she looked old again, the furrows stacked on her forehead.

"Then *who* is picking you up when you get in?"

"Nobody."

"Oh, that's terrible. Just terrible."

Having given the Rhodeses an unflattering portrait of his father's family, he didn't want them to get the impression that his mother's were careless trash, and so he explained that there wasn't anyone he could have called to pick him up: his grandfather Dougherty was dead, his grandmother in a nursing home. His closest relative was his mother's younger sister, Kathy, and she lived in Boston. She had phoned Dante at his apartment, while he was packing, and said that she and his uncle would drive down to Norwalk to see to the funeral arrangements. He didn't have to worry; leave everything to them. Dante was so grateful, he didn't want to impose on them by asking them to drive to Penn Station at rush hour.

"I wasn't criticizing anyone," Greer said. "I simply meant that it's terrible for you to get off the train with no one there. There's something desolate about that picture. We'd be happy to give you a lift. We've got a limo reserved."

"That's okay. I'll—"

"I insist," she said, in a tone that meant it. "It's on our way. It won't be any trouble at all. Do you have a place to stay?"

"My mom's house. I've still got a key."

"You're more than welcome to stay with us."

Julian grimaced and said, "Greer," speaking her name slowly, stretching the single syllable out for emphasis.

"It's only a suggestion, dear. It might be depressing for Dante to stay there," she said.

Dante *knew* it would be depressing, but when Julian gave him a look that practically commanded him to decline Greer's offer, he did.

"Whatever you think best." She appeared genuinely disappointed. "But don't hesitate to call on us if you need someone to talk to, need help with anything. After all, this coincidence is just too remarkable to be a coincidence. It seems almost fated, don't you think?"

LOWERING BENEATH a dark storm cloud, the sun cast a textured golden light over the Connecticut Turnpike, flashed off rear windows and side-view mirrors, and lit up the tops of the oaks and maples along the highway. They were not as green as the trees in the South. They had just begun to bud, and the sunlight falling through the nearly barren branches was somehow autumnal, its slant and amber color the hue and angle of endings rather than beginnings.

The limousine driver, a thickset, aggressive man, took advantage of every opening in the traffic, dodging from lane to lane, slipping the Lincoln into spaces that looked too small for a Volkswagen. But even he could do nothing once they reached the Mianus River bridge. Ahead, for as far as Dante could see, brake lights winked on and off like ruby stars in some elongated galaxy.

He would have to shower and change into his suit, then call a cab to take him to the funeral parlor. Would he have enough time? He imagined the censorious faces that would greet him if he walked in late, and the most censorious of all would be his aunt Kathy's.

He would save a lot of time if he didn't have to take a taxi. Maybe his mother's car was back at the house. But who could have returned it, and what about the keys? It must still be in the parking lot where she worked. He hoped it had not been broken into, or towed, or stolen. Did it belong to him now, and what was he supposed to do with it? Worrying about the car caused a horde of other anxieties to sweep over him. What about the house and the furniture? She had managed to hold on to the house after the divorce was final, scrimping to keep up the mortgage payments. Would Dante have to make them now? He couldn't possibly, not with his rent in Miami. He would have to sell the place, but he didn't have the slightest idea where to begin. The magnitude of the responsibilities that had been thrust upon him almost made him angry with her for dying on him so unexpectedly.

"Here! Right!" he said. The driver swung the Lincoln into the turn lane, cutting off another motorist, and barged into the line of cars stopped for the light at the end of the exit ramp.

"Sorry for the short notice. I was somewhere else." Dante heard his voice quaver with tension. He leaned forward in the seat, less to give further directions than to ease the acid pains shooting through his gut. "Make a right at the light, go down two more, and make a left."

Greer rested her hand on his shoulder and murmured to him to try to relax; he would get through this somehow.

"I was just thinking about a lot of dumb stuff," he said, and then directed the driver to take Flax Hill Road. "About my mom's car, her house, her things. What I'm supposed to do. It's like all that dropped on top of me in the last two minutes, and I don't know how to deal with any of it."

"It's hardly dumb stuff, dear, but one thing at a time. One thing, one moment, one day at a time." The platitudes sounded like the deepest wisdom simply because her lips had uttered them.

"If you want, we can give you a hand with those problems when the time comes," she added, and produced a business card from her purse. "I'm in real estate—the last refuge for middle-aged females who have too much time on their hands and don't know how to do anything else. Perhaps I could list the house for you. At least I could put you together with a good realtor."

They headed down Taylor Avenue, passing the streets Dante had walked in his childhood. The streetlights were on now, and the lights from the houses laid hazy, skewed rectangles across patchy lawns enclosed by chain-link fences. At a corner, a man in working clothes, shambling along with a grocery bag in his arms, paused to stare at the limousine—a rare sight in this neighborhood. When they pulled up in front of his old house on Avenue E, Dante felt embarrassed. The little Cape Cod was the shabbiest house on the block, and he couldn't believe it was the home he'd recalled so fondly. Was it different than when he'd last seen it? No—the difference was in the way he saw it; it was as if the limo's tinted glass had filtered out his memories of growing up here and given him the clearer, more objective vision of a stranger. A stranger like Greer or Julian. How did the house and the neighborhood appear to them? Pretty common, he imagined, maybe a little worse than common.

"Someone seems to be home," Greer said.

He had been too preoccupied with the house's appearance to notice the reason why he could see the peeling paint and broken shutter: the porch light and the lights inside were on. A tiny flame of irrational hope sprang up in him—an incredible mistake had been made, a dead woman had been misidentified as Margaret Panetta—and quickly fell when he spied the Ford Taurus with Massachusetts plates parked nearby.

"It's my aunt and uncle. They must've got a key some way."

"Well, at least you'll have company," said Greer.

After the driver pulled his suitcase from the trunk, he leaned into the car and shook Julian's hand, then took Greer's to thank her. With a gentle pressure, she drew his face close to hers and, holding him by the upper arms, lightly kissed his cheek.

"Oh, Dante, it's been . . ." Greer stopped herself, as if she wasn't certain what it had been. Her hands slipped down along his arms, and her cool fingers clasped his palms. "I truly hope this isn't the last we see of each other."

"That's right. Hope to see you again," said Julian, his florid face aglow in the interior light.

"And be sure to call if you need help with the house. Help with anything," Greer said.

He watched the long gray car drive off, the scent of Greer's cologne mingling in his nose with the smell of leather upholstery. He climbed the three short steps to the front porch and rang the bell. For no reason he could think of, a bright, bouncy Arturo Sandoval tune began to play in his head, and he shocked himself when he found his feet tapping in rhythm to the driving samba base line. His aunt opened the door, and when he saw her hard green eyes and her dark dress, somber as a nun's habit, the music stopped, and his foot grew still.

1 1

IN THE FUNERAL home's hallway, on a black announcement board, were the names of the dead and the visitation rooms in which they were being waked. Margaret Panetta was in the last one down the hall, the Sacred Heart Room. Dante went there, with Kathy and Will Malone beside him. One of the rooms overflowed with mourners, but only a dozen people were gathered in his mother's room. He couldn't understand it; she had been well liked at work, active in parish affairs. His heart swelled with anger, embarrassment, and disappointment as he walked toward her coffin past empty rows of folding chairs. He was upset more for her sake than his own, as if she were a once popular star whose final performance had drawn only a handful of fans, while the act next door had packed the house.

They had dressed her in a dark-green dress and a string of imitation pearls. Her hair was coiffed and lacquered in a sweep across her forehead, her cheeks glowed with the false ruddiness of the mortician's blush. A rosary wound around her large hands, folded over her midriff. There was an oppressively sweet smell—the flowers in the vases beside the two tall candles burning at each end of the coffin. It was the first time Dante had seen her since last Christmas. He wanted to think that she looked like an enchanted beauty, lying there all made up on a bed of satin, but the reality thwarted the desire: she looked more like a painted wax statue of herself.

With a nudge and a movement of her head, Kathy told him that he should go first. He approached the coffin and knelt to pray, but he could not keep his mind from wandering. He bowed his head and moved his lips in a mimic of devotion while he remembered her Christmas visit in Miami, and how excited she had been, seeing the Beach and the Art Deco district for the first time, how she had joked, the night she went to one of Dante's gigs, that maybe she would run off with a genuine Latin lover if only she could find one she could look *up* to.

He rose and bent over the coffin to kiss her. Her skin was stiff and cold, like paper, and the makeup's chalky taste repelled him. Raising his head, he noticed, showing faintly through the layered powder, plum-colored blotches under her eyes and on the left side of her forehead—bruising from the blood vessels whose ruptures had killed her. He turned and went to a chair and watched Kathy and Will kneel and cross themselves.

A short, dark-haired woman, accompanied by a short, stocky man, came up to him and said, "You must be Dante."

To his blank look, the woman asked if he recognized her and her husband. He shook his head apologetically.

"The Pietros," she said. "Paul and Donna? We used to live in the green frame place behind your house when you were . . . oh, you must've been ten, eleven then. We had a son a few years younger. Michael?"

He bobbed his head in recognition. Donna said that she and Paul had read the death notice in the *Norwalk Hour.* . . . What a shock!

Dante didn't know what to say to the Pietros, or how he was supposed to act toward anyone. He wished Greer were here. She would know.

Will and Kathy came away from the coffin and sat down, and the Pietros knelt in their place. Kathy was daubing her eyes. It somehow pleased Dante that his formidable aunt was susceptible to tears, and he wondered why none seemed to be in him. He hadn't cried after the first phone call, hadn't cried once on the train. He thought he should now and made himself recall little things about his mother—how she would sit cross-legged on the living room floor, like a schoolgirl, when she watched reruns of *The Mary Tyler Moore Show;* the wistful way she would listen to her old Beatles tapes and talk about how hopeful and optimistic life had been in the mid-sixties, before everything got dark and menacing. But no tears came.

A few more people came in—strangers, his mother's friends from work—expressed their sympathies and then stood around, talking quietly to each other. Will grew restless and said he was going out for a cigarette and asked if Dante wanted to join him. He glanced at his aunt for approval, and she gave a half nod, half shrug.

Outside, the two men stood on the walkway, under a long canvas awning that arched from the door to the curb. The air was chilly, and a light rain had begun to fall. Headlights and streetlights cast fuzzy reflections in the wet pavement.

"You okay, guy?" Will asked, lighting up.

"Yeah, sure." Dante paused for a beat. "No. No, I'm not. How could I be okay?"

Will exhaled a plume of smoke and laughed at himself.

"Yeah, you're right. Dumb question," he said in the flat, rough tones of south Boston, where in his younger days he had been a tough street kid, a Golden Gloves boxer. He shook his long head. "Man, like that, just like that, in a second," he continued, with a snap of his fingers. "Me and Kathy couldn't believe it. I thought I'd gotten used to it happening that way, but that was over there. You expect it to happen that way in a war."

Will had been with the marines, but he hadn't used Vietnam as a reason to fail. He'd come home, gone to vocational training on the G.I. Bill, and now owned a plumbing contracting business. Dante wondered what his life would have been like if his mother had married someone like his uncle.

"Will?" he asked.

"Yeah?"

"I've got to thank you and Kathy for everything. The way you arranged everything."

"Don't thank me. Thank your aunt. She did it all. You know her. Most organized woman on planet Earth."

"I wouldn't've had a clue where to start."

"Hey, guy, that's what family's for."

"Will, when I get back to Florida, would it be okay if I called you? Not a lot. Every once in a while?"

Rubbing the tip of his sharp, thin nose, Will feigned a look of surprise.

"Are you kidding? Hell, yeah, you can call anytime, if you can get through with the kids talking on the phone all the time. And next Thanksgiving or Christmas, you wanna spend it with Kathy and me, you let us know."

"I think I'd like that."

Will crushed his cigarette underfoot and stood for a moment, looking down at the flattened butt.

"We'd better get back inside, before the old lady starts thinking I dragged you out for a snort and made a real Irish wake of it."

Dante started to laugh, but without warning, he began to cry instead. Of its own accord, his congested grief broke up and burst from out of the tight, cold place in his chest. Will went to him and held him tightly. He pressed his face against his uncle's shoulder, and then a fury burned through him, becoming one with his sorrow, and he broke Will's embrace and kicked the side of the step.

"Aw, Mom! Goddamn it! Mom! Goddamn it all!"

He cursed, sobbed, and kicked at the same time. Will took him in his arms again.

"Hey, guy, c'mon. C'mon, Dante. Try to . . . She's all right now. She never suffered. You gotta believe that. You gotta believe she's gone to a better place."

Why did he have to believe any of that? The blood vessels had exploded inside her brain, she must have suffered, and why did he have to believe that her immortal soul had gone anyplace, whether better or worse than this one? He broke free once again and spun away, out from under the awning, into the cool drizzle. The rain mingled with his tears, and covering his face with a hand, he stumbled blindly into Father Talley's embrace. He knew it was Father Talley because he smelled English Leather.

"That's okay, Dante. Let it out now. It's okay to let it out," said the priest, patting his back. "But your uncle's right, you know. If anyone's got a place in heaven, it's Meg."

Dante dried his eyes with his sleeve, backed away, and looked into Father Talley's square face, set off by square, black-rimmed glasses. The priest had aged in the past couple of years; his curly hair was streaked with gray, and the flesh of his flabby neck folded over his tight cleric's collar like dough over the rim of a pie tin.

"Are you all right now, Dante?"

He nodded.

"It's good to see you again, son. Wish it wasn't under these circumstances."

"Good to see you, Father," Dante said, shaking the man's hand. But some anger was still in him, and he added bitterly, "You didn't have to tell me that, that Uncle Will's right."

"Because you already know he is or because you don't want to hear it?"

The scent of the priest's aftershave drew him back to his dream of the night before, back into that calm space when he had stood in a place he knew among people he knew. From out of a deep recess in his memory came a line from one of Father Talley's sermons. *We lose our faith when we step outside the radiance of grace.* He didn't know why those words came back to him, nor even what they meant exactly, nor what comfort they could bring him now, but he saw that his sorrow was for himself, as his anger was against God for allowing his mother to die so long before her time.

"I don't know," he said in delayed answer to the priest's question. "I'm not sure about much of anything right now, but I'm all right."

Father Talley laid a hand on his shoulder.

"Then shall we go inside? I'd like to say a few words about Meg, for those who won't be at the funeral tomorrow."

THE RAIN STOPPED sometime in the middle of the night, and his mother was buried in St. John's and St. Mary's cemetery on a clear morning warmed by a breeze that smelled of the advancing spring. Standing at graveside, Dante barely heard Father Talley's ritual invocation for Margaret to rest in peace and the perpetual light to shine upon her. He wept quietly but felt relief more than anything else when the coffin was lowered at last, beneath a stark temporary marker:

MARGARET MARY PANETTA
NOV. 6, 1946—APRIL 2, 1995

Will caught him staring at it and whispered that a permanent tombstone would be put in later—another thing Kathy had seen to. But Dante's mind was not on the tombstone. He found himself disgusted by the cheerful weather, whose dissonance with his mood and the mood of the occasion struck him as an insult. So did the traffic on the Post Road as the funeral limousine took him and his aunt and uncle back to their car. Just as a young man who falls in love for the first time feels that he is the first ever to fall in love, so Dante felt that he was the first young man ever to have lost his mother. He thought her death and his loss deserved everyone's attention, but then the limousine stopped for a traffic light at the entrance to a strip mall, where customers were carrying new books out of a Barnes & Noble, wheeling groceries out of a supermarket, lugging computers and other vehicles for the information highway out of a CompUSA store. The light changed. Red green. In a few minutes it would be green red. A thousand funerals could pass beneath it today alone, and it would go on changing according to its routine intervals. Red green red. All day, all night.

After they returned to the house, Kathy sat him down on the living room couch, then brought a folder full of papers from his mother's old bedroom. Installing her stout body beside him, she arranged the papers on the coffee table as neatly as cards at a bridge game. She managed her emotions like files in a software program; each of them was clicked on or off as necessary. The crisp movements of her hands, the concentrated look on her face, and her dry eyes said that she was done with grieving, at least for the present. All that could be done for her sister had been done; now it was time to attend to the living.

"It would've been nice if we had a few days before we got into this," she said, primly resting her hands on her knees, her black dress rustling. "But we've got to be going soon."

Dante looked toward Will, who stood near the living room door, leaning a shoulder into the wall.

"Can't leave three teenaged kids on their own for another day," his uncle said.

Pointing a dark-red fingernail at a fat envelope with the word WILL printed on it in Gothic letters, Kathy said that Dante was lucky his mother had been sensible enough to make one out. She had left the house, the furniture, her car, her savings account—in short, all that she had—to him. Kathy's lacquered nail fell on a second envelope, which contained his mother's certificate of deposit, and copies of the mortgage contract and something called an amortization schedule, and then on a third—an insurance policy. The policy was small, and every dime in it would go toward funeral expenses, said Kathy firmly. Meg had not saved much—what could you expect, she being a single mother with a mortgage? Twenty-five hundred and change. As for the mortgage, less than half of it had been paid off, so Dante would be wise to put the house on the market right away.

"The real estate market's way down from the eighties peak," she continued, "but you're lucky Meg and that *father* of yours bought this place in the early eighties, before the big run-up. They hit it at the right time. It's appreciated quite a bit." She gave the room an appraising glance. "I'd think you could net twenty thousand when all's said and done."

Dante felt ashamed when his heart leaped at the thought of twenty thousand dollars. Add that to the CD, and he would have more than he'd earned in the last year.

Will had noticed the change in his expression and pushed away from the wall to stand in the center of the room, his arms crossed over his chest.

"I'm gonna talk straight, guy. You're like me. High-school diploma only. That could still get you somewhere in my day, but nowadays it won't get you squat," he said, looking down the knife-edged slope of his nose. "Same with your barber's license. Great that you've got a trade, but I don't think you're gonna die rich. Don't blow the money once you get it. A new car, bimbos, whatever. Sock it away in something safe. You let that twenty Gs earn some interest, maybe you'd have enough to put a down payment on your own shop someday. Or maybe your own house."

"Very good advice," Kathy said. "The name of the lawyer who drew up the will is in the envelope. You'll need to see him to get everything settled. When you do, ask him for the name of a good realtor."

Eager to show that he had some business sense, he said that he knew a realtor who could sell the house. Kathy asked who, and when he answered that it was a woman he'd met on the train, she and Will looked at him with dismay.

"Please don't do anything foolish. Talk to the lawyer first. This is all you've got. Your mother would turn over in her grave if you lost it, and I'd come down here and wring your neck."

"I just said she *is* a realtor," Dante protested, irritated by the suggestion that he wasn't capable of making smart decisions. He took Greer's card from his wallet and showed it to Kathy.

"Her husband and her were the ones gave me the lift from Penn Station. She said she would list the house for me if I wanted."

"This woman meets you on a train, gives you, a perfect stranger, a lift, then offers to sell your house for you. What is she, a good Samaritan, or did she just like your looks?"

Dante almost laughed at that one. "Yeah, in a way she liked my looks. She's just a nice lady who wants to help me out. I told her my mom had died and that I didn't have a clue how to handle everything. The house and all."

Kathy's lips turned down, and her posture stiffened. "You could've waited to talk to Will and me. We don't want you taken advantage of."

"Taken advantage?" asked Dante. "Look at this place. It wouldn't make a garage in Fair Harbor. Paint's peeling, shutters about to come off. What would be in it for her?"

"This was your *mother's* house, and now it's yours. Maybe it would look a little better if you hadn't zipped off to Florida, leaving Meg to take care of it herself."

"Thanks, Kathy. Thanks a helluva lot for that."

"Okay, you two. No arguments. Christ, we just buried her." Will took a step forward and stood over them, a hand on each of their backs. "Kath, why don't you get into your traveling clothes? We've got to get on the road."

A few minutes later, she emerged from the bedroom in a sweater over jeans too tight for her thighs and hips. She dropped two suitcases on the living room floor and said she had to go to the bathroom. Dante picked up the luggage and carried it out to the car.

"I didn't mean to upset her," he said as Will opened the trunk. "I don't know, me and her, we never . . ."

"I know, the chemistry was never right," said Will. "But she cares for you, take my word for it."

Dante loaded the suitcases and looked up at the trees, their tops swaying gently. They were noticeably greener than they had been the day before, their buds, nourished by the night's rain, opening to the sunlight. He had only a few minutes, and then Will and Kathy would be gone and the question would haunt him ever afterward.

"I oughta put this to Kathy, but . . . My mom, before she married my dad, did she . . ." As Dante hesitated, trying to think of a diplomatic way to ask, Will slammed the trunk and looked at him.

"Did she have a kid, a boy, out of wedlock and put him up for adoption?"

Will dropped his eyes to the ground, then raised them. Dante couldn't tell if he was offended that such a question would be asked at this delicate time or was merely baffled.

"Yeah, it's a good thing you didn't ask Kath that one," Will said. "She's more Catholic than the Pope. I didn't know Meg before she married your dad, so I can't say."

"Right. But did Kathy ever mention anything to you? Drop a hint? I know my mom was supposed to've been a little wild back in the sixties. Kind of a hippie. Not like Kathy."

"Kathy never said anything; no."

"Would she have, if it happened?"

"After eighteen years, yeah, I'd think so. No secrets between us. Hey, Dante, where the hell did you get this idea?"

"The woman I met on the train. Her and her husband adopted a boy back in '66. Some home for unwed mothers up in Maine. He got killed in the Gulf War. They showed me his picture. I'm a dead ringer for him, almost."

"C'mon."

"Had my eyebrows, even. Mom's eyebrows. Kathy's. It was so weird. The only way I could figure it was that Mom had a kid she put up for adoption."

"So that's what you meant, this woman liked your looks." Will turned toward the house as Kathy came out the front door. "I'll tell you this," he said in an undertone. "Your grandmother wouldn't've let Meg put up a kid for adoption. She would've raised the kid herself before she'd let some stranger do it."

Kathy marched down the walk, and the two men stopped talking. Dante opened the car door and apologized for upsetting her and thanked her for all she'd done. They managed to part, if not amicably, then at least with no ill feeling. After she and Will drove off, Dante stood on the sidewalk, staring down the street long after their car was gone from sight. He was giving himself a few minutes to get used to their absence. Then he went back inside to confront the silence and aloneness he had been dreading.

He sat on the sofa and stared at the cheap prints and posters on the walls, the photographs on an end table. One was an eight-by-ten of the photo in his wallet, another was his graduation picture, a third showed him looking awkward in a rented tux beside the girl he took to the senior prom. He couldn't recall her name, except that it began with *A*. Ann, or maybe Alice. His relationships with girls in high school had been fleeting and shallow, and the passage into his twenties hadn't changed things. The only women he'd been with these past two years had been a couple of Cuban groupies who hung out in the clubs where Hector Baroso's band played regular gigs, two or three tourists whose desires to round out their Florida vacations with one-night stands Dante had been happy to fulfill. He wished he had a serious girlfriend now, a true friend and lover he could call and confide in.

Ten minutes passed. He could hear his heart beating and, in another few minutes, the sound of blood rushing through his head. The silence became as a living presence, its weight pressing down on him, urging him to lie down. He thought that if he did, he might never get up again. Stirring himself, he went into the kitchen and turned on the radio, tuning to the Newark jazz station he used to listen to instead of doing his homework. With Albert King strumming soulful electric riffs in the background, he found the lawyer's name—Tom Ahearn—in the envelope containing his mother's will and made an appointment for two o'clock that afternoon. Then he took off his suit, closed the drapes in his old bedroom, and fell into a restless sleep while some female singer wailed about the man who'd wronged her.

A little later, he woke with the same sensation he'd had on the train—of not knowing where he was. The bed he'd slept on for most of his life felt as strange as the bed in a motel. Nothing in the room looked familiar in the first few moments of groggy consciousness, not even the high-school hockey jersey in the closet, though his name was stitched on the back above his old number. The peculiar amnesia passed quickly, but it left an arid residue of fear on his tongue. Light-headed, licking his lips, he got out of bed and gave himself a passing glance in the dresser mirror. Cleft chin, dark-blond hair, eyes the color of newly minted pennies, the small rhinestone in his right ear glinting in the sunlight that sabered through the crack in the drapes. Dante Patrick Panetta. He put his suit on again. He supposed he ought to wear a suit if he was going to see a lawyer.

He went into the kitchen to turn off the radio, then noticed a note held by a magnet to the side of the refrigerator. It was a list, written in his mother's cursive hand. She had been planning to buy frozen spinach, chicken breasts, and Parmesan cheese—ingredients for one of her favorite dishes. Below were notes to call someone named Anne Califiero and a plumber to fix the running toilet. He wondered when she had written these reminders. Sunday? Monday, the day of her death? How far away death must have seemed to her, how she would have scoffed if anyone had told her that it was right around the corner, lurking like a mugger. He switched the radio off. The silence rushed in, and grief ambushed him again, striking his sternum with the force of a punch, driving him into a chair beside the kitchen table. With his elbows on the stained cloth, he sat sobbing for a full quarter of an hour.

When he was able to master his voice, he called Ahearn and said that he would be a few minutes late. It was strange the way the spells of grieving would seize him from out of nowhere, shake him, and then let him go.

The lawyer's office was in a trendy, rehabbed riverfront district, where the dingy exteriors of extinct factories converted into artists' studios and offices seemed to hold echoes of thudding machinery long silent, the shouts of grimy workers long dead. Ahearn, a slight man in his late thirties or early forties, with dark hair and elastic features, sat in a high-backed leather chair beneath two framed diplomas, one from Notre Dame, the other from Georgetown Law School. Dante mentioned that his mother once had hoped he would go to Notre Dame, but there had been no money for a school like that and his grades hadn't been good enough for a scholarship.

"Notre Dame's a little overrated. It's the image. The Fighting Irish and the Gipper and all that," said Ahearn with a wan smile.

The chair creaked as he leaned back and said that he and Dante's mother had worked together on a fund-raising committee for St. Mary's parochial school—a fact he seemed eager to establish to assure Dante that he was trustworthy. Three years ago, he continued, he'd convinced Meg to make out a will, even though she was young and in good health, and, sadly, his advice had proved sound. She had named him as executor of her estate, and because her estate primarily consisted of her house, all that meant was that he would represent Dante if he decided to sell the place. Any questions? Dante thought for a moment, gazing out the window at the Norwalk River, where the rusty barges moored end to end against the far bank looked like a layer of huge iron bricks.

"Do you know anything about a realty company called Bratton and Higgs?"

"They specialize in premier residential properties and commercial real estate. You know, eight-bedroom houses on the shore, shopping malls, horse farms, that kind of thing."

"So they're not shady or fly-by-night or anything like that?"

The lawyer pushed his chair backward and, with his chin raised, opened his mouth in silent laughter.

"I hardly think so," Ahearn said, and then he gave Dante some papers to sign.

HE WALKED DOWN Water Street toward his mother's car. No, his. The car, the house, the bank account, *his*. True, the Civic was not much of a car, the house not much of a house, and the bank account small, yet he had come into possession of all the things that proclaimed you had a place in the world. Odd, then, that he felt as displaced on these familiar streets as he did in Miami. He wondered if he could make a life for himself down there. Thousands had: the Cubans and Haitians and Central Americans who, like mangrove shoots bobbing on ocean currents, had floated to the Florida shore and managed to root themselves in the sand and loose limestone marl.

The slow city traffic bore him into the torrent hurtling down I-95. He had a lot to do before he caught the Sunday train back to Miami. Call a used-car agency, pack his mother's clothes and arrange for Catholic Charities to pick them up, fix the cockeyed shutter, cut the lawn, and put the house on the market. All these projects needed doing, but as he neared the turnpike, he headed north, away from his mother's house. His grief was there, crouched and waiting to pounce on him again from each small room. He just wanted to keep moving. Greer was right—there was a forgetfulness in motion. The first Westport exit flew by. In a few minutes, the sign for the next appeared. He took it on impulse, following the road into Sherwood Island State Park. On both sides, salt marshes opened up in broad swaths of green and yellow spartina. The road wound past a grove of tall pine and oak, their afternoon shadows striping the pavement, and dropped with the land toward the shore, beyond which the blue, wave-ribbed Sound reached to the Long Island side.

He parked and walked along the beach, packed hard by the receding tide and cobbled with broken mussel shells, which crunched beneath his feet. Now he knew why he had come here. This was where he had learned to surf-cast and where he had caught his first bluefish. It had been only a snapper, but landing the fish had excited him and had brought a rare and loving touch from his father.

He walked on for almost a mile, careless of the effect sand and sea wrack were having on his dress shoes, until a tidal creek barred his path. Upstream, the creek's falling waters split around a muddy island, where a great blue heron stood still and vigilant, its head and long neck forming a question mark. Faster than Dante's eye could see, the bird extended its neck and darted its beak into the current. It came up with a fish, quickly swallowed it, and resumed its motionless watch. He started toward the heron. It caught the movement with one yellow side-looking eye and, spreading its wings to the width of an armspan, tucked its legs beneath its tail and rose in elegant flight, lofting into the birches clumped where the creek curved away into the marsh.

Heading back toward the car, he listened to the clatter of mussels that gulls dropped on exposed rocks to crack the shells. The world of nature, like the world of men, was going on, indifferent to his tragedy; but this recognition, instead of fanning his bitterness, began to loosen the bands of sorrow from around his chest. For wasn't he going on as well, moving forward in time and space, breathing the air of the living world? As he left the park, his heart rose with a skein of Canadas winging out of the estuary to wedge up over the Sound, the wedge like a trail of smoke, ever shifting yet holding its V in the sinless April sky. They were heading north; soon he would be going south. If he wanted to. He did not have to return to Miami. Probably he would—his job was there, his apartment and possessions—but there was no obligation.

Coming to the turnpike entrance, he was a little disturbed to discover that his feeling of displacement had somehow mutated into one of freedom, as if his mother's death had released him from something. He recalled, with a prickling of shame, the many times, in high school and afterward, when he would stare at the rusting Cyclone fence separating his cramped backyard from the neighbors' and feel hopelessly trapped. The emancipation from his father's unpredictable violence had shackled him to his mother's workaday life of workaday people, drab and featureless and with horizons as restricted as the view from his bedroom window. He supposed his flight to Florida had been an attempt to win his independence, but it hadn't worked. With each weekly call, each monthly letter, he realized anew that his life was linked to hers by bonds as firm as the long tether of concrete that lay between them: bonds of love, of obligation, of his own need for her, that above all. Well, they were broken now.

IT WAS A WHITE brick building on the Post Road, with white pillars grinning at its entrance. Dante hadn't made a conscious decision to come here; when he'd seen the sign for Fair Harbor, the car seemed to steer itself off the turnpike. He mounted the stairs, a little intimidated by the display easels in the window, which showed manorial houses selling for prices beyond his imagining. He tugged at his sleeves and, leaning toward the window, combed his tousled hair. Then he entered a reception room with leather chairs grouped around a coffee table on which magazines and brochures lay in neat, glossy rows. A middle-aged woman seated behind a walnut desk peered at him over the rim of reading glasses strung to her neck by a silver cord.

"May I help you?"

He asked to see Mrs. Rhodes.

"And who may I say is calling?"

He told her. The woman, pushing her glasses to the bridge of her nose, checked an appointment book, then looked at him skeptically.

"I don't have an appointment. But she's expecting me. I think."

Picking up the phone, the receptionist pushed a button and said:

"Hello, Greer? Ann. There's a young man here to see you. I don't see his name in the . . . Yes, that's right. Mr. Panetta. Yes . . . All right, I'll tell him."

"Mrs. Rhodes is with a couple of clients right now," said the woman, somewhat thawed, the fissure of a smile cracking her gelid face. "She'll be another ten minutes or so, but she asked that you wait. Insisted on it, in fact. Please . . ." And she gestured at the chairs.

The leather arms enfolded him, the cushion buoyed him like a cloud. He browsed through *Town & Country*, which exhaled perfume, and then the brochures that advertised houses even grander than those in the windows: there were no figures in the space marked "Price," only the words "Upon Request."

What am I doing here? he asked himself.

Greer appeared in a dark-blue pinstripe suit, its skirt touching her knees, and blue pumps that made her appear elegantly tall. A string of pearls dipped into the plunge of her silk blouse. "I can show it to you then," she said discreetly to her clients, an unapproachable blonde and a slab of athletic beef in a forest-green blazer. The young man leaned toward Greer and murmured something. She shook her head solemnly. The couple did not look over thirty. Dante was amazed that two people only a few years older than he could even think of buying one of these places. They had to be trust-fund brats. He decided to hate them.

Greer escorted them out, then turned to him, her face brightening as she took both his hands in hers and, with a subtle pressure of her fingers, bid him stand. A scent rose from her bosom, like the scent in the magazine, only less aggressively sweet.

"I didn't expect you so soon."

He started to speak, but she continued:

"That's a lie, actually. I had a feeling you'd come today. I'll confess that I wanted you to, but you should have given yourself a few days," she said with a gravity out of phase with her smile. Her body inclined toward his, telling him that she wanted to embrace him. He supposed she didn't because he was here on business.

"I don't have a few days. Got to get back on Sunday," he said.

"Of course. Come in, then, and we'll talk." She took a step backward to look him up and down. "Well, I must say you look handsome in a suit. You're a clotheshorse."

He wanted to believe the flattery, as he wanted to believe that the pearls and smart business suit had been donned exclusively for his arrival, that her admiring eyes shone for him and not the lost son he resembled.

He followed her down a corridor between rows of desks. Looking at her hair, he again took up a pair of imaginary scissors. It was too shaggy, and there was too much of it. From the back, it looked like the gray mane of a fairy-tale witch.

She led him to her desk, took out a notepad, and asked questions about the house that he couldn't answer. No, he didn't know the original purchase price or what the property taxes were, and no, he hadn't the slightest idea how much to ask.

Greer laid down her pen and folded her hands.

"Well, then, I'll have to take a close look myself and come up with an asking price," she said pertly, then rose and slung a briefcase over her shoulder.

"You mean now?" asked Dante.

"As good a time as any."

She swept out and bustled down the steps and across the lot to her car, Dante feeling as though he were being carried along, like a light plane in the slipstream of a jet. He'd assumed she was going to follow him, but she didn't let him get near his car. Somehow, without a touch, she drew him into her Lexus. He sank into the leather with a pleasant sense of surrender. Greer got in and pulled out into the street. She pushed a button on the armrest, and the door locks clicked. He wasn't sure if he was her client or her prisoner.

"Why are you going to all this trouble?" he asked as they sped down the turnpike. "I saw those places you people sell. One-point-two mil. Price upon request."

She had put on sunglasses against the glare to the west.

"High end, low end—our inventory runs the gamut," she replied.

"Besides, we're on the MLS—the Multiple Listing Service. Every broker in Fairfield County will have a chance to sell the place."

"Whatever. You could be selling one of those mansions right now."

"All right. I'm a hard-hustling real estate saleswoman, always looking for a way to turn a quick buck, even a small buck," she quipped without a smile.

"That sounds like something my aunt would say."

"The one from Boston?"

Dante nodded and said, "I told her that you gave me a lift from the station and offered to help me sell the house. She said something almost made me laugh. She wondered if you were a good Samaritan or just liked my looks."

Greer opened her window a crack, shook a cigarette out of her purse, and pushed in the lighter.

"What do you think, Dante? Good Samaritan or like your looks?"

"I'll vote for Samaritan."

"You might vote for Samaritan, but you're thinking it's all because of your resemblance to Clay."

"It would make sense, wouldn't it?"

"I would have thought—no, I would have *hoped* that you would give me more credit than that," she said with a note of injury perfectly pitched to avoid sounding whiny while putting Dante on the defensive. Women could do that so quickly, so easily, he thought. "Do you think I'd be going out of my way if I didn't see something in you underneath?"

Smoke coiled around the back of her neck, then slithered through the crack in the window.

"You don't know anything about me," Dante said. "I could be a crook, for all you know. A con man. A psychopathic serial killer."

"Not to mention the possibility that you're a gigolo who preys on older women," Greer remarked with a snort. "Dante, dear, Bratton and Higgs has five branch offices and seventy-odd salespeople. I've been with them only four years, but last year and so far this year, I've been in the top ten."

He gave her a quizzical look. What did her sales record have to do with anything?

"Our clients tend to be the lions in the capitalist Serengeti," she replied. "They're used to having their way. If I weren't something of a lioness myself, I could be intimidated by them, but I can't let that happen because I have to make judgments about them. Are they serious buyers or sellers? Are they honest? Can they really afford a particular property or do they only look as if they can? In a phrase, I'm pretty good at sizing people up."

He said nothing, though he longed to know what judgments she had made about him, not as a client but as a person. For reasons he couldn't define, her esteem was important to him.

He entered the house without fear. Greer's presence kept the ghosts at bay. She whirled through the rooms, measuring them with an electronic device that shot an invisible beam from wall to wall and recorded the distance on a miniature display screen. The latest high-tech gizmo, she said. Fast, precise to the millimeter, and it obviated the need for all the bending and stooping you had to do with a conventional tape measure.

She descended into the cobwebbed cellar and inspected the oil heater, opened the breaker box to check out the electrical circuits, and turned on the washer and dryer to make sure they worked. Going back upstairs, she gave the kitchen appliances once-overs, opened and closed doors, and surveyed the bathroom. Dante cringed at the reproach of the broken hooks on the shower curtain and the rust stains in the bathtub. His mother never was much of a housekeeper, he said.

"Never explain, never apologize, Dante. I don't imagine your mother had the time or energy to play June Cleaver, scrubbing every spot," Greer said, then breezed into the living room, where she sat on the sofa, drew a listing form from the briefcase, and began writing. He took the moment to duck into his room and consult the paperback Webster's in his desk drawer. "Obviate" meant to make unnecessary. When he returned to the living room, feeling just a little smarter for having learned a new word, Greer was studying the mortgage contract and making more notes.

"I'll have to look at the records, find out what other houses in this neighborhood have gone for, to come up with an asking price."

She held up her pack of Benson & Hedges. He motioned that it would be all right if she smoked, and fetched a saucer from the kitchen for an ashtray.

"My aunt said that after I paid off the mortgage, I'd clear—"

"Mortgage *and* closing costs," she interrupted.

"Uh, what are closing costs?" he asked, feeling dumb again.

She gave him a quick seminar on brokerage fees, etc., then said

"Figure six to eight percent for those. You should have a profit mid to high twenties."

There was an interval of silence, and Dante heard the faint rustle of wool against nylon as she crossed her legs, the movement raising her skirt to uncover her lower thigh, its white flesh darkened by her stockings. The glimpse wasn't provocative but struck him as something he wasn't supposed to see. Fastening his gaze on her face, he said that twenty-five thousand plus was more than he'd expected.

"It isn't much these days, dear. Well, I'd say we're done for now. What are your dinner plans?"

The change of topic was too quick for him.

"Plans?"

"You are planning to eat, aren't you?"

"I suppose I'll grab something at a diner."

"*Diner?* Too dreary, Dante. Please have dinner with us. I'm going to do a pasta with shrimp, in a white wine and garlic sauce."

"You've done enough for me already."

"I've got to take you back to your car anyway. The house is only a few minutes from my office."

He understood then why she had maneuvered him into her car. The idea to ask him to dinner must have come to her at the office, and his car had been left behind to make it inconvenient for him to refuse. He was usually put off by feminine guile, but Greer's charmed him.

"Should I wear this?" he asked, gesturing at his suit. "Or can I change?"

"We're not formal. Most of the time we eat off TV trays in the den."

As he stood to go into his bedroom, she leaned toward the end table and looked at his graduation picture, her hand resting on its frame.

"Was it awful for you, staying here last night?"

"Not with my aunt and uncle here. It was this afternoon, after they left, when it got bad. I went to see a lawyer about my mom's will, and when I left, I couldn't stand the idea of coming back in here. That's how I ended up at your office. I was just driving around."

"I haven't been in Clay's room since he died. Julian has, the cleaning lady, but if I went there, I'm sure it would kill me, even now. Well, there I go again, unburdening myself when it's you who needs to." Her lips parted slightly and smoke curled from between them, rising to curtain her face before dissipating into filaments that wove and spun patterns in the house's quiet currents of air. "You know the offer to stay with us is still open. You're welcome to stay the night. You're welcome to stay till it's time for you to go back to Miami."

Dante frowned pensively. "I've got a feeling Mr. Rhodes wouldn't be too happy, having a houseguest he didn't expect."

"Julian will be delighted. He might not show it, but he will be."

"If you say so," said Dante, absolving himself in case Julian's reaction wasn't as forecast.

"That's wonderful, Dante. It'll be good for you. It'll be . . ." She didn't finish the sentence but, bending forward, clasped her fingers around her knees and suggested that he pack while she phoned her husband.

"So it won't be too much of a surprise," she added, bestowing on him the covert smile of a coconspirator. The trouble was, he wasn't sure what they were conspiring to do.

In his room, amid old, familiar things, he changed out of his suit and carelessly tossed it into his bag with his socks and underwear. Glimpsing through the window the light of the waning day and the diamond shadows the Cyclone fence cast upon the tiny province of his backyard, he felt a bittersweet melancholy and the quickening of anticipation—the emotions of departure and advent. This place now belonged irrevocably to his past. And what of his future? He couldn't say, but sensed that his acceptance of Greer's invitation implied a deeper commitment, that he was allowing himself to be drawn into a design whose shape and nature he could not clearly see.

THE ROAD RAN atop a bluff above the long black tongue of the cove that gave Fair Harbor half its name. There were big houses on both sides: a couple of modern places with plenty of glass and skylights invitingly aglow; sprawling colonials that made Dante think of founding fathers in wigs and buckle shoes. Two granite posts as squat and solid as goalies guarded the entrance to the Rhodeses' driveway. As he turned in behind Greer, his headlights illuminated a brass plaque on the left post. "Fastnet," it said. Beyond the gate, looming in the darkness, a massive frame house embraced by a veranda rose three stories to a mansard roof picketed by iron spears. A narrow tower stood square in the center, with a double door at its bottom and a long, arched window at the top, glowering down on a lawn shadowed by hemlocks. Lightless dormers jutted out from the roof's steep pitch, lightless windows rounded at their tops peered from under the front eaves, like blind eyes from beneath protruding brows. One of the three automatic doors in the detached garage rolled open, and Greer's Lexus glided inside. She climbed out, holding a grocery bag in one arm while she signaled him with the other to park on the apron beside the drive. When he got out and followed her up the walk, colored yard lights hidden in the hedges and flower beds blazed on with a festive, startling brilliance.

"I forgot to warn you about those," Greer said with a chuckle. "They're switched on by motion detectors in the alarm system."

The house looked more cheerful in the lights. Its pale-yellow walls were bright with the luster of a recent painting, gingerbread carvings curled in the corners between the pillars and the veranda beams, and the windows, trimmed in white, and the green shutters, all in their ordered places, sang to him a silent and soothing melody of proportion and harmony. A sign beside the front door repeated the name on the gatepost and declared that the structure had been built in 1859. That was the only numeral he saw; there was no address, which impressed and excited him. Houses here were distinguished not by the banality of street numbers but by names. Greer opened the door and flipped a couple of light switches. A glowing center hall, hung with oil paintings under hooded lamps, beckoned Dante to cross the threshold.

"Set your suitcase there. We'll bring it up later," she said, pointing to the foot of a wide staircase that climbed into the mystery of the upper rooms.

He tried not to gawk at the high ceilings, the paintings and furniture, as she took him into a kitchen as big as his mother's living room. French doors stretched across the back wall. Beyond them, a veranda overlooked the harbor, where the mast lights of moored sailboats gently swayed, like stars on pendulums. That he was standing here as an inhabitant, even a temporary one, amazed him. He recalled the summer he'd worked as a Federal Express courier and stood on doorsteps in Greenwich and Darien. Looking over people's shoulders as they bent down to sign for their packages, he caught glimpses of splendid interiors, Persian carpets on floors that shone like china. He had tried to imagine what life was like in those golden realms, filled with all the grace and beauty that were not his, though it wasn't the houses and the things in them that he wanted; it was the unbreachable security that they represented—the exemption from the soul-killing fear of poverty. He knew even then that his America was not going to be like his Uncle Will's, that he was in his place, a delivery boy on the outside, looking in. And the few times (usually in bad weather) some thoughtful lady or gentleman allowed him to step in out of the rain, he could almost feel a strange pressure in the interior air; it was as if the house were reacting to his presence, gathering itself to eject him should he overstay. No such atmospherics troubled him now.

Greer raised him out of his reverie, telling him to take a pasta pot out of a certain cupboard, fill it two-thirds with salted water, and set it on the stove. While he did this, she took the shrimp from the refrigerator, snatched a package of linguine from a cabinet, then set a bulb of garlic and a knife on a cutting board beside the sink, performing these movements like choreography.

"All set," she said. "Now let's have a look at your room."

It was on the attic floor—old servants' quarters, she explained, adding with an apologetic smile, "I hope you don't mind. I just thought you'd find it more private up here. There's a bathroom with a shower at the end of the hall."

He glanced at his room, which was narrow and as sparsely furnished as a monk's cell, with a single bed, a nightstand and lamp, and a plain dresser that looked as if it had been made when the house was built. The dormer window offered a view of the front lawn and the street.

"I'm not putting anybody out, am I?" he asked, somewhat hopeful that the Rhodeses employed servants. A butler and maid would have completed the picture he had of their way of life.

"Oh, heavens, no. Clay's nanny had this room when he was small, but she's been gone for years." Greer stepped past him, fluffed the pillow, and turned down the bed. "And we never did have live-in help. Isn't necessary anymore. With all the cleaning services, who needs a housekeeper? Who needs a gardener when there are scads of landscaping services? And I'd rather do my own cooking. Kind of lonely, though. Be nice to have a staff just for the company. Ah! Towels!"

She went into a linen closet in the hall and got the towels and set them on the dresser.

"Dinner'll be at eight. Julian's working late tonight. Having cocktails with some movers and shakers."

Dante undid the bungee cord on his suitcase.

"What's he do?" he asked. Having cocktails wasn't his idea of work.

"He has a seat on the exchange."

"The stock exchange, you mean?"

"Of course, dear," Greer, withdrawing from the room, replied archly, the pained look on her face telling him that in this world you didn't ask what people did for a living. He could tell he was going to have a tricky time, figuring out the rules and customs.

He lay on the bed, the former nanny's bed. A nanny! He pictured a Jamaican woman, like the ones he'd seen wheeling infants down the sidewalks and lanes of Greenwich and Darien. He could not imagine what it must have been like for Clayton to grow up in the spaciousness of Fastnet, with a nanny and without ever feeling embarrassed for his mother as she tried to maintain her dignity while explaining to some bank officer on the phone why the mortgage or car payment would be late again this month.

GREER WENT OUT of her way to make the dinner special. It was served not on TV trays in the den but in the dining room, with candlelight, her best china and silver, and wine in a crystal decanter. Dante, Greer, and Julian sat clustered at one end of a cherrywood table in which their reflections moved with the shimmering reflections of the dimmed chandelier, the candelabra, and the candles and their steady flames. There were sixteen chairs at the table, four more lined up against one wall, two on each side of a breakfront on which silver urns and bowls gleamed like trophies.

Julian, doing his best to make him feel welcome, quipped that he hoped Dante would stay the month. This was civilized dining! By God, it was good to eat like white people again, he declared jovially, drawing a "Julian!" from Greer as she set the salad bowl on a trivet. He sloughed off the rebuke with a wave and said he couldn't recall the last time he and Greer had eaten in the dining room. Oh, when they entertained, but they didn't entertain very much anymore. Now, his parents, well, they ate formally every night, he added, a hand going to his red and fleshy throat to indicate a necktie (though he had doffed his tie and suit jacket). People ought to do more of that . . . ah, these were vulgar times. Dante gravely nodded his agreement with the benefits of dressing for dinner— though he'd never seen anyone do that except in old movies—and carefully watched which fork Julian picked up when Greer served the salad.

Julian asked what sports he played—he looked in good shape. None.

There wasn't time with his day job, band rehearsals, and engagements. He had played on the high-school hockey team his first two years, but quit to work after school and help his mother make ends meet.

Coiling linguine around his fork, Julian inclined his head and turned up a corner of his mouth, as if he hadn't quite understood, so Dante elaborated, telling him that he'd worked as a housepainter his junior year and loaded trucks for UPS the next, and begun playing professionally when he was eighteen to bring in extra money.

The fork vanished into Julian's mouth, and he chewed slowly.

"You know, Greer and I . . . a bubble—I guess we've lived in a bubble all our lives."

Dante gave him an inquisitive look.

"I think he means that we've been lucky and that we know a lot of lucky people," Greer explained. "Kids who don't have to work after school to help their families pay the bills."

"Not all luck," Julian drawled. "Some hard work went into it. Taking advantage of opportunity when it knocks. Loaded trucks, eh? *That* must be where you got those shoulders."

Dante asked if he had gotten his playing football.

"Football? No. Eights. Prep school and Dartmouth. All four years both places."

He did not want to reveal his ignorance by asking what "eights" was, but his expression must have betrayed him, because Julian pushed his chair back and began making rowing motions.

"Crew. An eight-man racing shell," he said, continuing to propel the chair down some imaginary river. "I've got an Alden in the boat shed out front. Ought to . . . This . . ." He patted the belly that made his white shirt resemble the surface of a mega-egg. "Get rid of this. Ought to do more rowing. Or maybe load trucks. Ha!" He paused, spearing a shrimp from its nest of linguine. "How did you ever . . . I mean to say, if you did work like that, how did you get into this hairstyling thing?"

His eyes, clear and probing from beneath his heavy lids, gave the impression that he was more than casually curious. Dante, confident that he had settled any questions about his masculinity, said he had taken a course in hairstyling because he figured he'd be more employable if he could do women's hair as well as men's.

"That was after the first place I worked in Miami. It wasn't really a barbershop. A lot of guys would come in, but not for haircuts. Went straight to the back room to get the line at Hialeah, or at the dog track, or on the Dolphins and the Heat. I figured it was only a matter of time before the place got raided."

"How *interesting*. You mean it was run by the Mafia?" Greer, her fork poised over her plate, her lips slightly parted, silently invited him to tell them more about his brush with the underworld. He was beginning to feel as if he were undergoing a background check.

"I guess it was run by the mob. I don't know. Nobody said a thing to me, except to tell me not to pay attention to what was going on. I wasn't supposed to see no evil."

She flinched again, as she had on the train, and this time he realized the reason for it. His mother often had reprimanded him for the same mistake.

"Any," he added. "Wasn't supposed to see any evil."

When it was time to clear the table for dessert, Dante started to rise, but she motioned to him to keep his seat.

It was awkward to be alone with Julian, who fidgeted and allowed his glance to dart around the room, as if some corner of it might yield a topic of conversation. Dante tried to rescue him from his discomfort by complimenting Greer's cooking.

"Here's the proof," said Julian, patting his stomach again. "One seventy when we got married, thirty years ago; thirty-one next month. Two-oh-five now." He took a sip of wine and looked wistfully into the glass. "Thirty-one years . . ."

"Were you married here?" asked Dante, wondering why they had adopted so quickly after their wedding. He imagined a tragic discovery of sterility or infertility.

"No. Up on the north shore. That's where Greer's from. She's a Braithwaite, old north shore family. Been there damn near since the *Mayflower*. Marblehead. And here she is."

She backed through the swinging door to the kitchen, bearing a tray of coffee cups and dessert bowls, from which peaks of vanilla ice cream rose, blanketed in raspberries.

"So what did you two talk about while I was gone?" she asked as they began to eat. She seemed eager for Dante and Julian to get on together.

"Your cooking, and all complimentary," said Julian.

"I should hope so, after all those classes. I don't believe in false humility," she informed Dante, then attacked her dessert with gusto, consuming half of it before she paused and asked if he did any fishing in Florida.

"Some. Not half as much as I'd like."

"Like to fish?" Julian inquired hopefully.

"Love it. My dad and me used to surf-cast on the Sound. Couple of times he brought me to Montauk when the blues were blitzing."

"Been there for that. Crowded, though . . . Too much shoulder-to-shoulder for me. Get as much action on the Vineyard and not as crowded."

"Never got to the Vineyard. Like to someday. Heard the stripers there are something else in the fall run. I'd rather catch stripers than bluefish any day of the week."

Julian softly gaveled with his hand. "Couldn't agree more. Great fish, the striper. Not as great as the bonefish. Can't beat the bonefish, but stripers . . . Close second in my book."

Greer sat in silence, smiling benignly.

"I've never tried bonefishing," Dante said, recalling the weekends he'd tossed a line from bridges high over ocean channels, jostling amid the salty reek of bait buckets for a spot at the rail with trailer-park crackers, poor blacks seeking relief from the fiery confines of Liberty City and Overtown, Cuban refugees only weeks ashore from their rafting voyages, while far out on the emerald flats, sportsmen in chartered skiffs conducted silent symphonies with their fly rods.

"Your number, be sure to leave it with us before you head back. Give you a call next time I'm down there. Take you out on a trip." Julian was becoming more relaxed and expansive. "Take you out on the Sound this Saturday, but my boat's in the yard."

"I couldn't go anyway. Too many things to do. Pack my mother's things, figure out what I'm going to take with me from the house, the furniture—all that."

His spirits instantly fell, the vision of racing with Julian into waters where the big bonefish tailed dissolving into a doleful picture of himself filling packing boxes with all the bric-a-brac of a life that had ceased. His mood changed the mood at the table, and for a while, no one spoke. Then Greer perked up, her head turning with the quick, open-eyed movements of an alerted bird's.

"I'll help you with all that," she stated.

Dante gestured that it wouldn't be necessary.

"Nonsense. Two of us working together, we'll get it done like that." She snapped her fingers. "I can take some time off from the office."

"Greer . . . ," Julian began to say.

"Please, dear . . ."

"You don't have to," Dante said.

"I know I don't *have* to. If I felt obligated, I suppose I wouldn't do it. I *want* to. Now, what do you say we go to the den so I can have a cigarette? It's the only room in the house Julian lets me smoke in."

It looked more like a library, or a room in a posh men's club, like one Dante had seen on a TV commercial. Above the mantelpiece, a man wearing white whiskers and a black coat sternly gazed out of an oil portrait cracked with age. A gold plate at the bottom identified the subject and gave the date of the painting: Elliott Braithwaite, 1795. Greer, sitting down with her cigarette, said that he was an ancestor of hers, a sea captain who'd been born in the English town of Fastnet.

"He came to America as a boy and went whaling and then found out there was more money to be made building ships than sailing them. When he got his pile, he built quite a grand place near Marblehead and called it Fastnet. It burned down ages ago, so when Julian and I bought this place, we decided to christen it with the same name."

"How did you find out all that stuff about him?" Dante asked. He was captivated not by the iron set of Elliott Braithwaite's jaw, nor by his gray, unyielding sea dog's eyes, but by the fact that Greer knew the name and life story of an ancestor so remote. Christ, he knew only sketchy details about his grandparents, and of those who preceded them he knew no more than a Peruvian Indian knows about his Inca forebears.

"Some of it's written down." Greer pointed vaguely at a bookcase. "The rest of it's stories passed down, generation to generation."

Julian drew a decanter of whiskey from the liquor cabinet and, settling into a chair, held up the amber vessel.

"Care for a shot?"

Dante accepted, watching with mild alarm as Julian filled two short glasses to the brim. He hoped he wasn't expected to finish all that; he'd be a babbling, staggering fool.

Julian took up the TV remote. "Okay with everybody if I check in on a basketball game?"

"Do we have to, dear? That's such a conversation-killer, that damned television."

Dante suspected that was why Julian wanted it on.

"Maybe Dante likes basketball. Follow it much?"

"Perhaps Dante would prefer a hockey game."

"No. That's okay. Watch whatever you want. It's, you know, your house."

"But we'd like you to feel at home here, to feel that it's your house," she said.

"The basketball's okay, really," said Dante—unnecessarily, as Julian already had it on: a game between the Knicks and the Sixers.

He tentatively drank his scotch, which slipped down his throat with a warm, smoky seductiveness, and feigned interest in the game. During a commercial break, he began to feel drowsy—the effect of the whiskey, the meal, and the emotional ups and downs of the day. He was about to excuse himself when, out of the corner of his eye, he noticed that Greer appeared ill: elbows on her knees, head bowed, she sighed and massaged her forehead.

"Greer, are you . . . ?" Dante started to say.

"It's nothing. Tired is all." Her thumb and forefinger forming a hoop above her eyebrows, she sighed again. "Awfully tired."

"Too much today, Greer," said Julian. "You're always taking on too much."

"It's not that," she said, a little snappishly. "It's . . . Oh, Dante, I'm sorry. I'm usually quite in control, but just now, seeing you in this room, in that chair, in this light . . ." She hesitated, her glance sliding toward a long, leather-topped desk behind him, on the far side of the room. He sensed what she was looking at but didn't dare look himself; instead, he half rose, intending to remove himself, since his presence seemed to disturb her.

"No! Please stay right where you are," she said fiercely, and raised her palm. "It was just a moment, past now . . ."

All this was entirely too much emotionalism for Julian, who cleared his throat, scowled, and said that maybe it would be a good idea if they all went to bed.

"But it's early! Oh, there, I've gone and spoiled a perfectly fine evening."

Dante assured her she hadn't, and insisted on doing the dishes. She refused: he was their guest.

"I'll give you a hand. The woman has only one speed. All ahead full," Julian said with an indulgent shake of his head, and followed her to the kitchen.

Dante did not go immediately upstairs but crossed to the desk and stared again into his double's face. Three photographs sat on the leather surface. One showed Clayton, wearing a blue blazer with a prep-school crest, flanked by a younger, slimmer Julian and a ravishing Greer, her hair as long and wavy as it now was, but a rich chestnut instead of gray; in another, she and Clayton were windblown and squinting into the sun as they sat beside each other in a small sailboat; and in the last, he was in black tie, accompanied by a tall, auburn-haired girl in a low-cut ball gown, with what appeared to be a hotel ballroom in the background.

Looking at the pictures made Dante uneasy. He left the den, bounding up the stairs to his bare chamber, where he took off his jeans, put on his suit, and stood in front of the dresser mirror, striking Clayton's pose: a hand in a pocket, the other around an imaginary waist, his head, with a lock of hair falling carelessly over his brows, inclined just a little to the right, his lips forming a faint, smug smile. He had it all down right, but he looked stiff and counterfeit. Kind of like knowing all the notes to a song but playing it square, he thought. The negligent grace wasn't there, that air of polished unconcern. Those came from within. But might they be learned? he wondered. Clayton must have learned those mannerisms until they came as naturally as flight to a bird.

He undressed and, the attic floor being stuffy, opened the window. Spring's advance was accelerating; the night was warmer than it had been only hours before, and a fog rising from the harbor sent vaporous ribbons across the lawn and the street. The bellow of a lighthouse foghorn came from far out on the Sound. Now and then, as the sailboats in the harbor rocked on a swell, halyards chimed against aluminum masts. To this sea music he lay down, feeling cozy and safe, delighting in the caress of the crisp bedsheets. The meal lay heavy and warm in his belly, radiating throughout his body the contentment of a well-fed child, and the liquor in his blood drowned his mind in a flooding tide of happiness, a tide that drew out in its ebb the last grating sands of this day's grief. There would be grief tomorrow, and the next day, but this one's was gone. His only regret, as sleep fell upon him, was that he would have to leave.

ON SUNDAY MORNING, while Julian was at church—Greer owned that she didn't care for "all that high Episcopal ritualism"—she came into Dante's room as he was packing. A dark-blue garment bag was slung over her shoulder. She wasn't her usual self but was nervous, almost shy. He asked if anything was wrong. She shook her head and requested that he do her an unusual favor.

"As long as it isn't illegal," he joked.

She smiled wanly and, in a halting voice, told him that when Clay came home on leave, before he'd begun flight school in Pensacola, she had taken a photograph of him on the back lawn in his uniform. The picture got ruined a couple of years ago—her cleaning lady had accidentally knocked it off her bedroom bureau, into a bucket of detergent. And she couldn't find the negative anywhere. She had plenty of pictures of Clay, as Dante must have noticed, but that one had been of particular sentimental value, the first she'd taken of him in his uniform.

"This is it," she added, extending the arm with the garment bag. "I was wondering if . . . Oh, I'll understand if you won't, even if you think I'm a little off my rocker for asking, but I thought . . . we aren't likely to see each other again, so perhaps you'd be willing."

Dante made an expression he knew must have looked stupid—a cartoonlike grimace.

"Greer, excuse me and all, but that's not 'unusual'; it's kind of weird. I wouldn't feel right about it, like I'm an . . . Y'know?" He looked aside to avoid her eyes, which were appealing one second, demanding the next, and switched from appeal to demand and back to appeal so rapidly he couldn't tell the one expression from the other.

"But I'm asking you, so you wouldn't be an impostor really. And it would only take a few minutes of your time. Is it too much to ask?"

"You'd know it was me anyway. I mean, if somebody saw it, what would you say?"

"No one would. It would be for me and Julian only. On my bureau. Very well, then. I understand. I'd probably feel exactly the way you do."

She bit her lower lip and turned to leave, her shoulders sagging a little. There was something about her—not persuasiveness, but a quality he couldn't give a name to—that made it difficult to deny her.

"Wait a sec, Greer. I suppose, after all you've done for me . . . I suppose it's not too much to ask. Will anyone see me?"

"No. I promise."

She supervised his costuming, made him take off his earring because the navy would not have allowed it. Despite her assurances, he felt as if every eye in town were on him as he posed on the back lawn in the blue-black jacket with the brass buttons and gold stripe around the sleeve, the white cap with its brass anchor and shield.

"I'm going to take four or five frames, bracket the shot to make sure I've got the light right," she said.

"Sounds like you know what you're doing."

"I'm a pretty good amateur photographer. It's my hobby, like my dad." She shifted sideways and bent her knees. "Now turn toward me a bit, and a little more of a smile. . . . That's it. . . . Oh! There it is! Perfect!"

She removed the cap and daubed at the sweat that had broken out on his forehead, though the temperature was only in the high fifties.

"Try to relax, dear. I know this is difficult and strange, but do try not to look as though you're facing a firing squad."

He did feel close to that: if Clay Rhodes could see him, he would swoop out of heaven in a ghost fighter plane and machine-gun him for this impersonation. He couldn't believe he'd been talked into this.

She took another frame, changed the settings, and took another. Pangs of anxiety shot through his chest, timed, it seemed, to the clicks of the shutter. Looking into the lens, he had the unsettling sensation of not recognizing himself; the still more unsettling sensation that his very identity was somehow being drawn out of him, soaking through the uniform with his sweat, evaporating into the cool spring air.

When it was over, she thanked him with a somewhat apologetic smile. He went back upstairs, changed into his own clothes, put his earring on, and was Dante Patrick Panetta again.

I I I

HERE IT WAS, only mid-May, and already as steamy as the worst August dog day up north. Outside, the sun bombarded the asphalt plain of the Dadeland Mall, its rays ricocheting off car roofs and windshields— a glare of metal and glass, bright and explosive. In shorts and sandals, afternoon shoppers moved in a languid daze under the arcades or scurried across the parking lot as if they were fleeing a downpour. Sheltered from the storm of heat and light in the air-conditioned NuWave, Dante was the climatic opposite of the Arctic dweller snug in a cabin during a blizzard. He finished a razor cut for a customer with thick, straight black hair. Razor cuts were his specialty, and he enjoyed giving them; it was more satisfying than cutting with electric clippers. The deft strokes of the honed blade, transforming a shaggy crop into something pleasing and attractive, made him feel like a woodworker carving by hand instead of with power tools.

He whisked his customer's collar, then turned him in the chair and held up a hand mirror so the man could see the back of his head. After he nodded, Dante whipped the apron off with a flourish, the clippings falling to the floor, and offered an appreciative "Thank you, sir," when two dollars were slipped into his palm. It was funny, he thought, how some customers tipped as if it were a bribe.

No other customers were waiting; this was the slow period of the day, between lunch and the time when the stores closed and salespeople came in for haircuts, perms, manicures. As Dante swept up, Alicia, the flashy graduate of a flashy cosmetology school, was prancing around her customer, a thirtyish woman, with a whirring blow dryer. Sandy Castro was rapidly conversing in Spanish with a cute little *chica* who, sitting stiffly under an egg-shaped dryer, looked like a nervous volunteer in a brain-wave experiment. Rose Vargas and Ginnie Cardenas tidied the bottles of shampoo, hair coloring, and perm solutions on the counter, while they heatedly discussed Rose's problems with her boyfriend.

Finished with the broom, Dante went into the back room for a coffee break.

". . . and it was outrageous," Frank Romano was saying to Gil Webber and Ida Marquez. Romano, camping it up (though he could act as straight as a Brooklyn fireman when he wanted to), tossed his head back and spread his olive-skinned arms wide, as though offering himself for crucifixion. "I am telling you, absolutely out*rageous!*"

Seeing the sludge in the coffeepot, Dante emptied it in the sink and started to make a fresh pot.

"Well, are you going to tell us or treat us to more foreplay?" said Gil, whose small head, neat mustache, and short sideburns gave him the priggish good looks of a British officer in a World War II movie.

He, Romano, and Ida were in their late thirties and formed a clique with seniority at the salon. They occupied the only chairs in the room, so Dante remained on his feet, leaning against the lunch table.

"Serial killers," said Romano. "Men who've committed the most baroque atrocities you can imagine. Absolutely rococo rapes and murders."

"She didn't have serial killers on!" Ida protested.

"No, *no.* Women who fall for them while they're in jail. Six serial-killer groupies. Men who kill and the women who love them. These are noncarnal relationships. Unions of mind and spirit," Romano said, and let out a sharp laugh.

"The outrageousness. Let's hear the outrageousness," Ida demanded, her soft *t*'s and slightly rolled *r*'s the only remains of her Central American accent.

"Patience. I have to set the scene." Romano crossed his legs and, shifting in his chair to face his companions directly, turned his back on Dante. "Whoever did their hair ought to have been prosecuted. Teased to death. One of these creatures looked like she had her finger in some invisible electrical socket, and another one had this absolutely frizzy blonde bushel basket on her head. Honey, they looked so awful it made me feel sorry for the serial killers."

Ida bent over, laughing.

"It wasn't that funny," said Gil.

"The way he says it, that's what makes me laugh. So what happened? How do these women get to fall in love with serial killers on death row?"

"Interested, Ida?" Gil asked with an exaggerated rise of his thin eyebrows.

"No. How about you, *mi maricón?*" she replied in a genial, kidding tone that drew the venom out of the pejorative.

"They write letters to these guys. They become pen pals, and romance blooms," Romano said. "They even get engaged by mail. What happened was, two of these women, Socket Finger and Bushel Basket, fell for the same murderer in, I think, Texas. He killed prostitutes and minced them in a blender or something. Sally Jessy asked Socket Finger what she saw in this butcher, and she said"—Romano, miming a woman fluffing her hair, put on a deep-in-the-heart of-Texas drawl—" 'Wal, ah luuve him on account of he's so inner die-rected. He knaows what he wants out of lahf and he went out and got it.' I swear, that's what she said. Inner directed. She was absolutely a trailer-park homecoming queen, but she had the psychobabble down pat. Inner die-rected!"

He, Gil, and Ida broke into laughter. Dante filled a paper cup with coffee and crossed the room in two steps to rummage through the magazines on an end table for his copy of *Down Beat*. There were dog-eared copies of *Glamour* and *Cosmo*, of trade magazines and fan magazines for Spanish-language soap operas, but *Down Beat* was missing.

". . . and then the other one, Bushel Basket, said, " 'Ah doan thank you know anythang about him, cuz he doan luuve you the way he does me.'" Romano went on: "That did not go down well with Socket Finger, who jumped out of her chair like she'd been goosed. 'He doan luuve you atall,' she shrieked. 'He tole me that in his last letter, that you doan mean half as much to him as ah do!'"

"Can I break into this important discussion and ask if anybody's seen my *Down Beat*?" Dante asked.

Without looking at him, Ida gestured impatiently for him not to interrupt.

". . . Then a fight broke out," Romano continued. "It was *delicious*. A catfight over a serial killer! Sally Jessy yelled for calm. 'Now, ladies, please, let's not lose our heads.' Something like that. Can you imagine? *Ladies!* What a hoot! Sally Jessy got an F-minus as referee, because Socket Finger stormed across the stage and slapped Bushel Basket in the face, who punched her back, and honey, I do mean punched. Socket Finger went down, but not before she grabbed the Bushel by all that hair and pulled the blonde down with her, and there the two of them were, clawing, pulling, and scratching right there in front of Sally Jessy and ten million people in TV land."

"No!" Ida was rapt. "Like that time on *Geraldo* with the Nazi guys?"

Romano raised his hand in oath.

"I was thinking about our hero. A two-timing serial killer, a serial killer with a cheating heart, watching from his jail cell while those two fought over him on national TV."

"You done now?" Dante asked. "I had a Post-it note on that magazine. My name and 'Please do not remove,' and now somebody's removed it. It was here this morning."

"Why don't you look for it in front," Ida said irritably, then returned her attention to Romano and asked, "So who won?"

As he walked out, Dante heard Romano say, "I don't know. They went to a commercial. . . ."

Cutting quickly across the parking lot toward an Eckerd's, he watched his shadow and the shadows of other pedestrians moving over the glutinous asphalt, slipping under cars, as if even insubstantial things needed shade from the sky-whitening sun. Eastward, somewhere over the Atlantic, a range of cumulus towered, teasing the land-bound with visions of rain and relief. He leaped into the drugstore as if it were a swimming pool, looked for *Down Beat* in the magazine rack, but didn't find it. The woman at the register told him that the store didn't carry the magazine.

Back outside, sweating through his white smock, he realized that he could live in Miami for the next twenty years and never consider this seasonless city—with its palm trees rattling in winds that blew on you like dog's breath, its babble of exiles' tongues, its shrinking enclaves of aging, displaced New Yorkers in transit toward death—as a real place, much less as home. When he returned to the NuWave, Sara, the receptionist, greeted him with a secretive glance and motioned with her head at a woman who was sitting against the back wall, tapping her feet impatiently.

"That's not my appointment," he said with a look at the clock. "I've got Paula Rodriguez. Don't know who that is."

"I didn't mean her," replied Sara, jerking her head again, in the direction of Consuela's office. "She wants to see you."

"What for? She's mad because I stepped out for ten minutes?"

"Don't know," answered Sara, shrugging. "She said you should see her when you're done with your appointment."

Paula Rodriguez came in and asked for her usual layered haircut. Dante clipped and combed in a state of anxious anticipation. He ought not to have left the shop; it was a minor transgression when no customers were waiting, but he couldn't afford even minor transgressions. He was on probation because, about a month earlier, he'd botched a perm for a young woman who was auditioning the next morning for a reporter's job on a local TV station. She was under the dryer when Greer phoned. Dante reminded her that he'd asked her not to contact him at work; Consuela was strict about her employees taking personal calls. Greer apologized but said the matter was urgent: yesterday, after a night of heavy rain, she had shown the house to a young couple and noticed plaster flaking off the ceiling in his mother's old bedroom. She'd dropped the ladder to the attic crawl space, climbed up there herself with a flashlight, and discovered two leaks in the roof. Water had puddled overnight and soaked through the attic floor. The house was going to need a new roof. A new roof! Dante said that would wipe out the CD he'd inherited. He couldn't afford it. Greer offered to cover the costs out of her own pocket and deduct them from the proceeds of the sale—with his written approval, of course. Talking to Greer, he did not hear the egg timer ring, signaling that it was time to take the dryer off. The other stylists, busy

with their customers, paid no attention to it. After he hung up, Dante
went back to his customer, looked at the timer, its dial on 12, then at the
clock. Sick to his stomach, he raised the dryer off the young woman's
head and removed the cotton swaths and rollers. The aspiring TV reporter shrieked. Her hair had been transformed into a frizzy horror,
something between a badly done Afro and a fright wig. She started sobbing; she couldn't possibly go to her audition looking like this; her career was ruined before it had begun. Dante felt terrible for her, offering
to work overtime to repair the damage, but she stormed out. He felt
worse for himself the following morning, when the woman's father
came in, threatening Consuela with a lawsuit if his daughter did not get
the job. After he left, Consuela took Dante aside and warned that he was
"skatin' on berry tin ice." She didn't think the man would make good on
his threat, but if he did, Dante himself would be looking for a job.

He made a distraught call to Greer that night from his apartment.
She fell into a fit of apologies and self-blame; she was so, so sorry for
phoning him at work, and if he lost his job because of her, she never
would forgive herself. Her contrition was so heartfelt that he found himself consoling her. She wasn't to worry, no lawsuit would be filed, he
wouldn't be thrown out of work.

He wondered about that now. His heart thrummed as he cleaned up
after finishing Paula's hair, then knocked at Consuela's door. He knew
the worst was coming when he saw the expression on her broad, matronly face; it was a look of regret, not anger.

"Si' down, Dante," she said, motioning at a chair beside her desk, its
surface hidden under stacks of bills, order forms, and cosmetic catalogs.
Tiny and windowless, the office was stifling, even with the air-
conditioning on.

"You remember a cus'omer named Eileen Kaufman? You did her
hair about a month ago? She's from New York? Har'sdale, New York?"

"Hartsdale? I know the town, but I don't remember any Eileen
Kaufman."

"Well, she remember you," Consuela said sternly, and handed him an
envelope bearing a Hartsdale postmark. Inside was a typewritten letter,
dated May 5, and two Polaroid photographs showing the top of a female
head, which, Dante presumed, was the writer's. In one photograph, the
woman's maple-blonde hair was long, wavy, voluminous; in the second,
it was tightly curled and thin, with small scabs blemishing patches of

exposed scalp. He read the letter with disbelief and, laying it on the desk, said:

"I don't remember this lady. I don't remember anything about this."

"Like I say, she remember you. Not your name. But she says in there, tall, young, diamond in his ear. That's not Frank, not Gil."

"Connie, I would remember giving a body wave to a blonde from New York. We don't get that many customers in here from New York. I'd remember her and I don't, honest to God," said Dante. A pleading, almost whining tone had entered his voice, and he despised himself for it.

"Yeah, sure, okay. But why does this woman write this to me? If she wants money back, or maybe for me to give this sister she says she got in Miami a free perm or something, or maybe even to sue me like that other girl, then maybe I'd think she's trying to pull a fast one. But she don't want anything, just to tell me that the NuWave's not going to get her business next time she's here, and not going to get her sister's business, or none of her sister's friends."

Dante stood suddenly, propelled to his feet by an urge to pace; but there wasn't any room, and he dropped back into his chair.

"She says she wanted a body wave, that I gave her a curly perm instead, and then she got blisters on her scalp and her hair started to fall out? That night? If that happened, why didn't she come and show us the next day?"

"You read the letter. She got to get the plane the next morning," Consuela said with a shrug of her stocky shoulders.

"Then why'd she wait so long to say anything? Is this her idea of a joke?"

"A joke?" she said, pronouncing it "choke." "Why she would make a joke like this? Dante, this is the second big problem I got with you. This place, it's got a good reputation, y'know?" A crease formed on her low, flat forehead. "So you got something to say for yourself, besides saying you don't remember none of this?"

A wavering note stole into Consuela's voice, and he sensed that if he begged her, played on her pity, he might talk her out of doing what she did not want to do in the first place. But what could he say? That he was sorry for something he was certain he didn't do?

"Connie, you want to fire me because of a dumb letter, go ahead. I don't think it's fair, but go ahead."

"Not fair? First you make a mess that got me nearly sued, now this. Not fair?" She laid her palms flat on the desk, her gaze fixed on the pile of colorful catalogs. "I tell you what, Dante. You shouldn't say nothing more to make me mad, because there's two things I want to do for you. You need a recommendation, you got it from me. And you can finish out the month here while you look for something else. I don't say nothing to anybody. Let them think you quit."

He considered the promise for a moment or two. Of course, the secret wouldn't keep more than a few days. He pictured Frank, Gil, and Ida gossiping about him in the back room, embarrassed looks from Alicia and Rose, and all of them straining to pretend that they didn't know. He unbuttoned his smock, stood to pull it over his head, and draped it on the chair.

"Thanks, Connie. You know where to send my check," he said, and left.

Driving to his apartment in Sweetwater, the distant cumulus reflecting the fire of the low sun, he wondered why he did not feel what you were supposed to feel when you got fired. Instead of fear, shame, and remorse, he felt only a sense of relief. He hadn't liked working at the NuWave anyway—too slick and trendy, too unisex somehow, no place for him. Heading north on Fifty-seventh, past the palmy sanctuary of the university campus, he managed to convince himself that his prospects weren't so bad. He had been out of work before and survived. He would survive this. He still had the band, money in the bank from the sale of his mother's car and the remainder of her CD, and unemployment compensation was good for six months. Surely he'd find another job in six months.

His optimism continued until he stopped for a traffic light at the intersection of Fifty-seventh and the Tamiami Trail, where he was startled by a knock on the side window. Turning, he saw the face of a derelict with sunken eyes, their pupils squeezed down to the diameter of a crab's eyes by the unrelenting light. Broken blood vessels spread across his unshaven cheeks, and he held at his waist a cardboard sign with the message "Lost Job. Will Work for Food." Dante looked again at the traffic signal, for the sight of the man affected him as the sight of a horribly wounded casualty affects a soldier marching up to the front. The light changed, and he turned onto Tamiami with an inner fluttering that was not ordinary butterflies; it felt as though a panicked aviary were beating its wings in his belly.

The Tamiami carried him through an architectural bloblandia of commercial strips and under the Palmetto Expressway. Nearing the urban margins, beyond which the saw-grass savannas and gator-haunted swamps of the Everglades spread out in humid desolation, he turned off Tamiami into his neighborhood, a part of Miami that never made it into the travel magazines. Most of the scars from Hurricane Andrew's stupendous vandalism had been erased, but the misnamed Sweetwater still looked temporary and provisional, as if it were inviting obliteration by the next big blow. On treeless streets, cinder-block houses with windows covered by scrolled iron burglary bars, like ornamented jail cells, baked under the naked sky, and watchdogs prowled behind the chain-link fences of sun-ravaged yards.

He pulled into his apartment complex—three flat two-story buildings arranged in an H—and the modular dull-ocher walls gave the same impression of impermanence as the cinder-block houses. In his ground-floor studio, he showered, changed, packed a bag for the weekend gig in Key West, then pulled from a locked closet his most precious possession, an Alembic electric bass. It looked beautiful in its felt-lined case, its dark, polished body showing a grained and tinted reflection of his face. He strapped the instrument on, its weight pleasurable on his shoulders, and ran through various bass lines—a straight-ahead blues, a samba, a funky salsa—to kill time before Hector picked him up in the van. He was looking forward to the gig and thanked God he had it to distract him as well as to bring in a few extra dollars. The distraction was at least as important as the money. Music always had given him solace and escape. When he was playing, even alone, he lost awareness of his surroundings and of his aloneness. He soared on the wings of notes and chords into a realm where he conversed musically with artists and composers he'd never met but felt he knew. With an instrument and a page of sheet music, he could be by himself and feel as though he were in a crowd of friends.

But he couldn't concentrate this afternoon; transcendence eluded him. The sunlight, no less fierce for its lateness, slashed through the blinds and laid bright ribs on the walls, barren except for posters of Miles Davis, Stanley Clark, and Eddie Palmieri. The light exposed the small rips and stains on the secondhand furniture. He couldn't complain about the rent for this place—two-forty a month—and it certainly was preferable to the streets and underpasses where the ghostly derelict dwelled; but there was nothing in it to affirm his possession, and its cold, somehow menacing blandness seemed the image of his rootlessness and displacement. He was adrift in his own life, a landscape bare of prominent features.

He needed to take immediate action and regain control of things. No, to *gain* control, for his destiny had never been in his hands. He remembered his uncle Will's advice, and an idea grew in his mind, moving him to pick up the phone and call Greer.

As soon as he heard her accent, his uneasiness began to fade. It was as if he were hooked up to her, like a transfusion patient to a donor, the self-assurance in her voice flowing through the telephone lines into his bloodstream. He asked if there had been any progress. She replied that there had been an awful lot of activity. Salespeople from other realtors had shown the house to a dozen people, but, well, the low end of the market, like the high end, was a difficult sell.

"You mean even with the new roof . . ."

"Dante, the place will sell. It's been on the market less than two months." He loved the way she said "market," with a slight rounding of the *r*. "It *will* sell, eventually, I promise you."

"What do you mean, 'eventually'? Like a year?"

She must have heard something in his tone, because she asked if anything was the matter. No, he answered, and told her that he was thinking about using the profits to open his own shop. Maybe it was time he went into business for himself, became his own boss, the one who did the hiring and firing rather than the other way around.

"That's enterprising of you," she said. "Not to be a wet blanket, but have you looked into what your start-up costs would be? A salon—there's all that equipment, the furniture, supplies."

"I'm not thinking about opening no salon—"

He heard what sounded like a loud sigh.

"All right, *any*," he said. "I'm thinking about an old-fashioned barbershop. Striped pole. Bottles of hair tonic. *Sports Illustrated* for the customers to read while they're waiting. No chrome and glass and jivey *Cosmo* girls dancing around with blow dryers."

"Some people might consider that sexist," Greer said. "What brought on this entrepreneurial spirit?"

He paused because he did not want to confess the truth, but she somehow intuited it.

"Oh, Dante, you didn't lose your job?"

He nodded, as if she were sitting across from him, which he wished she were. Then he told her everything.

"You ought to march right in and demand your job back," she said when he finished, and she sounded as indignant as his own mother would have under the same circumstances.

"Too late. I kind of burned my bridges."

"Dante, it sounds fishy."

"How so?"

"If that woman really was losing her hair, she'd have a right to demand compensation. Medical expenses, pain and suffering, the usual. The fact that she didn't makes me wonder."

"About what?"

"Oh, dear, you can be so naive. I seem to recall your telling us that you were the only straight guy in the place. Six Hispanic women and two gay guys. You don't fit in. Maybe this Consuela person was looking for a pretext to fire you. Maybe she created her own pretext, put someone up to a hoax."

He was a little shocked that Greer would think Consuela capable of such deviousness.

"I can't picture Connie being that rotten," he said. "And if she was, I sure as hell wouldn't want to work for her. I'd as soon try hacking it on my own, if I can get the money together."

There was a knock. He stretched the phone cord across half the room, listening to Greer say, "I want you to consider something," as he opened the door, admitting a blast of oppressive air. Framed against the sunset, a gold chain glittering amid the black hair curling in the vee of his open-necked shirt, tall, paunchy Hector looked more like a sleaze out of *Scarface* than a bandleader.

"Greer, I've got to go. Got a gig in the Keys this weekend—"

"Just give me a moment," she replied. "There's a place for you right here in this house till you get on your feet. If you want to open your own shop, think about opening one back in Connecticut. Someplace you know. I could help you find commercial space to rent, and at a bargain. I can help smooth the bumps in the road."

He was too stunned by her offer to respond, and Hector was pointing impatiently at his counterfeit Rolex.

HE WAS RIDING in the back of the van with Enrique Torres, the timbal player, and Hector's cousin Barron, who played horn. Behind the seat, sharing space with speakers and amps, the band's instruments lay cased and at rest after hard use through two nights and six sets: Barron's and Hector's trumpets; Dustin Cervantes' alto sax, Tony Alvarez's tenor, and Dante's Alembic. Jaime Lopez's keyboard, Jimmy Montagna's set of traps, and Pete Sanchez's congas were in the U-Haul trailer that wagged behind the van like a fat steel tail. The Overseas Highway was nearly deserted at this late Sunday hour, plied only by those who traveled at night out of preference or necessity, and the musicians sped northward at a steady seventy-five miles an hour. Motel signs cast their lights across the road, in places lapped by water on both sides, low-tide reek filtering through the air conditioner to mingle with the stench of the Marlboros that Hector and Dustin, in the front seat, smoked constantly, the twin red tips tracing the patterns of their gestures as they spoke in a staccato patter. Dante caught a phrase here and there, but otherwise he hadn't the slightest idea what anyone was saying. Full of good intentions, he'd taken a few Spanish lessons at Dade Community College after he got to Miami, and soon discovered that the language spoken on the streets bore as much resemblance to what he was learning as Jamaican patois did to an anchorman's English. It was *Cubano*—turbocharged, frantic Spanish that made the most ordinary conversation sound like a tape of a 911 call to the Havana police, played on fast forward.

Dante had the impression that his fellow bandsmen were engaged in a more or less genial argument, with Hector, Dustin, and Tony—the brass—on one side, and Enrique, Jimmy, and Pete—the percussionists—on the other. Barron and Jaime seemed to be the referees, now and then offering commentaries in support of one point or another. Squeezed between the well-fed Barron and the lean and lupine Enrique, Dante sat silent in an isolation booth of incomprehension.

They shot through Big Pine Key, Hector ignoring the signs that warned: SLOW! ENDANGERED KEY DEER. The conversation had changed. Now the musicians were swapping jokes, or so Dante surmised from the laughter that interrupted the chatter. He wondered if he might be the butt of some of the humor, because he'd twice missed his cues during the gig, once on Saturday night and again tonight. He couldn't stay focused on the improvisational parts; he'd been off in a private mental space, picturing himself stepping through the door Greer had opened, a door to as secure a future as he could hope for.

He wished he could get back into that space right now, so he could ignore the opaque babble, the meaningless (to him) laughter. Soon they were on the Seven Mile Bridge, speeding toward Marathon Key. Driving the long span at night always unsettled him, and Hector's driving heightened his nervousness. Besides doing twenty over the limit, he kept taking his eyes off the road to look at someone, steering with one hand, and not even with his hand but with his wrist, resting lightly on the wheel, while the cigarette in the other hand continued to make eccentric twirls in the darkness, like a faulty July 4 sparkler. About a mile ahead, an eighteen-wheeler was booming down the incline where the bridge soared into a high arch over the channel.

"Hey, Hector!" Dante said, almost shouting over the others and the samba crackling on the radio. "Watch where you're going!"

Hector raised his glance to the rearview mirror.

"Hey, what do I got? A back-seat driver?"

"Just keep your eyes on the road."

"Don't gotta," Hector said, half turning toward the back, his dark face with its slash of a grin illuminated by the oncoming truck's headlights. "Know where I'm goin'. Meeammee! Goodbye to Key West and all those *maricones*. Hello Meeammee!"

The truck thundered by, buffeting the van with its wind.

"Meeammee!" shouted Pete Sanchez, hands flashing over imaginary congas, and then Dustin, Enrique, and Tony echoed him. "Meeammee! Meeammee!" They sounded as giddy as exiles returning from a long banishment.

"Okay. Miami. Let's make sure we get there," Dante said, hoping to keep the conversation in English. "Man, we've got nothing but water fifty feet below and on both sides."

Hector made a remark in Spanish, and gusts of laughter flew from everyone but Barron.

"What's so funny?" Dante asked him. He liked Barron, at forty the oldest member of the band and a Latin musician of the old school. He had a dignified air and played with restrained passion, not with the unbridled heat of his younger cousin.

"Hector said that he sure hopes we've got water on both sides, because we're on a bridge."

"That's funny?"

"They think so," said Barron.

The van climbed the arch. The road rising ahead appeared to touch a constellation low on the northern horizon. Below, with every ripple ironed out of it by an offshore breeze, the Atlantic resembled a vast prairie of smooth snow in the light of the full moon. The whiteness infused Dante with nostalgia for the Connecticut winters of his boy-hood—the bracing winds off Long Island Sound, the sparkle of branches encased in frost on clear February mornings. There was something real and honest in the rigor of a New England winter, as there was some-thing fantastic and false in the perpetual Florida heat and sunlight—a kind of Disneyland of climate. He imagined how a Christmas at Fastnet would look. The harbor dark blue against white banks, gulls at rest on slender floes of ice.

Hector slowed down for Marathon Key, a speed trap, but didn't stop talking. Nor did the others. Except for Enrique, who'd come over from Cuba on the Mariel boat lift in 1980, everyone in the band had been born in the U.S. or had come here as an infant. Why the hell did they have to speak to each other as if they'd left Havana yesterday morning?

"Hey, Hector—"

"Yo! The back-seat driver speaks again." Hector raised a hand, cutely signaling for silence. "What is it now? I'm goin' too fast, too slow? What?"

There was a bite in his voice, and it definitely was deliberate—a re-minder that he hadn't forgotten Dante's missed cues.

"Do you know what 'obviate' means?"

"What?"

" 'Obviate.' It's a verb. Know what it means? Anybody here know?"

Enrique turned his gaunt and sallow face toward Dante.

"Mang, whadafock chew talkin' 'bout? Oviate?"

"*Ob*viate," Dante said.

"This is like school," said Dustin, a fair-haired Cuban, a descen-dant—as he frequently reminded people—of pure Castilian Spaniards. "A pop quiz."

"Right," said Dante. "English class. We're in the U.S.A. Thought it'd be fun if for a change we all *habla* a little *inglés*."

"Okay. Obviate." Dustin turned to look at him earnestly from over the front seat. "That what women do when they got their time of the month?"

"You're thinking of ovulate," Barron remarked, chuckling.

"Oh, hey, the professor," said Dustin sourly. Barron taught jazz part time at the University of Miami. "You're so smart, what does it mean?"

"Give you a hint before you give up," Dante said. "That arch they put into the Seven Mile obviates the need for a drawbridge."

Dustin frowned, pondering this for a couple of moments. Then he shrugged.

"It means to make something unnecessary," Barron explained. "They built the new Seven Mile with an arch so they don't have to raise a draw-bridge every time a sailboat wants to pass through, like they did with the old highway."

"Yo! Cuzzy! You're smarter than I thought," said Hector. "So tell me somethin'. Can this obviate make some*one* unnecessary?" He flicked a mirthless grin into the rearview mirror.

"Give me a for example."

"Sure. For an example, if a bass player misses his cues and everybody but him comes in when they're supposed to, could you say that particular bass player is obviated?"

Dustin lowered his blond head, pretending to duck or cringe.

"Whoaaaa, here it comes," he said.

"How 'bout you, Dante?" Hector needled. "You say a bass player who misses his cues is obviated, or what?"

An expectant hush fell over the musicians. Dante felt as if everyone were looking at him, though no one was.

"I don't hear no answer from the English teacher."

"C'mon, Hector," Barron said. "This isn't cool."

"I'm cool, cuzzy. A cool breeze blowin' out of the Florida Keys, tryin' to get an A in English class."

They were in the sparsely populated Matecumbe Keys, and the un-lighted highway, its reflecting lane markers glowing like cats' eyes, cut a gallery through mangrove thickets that looked solid in the darkness. Here and there, taller than the mangroves, thatch and coconut palms leaned, moon-silvered fronds moving, then not moving, in the spas-modic breezes. Dante wanted to tell Hector to pull over and let him out of the car, but the pall of silence hanging over everyone checked him from giving in to his injured feelings; it signaled that the band was on his side, in agreement with Barron that Hector had been uncool, out of line. If he'd had anything to say, he should have said it to Dante in private, not humiliated him in front of everybody else.

Hector did not like the quiet. He tried to start a conversation and failed. When the glimmer of Islamorada appeared ahead, he banged his forehead on the wheel in mock chastisement and said:

"All right, all right! Hector should've kept his mouth shut. Hector's fucking sorry. Yo! Dante! Hear that? I apologize. I was just kiddin' anyway, just jerkin' your chain. Are you cool?"

"Yeah," Dante said, without conviction.

"Okay, you're cool, I'm cool, and Islamorada's our halfway point. How about we all have a beer and lighten the fuck up for the rest of the trip?"

The Lorelei was an anglers' hangout on the bay side. The band went to the tiki bar outside, empty of other customers except for two drunk fishing guides with tanned faces reddened by rum.

The towering brunette bartender's glance roamed over the musicians; in their loose-fitting sport jackets, gold chains, and leather shoes, they looked incongruously urban beneath the thatch roof and bamboo rafters.

"Know what you're thinkin', but we aren't," Hector said, meaning Miami drug dealers. "Meet Hector Baroso's Latin Jazz Band." He offered a brilliant smile and extended his hand, as if he were introducing the band onstage, then whipped out a business card and handed it to the bartender. "In case this place needs some livenin' up some weekend. Sambas. Merengue." Palm pressed flat against his belt, the opposite hand held level with his ear, his shoulders swayed in rhythm with his hips. "*Ohe!* We cover 'em all. Puente, Irakere, Palmieri."

"Cut the advertising," the bartender said. "This place, it's rock 'n' roll or shit-kickin' music. What'll you have? We're on last call."

Hector, making a concession to safe driving practices, ordered a Coke, Barron asked for a scotch, and Dante a beer. He stood leaning against the bar, staring past the line of seated musicians toward the docks, where streamlined skiffs were moored gunwale to gunwale, their hulls glistening in the dock lights, powerful outboards tilted up under aluminum poling platforms. He saw himself in one, booming across Florida Bay at fifty knots for the bonefish flats—a sportsman like Julian. Hector nudged him and said in an undertone:

"Hey, Dante, I really am sorry, man. It's just that I felt you was, you know, makin' fun of us, teachin' us English like we're . . ."

"Somebody I know told me 'never explain, never apologize.' "

"Well, I'm splainin' and apologizin' anyway."

"No problem. I'll apologize too. Been having a tough time concentrating."

"Sure, sure. With your mama dyin', gotta be a tough thing."

"But I don't think anybody in that audience even noticed. Those cruise-ship tourists," Dante added, and realized that he ought to have kept quiet. Hector's brows rose and fell, he flicked sweat from beneath his low, dense hairline with his fingers.

"That crowd wouldn't have noticed if we started playin' the 'Star-Spangled Banner,' but the thing is, *I* noticed, the band noticed."

With his head, he motioned for Dante to take a walk with him.

They strolled to the end of one of the docks, Hector with his hands in his pockets, his loafers clumping on the bleached planks. A dock light shone into the water, disclosing fat mangrove snappers darting into schools of glass minnows that flashed like new dimes in their flights from the snappers' jaws.

"Thing is, it isn't only that you missed the cues," Hector continued.

"I dragged the band down on 'Night in Tunisia,' I know," Dante cut in.

"Supposed to be up tempo, you're down, and you do that in front of an audience that's not a bunch of cruise-ship bozos from Ohio, that's hip, they'll notice." Hector paused, gazing down as if to study the drama of marine predation below. "So is it just your mama, or somethin' else?"

"Lost my day job. Fired," he said indifferently.

"*What?* Why you didn't say nothing, man?"

"Because I didn't want to bum everybody out for the gig."

"It's a bummer, all right." Hector shook his head in sympathy and signaled with a glance at his watch that it was time to get back on the road. "You okay with cash?"

Dante nodded; the last thing he wanted or needed was charity. They strolled toward the bar to round up the band.

"Well, hey, things aren't so bad. Long as people got hair, they're gonna need to get it cut, right? You'll find somethin' else. I got a cousin, he's a barber in the Gables. Lotta customers with big bucks, big tips. Maybe they got an opening. I'll talk to him if you want."

Dante wasn't thinking about employment; he was thinking about fishing again. He remembered a fifty-year-old he had fished beside one afternoon from a bridge in Key Largo. With a beer gut, skin the shade and texture of brown wrapping paper, and white in his hair, he was hurling curses at the sea because it hadn't given him any snappers for dinner, and he couldn't afford the five bucks a pound they charged in fish markets. Dante thought with conviction that this memory was a prophecy of his future, and it forced his conscious mind to acknowledge the decision his subconscious already had made.

"Don't bother," he said to Hector's offer, and dropped his half-drunk beer into a trash barrel outside the bar. "I'm going home."

"We're all goin' home," Hector said, then called to the others to drink up and pay up.

"I mean *home*," said Dante. "I'm quitting the band, Hector."

WAS IT POSSIBLE to be perfectly sane in every corner of your mind but one, and in that one to be utterly mad? Julian lay in bed, staring at the ceiling light, his belly roofed by a slim volume of a Civil War soldier's letters home. The human mind wasn't so tightly compartmentalized that derangement could be quarantined to one small part while the other parts remained healthy in every respect. The madness would spread to the rest eventually, wouldn't it? These were questions he had asked himself often since Clay's death, questions he with his mathematics degree and long years of stock trading was ill equipped to answer. A few years earlier, when Greer began making almost nightly pilgrimages to Clay's room, he consulted a psychiatrist about her condition. Dr. Mowbry, a tall, bald man with the physique of an anorectic monk, was supposed to be one of the best shrinks in Manhattan, but all he said was that he would have to talk to Greer in person before giving an opinion.

Julian need not have paid a hundred fifty an hour to talk to a professional; the answer was with him every day. Greer proved that it was possible to be sane and insane at the same time. Maybe "insane" was too strong a word; on the other hand, "peculiar" seemed too mild. At Bratton and Higgs, in the Colonial Dames, and among her friends on the civic and club committees she belonged to, she was known as a competent, energetic woman, a woman with Yankee granite in her marrow, clear of eye and head. Only Julian knew about that hidden mental chamber in which the demons of her grief danced and shrieked.

She never had been rational about Clay, loving him with the maternal equivalent of an obsessive passion that was ever attended by the fear of losing him. Every childhood cold, cough, and fever became a life-threatening disease to her mind. By the time he was ten, Clay had become as familiar with doctors' offices and emergency rooms as an invalid, his little body examined and reexamined for diseases that existed in his mother's imagination. And yet, when she and Julian discovered that they had a real problem to confront, she refused even to acknowledge it. Julian disliked Dr. Mowbry's term—denial—because it suggested what criminals and corrupt politicians did under questioning. He preferred to think of her blindness as a frailty, the unconscious vanquishing of her capacity to see things as they were by her desire to see them as she wanted them to be. That took the willful, illicit edge off the lies she told about Clay, to herself and others.

Willful or not, her inability to face the truth about their son perplexed Julian. He thought of her as the family liberal, always ready to defend the poor, the luckless, the outcast. She ought to have been accepting of Clay, but her liberalism applied only to other people, or to ideas. When it came to her own life and the people in it, she was the family Tory, cleaving slavishly to the antiquated customs, traditions, and attitudes of her class. Almost from the day they had brought Clay home from the adoption agency, her mind hastened far into the future, charting the course his life was going to take. She was an imaginative woman, but her imagination failed her when she drew up that map: Clay was going to follow the road rutted and worn by generations of privileged Eastern kids. There would be tennis, sailing, and riding lessons; he would go to the right summer camps, the right prep school and college, marry the right girl, and produce a brood of fair grandchildren for Greer to dote on. She had begun to think about his wedding when he was barely into puberty. How old was he that afternoon the three of them went sailing with the Conklins? Not more than thirteen. A wedding party was in progress as the Conklins' yawl cruised up a harbor in Rye. Striped tents pitched on the lawn of a Georgian mansion. Guests strolling across the sparkling grass. Groomsmen in blue blazers and bridesmaids in pink posing for photographs beside the glorious couple, anointed by a promising summer sun. "Oh, isn't that just *perfect*? Take a look, darling," Greer had said, passing binoculars to an uninterested Clay. "That's how your wedding is going to look someday."

She was enchanted by images, and the picture of nuptial perfection seized her imagination entirely. She referred to it often in the following years, pointing to the spot on their lawn where the tent would be pitched, and speculating about the oohs and ahs boaters in the harbor would utter when they beheld the sight. Christ, she was summoning up that vision long after Clay had been expelled from Hotchkiss and it became obvious that there never would be a wedding, or any grandchildren.

Julian was a Hotchkiss alumnus, class of 1956, and a generous contributor to the annual fund, so Broadhurst, the headmaster, thought it diplomatic to explain the reasons for Clay's expulsion to the Rhodeses face-to-face rather than in a letter. At the end of the meeting, when Broadhurst suggested counseling for Clay, Greer's lips pulled into an eerie smile and she asked, "Whatever for?"

The headmaster coughed and, misunderstanding the gist of her question (as did Julian), said that he realized attitudes were changing, that a lot of people no longer considered behavior like Clay's and the other young man's as, well, abnormal. Nevertheless, the school had standards. . . . Well, now, put it this way: If Clay and a female had been caught in the dorm, the results would have been the same— "Please don't think I'm tolerant about this," Greer interrupted. "I understand that smoking marijuana on campus is grounds for immediate expulsion, but I'm not at all convinced that Clay has a drug problem and needs counseling."

Broadhurst and Julian exchanged alarmed and baffled looks. "Mrs. Rhodes, possibly, in the interests of sparing your feelings, I wasn't quite clear enough." The headmaster spoke firmly, but his nervousness was betrayed by his flickering eyelashes. "Clay and his classmate are being expelled not only for a drug violation but for sexual misconduct. . . ." Greer sprang from her chair, and Broadhurst flinched, as if he were about to be slapped. Wasn't it enough, she said, that Clay was being kicked out? Did Broadhurst have to humiliate her by repeating that other kid's lies? Whatever went on, it was his fault, that lying pervert had roped Clay into it, gotten him stoned so he didn't know what he was doing. For Broadhurst to repeat that trash as if it were gospel was worse than humiliating; it was slander against her and her Clay, and there were laws against slander. If Broadhurst allowed such . . . such *calumny* to remain in the record and a word of it to get off campus, he would be talking to their lawyer next.

That was the theme during the dreadful drive home. Slander. Calumny. Lies. Julian was too stunned and shamed by Broadhurst's revelations to speak, except when Greer repeated her threat to get their lawyer on the case. "You will not!" Julian had said. "Do you want to see this dragged into the courts?" What about Clay's future? she countered. Sexual misconduct! They made it sound like he was some sort of criminal, when the real criminal was that other kid (ever afterward, he would be known only as the "other kid"). She did not want a god-blessed word of those ugly lies to stay in the school's files, and if Julian could not set the record straight, then she would have no choice but to call a lawyer. He could not bring himself to remind her that it had been an act of mutual consent. He was afraid of sounding disloyal—and of her fury turning on him.

His mission was clear, and the next day, after he'd helped Clay pack his things, he accomplished it in a quiet meeting with Broadhurst. The fact of the expulsion could not be erased, the drug charge would remain, but the sordid details of the other were expunged, the record brought into conformance with Greer's illusions. Julian supposed it said something about them and the world they lived in that a narcotics violation was more acceptable than a homosexual act. Looking back on his life, he could forgive himself a lot, but not for acting as accomplice to his wife's blindness. Nor could he forgive his lack of understanding toward Clay. After he drove the kid back from Hotchkiss, he dragged him into a figurative woodshed and brought him to tears, telling him that he was ungrateful and morally defective and that if he ever did anything like that again, he would destroy his mother. Clay knew he was adopted, and the accusation of ingratitude was not lost on him, nor was the threat that Greer's emotional survival depended on his keeping up appearances. Julian had condemned him to a double life, to becoming a kind of accomplice himself. The incident was never mentioned again, and when anyone asked Clay why he'd left Hotchkiss for the public high school, he dutifully parroted Greer's script: prep school was too isolated from the real world.

He went on to Denison and dated a parade of girls (he was good-looking, a superb tennis player, and his indifference to women attracted them). He kept his other life hidden, like a spy in enemy territory. When he was home on school vacations, he went into New York a lot, saying only that he was going to see "friends." Once, Julian answered a phone call and heard a male voice say, "Clay, honey?" When Julian identified himself and asked who was calling, the line went dead. He pictured an aging queen, setting down a telephone in some tricked-up apartment.

In those days, Julian spent a lot of time feeling sorry for himself, feeling somehow betrayed. But now he realized how difficult things had been for Clay, the strain he must have been under. Greer frequently played matchmaker with the daughters of her friends. If Clay went out with a girl more than twice, she, full of hope, would ask him if the relationship was getting serious. Clay always answered no, and Julian himself felt like slapping Greer when she responded with cheery comments like, "Oh, that's probably a good idea, darling. No sense in getting involved too early—it's best to play the field at your age." A measure of love is the suffering one person is willing to undergo for the sake of another. By that standard, Clay must have loved his parents a great deal, more perhaps than they loved him. And, possibly, he was trying to do more than give them what they wanted, or at least its appearance. Maybe he was trying, with all those girls, with the letter he'd won on the Denison tennis team, with the painfully false masculine bravado he sometimes affected, to become what he wasn't and couldn't ever be.

Home on spring break in his senior year, he surprised them when he announced his plans to enlist as a naval aviation cadet after he graduated. Greer was concerned. Flying for the navy would be dangerous. Without the draft breathing down his neck, there was no need to go into the service; wouldn't he be better off finding a regular job somewhere? But she, the daughter of a World War II bomber pilot, could not keep a hint of pride and admiration out of her voice, or a look of vindication from glinting in her lucid blue eyes. Here was unimpeachable testimony that the incident at Hotchkiss had been an aberration; young men who were "that way" wanted to become choreographers and interior decorators, not fighter pilots. Julian still wondered, though it was useless to wonder, what might have happened if she had protested the decision with more conviction, if she hadn't, with her proud looks and tone of voice, encouraged Clay. He wondered as well what might have happened if he'd overcome his own inhibitions and spoken candidly to Clay later that evening. An uneasiness had fallen over him, almost like a premonition of disaster. He went up to Clay's room and asked what on earth had motivated this decision to enlist, as a pilot, no less. Clay jerked his head at the model planes he'd built as a kid and said that he'd always been interested in flying. Gramps got him interested—his glance drifted to the photo of Greer's father, in a fleece-collared bomber jacket, that hung over his dresser. Gramps was helping him pay for flying lessons on weekends, at an airfield near campus; he was going for his private pilot's license. Julian counseled that buzzing around in a Piper Cub as a hobby was one thing, flying high-performance jets quite another. Clay had to be sure he knew what he was doing.

Ten or fifteen seconds of uncomfortable silence followed. Julian grew a little short of breath; a tiara of sweat formed above his eyebrows. The prospect of uttering what was in his heart, to say nothing of the awkwardness of the subject, terrified him.

"It's not going to change things," he managed to say. "If that's why you're signing up—to change things—it won't do it."

"What're you talking about?" asked Clay, his hands going into his pockets, his lean body falling into the insouciant pose he struck so easily.

"You know . . . Change the way . . . Well, you know . . ."

Clay shrugged slowly and squinted with one eye and screwed up a corner of his mouth. Julian couldn't tell if he was genuinely puzzled or if his bemused silence was a challenge: he wasn't going to respond until his father spoke openly and clearly. How Julian wanted to! He wanted to tell Clay that he should not take such a risky step merely to win his parents' approval or (as Julian suspected was the greater motive) to prove something to himself. He wanted to say that he loved and accepted Clay no matter what, but just when the right words seemed ready to fly freely from his lips, he saw his own father in his mind's eye, a pale finger raised to pale, closed lips. They had never been able to open their hearts to each other. Julian had been about Clay's age when the Colby girl he'd been engaged to returned his ring only two months before the wedding. His father took him salmon fishing in New Brunswick to console him and talk things over, man to man. In the intimacy of a fishing cabin, the subject of his broken heart seemingly could not be avoided, but they managed to dodge it, gossiping about other guests at the lodge, discussing river conditions and which flies to use. That kind of reticence was in their blood, he supposed, a legacy too old and ingrained to overcome.

Julian glanced at the photo on Greer's bureau, the old one of Clay in his uniform that she had had restored recently, and then raised the collection of Civil War correspondence and read: "Dearest Mother and Father . . . How I miss our farm. . . . Camp life is hard and dreary, and there is little to do but drill, drill, drill. . . . There are rumors that we are to go into battle soon. . . ." This was one of the last letters written by Private Elias Sutter, Connecticut Volunteers, killed in the assault on Fort Wagner in 1864. Oh, the pain . . .

He and Greer had received a stark mailgram first, then a letter from Clay's commanding officer, explaining the circumstances. He'd tried to be euphemistic, but the details were repulsive nonetheless. At first, Julian was too numbed to speak, Greer too numbed for tears. Clay's body was flown back to the States from Italy, and he was buried in the Episcopal cemetery, on a clear, windy February morning, with only his parents and surviving grandparents attending. Julian and Greer told the older people nothing about the contents of the commander's letter, except that the cause of his death was under investigation. That night, she locked herself in Clay's room and stayed there till morning, crying softly but without cease. There was nothing Julian could do or say to console her. He stood outside the door for hours, listening to her sobs. When she emerged, she shredded the letter and burned the shreds in the fireplace. No one is ever going to know, no one, she'd said.

He had no inkling of the fiction she'd concocted until the afternoon Foster and Meredith Conklin stopped by to offer their condolences. All they knew was what Julian had told them on the phone: the bare and terrible fact that he had been killed overseas—no, not in the Persian Gulf, but aboard his ship in the Mediterranean. He couldn't bring himself to say more. On the phone, the Conklins had been gracious enough not to press him for more information, but during their visit, Meredith could no longer suppress her curiosity and asked what had happened. Julian was fumbling for an answer when Greer, rising to refill their coffee cups, launched into the tale that would become her authorized version: the flameout, the plane crashing into the sea. Julian listened, struck dumb by the boldness of the falsehood. The story flowed too smoothly to be the product of the moment's inspiration, and he noticed that she did not overembroider, say, by claiming that Clay had been shot down in action rather than in a training accident. That gave the fable just the right prosaic touch and made it more plausible. She must have been working on it for days, polishing and fine-tuning. In the end, Julian concluded, it was pride, family pride and pride in herself, that suborned her to commit a kind of perjury about Clay's death. She was a Braithwaite after all, and that family were talented revisionists, rewriting the chapters of their family history they found sordid or shameful or in some way disconsonant with their high conception of themselves.

They had an awful quarrel after the Conklins left. Where had she come up with such bald-faced lies? Julian shouted. What did she think she was going to accomplish except to shame them further when the truth came out, as it was bound to? She hollered back at him: What were they supposed to tell people when they asked? The trash in that ship captain's letter? What was she supposed to say to their friends, to her father? Ah, yes, her father, Julian thought. That Madison Avenue carnivore after whom she'd named Clay. The hero who'd won a Distinguished Flying Cross, piloting his flak-sieved Mitchell back to England, his copilot and a turret gunner dead. All right, said Julian, what was she going to tell her father? Clayton Braithwaite already knew about his grandson's naval career. What would she say to him? She wasn't to repeat that story again. He forbade it. She laughed. He *forbade* it? What the hell century did he think he was living in?

Contrary to his prediction, the facts never did come out. The navy had had its share of scandals; it kept the investigation confidential and the court-martial out of the media. And Julian once again served as Greer's accomplice, keeping his mouth shut when she repeated her fable to their neighbors the Seavers and Crandalls, and to her friends in the Colonial Dames.

The telling and retelling of Greer's story exercised its brittle limbs of fraudulence and made them stronger. Julian, who thought that thirty years on the stock market had taught him everything about the human capacity for self-deception, realized that Greer had come to believe in her own lie. It attained the power of myth, and he learned to accept its necessity. It helped her get through each day. He was more ambivalent about her visits to Clay's room, which she had turned into a morbid shrine. Two or three times a week, she would sit in there amid Clay's photographs and model planes, murmuring her thoughts and feelings, telling him about births, deaths, and marriages among the families who'd known him, about the things she and Julian had seen on their trips. She would come out fifteen or twenty minutes later and carry on with the rest of her day, as if holding a one-sided conversation with a ghost were no more unusual than chatting on the phone with a friend. This behavior, which had impelled Julian to consult Dr. Mowbry, still disturbed him. It had gone on for too long. She couldn't let go of the past or her grief, and so her grief would not let go of her. Sometimes he feared that she would take her visitations to the next level: bring in a medium. She hadn't gone that far, but this week, things had taken an unexpected and alarming turn.

From down the hall came the sound of Clay's door closing and then Greer's footsteps, quick and decisive. Julian propped himself up in bed and pretended to be reading. She entered with a velvety rustle of her burgundy robe, the gray fall of her hair clashing with her slender figure. Another of her contradictions, he reflected. She refused to color her hair and sneered at the vanity of women who had face-lifts, but she wouldn't allow time's ruinous hands to touch her body. She went to aerobics class three times a week, played tennis, and rowed Julian's Alden on spring and summer weekends. She looked her age from the neck up and twenty years younger from the neck down, and Julian was envied by his friends, whose wives had either gone to flab or dieted themselves into concentration camp models. Being married to a woman other men found attractive used to fill him with pride, but looking at her now only brought a dryness to his mouth—the ashen taste of regret. They hadn't made love since Clay's death, though they'd tried. Their fingers would touch, their lips, but then they would feel Clay's presence, lying between them like an invisible bundling board, forbidding them from taking any pleasure in each other.

Peering over the book of Private Sutter's letters, between the bedposts, each like a tall oaken candlestick, he watched her at the dressing table, her head inclined to the left as she brushed her hair on that side.

"I suppose you had a lot to talk about tonight," he said.

She yanked the brush, its bristles crackling with static electricity.

"Please don't make light of it, dear."

"I wasn't."

"There was a tone in your voice."

He laid the book down. "Of what?"

"A kind of weary sarcasm."

He wasn't aware of sounding weary, but he supposed the sarcasm was there—an attempt to mask his nervousness. He was going to do something he hadn't done in five years—deny her what she wanted—and he wasn't sure he was up to it.

He rose from the bed and buttoned his pajama top to hide the belly that gave him a look of old-fashioned prosperousness in a suit but was merely an unsightly bulge when exposed. He didn't think he could say what he had to with authority if he was half dressed and barefoot, so he put on his robe and slippers, then stood behind her. She set the brush down and looked steadily at his image in the glass.

"I was talking to myself really," she said. "Trying to sort things out. Trying to get an idea of how I'd feel if I moved Clay's things out and let Dante have his room."

This part was news, and it caught him off balance.

"Move Dante into his room? When did you get that idea?"

"I've been thinking about it. I've been thinking that maybe it's time to—" She stopped herself. His reflected gaze meeting hers, he waited for her to finish.

"Anyway, I don't think it would be inappropriate," she went on. "Do you?"

He certainly did. Yes, it was past time to put Clay's things in a trunk and clear out his room, but the idea of his look-alike sleeping there gave Julian chills.

"You're leaving one important person out of your thinking, and that's Dante," he said. "How would he feel? If I were in his shoes, it'd make me damned uncomfortable."

"He wouldn't know it's Clay's room," she said matter-of-factly, as if Dante's ignorance justified her.

"Don't you think he ought to? Don't you think it would be the right thing to ask him how he'd feel about it?"

"It's our house after all, so the right thing is what we say the right thing is." He watched her raise her chin—that smug movement with which the Braithwaites expressed their right to make their own judgments about what was ethical. "Anyway, dear, which room we put him in isn't a moral issue."

It wasn't the issue at all, thought Julian, moving over to the chaise. He sat down.

"I'm going to say something; not to argue it, just to say it. I'm upset, damned so, that you didn't talk to me before you invited Dante to stay with us, or whatever you told him." He was fighting the impediment that derailed his trains of conversation in stressful moments. "I'm not asking you to apologize. I've . . . For so long now, I've given in to you, you must've assumed it would be okay with me. Well, it's not."

"Given in to me? Given in to me?" she asked, tucking into the second utterance a dual note of indignation and incredulity.

"Greer, this business about Dante—"

"No, wait a second. What have I demanded that you've *given in* to?"

"We've never talked about this—why start now?"

Raising her hands, she motioned to him to go ahead and talk.

"That Hotchkiss thing. You wanted me to . . . and I did. I shouldn't have, but I did." He felt stupid and defeated; she'd diverted him. "And when Clay joined up, the navy people, when they checked into his background, they would've found that stuff if it had been in the records, and he wouldn't have gotten in."

Now, crisply and emphatically, she spun on the settee and faced him.

"Please finish the thought. Let's really put things on the table. Clay wouldn't have gotten in and he'd be alive today. In other words, I killed him, with your reluctant help."

A gas pain shot through his lower abdomen.

"Jesus Christ! That isn't what I meant," he insisted, wondering if she was ascribing to him an accusation she'd made of herself. "All I meant was, you wanted the records cleaned up and I didn't argue."

"Sure. And not because I demanded it. Because you didn't want that garbage in there any more than I. Well, what else do you want to indict me for?"

"What you've told people about the way Clay died. That crazy story. And I'm not, for Christ's sake, indicting you. Not criticizing, even. I've gone along with you. Never hinted at the truth to anybody."

"I would hope you wouldn't want people to know."

"Maybe not. But sometimes I wanted to talk to somebody about it—what happened. I've kept it bottled up inside—"

"And you think I haven't?" She rose, folding her arms over her bosom. "Do you really think that I don't remember, every goddamned day of the year, how Clay was . . ." Moving toward the bed, she briefly touched her lips with the back of her hand, showing a palm braided with cracks. "All right, I can't bring myself to say it, but that doesn't mean I don't know it. What was in the captain's letter and in the investigation . . . I can see it—not the words, no, no, but what they described. *It*. I can even feel it happening sometimes, like it was me who that sick bastard . . . It might as well have been. . . ."

Her voice faltered and her body leaned, as if she were about to throw herself on the bed. Julian thought she was going to break down, but then she drew on the Protestant Yankee's heritage, both gift and curse—that old, rigorous restraint of emotions. Like a spectator at some contest, he watched her grapple with her sorrow and her rage, gain leverage, and subdue them, all in a few seconds. He wanted to applaud her triumph as, cool and composed again, she turned toward him and said:

"I am perfectly aware of the truth. I can bear knowing it. What I can't bear is anyone else knowing it. They don't have a right—it's none of their business. And all right, I've lied, fine, I've lied, but it wasn't to protect myself or us, but Clay. *Clay*."

"Clay," Julian echoed dully.

"When people thought about him, I wanted them to have beautiful memories of him, not a lot of sick, stinking innuendos in their heads, not thoughts about the way he died. It was bad enough we had to tell Dad, that Dad had to carry that to his grave."

"Well, we couldn't have given him that fairy tale, could we? Not that we told him the full truth, either."

"Oh, really?" she said. "How do you know? We'll never know what happened on that ship, because it was just the two of them. Clay and that *thing*. It could have been just the way I told Dad. . . . Oh, hell . . ."

"All right, all right," Julian said hotly. "Then why couldn't you have told other people what you told your father? Why that damned fairy tale about flameouts, a crash?"

Greer blushed, as if embarrassed now by the outlandishness of her invention, but she recovered herself in the next moment.

"Because people still would have had their stinking little suspicions. So I just took the thing as far from reality as I could."

The floor creaked in its usual spot as she glided toward him. Sitting on the edge of the chaise, she rested her hand on his knee, but he went stiff at her touch, swung his legs aside, and planted his feet on the warm oak planks.

"What's wrong?" she asked.

"Nothing."

"Dear, you positively cringed."

"All this time . . . Five years . . . I guess I didn't realize it was so deliberate. I kind of thought that it was your way of living with the thing, that you needed to believe it yourself. But what you just said, it sounds so calculated, like an alibi."

"You'd prefer to think of me as a little nuts? Deluded? Your poor little Greer?"

"Oh, Christ," he said, and returned to the bed, hoping she didn't follow him. He did not want to be too near her. The curtains, billowing in a breeze from the harbor, pulled against their sashes. A powerboat snarled out on the Sound—probably a striped-bass fisherman, heading for Pennfield Reef. Julian wished he were there, on the black waters, under the stars, for the room felt stifling despite the breeze. Ah, what would their lives have been like had they dealt with things honestly years ago? Clay might still be living, and they in any case happier than now, cloistered with their musty secrets, like two conspirators covering up an old crime.

"We should have faced things right off the bat. At Hotchkiss," he said. "When I think about the way things are these days . . . That congressman up in Massachusetts came right out and said he was gay and gets reelected. Maybe it's not something to brag about, but ashamed about . . . ?"

She, lounging back on the chaise with bare ankles crossed, took a cigarette from the pack in her pocket and dragged on it unlighted.

"Go ahead, fire it up," he said.

"I'll stick to the rules. And what was there we should have faced right off the bat? If Clay had been gay, I wouldn't have been ashamed. The point is, he wasn't."

Here's delusion, thought Julian.

"He was intoxicated, dear. And what happened, that's a story as old as prep schools," Greer persisted. "It's practically a tradition in England."

"What about what happened on the ship?" he asked, though he didn't want to pursue the matter anymore. Arguing with her on this question was like arguing with a religious fanatic.

"Didn't we just go through all that, or was I imagining things?" She snapped the cigarette in two between her crossed fingers, then tossed the pieces out a window, onto the lawn where, in old dreams, wedding tents had been pitched and toasts made and guests had sauntered in the sun. "Why are we raking all this up?" she asked, turning and leaning against the window frame. "I want to talk about the future. What are your objections to Dante?"

"He wouldn't fit in with . . ." Julian made a sweeping gesture to indicate the world beyond the room, the world they lived in. "He seems a little rough around the edges."

"Well, those can be smoothed out, sanded right off of him, I'm sure. You know damned well what I meant, dear. Not to *him*—to his living under this roof. Oh, to have someone else here again, even if it's only for a while. All this space, this emptiness."

"Another place. We could move, a smaller place, a new place, where there aren't all these reminders," he said, though he was aware that a move was totally out of the question. So out of the question that she didn't even react to the remark, as if she hadn't heard it.

"There's a time of day, usually when I get home but before you do, five to seven, especially in the fall, when we start to notice how short the days are getting and the light falls in a certain way, it gets a certain deep golden color on the marsh grass across the harbor. . . . That time, when I come home and hear nobody, don't hear a thing except, I swear,

I can hear the air moving in the house, whispering . . . It's desolate, desolate. . . ."

"Oh, God, Greer."

"What would be so terrible about Dante staying here for a while? What?"

He began to muster his objections, knowing perfectly well he was going to surrender to her. The gas bubble burned again below his navel. He wanted a drink.

I V

EARLY ON A Sunday morning—exactly a week after he'd quit the band—Dante left for Connecticut with his clothes, CDs, fishing rod, and Alembic in the trunk of his '81 Mercury. He did not feel that he was moving over I-95; that long, linear slab of pavement seemed to be moving swiftly under him, conveying him to a new life. He made the drive in record time, arriving at Fastnet the following night. When he got out of the car and the yard lights blazed on, as if to illuminate his way across the hemlock-shadowed yard, he allowed himself to pretend that he was coming home after a long absence.

Julian's greeting was a little cool, but Greer's embrace more than compensated. She took him upstairs, not this time to the attic but to a second-floor bedroom at the end of the hall. A guest room, he supposed, and seldom used: the walls were bare of pictures, though he spotted squares and rectangles, lighter than the rest of the walls, where pictures once had hung. After unpacking, he joined the Rhodeses for a drink downstairs, told them the trip had been uneventful, and learned that a young couple had shown a lot of interest in his mother's house; if they qualified for a mortgage, they probably would make an offer.

"You just could be on your way to owning your own shop," Greer said with an encouraging smile, and raised her glass.

Dante raised his in return, but after driving fifteen hundred miles in two days, he was made dizzy by the mere smell of scotch. He excused himself, went to bed, and fell immediately asleep to the music of the sea. He woke late the next morning to the same sounds of gull cries and chiming halyards. A window across from the foot of his bed overlooked the cove, and it was as if he had opened his eyes to a three-dimensional seascape, flooded in summer light. He stretched and yawned and, going to the window, opened it and thrust his head outside. Long and narrow, the cove curved gently past the brick buildings and colonial houses of Fair Harbor Center, past a marina and a dock and muddy shoals, in which oystermen's stakes stuck out like straws. Beyond, the constricted passage opened onto Long Island Sound, appearing as boundless as the ocean on this morning whose humid haze cloaked the New York shore. A feeling he couldn't name stole into him. His luck was changing, and he sensed new possibilities lying ahead, possibilities he could not have imagined a month before, though they were as vague—and as tantalizing—as the land forms he glimpsed through the haze on the horizon. Now he could identify the feeling. It was one that should have been his by right of his birth date—the special happiness of being young.

For the first few days, he basked in it, and in the somewhat illicit pleasure of being unemployed without the usual anxieties. To avoid straining the Rhodeses' generosity, he insisted on paying his fair share of the grocery bills, funding his contributions out of his small inheritance, now diminished by his travel expenses and the two forty he'd had to spend on his last month's rent in Miami.

He wasn't wired for prolonged idleness, however; his conscience began to needle him, and he started looking for a job. First, he called on barbershops and hair salons near Fair Harbor, then broadened his search, ranging farther and farther until, two weeks later, he found himself reading the New Haven want ads. There weren't any openings anywhere. A salon in Westport—a trendy place much like the NuWave, but he couldn't be choosy—took his name and number; so did DeGrasso's, a venerable barbershop in Stamford, with seven chairs and a manicurist. It was much more his kind of place, but the owner, Dave DeGrasso, a big guy with a grin that kept breaking through his somber gray beard, didn't hold out much hope. "Two words we don't know how to spell here are 'turnover' and 'retire,'" he said, and jerked his thumb at an old man shaving a customer in the last chair. "See that guy there? Nick Demaris. Started here after he got out of the army in '47." Dante left, disappointed but promising himself that if ever he had a shop of his own, it would look and smell and feel like DeGrasso's.

That dream of independence appeared to be as far away as ever. The young couple had been denied a mortgage. Some problem with their credit record, Greer said. No one else had shown any interest in the house, despite its new roof. It seemed to resist being sold, as if it had a mind of its own—or as if his mother's spirit haunted the place and drove people away. Greer had a more prosaic explanation: the state's economy remained flat, and interest rates, having fallen in '94, had ticked up again, which affected low-end buyers most. Again she counseled patience; some houses were on the market for two years.

Dante's optimism flagged a little. Well, at least he now had, between him and the yawning chasm where people lined up for food stamps and waited for the repo man's knock, a net stronger than next week's paycheck. But for how long would the net remain? Greer's invitation to stay as long as he wanted couldn't be taken at face value; he would wear out his welcome if he didn't find work soon. Maybe it was wearing out already. She was as warm as ever, but Julian had become more distant, barely saying hello and good night—a sure sign that he was getting impatient with having an idle boarder in the house. To make himself useful, Dante did odd jobs around the house—those his limited skills allowed. He repaired a couple of light switches, fixed a leaky faucet, replaced a screen. And Greer, as aware as he of her husband's attitude, made it a point to call his attention to these small improvements. "Dante got that light switch in the den working again," she would say. Or: "The torn screens in the sunroom are fixed, thanks to Dante." He was beginning to feel like live-in help.

One day, she was inspired to paint his bedroom. She said that it had been Wedgwood blue with white trim originally, and she wanted it restored to those exact colors. She did mean "exact." He had to make three trips to a Westport paint store, mixing and remixing, before he got the shade right. She took the next day off from work and, her hair pinned up beneath a red kerchief, helped him move the furniture into the hall and throw tarps across the floor. With the radio playing, they laid on the primer coats amid a clutter of pans and paint cans and trim brushes. "This is fun!" she declared, pushing a roller up and down a wall with long, exuberant swipes. She had two closings the next day, so Dante applied the finish coats by himself. That was just as well: as a housepainter, Greer was more enthusiastic than competent. She returned home late in the afternoon and made a circuit of the room, inspecting the trim and mullions. He thought he'd done a pretty good job—hardly any smears or splashes—yet his heart beat with a real fear that she would find fault with his work. When she pronounced it "perfect, just perfect," the rhythms of his heart changed, and he realized that he wanted to please her, not to ingratiate himself but simply because pleasing her made him happy.

The following day, as he was moving the furniture back in place, she presented him with a large gift box, decked out in a green ribbon.

"You deserve something for the good job you did," she said, with a look of anticipation. "Well, are you going to open it?"

Inside were a blue polo shirt—the prefaded kind—and a pair of khaki slacks, with the store labels removed. The clothes exhaled a faint, indefinable, but pleasant smell.

"Try them on. I had to guess, but I figured you were about . . ."

"Clay's size," he said.

He took the trousers out of the box and held them to his waist and said they looked long enough.

"On, Dante. Try them *on*."

When he came out of the bathroom, she looked at him appraisingly, then thumped rapidly down the hall and returned with her camera.

"You look great. Now let's have a picture of you. A picture of you in the bright new room you painted."

"A picture?" He gave her a nervous blink. "It's just a room; it's not like it's a work of art."

"Over there. The light's just right. By the dresser," she commanded, with a fluttering of her thin, cracked fingers, like those of a woman who did physical labor, except for the smooth red nails filed to perfect ovals.

He complied. Greer backed toward the door, adjusting the focus and telling him to loosen up. He rolled his neck and shrugged a couple of times, but immediately he fell back into his stiff posture.

"There you are again, looking like you're facing a firing squad."

"This is me you're takin' the picture of this time, right?"

"Tak*ing*. Yes. Yes, it's you. That last time, that was the one and only time I'd ever—" She stopped herself. "Here's what I want you to do. Put your elbow on the dresser and kind of lean toward it, the other hand on your wrist. . . . That's it. Now cross your ankles, make a figure four with your legs. . . . There you go, good."

Flattered by the attention and her approval of his pose, he broadened his grin. Too much teeth, she said. Just a subtle smile, please . . . Scuttling backward again, she looked at him with her head cocked and her lips pursed. Something was needed, a little prop. . . . The bare dresser against the bare wall—it looked too stark. . . . Again the rapid thump as she went down the hall. A minute later, he heard things being moved around above him, in the attic storeroom.

"What are *those*?" he asked when she came back. He'd thought she'd gone to fetch a vase or one of those antique porcelain washbasins.

"What do they look like?"

"Model planes?"

"And this is a photograph," she said with gentle mockery, holding up a picture in a desk frame. She set it on the bed and made one of the planes swoop in mock flight. It was a bomber from the old days, with little plastic propellers and machine guns sticking out like wasp stingers from glass bubbles in the tail and on the fuselage.

"It's a Mitchell, a B-25, and this," Greer said, raising the other, larger one, "is the famed Flying Fortress, a B-17." Playfully mimicking the gut-tural roar of a prop engine, she buzzed Dante's head with the B-17, then landed it and the B-25 on the dresser. "My father flew both in World War II."

She set the photograph on its easel between the models. It showed two men, both wearing crushed caps, leather jackets, and rakish grins, kneeling in front of several other men, in what looked like mechanics' coveralls. Behind them loomed the nose section of a real-life Mitchell bomber. Under the checkerboard Plexiglas of the pilot's cabin was a painting of a blonde in a one-piece bathing suit, she winking lewdly over the words "Yankee Lady."

"My dad's the one on the left, the captain," Greer said fondly. "He named the plane for my mother, but that bimbo in the swimsuit isn't her, I assure you. Dad used to stay in this room when he visited us. That picture used to be right where it is now."

"Is he . . . ?"

"A little more than a year ago. Would you mind terribly if I left the picture there, right where it was, with the models?" Her plaintiveness touched him and made him feel guilty for reminding her that his mother's picture had been on the dresser before they started painting.

"Oh, God, that's right!" She took the camera from around her neck. "Just let me get a few more shots of you, and then I'll bring that stuff back upstairs."

When she was through, Dante, wary of acting ungrateful, had second thoughts; if she wanted the models and her father's photo on the dresser, that was fine with him. It was, after all, her house.

"But it's your room," she said.

"Well, yeah, for right now, but after I'm on my feet and all . . ."

"You'd leave?" Before he could answer, she turned aside abruptly, almost angrily, and stood profiled to him, her arms crossed under her breasts. "I did say for as long as you liked, and I meant it."

He wondered if he'd been trolling for this reconfirmation. Then she said, facing him once again:

"You do like staying here, don't you? We certainly like having you here. This place has been so quiet for so long, so deadly quiet. If you could know how glad it makes me to hear you coming down the stairs for breakfast. Or the painting we did yesterday—I really liked that, working with you to brighten the place up. Don't misunderstand the way things are between me and Julian. We get along, but we always talk about the same things, we each know what the other is thinking, and it's just been the two of us the past five years; in a way, longer, if you count the time Clay was away at school and in the navy. Two of us, alone together, in seven-plus thousand square feet. We could turn this place into a bed-and-breakfast and people wouldn't get in each other's way. Oh, my, I'm going on a bit."

A silence fell over them, a kind of invisible box in which he and Greer stood motionless. Something more needed to be said, and he turned toward one of the night tables and asked how his mother's picture would look there.

"Fine," said Greer. "She'll be closer to you when you go to sleep."

"That's where it goes, then. So that solves the decorating problem."

"You're sweet, Dante. You've got a very good heart. That was one of the things I saw in you almost immediately. You've got a good heart, and both Julian and I could use someone like that in our lives."

And then, under the white ceiling with its new gloss, he blushed as she rose on tiptoe and kissed him on the cheek with her cool, slender lips.

After she left—to get the pictures developed, she said—he changed back into his work clothes to clean up the brushes and rollers. As he folded the polo shirt and slacks into their box, he sniffed again that vague, pleasant aroma and put his nose down to identify it. Woody. That was as close as he could come to naming it. Like the smell of fresh new wood. Probably from the store shelf.

THE PHOTOGRAPH, blown up to an eight-by-ten, appeared on his dresser two days later on one side of the model planes, the picture of Greer's father on the other.

THE NEXT WEEK brought a heat wave that bled the sky into an anemic blue, causing Dante to feel that the Florida climate had followed him north. Greer took it upon herself to keep him busy in between his handyman tasks, which seldom lightened his burden of idle time by more than two or three hours a day. She put him on a camp counselor's regimen of tennis and sailing lessons, the former administered by a pro at the Rhodeses' country club, the latter by Greer herself, in her Greenwich twenty-four. She was mad for exercise, despite her addiction to cigarettes. Unless it was raining or blowing hard, she changed into shorts and a tank top immediately after coming home from work and rowed the Alden in the lingering light of the long midsummer days. From the rear veranda, Dante would watch her carry the green-and-white shell, with its dagger-pointed bow and stern, down to the floating dock in back of the house. She would climb in delicately, to avoid capsizing; then, her muscles flexing, she would row through the harbor with strong, graceful strokes, the feathered blades of the oars sometimes skipping over the still water with a hissing, crackling sound. Half an hour or forty-five minutes later, the same sound would herald her return from open water. One final stroke would send her gliding into the dock, the raised oars held parallel over the stern deck and strands of water dripping from the blades, like tinsel. He liked to watch her climb out and take off her cap and toss her hair, her sweat-stained tank top clinging to her—a sight that caused him on one or two occasions to compare her figure with his mother's.

He remembered Mom's lumpy thighs and upper arms when he took her to the beach on her visit to Miami, the matronly sag of her breasts beneath her bathing suit, the coarse thickening that was stealing into her face. He didn't like himself for remembering her this way, or for awarding her second place in his private beauty contest: it was like a betrayal.

He was shocked one day to discover that he resented her for letting herself go, and in more ways than physically. She had resigned herself, in the last two or three years of her life, to never marrying again and to a dead-end job, and had found a kind of gray contentment in her resignation. For all the liveliness she'd shown in Miami, she had pretty much given up, satisfied to sit out the rest of her life and keep her losses to a minimum. He couldn't imagine her rowing a small, tippy craft alone on open water after work, or doing anything other than what she used to do: watch television for hours, often consuming half a bottle of cheap white wine before the eleven o'clock news. Of course, it was unfair to compare her with Greer. Greer had money, and money made you confident. Money kept you looking good way past the age at which other people started looking bad. People with money didn't wear out as fast as those without it.

On the day of his first tennis lesson, Dante drove to the Rhodeses' country club wearing a white outfit Greer had given him for the occasion. He went down Harbor Road, crossed a bridge, passing an old grain mill now converted to an office building, then followed the road to a shady little street that eventually broke into a plain of fairways glistening under silver umbrellas opened by the sprinklers. Stopping at the guard shack, occupied by an elderly man wearing a uniform and thick glasses, he suddenly had the sensation that he was an impostor, in a disguise so thin that even the half-blind old man would see through it. "I'm a guest of Greer Rhodes," he said to the security guard's silent inquisition—and was surprised when he was waved through without having to identify or explain himself any further. It was like being in a fairy-tale kingdom, where magic words opened castle gates.

The instructor came out of the pro shop, carrying what looked like a shopping basket that was full of tennis balls. He was a tanned, wiry man in his early thirties, with reddish curls, and drawled that his name was Pernell Stokes, but everyone called him Perk. Leading Dante toward the first court, which a sign on the chain-link fence declared was "reserved for instruction," Perk devoted the first half hour to such ABCs as proper grips, rules and scoring and court geography. When Perk started him on ground strokes, just as two impressively skilled young women, the one short and blond, the other tall and black-haired, started playing singles on court three, Dante wished he could make himself invisible. Though he hadn't played many sports in high school, he'd been very good at those he did; but all grace and coordination deserted him at tennis. A part of his mind floated out of his skull and, as it were, began to video-tape him, so that he could see himself, swatting futilely. The women sent their ball back and forth in hard, flat trajectories, while he stumbled after the balls Perk hit to him one after the other and which he either missed altogether or lobbed onto the girls' court. When enough balls cluttered their backcourt to pose a hazard, the taller of the two hit them back to Perk, registering irritation and reproach with each swing of her metallic-blue racket.

As Perk refilled the basket, Dante watched the long-limbed girl rise and stretch to serve. The ball sizzled over the net, which she rushed to volley her partner's return. "Game," she said. The choreography of the genteel combat thrilled him; so did the sheen of her hair in the sunlight, her contained stride as she returned to the baseline, dribbling the spare ball with the racket in a silent celebration of her victory. Every move she made was certain and economical, exuding a kind of sovereignty. When, in another fierce attack on the net, her skirt flew up, the flicker of her white panties, as fleeting and mysterious as a running doe's tail in the woods, was almost more than he could stand.

"If you're gawking at her because she's good-looking, fine," Perk said, leaning over the net in the confidential manner of a racetrack tip-ster. "But if you're looking at her game, forget it—you'll only frustrate yourself. That gal was hitting forehands before she was out of Pampers."

"Know her?"

"Penny something. Cunningham, I think. I've only been here a year, and I haven't got all the members' names down right."

"So she belongs?" asked Dante, glancing sidelong at the jet-haired Penny. He might have been imagining things, but she appeared to be looking at him, with more than casual interest.

"Cummings, that's it," said Perk. "Penny Cummings. Her parents be-long. Don't know about her. Let's take a break and then start the second hour."

"The second hour?" Dante had hoped his torment was over.

"Mrs. Rhodes signed you up for two hours. Two more tomorrow, and two on Friday. Total immersion."

Penny and the blonde were playing the next morning when he showed up for his lesson. He missed the ball less often, but that was his only improvement. When, after he'd fanned a backhand, the racket flew from his slippery palm, he came within an inch of smashing it against the fence in frustration. To make matters worse, the two girls were taking a break and watching him. Never had he felt so inept and out of his element, but they looked relaxed and natural, claiming possession of the court even while doing nothing. It reminded him of the way gifted musicians who know they're good possess a stage before they've played a note. Perk amiably counseled him not to take things so seriously; he was doing no worse than most beginners, and anyway it was only a game. But it had become more than a game to him: The previous night, after reporting to Greer that he didn't think he could get the hang of it, he learned that Clay had been captain of his college tennis team. She showed him gleaming trophies. Not that she expected Dante to win tournaments—he should only learn to play well enough to participate without embarrassing himself. There was a social value in tennis, she'd said. It would give him something in common with people, meaning, he supposed, the kind of people he was likely to meet while he was living with her and Julian. Saying she was confident he would master the sport in time, she left little doubt that that was her expectation. So with each failed stroke, he felt he was letting her down; each was a sad measure of the difference between him and his shining twin; each withdrew a few more dollars from his account of self-confidence, marginal to begin with. If he couldn't learn to play a simple game, how could he expect to accomplish anything in this new life of his? It was crazy, he knew, but his opinion of himself now hinged on his ability to hit a little yellow ball with skill, and the great world, in which he never seemed to find his place, had concentrated itself into this fenced enclosure of green rectangles.

After the lesson, Dante toweled his head and went into the pro shop for a Coke. He sat on a director's chair, facing a window on which condensation made a miniature mountain range, and felt his shirt growing crusty with dried sweat. It was supposed to hit a hundred today, Perk said, busying himself with something behind the counter. This heat was worse than Florida, where he taught during the winters. Dante mentioned that he'd lived in Miami, and was about to begin a small-world discussion when, through the false frost on the window, he saw the two women striding toward the shop, their tennis bags swinging jauntily from their shoulders. He wanted to flee, as if he'd done something disgraceful.

From a distance, Penny looked every bit of six feet, the short, pleated skirt exaggerating the length of her legs. But as she stood next to Perk to pay for her court time, Dante saw that she was only about five-nine.

She had high cheekbones, a coppery complexion. He thought her gray eyes, giving off flashes of aquamarine, were a little too deep-set, her nose too aquiline, and her lips too thin, suggesting a severe nature; yet these flaws somehow complemented each other, saving her from a conventional prettiness and creating an arresting beauty. He barely noticed the blonde, and she faded even from his peripheral vision when Penny turned to him and said:

"You've got to be the guy who's staying with the Rhodeses."

He didn't answer, flustered by the question and by the striking directness of her gaze.

"You are, aren't you? Or am I making an ass of myself?"

"Well, yeah . . ."

"Which? You're the guy or I'm an ass?"

"You're not an ass. Not shy, either. How'd you know?"

Her mouth turned down at a corner, into a tight, slashing smile.

"Kidding, right? It's like everybody says, like Clay Rhodes got stuffed into a copy machine and you came out of the slot."

He wasn't sure he liked the image of himself as a Xerox copy. He also didn't realize that he was famous. He'd met a couple of the Rhodeses' neighbors, the Seavers and the Crandalls, and some friends of theirs from New York—the Conklins, he thought—but no one else.

"Who's this everybody?"

"A few people from town, the club. Word gets around. Hope I'm not embarrassing you, but would you mind standing up a second?" she asked, then added as he got to his feet: "Damn, you're even about the same height. Wouldn't have believed it if I didn't see it."

"Who are we talking about here?" asked the blonde, in a voice an octave higher than Penny's.

Penny gave an awkward little shrug, which charmed Dante for some reason. Off the court, she wasn't quite the formidable female animal, all lithe movement and lightning reflexes.

"A guy I knew when I was a kid. Clay Rhodes. This guy could be his twin brother."

"This guy's name is Dante Panetta," he said, with a quick stab of his hand that startled Penny. He hadn't meant to be so aggressive but was eager to assert his own identity. He was tired of being gawked at.

"Dante. Neat name. Penny Cummings." She leaned backward, as if to avoid getting too close to him, and shook hands with all the strength he would have expected from a woman who hit forehands like hers. "This is my roommate, Marcia Williams."

"A double, huh? You mean to say there's two of you in this world?" asked Marcia, looking him up and down flirtatiously. "Two means there's enough to go around?"

"Marcy! For Christ's sake!" Penny chided, as Dante blushed. "There aren't two anyway. Clay was . . . He died a few years ago."

Marcia attempted to alter her expression to conform to the somber revelation, but she failed.

"What a waste, is all I've got to say. Proves that life isn't fair?" Her voice had an annoying, girlish cuteness, rising at the end of sentences so that statements sounded like questions.

"You're incorrigible," Penny said. "It was really sad. His mother . . . We wondered for a while if she was going to get through it."

Since the topic of Clay was apparently unavoidable, Dante decided to paddle with the current and asked if Penny and he had gone to school together.

"School? No. He was five years older," she answered, and inclined her head with a slow, almost wistful movement. "Didn't date him, either, if that was going to be your next question."

"It wasn't."

"I suppose I had a crush on him. Most girls did, but by the time I was old enough, I knew it was hopeless."

There was something unfinished about the last remark. Her eyes moved back to Dante's face, flustering him once more.

"Mind if I get personal?"

Dante shrugged his approval.

"Isn't it a little weird for you, staying there? If it were I, I'd find it way too weird."

"No, it's not too . . . Well, yeah, sometimes it gets weird when I look at the pictures of him in the house."

"That would give me the total creeps," said Penny. "You must have a strong sense of yourself, because if I was in that spot, I'd start to wonder who I was."

He thought of a line—"I'd like to find out more about who *you* are"—but a fortunate governor in his head checked him. Instead, he complimented her tennis game.

"Changing the subject, are you? I'm not Steffi Graf, but I do okay."

She leaned over the counter, in which wristbands and headbands shared the shelves with clear plastic ball containers, and asked Perk for a pencil and paper. "Want a free lesson sometime, give me a buzz," she said, handing him her phone number.

He didn't dare allow himself to think that this invitation meant anything beyond its face value.

"Maybe you two could hit after Friday's lesson," Perk offered, then added, with a silly goggling of his eyes, "I'll bet Dante would rather see your face on the other side of the net than mine."

"You're a lot cuter," Penny quipped, playfully bouncing her racket on Perk's dense russet curls.

Late that afternoon, lounging in the cockpit of her Greenwich, her bare feet with their lacquered nails propped on a cushion and a browned arm looped over the tiller, Greer agreed that Penny was beautiful in an exotic way. Amanda—her mother—had hair that color, like carbon or lamp black.

"She's part French; her father came from Charleston. Amanda Duquesne. That's where it came from, the French."

Dante brushed the side rails with varnish, the sailboat as steady as if on dry land, moored by its orange buoy in a calm cove dramatically narrowed by the ebbing tide. In the soft, horizontal sunlight, the snails in the mud banks resembled lumps of gravel embedded in fresh, hot tar. Egrets stalked the shore, occasionally plucking crabs with their long beaks.

"I was thinking she might have some Indian blood—the high cheekbones, the coppery skin," he said.

"I think it's the French, but you never know. Her family goes back as far as mine. Could have been a squaw in the woodpile somewhere along the line."

This fostered in Dante's mind a picture of one of Penny's Puritan ancestors, driven berserk by a diet of oatmeal and Christianity, fleeing into the woods to ravish some Pocahontas. He ran the brush over the varnish he'd just applied, trying to smooth it out.

"It says on the can you shouldn't put this stuff on in hot, humid weather. Look, it's bubbling up."

"Then quit and wait for a cooler day," she said. "God, it is hot. I can close my eyes and feel like I'm in a Conrad novel, anchored in the mouth of a jungle river."

He tapped the cover tight with a hammer and dipped the brush into a container of mineral spirits. Sometimes Greer's references to books and authors he'd never read irritated him.

"My take on it is, she wouldn't have given you her number if she weren't interested in something more than improving your ground strokes."

"You think so?"

"Well, we've got to consider that women these days are more used to dealing with men on an equal footing than in my day. There's a certain androgyny at work. She might have given you her number with no more thought than if she'd given it to another woman," Greer said. "No sense in second-guessing. Wait till Friday, see what develops."

"What can you tell me about her?"

"You seem quite smitten with this gal, for having talked to her for only a few minutes."

"I'm just . . . I don't know. Ever since Mom died, I haven't thought about women, and Penny . . ."

"At least got you thinking. A guy could do a lot worse than her. She's always had a certain poise, a kind of self-possession. Wonderful athlete, as you saw. Also bright. She was Phi Beta Kappa at Smith and just got out of graduate school last month. Art history, I think her mother said. She wants to teach, maybe work in a gallery."

If Dante had entertained any serious hopes, the weight of this intimidating résumé threatened to crush them.

"You know, Clay came up, naturally. She said she had a crush on him when she was younger."

"A lot of girls did," said Greer, with a fond smile. "Clay had so many girlfriends. He'd bring a new one home every time he was on school vacation or back on leave from the navy."

"Yeah. Penny said that by the time she was old enough for Clay to date her, it was pretty hopeless."

A line appeared between Greer's eyebrows, and she cocked her head slightly aside, as though listening for some distant sound.

"Meaning that he had so many girls, she didn't have a prayer?"

"Guess so."

She filled a plastic wineglass from the bottle on the cockpit deck, sipped, then poured it out into the running tide, saying that there was nothing worse than warm white wine.

"I've got an inspiration," she added. "The club's having its summer dance next weekend. Why don't you ask her?"

"To a club I don't belong to?"

"As long as you're staying with us, you've got privileges."

"Right. Me, an out-of-work barber, asks this Phi Beta whatever, this hotshot with a master's degree, for a date."

With a finger, Greer shaved a mustache of sweat from her upper lip and said, "Don't sell yourself short. You're an awfully good-looking young man—if anybody can say that, I can. And you might not be a Phi Beta Kappa, but you do have a head on your shoulders."

She plucked the bungee cord that held the tiller fast when the boat was moored.

"We'll get no wind this evening, so sailing school's postponed till the doldrums lift. But the light, dear, is perfect. Let me get a picture of us together. Sit on the port gunwale, would you?" she asked, withdrawing her camera from her beach bag. She focused, positioned the camera on the starboard seat cushion, and set the automatic timer before sitting next to him.

THE WEATHER broiled on through Friday. The whole northeast, Maine to Maryland, steamed like Brazil. Experts on TV and radio spoke of massive lesions in the ozone layer, of a greenhouse effect that would transform the planet into a huge spherical sauna. From Dante's point of view, these vast, malign climatic forces had gathered for only one reason: to deprive him of Penny's company. A message was waiting for him at the pro shop: she'd canceled their tennis date because of the heat. Relief balanced out his disappointment. Now he wouldn't have to ask her to the club dance, which he suspected would be pretty cornball anyway, like the gigs he'd played at yacht and country clubs around Miami. Silver hairs would be creakily two-stepping to big-band tunes out of the dark ages, aging baby boomers requesting hits by the Beatles and the Beach Boys.

Magic happened on the court, and he regretted Penny wasn't there to see him. He began to hit steadily over the net—loopy strokes that she would have returned with her eyes closed, but they were consistent. He rallied with Perk, his body at last obeying his brain. Perk congratulated him—his play had come up a level overnight.

He drove back to Fastnet, his spirits and his faith in himself restored, went to the phone in the den, and called Penny. He told her he was sorry to have missed her and joked that it was a good thing she'd canceled; he'd improved so much, he would have run her ragged.

"You guys played two hours in this muck?"

He thought, or hoped, he heard admiration woven into the disbelief in her voice.

"Us Floridians are used to this."

"You're from Florida?"

"Only lived in Miami a couple of years. I'm from Norwalk originally."

"Hey! Marcy and I are renting a house in Rowayton," she said, mentioning the shorefront community that was fifteen minutes by car and three or four income levels up from his old neighborhood.

"If it cools off, think you'd be free to give me that lesson?"

"Sure. I'm just chilling out from the job hunt, waiting to hear back."

"Exactly what I'm doing," he said, and immediately wished he hadn't. It wasn't a lie, but it wasn't quite the truth, either.

"It's a bitch, isn't it? Six years of school, and you think the world's going to beat a path to your door, and then you find out that you're the path. I had interviews with two galleries in SoHo, who were supposed to get back to me two weeks ago, and still not a word. So what was your major?" Abruptly, she let out a deep, rolling laugh. He loved that almost mannish voice of hers. "I do *not* believe I asked that. 'What was your major?' "

"Yeah, hey, no problem," he replied with a false chuckle, grateful that he didn't have to answer. A worm of nervousness crawled through his gut while he stood dripping sweat amid the cases full of books, each volume a reminder of all the things he didn't know, just as the photos of Clay, an arm's length away on the desk, were reminders of all the things he wasn't. And then he saw that the boyhood picture of Clay on the sailboat with Greer had been replaced by the one she'd taken of herself and Dante a few days earlier. How should he feel about this substitution? Uneasy? Flattered? Had he wrongfully taken his double's place? But he hadn't. Greer had put it there.

"Hello?" asked Penny. "Still on the line?"

"Yeah, yeah."

"Guess you didn't major in communications."

"Sorry, I just saw something. It's nothing. . . ."

Then an image came to him, and it was as clear as the photos: Clay, on a summer day long past, standing in this very room in tennis shoes powdered with the artificial dust of the courts, speaking to one of his many girlfriends. Without conscious command, Dante's hand rose to rustle a lock of hair over his forehead, his body fell into a careless slouch, his lips threaded into a thin smile.

"Why don't we pick a day for that lesson?" he asked, with the eerie sensation that a ventriloquist was speaking through him. "How's Wednesday sound? Nine?"

"Wednesday nine? Sure. See you."

"Greer told me the club's having some sort of dance next weekend. Looks like I'll be going with them. Be great if I saw you there."

He was striving for a nonchalant tone to go with the nonchalant pose, but the sensation of being a talking dummy upset his equilibrium.

"Those club dances are okay if you're over forty-five," Penny said, but there was no period on the sentence—an invitation to persuade her.

"You know, I was thinking the same thing myself a few minutes ago. I played a couple of gigs like that in Miami."

"You're a musician?"

"Jazz. Latin stuff mostly, but I do mainstream."

"Hey, great. Love jazz, which used to make me odd girl out with my undergrad peers," she said, putting a comical twist into the last word. "Alternative, grunge, Kurt Cobain moaning about the rotten world in his ripped jeans? No, thanks. Miles Davis any day."

"So are you going? The club, I mean?"

"Let me get something straight. Am I being asked for a date, or what?"

"Right. I'm asking you for a date."

"Then it looks like I'm going. We'll talk more about it Wednesday, okay?"

He hung up with a happy terror.

"I'M NOT, you know, sure how to handle myself."

"Dear, the way you look, all you have to do is make sure you don't belch or pick your nose," said Greer, sharpening with her thumb and forefinger the points in his pocket handkerchief. "Do let me get a shot of you and Julian together before you leave. Lord, you could be a male model."

She, in a silk bathrobe, her hair piled up under a towel, gave the compliment with pride, for the figure Dante saw in the dressing mirror was largely her creation. She had given him the double-breasted blazer, the cream-colored trousers, the burgundy tie and matching kerchief. Her self-assigned role as his wardrobe mistress made him feel childish, as if he weren't capable of picking out his own clothes, but he liked the result—although the outfit looked like something out of those nostalgic Ralph Lauren ads. The classic look, Greer called it.

"Anyway, what are you worried about? I thought you two hit it off on Wednesday."

"I don't know if we hit it off. We didn't not hit it off. Kind of neutral. We rallied, she gave me a few pointers, we grabbed a sandwich at the deli, talked a little."

"What about?"

"Things. How you and me run into each other on the train, and—"

"Dante! How you and I ran into each other," Greer rebuked. "You're not going to get anywhere with a girl like Penny if you insist on talking like a dropout."

"Okay, okay. You and I. We talked about jazz. She likes jazz."

"Good. You've got something in common."

"But maybe that's about all. She didn't ask me what I do, but she's bound to, and I'm going to feel dumb, telling her I'm a barber."

"Ah, that again." Greer sat down and, clasping her hands around her crossed knees, squinted at him. "Let me tell you something about a woman like Penny. I know, because I was like her when I was her age, and I suppose my mother was too. They're raised and schooled in a certain way, certain expectations are laid on them, or maybe they lay those expectations on themselves, but when they're twenty-something, they're in a mood to experiment with alternatives. The ones with a social conscience spend a year or two teaching in Appalachia or do social work in the ghetto. The wild ones run off for a brief fling to the Caribbean and sleep with black guys; and the ones in between will start seriously dating men who aren't quite right for them, men who haven't been schooled and raised in the same way, who are a little different. What they have in common is that ninety-nine times out of a hundred, they come back to what they're used to, what they expect. They find that they can't break the mold, can't do without the cedar-shake colonial starter home, without the Junior League, without some husband who's a lawyer or in finance and has four Waspy names, like Julian Blaine Selkirk Rhodes."

Dante said nothing, his brain tumbling in the surf of her words. Which of those categories had she belonged to? The social worker, the renegade trysting with Rastafarians, the girl who'd turned her back on a youthful passion for a dull but suitable husband? He was bothered by the way she'd said Julian Blaine Selkirk Rhodes, each name dropping with the distinct, crystalline shattering of a glass on the floor.

"I've confused you, haven't I?" she asked.

He nodded.

"I'm trying to tell you that your instincts that you'd be wrong for Penny, as a serious relationship, are on the money. But there's a right way to be the wrong guy."

Serious relationship? he thought, moving toward a window to catch the breeze from off the water. Was that what he hoped for? He supposed so. Never had he been this anxious to make a good impression, this concerned about a woman's opinion of him.

"So what's the right way to be the wrong guy?"

"You don't have to tell her you're a barber, if the subject comes up. You're not cutting hair right now, are you? And even when you were, you considered yourself a jazz musician first. That's what you emphasize. She likes the music, and with her art history background—well, that suggests a kind of genteel bohemianism. She might be intrigued by someone who plays professionally. And the Latin part, Miami. There's a certain romance there—Latin brass playing under the swaying palms. That's your entrée. That's how you get your foot in the door."

Silent, he looked at the harbor, like a plate of rippled brass in the wind and the waning light.

"You wouldn't be lying or pretending to be something you're not." She rose and joined him at the window, and for a moment or two, lost in thought, she gazed down at the lawn, gently sloping toward the seawall. "I know it's not my place to say this, but I'd like nothing better than to see you dating a girl like Penny. At the same time, I would want you to have both eyes open. I wouldn't want to see you get hurt."

"Hey, I can take care of myself," he said.

"Oh, I'm sure you can. Just some advice from an older woman. Pardon me if I'm acting a little possessive, but after all, I was the one who found you."

And she caressed his cheek, the tenderness of her touch voided by the iciness of her fingertips, which made him flinch. A hurt look passed briefly across his face.

"Your hands are freezing," he explained apologetically.

"Lousy circulation. Another reason I should quit smoking." She put her hand in the pocket of her robe, as if to warm it up, but then she pulled out a key and held it in front of him.

"Oh, hell, Greer . . ."

"Best foot forward. You can't—"

"Pick her up in a rusted-out fifteen-year-old Mercury," he said, finishing for her.

Penny and Marcia rented a white shingle cottage on a private lane near a salt marsh. Dante, less nervous than he'd expected, swung the Lexus into the drive and went up the walk, while an osprey turned predaceous circles over the marsh and bees swarmed around the pale-blue and lavender hydrangeas in the yard. He rang the bell and heard Marcia call out, "Hey, Pen, he's here."

Penny appeared in the doorway, in a low-cut dress and scarlet-sequined bolero jacket, both the same charcoal black as her hair. Her heels brought her eyes, their gray-green lucidness heightened by a hint of liner, almost level with his. Her lips, painted to match her ruby earrings, looked fuller and less severe. The contrast of red and black had utterly transformed the breezy, athletic girl he'd met on the courts into a figure of allure. On the drive down from Fair Harbor, he'd rehearsed several lines of what he thought was sophisticated flattery—lines he imagined a Clay Rhodes might have spoken—but the sight of Penny gave him stage fright. He couldn't recall a word, and blurted out:

"Damn, you look gorgeous!"

She smiled and said he looked pretty good himself.

"Amen to that," said Marcia, looking up from the television. She gave them a wink goodbye.

Penny's heels forced her to shorten her long stride and accentuated the curve of her calves, and her hips swayed beneath their sheath of black silk. Dante hung back, momentarily entranced, then made an awkward lunge to get to the car door before she did. He didn't know many women who expected, or even wanted, chivalry, but he was in uncharted social waters and decided to play it safe.

"Hey, an old-fashioned guy," she said in that wonderful mellow voice, and settled in, her dress rising past her knees. He'd seen more of her in her tennis skirt, but there was in the whisper of silk on nylon, and in the teasing glimpse of her thighs, a mystery that made him a little light-headed.

He drove cautiously up the turnpike, stretching itself through the gathering twilight, past long corridors of trees and high wooden walls raised to protect suburban backyards against the noise and danger of traffic. Penny warned him, in a friendly way, that she was a pretty good ballroom dancer, having endured five years of dance classes when she was a girl. She was used to leading, because most men her age, and even those a good deal older, didn't have a clue when it came to fox-trots, waltzes, and the lindy. With relish, Dante told her that his mother had taught him those dances, as well as those from the sixties and seventies, and he'd learned Latin dancing in Miami, everything from the bossa nova to salsa. Penny didn't have to worry—he knew how to lead.

He took his eyes briefly off the road and noticed her looking at him with an amused smile—the sort of expression a schoolteacher might bestow on a charmingly boastful schoolboy.

"My mom loved to dance," he went on, compelled to say something. "My aunt told me that when she was young and out in a disco, everyone would clear the floor to watch her."

"Are your parents still in Norwalk?"

He paused, calculating how much of his history to reveal.

"No. My aunt and uncle are in the Boston area, and . . . See, my mom died suddenly in April. A stroke."

"A *stroke*? My God, you didn't say a thing about that the other day." He gestured that he was past the worst of it now and said that he would always be grateful to Greer for helping him get through it.

"She's really what you'd call simpatico, and generous. She's always been like that?"

"I suppose. She was okay with me when I was a kid," Penny stated, a little flatly, he thought. "Listen, Dante, I'm not sure what sort of relationship you and she have, but it might get a little weird for you tonight. There's liable to be people there who knew Clay."

"I'm getting used to that," he said, though he wasn't sure if he was prepared for an onslaught. "How about you? Will it be weird for you?"

"Don't think so. My parents will be there, and I've already warned them to, you know, not make a big deal. Just take you for who you are, not who you look like."

The country part of the Fair Harbor Yacht and Country Club—the tennis courts and golf course—was familiar to Dante. Tonight he got his first close look at its maritime heart and soul: a rambling two-story building that lay beyond the fairways, atop a low hill on a rock-belted point shaded by oaks eighty feet high. Its divided-light windows shining in the violet dusk, its weathered shingles possessing a retiring charm, a little knocked about at the edges, the whole structure had none of the sleek, aggressive glamour of the clubs he'd played in Boca and Fort Lauderdale; it was bathed in an ambience of money too old and secure to feel the need to advertise itself. Hooded yard lights burned on both sides of the drive, and the car seemed to ascend on glowing rails toward the portico, where two valets waited beside a board on which car keys hung from brass hooks. Dante was proud to pull the Lexus into the line of BMWs and Audis. His pride swelled when he handed the keys to one of the valets, who ogled Penny and then, with a quick leap of his eyebrows, told Dante that he'd done very well for himself. "Take good care of that car," he murmured, and tipped the man five dollars. The valet's eyes widened, and it occurred to Dante that he'd overdone it. He checked to see if Penny had noticed his extravagance. She hadn't; she was looking toward the point, where a ship's mast converted into a flagpole blazed in spotlights. Signal flags flying from the guylines that extended from the tips of the yardarms to the base of the pole formed an inverted triangle of colorful snapping cloth.

"That's probably my favorite place in the world, especially on summer evenings," Penny said softly. "To sit there under those trees, with a drink, a breeze blowing, watching the sun go down—it doesn't make me happy. It *is* happiness. We'll have to do that one of these days, and you'll see what I mean."

"Sure, sure," he said, delighted that she wanted to share the experience with him.

They passed through a large foyer, its polished wooden floor sending back dark reflections of themselves, and entered the ballroom, where packed tables ringed a dance floor sparsely populated by couples shuffling to "They Can't Take That Away from Me." The band was a nonet in white dinner jackets. Penny and Dante exchanged crooked smiles— the music was going to be as hokey as they'd expected, yet they had to acknowledge that there was something touching and sweet about that tune. Penny stood at the edge of the bandstand, her neck craned, and said she was looking for someone she knew, someone, that is, who wasn't over forty or under eighteen, for the room was full of gray or graying heads, intermingled with towheaded adolescents, the girls looking older than their years, the boys in jackets too short for their gangly arms.

"Don't see a soul; let's take a look and see who we find," Penny said.

As he trailed her through the maze of tables, he heard Greer's voice behind him.

"There you two are!"

She was in a blue dress and spectator pumps, her hair piled up so that it resembled a pewter helmet.

"Penny! How are you? It's been . . . I think it's been since you left for grad school. What is that? Two years?"

"Two. Right," said Penny, and the women embraced in a cloud of mingling perfumes.

"We're sitting with the Crandalls and your parents. Come on and join us."

Penny got her long legs from her father, Alan, who loomed like a lean sequoia when he stood to shake Dante's hand. The man must have stood six-five. He had a low, straight hairline and blue eyes that glared frostily out of sockets deep as caves. His lips were thin, like Penny's, but where hers suggested severity, his proclaimed it, drawn over his jaw in two rigid lines that looked never to have been bent by a smile. Gazing down on Dante, he ignored his daughter's request and said the resemblance was incredible, all right. Never seen anything like it. Greer chimed in with a "Yes, isn't it just the most remarkable thing?" Dante grinned nervously and sat beside Penny's mother, who had puffy eyes and a slack chin that looked to be the result of too many cocktails before dinner—and indeed, two glasses, each with a twist of lime floating forlornly on melting ice cubes, stood beside her place setting.

When the introductions were over, Penny asked for a white wine. Dante navigated to the bar, somewhat relieved to be out of her father's presence, and ordered the wine and a beer for himself. As he waited for his change, someone tapped him on the shoulder and said in a quavering voice:

"Welcome back."

He looked into the face of a stooped old man wearing a black, brass-buttoned jacket, white duck trousers, and a tie with tiny anchors on it.

"Jim Ingram," said the ancient mariner, his eyes crinkling behind tortoiseshell glasses. "You probably don't remember me. . . . Been years. . . . Out of the service now? Navy, wasn't it?"

"You've got me mixed up with somebody else," said Dante, sweat erupting on his forehead.

"What? What? Aren't you—?"

"Never in the service. Excuse me."

He took the change and hurried away from the baffled old man, back to the sanctuary of Greer and Julian's table. The Crandalls had returned from the dance floor, Susan, with her raucous laughter, and her husband, Don, who had wrestler's shoulders and a voice that had only one, thundering pitch, even when he was speaking to people right beside him. He was in the market, like Julian. The Crandalls and Greer were the most animated of the group. Julian, looking as if he were dressed for a Christmas party in his greens and reds, was subdued, somehow insubstantial for all his bulk, and the Cummingses acted as if they wished they were somewhere else. Amanda worked on a third gin and tonic with quiet determination. Alan, as remote in his height and frigid personality as a monk on a mountaintop, hardly spoke a word to her or to Penny, whose glance kept wandering the room for a table of friends she and Dante could join. He was content to remain where he was, afraid of bumping into someone else who would mistake him for Clay.

Nevertheless, he asked Penny to dance. There was no choice, after bragging about how good he was. Feeling blessedly invisible among the circling couples, he led her through a fox-trot and then a version of "Stardust," which drew some dancers into close embraces. He pressed his hand against the small of Penny's back, testing for resistance, found it, and relaxed his grip. A camera flashed once, twice. Looking over Penny's shoulder, he saw Greer, snapping away. The band turned to swing—a tight, smooth rendition of "In the Mood," a number he'd played at a few wedding gigs. He twirled Penny with double turns, inside and out, she laughing when he let go of her hand and spun on his heels, timing the move to take her hand again on the beat.

With the next tune, "Sentimental Journey," Penny quipped that these musical museum pieces would make her ready for Kurt Cobain. "Let's take a break and get a drink."

She ordered another white wine, and chided the bartender for filling only two-thirds of her glass. Scowling, he topped it off. Dante slipped a dollar into the tip cup, asked for a beer, and started toward the table. She tugged at his sleeve and asked that they not go back just yet.

"You and your parents . . . everything's okay? I guess I shouldn't ask that. I meant it's okay with them you're out with me?" he asked.

"They're like that toward everybody, toward each other. Stiff as broom handles." She drained half her glass. "You should have seen Sunday dinners at our house when my sisters and I were in school. Dad in a tie, Mom in her pearls, foot-long candles on the table, drinks before dinner and hardly a damn thing to eat at it, and nobody saying much, just the clink-clink of silverware on china."

She actually shuddered. Dante swallowed an impulse to tell her that there were domestic sounds a lot more terrible than the clink-clink of silverware on china. Then he saw the ancient mariner approaching, took Penny's arm, and pulled her onto the dance floor before she could put her drink down.

"You must really like this song," she said.

"Not a whole lot."

It was the Beatles' "Yesterday": the band was advancing chronologically.

"Then what was with the Conan the Barbarian routine?"

He told her. She finished the wine with one quick swallow and back-stepped toward a table, on which she set the glass. Leaning back in his arms, she gave him a look at once beguiling and disconcerting. It was as if she saw right through him and yet was charmed, or at least amused, by what she saw.

"Warned you it could get weird, didn't I? I don't know much about you, but you seem like a pretty good guy."

"I do?"

"Yeah, so maybe one of these days you can explain why you're putting yourself through all this weirdness."

One of these days. Taking those words as another sign of encouragement, he wrapped his arm around her waist, and she yielded this time, drawing near enough for him to feel his warmth and hers fusing in the slender space between their cheeks. The vocalist was crooning now, and he decided that he liked "Yesterday" after all. Its sad but hopeful lyrics, flowing with the lilt of clarinet and guitar, flooded into him—a living stream of sound that cleared the vision of his heart, allowing him to see the promise he'd half beheld beyond the water on that hazy morning. All that he wanted, or thought he wanted, had become incarnate in this black-haired woman with the sea-gray eyes that smiled and pierced and altogether enchanted him.

Then the music stopped, the band took a break, and someone announced that dinner was being served. The rapture was broken, though a remnant of it lingered as Dante and Penny joined the chain of people shuffling toward the buffet table, behind which kitchen staff spooned out curried chicken and potatoes from chafing dishes and a guy in a chef's hat deftly sliced a pink-hearted roast. The smells made Dante ravenous. While he heaped his plate, a blandly pretty blonde with a nose as edged as an envelope swooped toward Penny and greeted her with a piercing "Penny Cummings!" The two women hugged. Penny introduced her—Beth something, an old friend from school—and Beth something introduced her date, Todd, who was tanned, freckled, and of average height, but with a thick neck and broad shoulders that projected raw leverage. He wore an irritatingly confident grin. Actually, Todd and Beth both irritated Dante: he resented their intrusion into his and Penny's private space.

Penny talked them into joining her and Dante for dinner. The two girls sat together, Todd on one side, next to Alan Cummings, Dante on the other, between Penny and Julian, whose plate was heaped with slabs of roast beef, a mound of potatoes.

"My father . . . he always"—Julian's hand wafted over his dinner—"he had a saying: 'A lean horse for a long race,' but I . . . it looks like—"

"Like you're going to settle for a short one," Penny's father said, with a sternness unrelieved by even a hint of good humor. "Don't live to eat, eat to live—that's a saying for you."

"Dad, let's not moralize about eating dinner," said Penny. "Let's try to have a pleasant time."

Alan reacted with a keen silence, as if her innocuous remark had been impudent. Dante began to change his mind about domestic unhappiness. If he had to choose between this human glacier and his raving, roving father, there wasn't any doubt about whom he'd pick.

The band opened the second set after dessert, offering a chance to recapture the spell of an hour earlier. As Greer, Julian, and the Crandalls went to the dance floor, Dante leaned toward Penny and said:

"How about we join them? If you know your stuff, you'll recognize this tune."

"Coltrane's version of 'My Favorite Things,'" answered Penny, looking at him bewitchingly over her brimming glass. She turned to Todd and Beth. "Dante's a jazz musician and he's tutoring me."

"No kidding?" Todd pushed back from the table and stretched his arms to the sides, his compact chest expanding to make oval-shaped openings around his shirt buttons. "Guy I went to Cornell with played in a jazz combo at school."

"You're a Cornell man?" Alan asked.

"Class of '88," replied Todd.

"Fifty-eight." Alan extended his long white hand—for him the equivalent of an embrace.

"So did you start playing jazz in school?" Todd asked Dante.

With Greer and Julian absent, he could not help himself.

"University of Miami," he replied.

"Old Suntan U? My roomie at Brooks and the guy across the hall went there. Eddie Jensen and Drew Koonitz. Maybe you knew 'em? They would've been there from '84 to '88."

He was aware that Todd wasn't suspicious and testing him; nevertheless, his heart thrummed as he rapidly calculated when he would have graduated.

"No, I was class of '92."

"Brooks, eh?" said Alan. "I was right next door, at Phillips." Turning to Dante, he tweaked his mouth into a semblance of a friendly smile and asked, "How about you?"

"What about me?"

"Where did you prep?"

Penny winced. "Where did you *prep*? Dad, you can sound so retro sometimes."

"Barber college," Dante said with a little bit of a defiant sneer.

Alan's smile vanished. "Was that supposed to be funny?"

"No, sir. I went to barber college. I'm a barber," Dante said, as Greer and Julian returned to the table with the Crandalls. He felt that this disclosure made up for his lie, though it didn't quite.

"You'll pardon me if I'm a little confused," said Alan, with a stare as penetrating as Penny's but lacking her gentleness and forgiveness. It had the quality of cruel exposure, a ransacking of one's interior for weaknesses in one's defense. "I thought you were a jazz musician, that you studied it at—"

"Oh, he's not a barber anymore," Greer leaped in, as if she'd been taking part in the conversation all along. With a certain tension in her face, she looked quickly from Dante to Penny to Penny's father. "That was his day job in Miami. All performing artists have to have a day job. Why, half the actors on Broadway are waiters and waitresses during the day."

Dante listened in silence. Greer's airbrushing of the facts, transforming him into a "performing artist" equivalent to a Broadway hopeful, struck him as somehow more fraudulent than the outright lies he'd told.

"Well, now, I'm still confused, but let's drop it," Alan said.

Taking Penny's hand, Dante fled to the dance floor.

They were silent through half the song, until she asked, "*Were* you trying to be funny? Because if you were, it didn't come off."

"I felt like he was interrogating me."

"It's his style. He never gets out of the courtroom. But look at it from his point of view. You're his youngest daughter's date. He'd like to know something about you."

When the tune ended, she nudged his arm and suggested they get some fresh air.

They went out onto the terrace, where a middle-aged couple were resolving a quarrel in subdued voices, and descended a few steps to a fieldstone walk. The pennants cracked smartly from the spotlighted mast, giving it the look of a festive crucifix. Under the vast audience of the stars, Long Island Sound, usually as placid as a lake in the summer doldrums, was ruffled by countless whitecaps. Spray blew skyward as waves crashed against a kind of natural jetty called the Sailors' Caps because its rocks were round and flat-topped.

"And *I'd* like to know a little more about you too," said Penny, as though there hadn't been a break in their talk.

"All right. I did go to barber college. Cut hair is what I did to pay the bills when I was playing, bar gigs mostly, a few cheap dates at Cuban clubs in Miami," he said as they passed under the oaks, whose wind-tossed branches made a shuddering darkness. "And I didn't go to no—any—University of Miami. A guy in the band I played with taught jazz there part time. That's how I came up with it."

"Why?" Penny asked, her heels clicking on the walkway and then on a concrete pier.

"I don't know. Guess I felt out of it at dinner. The way everybody was talking. Cornell '88, Cornell '58. Everybody sounded kind of snobby." There was a short silence, and he added, over the creak and squeal of the club's launches against the pier's pilings, "I don't mean you."

She stood, cuddling herself against the wind.

"Cold?" he asked, hoping for a chance to do something gallant, like offer her his jacket, but she shook her head.

"Sorry to say you'd have been right to include me. I am something of a snob, not a bigot, and maybe not much of a snob, but . . ."

Her voice trailed off, and she looked fixedly at the harbor, as though something had gone wrong out there, a boat adrift perhaps. But all the vessels lay fast to their moorings, the bare masts of the sailboats like giant metronomes in the constancy of their rocking.

"I was worried about what you'd think," Dante said. "Like you wouldn't take me seriously if you thought I was some——"

"Bullshit is what I don't take seriously. And bullshitters."

She made this declaration plainly and without a trace of anger, as if she were talking about a TV show she didn't like, and it was the awful neutrality in her voice that caused him to lose hope. She didn't feel a thing for him. What a fool he'd been to think he could possess her! But no sooner had this despair washed over him than its opposite poured into its wake. If she wasn't attracted to him, at least a little, then why did she want to know more about him, why the invitation to share a sunset drink at her favorite spot?

"I made up for it, didn't I? Five seconds later, I set things straight. Okay, ten seconds," he pleaded as, returning to the clubhouse, they entered again the unstable darkness beneath the trees. A muted horn, muted further by distance and the rustling branches, was playing a ballad.

"Sounds like Miles. 'Kind of Blue,' " Penny said, pausing.

"And just so you know the whole ugly truth, I didn't prep anywhere. Graduated Norwalk High, and just barely. And my dad was a sometime welder and a full-time drunk who took off on my mom and me when I was twelve, and we were damned glad to see him go."

Dante, with a kind of gleeful determination to make his background sound worse than it was, started to say more, but Penny laid a finger on his lips.

"Your honesty's appreciated. Keep it up. For your sake. You've got yourself in a funny spot, and you'd only make it worse by being a phony."

"What do you mean?"

"People could wonder—this is blunt, but what the hell—that you're sponging off Greer and Julian. Taking advantage of a lonely couple who lost their son, who you happen to look like."

Dante asked if people *could* wonder or *were* wondering, and if she was among those wondering.

"To answer: could. And as for me . . ." Suddenly, she cupped the back of his neck with both hands and kissed him, chastely, briefly, but on the lips, there in the quaking darkness, to the broken notes of the muted horn.

"A sign of my faith in your character," she said, with a coy laugh to warn him not to take what she'd done too seriously. But he did.

"So who was that you just kissed?" he asked.

"You. Not my schoolgirl crush. He sure as hell wouldn't have liked it."

"Right. You were the little kid, he was the awesome stud with the harem. That's what Greer told me. He brought a different chick home every week."

"She told you that? Greer and her . . . You'd think that by this time she would . . ." As Penny's speech faltered, her hand slipped lightly into his, more, it seemed, for reassurance than out of affection. "He did have lots of girls, and every one was a beard, part of the act he put on for his mom. Shit, I've had too much to drink."

He squeezed her hand, both to feel it more firmly and to coax her to go on.

"All right, as long as we're truth-telling. He was gay."

"What? How could he be gay? He was a fighter pilot. Whoever heard of a gay fighter pilot? *Top Gun* in drag? C'mon."

"I don't know any fighter pilots, gay or straight, but hey, if you read the papers, you know the service is full of closet cases. Don't ask, don't tell, right? And Clay was a closet case, because Greer and Julian made him one, Greer most of all. Everyone in town knew, but nobody let on that they did, because of the way Greer was about him. *Is* about him. God, when Clay was at Denison, she'd tell my mother about the latest cutie he was dating and how she hoped this one would be *the* one. She was talking marriage, would you believe, and my mom had to play along because she knew Greer would hate her if she threw the truth in her face. I don't know if you've seen that side of her yet, but she can really be bitchy when she doesn't get her way or somebody tells her something she doesn't want to hear."

Dante was silent, remembering the way Greer frowned the week before in the boat, the coded looks that had passed between her and Julian on the train.

"Dumb, isn't it?" Penny continued. "Nobody *cared*. A lot of people in Fair Harbor probably have a gay person in their families. The only one it made a difference to was Greer. Oh, I can understand why. It was her only kid, adopted on top of that, and she wanted grandchildren someday and maybe the family name to be carried on. Clay was a hyphen, you know. Clayton Braithwaite-Rhodes."

She tugged at his hand, then let it go, and they started slowly toward the terrace, upon which the panes in the glass doors laid tiles of amber light.

"I'm being a horrible gossip, but after Clay's plane crashed there was an ugly rumor going around that it wasn't an accident." She lowered her voice. "That Clay found out he had AIDS and—"

"C'mon. That's a little too much."

"I never believed it myself, but you can see how it got started. Clay was always trying to live up to Greer's expectations; he wanted to keep the truth from her as much as the rest of us. . . . As much as you're going to have to, it looks like."

"How the hell can I do that?"

"As long as you're under that roof, with great difficulty," Penny answered, raising one foot to the terrace step, and even the elegant S formed by her hip, thigh, and bent knee wasn't enough to distract anything more than his eye.

"After what you said, I don't see how I could trust a damn thing she says."

"Sure you can. Off the subject of Clay, she's as honest as anybody else. Look at it this way: Clay's gone, she has her illusions about him, let her have them. And then think about me. You let on that you know, she'll figure out in half a heartbeat you heard it from me, and I don't want to deal with that."

"Then you shouldn't have told me in the first place," said Dante, with a note of grievance.

"I figured you'd find out eventually, so better that you hear it from a friendly witness. Basically, I like Greer. Like you too," Penny added, with a thrilling quickness. "I wouldn't want either of you to hurt the other, and you both could get hurt if you said the wrong thing about her darling boy."

THE HIGH WINDS continued all the next day. Julian, Greer, and Dante ate a breezy lunch on the back veranda, Greer probing for details about Dante's evening, while he, doing his best to pretend that he didn't know what he now knew, made noncommittal comments about Penny's dancing. Greer said they looked splendid on the dance floor; she couldn't wait to get the pictures developed. And where had they disappeared to after dinner? Went for a walk, Dante answered, tempted to tell about what he'd learned on that stroll. Then she asked if he was going to see Penny again. Yes; she was going to give him another tennis lesson, but he didn't think things would develop between them—though he hoped they would. He was the downtown man, she the uptown girl. *Stop* worrying about that, Greer admonished, wielding a pickle like a teacher's pointer. Only last year, the daughter of a friend of hers, a thirty-year-old *lawyer*, had married a *carpenter* who was seven years *younger* and a *Jehovah's Witness* to boot. The old distinctions didn't count for much anymore, things were more open now, and oh, wouldn't it be wonderful if he and Penny continued to see each other and he brought her to Illumination Night in September? Illumination Night, she explained, to Dante's bemused silence, was the club's final event of the season, held on the weekend closest to the last day of summer. There were picnics and barbecues and then the climax—the lighting of lanterns all along the beach. It was a beautiful ceremony, almost pagan—all those lanterns flickering on the darkened shore to mark summer's end—a perfect setting for a budding romance.

Julian got one of his fits of temper, crumpling his napkin and telling Greer in his low rumble to stop pushing Dante and playing matchmaker. And in fact Dante did feel she was pressuring him—in contrast to her cautionary advice of the night before. He wasn't sure what accounted for the change.

Penny's prediction that he would keep his knowledge secret only with great difficulty proved accurate, at least for the first few days after he'd come into possession of it. It burdened his conscience, as if he were holding stolen property, and feigning ignorance brought an artificiality to his relations with Greer, once so natural. Had she merely withheld the truth about Clay, his confidence in her would not have been damaged; but she had uttered her lie with such conviction, almost as if she believed it herself (as part of her probably did), that he felt betrayed. And she'd betrayed more than him: Clay as well. To deny the truth now, so long after his death, was a little like trampling on his grave, and what kind of woman would do that to a son she claimed to have adored? *Had* she adored him? For Dante noticed that another picture had been substituted on the desk in the den: the shot she'd taken before the dance—of him standing beside Julian in the double-breasted jacket—had replaced the one of Clay in his prep-school blazer.

A week later, he received a letter from Ahearn, the lawyer, attached to a dismal and alarming notice from the bank: the June and July mortgage payments on his mother's house were overdue; continued nonpayment would compel the bank to begin foreclosure proceedings. Ahearn tried to soften the blow: he shouldn't worry about foreclosure for the immediate future. The bank wanted cash, not a house on its hands, but he advised Dante to reduce the price and get the place off *his* hands as quickly as possible. Finally, he wrote, he'd taken a ride past the place; it could use a face-lift. Dante had done nothing to the house for the past several weeks except cut the lawn. He felt feckless and ashamed when he drove to it the next day. While he'd been playing home handyman at Fastnet, he'd neglected his mother's—no—his house. How could he have failed to notice how blistered and scaled its exterior had become in the extraordinary summer heat? Borrowing an extension ladder from Julian, he bought primer and paint and spent the next four days in penitential labor, scraping and painting under a scorching sky. As he worked, he had an odd sense of disconnection from the roof and walls that once had been the shelter and center of his life; he might have been a hired workman, painting a stranger's house. Only once, on the last day, while he was cleaning spots from the windows and peered into his mother's old bedroom, did an emotion clutch at his throat: not grief, or nostalgia, but a feeling of final separation. For the past three months, her soul never had seemed far from him; now he sensed it, hurtling irrevocably away.

As he packed up to leave, the retired couple from the duplex across the street, the DeSantises, he a stocky, bald man with ribbons of white hair above his ears, she a dour woman with a broad peasant body, watched him from their front porch, where they always spent hot afternoons. Old man DeSantis called out that he was glad to see Dante fixin' up the place, it was gettin' to be an eyesore, makin' the neighborhood look bad. Hell, ain't nobody was gonna buy a place lookin' like that . . .

DeSantis's speech rasped in his ears, grown used to the cultivated accents of Fair Harbor, where no one ever shouted to a neighbor from across a street. He called back that he hoped the house would sell now, and drove off, feeling lucky as a fox that's escaped a trap as he went past the shabby corner grocery and the worn wooden houses with their side staircases rising to attic apartments.

Greer dropped the asking price. Dante would practically be giving the place away, she said, but what choice was there? She also offered to pay the two months' mortgage in arrears and to forgive his debt for the roof repairs, offers he accepted after making a pretense of refusal. These gestures reawakened him to the benefits of their relationship and caused him to soften his judgment. What she chose to disclose or conceal about her son was her business. He still felt awkward around her, still was tempted to ask why she'd lied, but he convinced himself that pretending not to know the truth was no worse than what her friends had been doing for years. If they could live with that, so could he. He was even flattered that Penny had entrusted him with the secret. Sharing it was a kind of privilege that made him feel more a part of life in Fair Harbor; it ratified his citizenship.

And so did the replacement of the final photograph. Now, instead of the picture of Clay in black tie beside the auburn-haired girl, there was one of Dante and Penny at the club dance. He decided to feel flattered and not uneasy about this incremental taking of Clay's place. It seemed fitting. He wondered again if there might have been a blood tie between him and Clay, and the possibility did not discomfort him as much as when it had first suggested itself; it appealed to him. A physical kinship would give him a kind of secondhand claim to Greer and Julian as family. After all, Clay had not been born to them but was given by an adoption agency that just as easily could have given him to another couple. There had been nothing fated about it. It had been a lucky accident really, like drawing a winner in the lottery—or a chance meeting on a train.

In the following days, he moved through Fastnet with a deeper sense of belonging, even possession. He loved to look at the house when he and Greer came in from sailing: the spiked rails picketing the roof, the pillared veranda, the clipped lawn sloping toward the seawall's mortared stone. He thought his love gave him some claim to it, and if not love, then the title granted by his sweat: each warped door he'd planed and sanded to fit true again, each wall painted, each crack patched, increased his equity.

His possessiveness radiated outward to the town itself, as he grew more familiar with its streets and lanes, winding beneath oaks and maples along paths trod out of the wilderness by colonial cowherds and still bearing quaintly colonial names like Redcoat Lane and Tory Hole Drive. Meeting people who'd known Clay continued to be an ordeal, but after the ritualistic gasps and astounded looks, they seemed to accept him as himself. Kay Munson, the short, stout postmistress in the red-brick post office in Fair Harbor Center, called him by his first name whenever he came in to mail a package or purchase stamps for Greer or

Julian. So did Maynard and Joan Hall, owners of the hardware where he bought tools and parts for his home repair projects, and Dale Perkins at the boatyard and marine supply store across the street from the post office (Perkins Ships' Chandlery, it called itself, as if it still equipped whaling ships and schooners instead of the yachts of stockbrokers and investment bankers). He had an address, a checking account, people who knew him. His place.

The notice from the bank, however, was a reminder of what he didn't have and needed to get: a job. Penny's remark also haunted him: he didn't want the Munsons and Halls and Perkinses and others to begin thinking of him as a mooch. He phoned the barbershops he'd called on the previous month—fifteen altogether. Two or three told him to call back in a few weeks, but there were no openings now. He gave De-Grasso's another try; the owner said he still didn't know how to spell "retire" or "turnover." Music seemed Dante's only hope. He hadn't played a note since quitting Hector, except for half an hour's daily practice in his room, where he would run through scales and chords, accompanied by the piercing cries of gulls. He made the rounds of music stores in Westport, Norwalk, and Stamford, pinning a summary of his qualifications to bulletin boards already papered with flyers and three-by-five cards from out-of-work musicians. There was something pathetic and desperate about those advertisements, especially the ones that strove for cute originality. *Dyno-Mite Guitarist! Can Play It All . . . Rock, Funk, Jazz, or just plain Kun-Tree. Call . . .* Dante's efforts yielded an audition with a rock band that needed a back-up bassist, and two fill-in gigs—a wedding reception in New Canaan and a bar mitzvah in New Haven. His net was two hundred dollars.

His ever shaky self-esteem began to suffer again, more so after Penny landed a plum job as assistant to a prominent New York dealer who bought art for corporations and major collectors. She'd told Dante at one of their morning tennis practices, and he congratulated her, and she, sensing that he was down on himself, praised his progress at the game. He was a natural; if he'd started when he was young, he would now be able to beat her easily. Charitable flattery wasn't what he wanted from her, but another impulsive kiss, or for her to make good on the promise of an evening drink under the oaks. She seemed a little reserved around him lately, as if calculating whether he was worth taking a chance on. He thought this hesitancy began on their first tennis date after the dance, when she saw the envelope on the dashboard of his Mercury. State of

Connecticut. Labor Department. Bureau of Unemployment Compensation.

How was he to spare himself further humiliations? The answer came from Julian, who surprised him late one weekend afternoon by inviting him to go fishing. Drifting with the tide past the Norwalk Islands, they cast for stripers in rock-bottomed shallows or in coves skirted by beds of long, green eelgrass. After an hour without a strike, Julian set down his rod and wiped his face with a bandanna and told Dante that he hadn't taken him fishing for the fun of it.

"Your staying with us . . . I guess it's obvious that I'm not happy with the arrangement, but I'm putting up with it as best I can," he added with unusual and brutal clarity. "Because . . . Greer . . . I love her, all right? And you might say I owe her, too. My family . . . Nowhere near the money hers had. She gave me a loan from her trust fund to buy my seat on the exchange, and her father helped us with the down payment on Fastnet. All right? So I've gone along with her on a lot of things, and you're one of those things. Sorry if that sounds . . . Well, I thought it best to be frank."

Dante nodded.

"I was against your staying for your sake too. Didn't think it was fair to you, but here you are." He was unable to match his direct words with a direct look, and his hooded eyes canted toward the stone tower of Sheffield Island lighthouse, painted by the falling sun. "You make Greer happy, something I haven't been able to do for a long time. Been years since I saw her this upbeat. That's why you're here, but I can't have you . . . Now look, I appreciate the work you've done around the house, but—"

"I need to get a job," Dante interrupted, relieved that he wasn't being evicted. "I've been trying, Mr. Rhodes."

"I know that, but it doesn't look like barbering is exactly a hot profession these days. And since I'm being up front, I don't see what the hell kind of future there is in it anyway. As for opening your own shop, we don't know when that house of yours will sell, or for what, and I doubt you'll realize enough to capitalize yourself. At any rate, you've got to do something."

He came to the point at last. Don Crandall had told him that there were openings in the back-room operations at his firm. Working in the back room of a brokerage house was clerical drudgery, but a job like that would give Dante a steady income, a foot in the door of the securities industry. He could find out if he had a talent and liking for the business. If he did, he could study for a broker's license test—it was called a Series Seven exam—and if he passed, he would be qualified to make market trades and move out of operations to where the real action was. The real money too.

A stockbroker! How could he ever be a broker? he asked. He didn't have a degree. Don't need one, Julian replied brusquely. All you need to do is pass that test. Sure a degree gave a certain social status, helped you to network and to understand your clients' needs, but a young man or woman with a quick mind, a willingness to put in long hours, and an ability to speak clearly and effectively could make a career selling stocks. Julian laughed sheepishly. Yeah, he knew what Dante was thinking: he himself didn't speak very clearly or effectively. That's why he wasn't a salesman but a floor trader instead. On the floor, about all you ever had to say was "Bid."

"But we're getting way ahead of things," he added. "I can call Don tonight and arrange an interview first thing Monday morning. What do you say?"

All of this was more than Dante could absorb, and he was silent for a moment, staring across the flat gray water toward the New York shore. How near it looked on this clear afternoon, as though he could touch it. He gave Julian the only answer possible.

V

DISKANT PLAICE & PARSONS' branch office was in one of the stark new buildings that had transfigured downtown Stamford in the boom years of the eighties. The glass and concrete cliffs, topped by the names of telecommunications firms, insurance companies, and hotel chains, towered incongruously over the venerable dome of city hall and the First Episcopal Church, its granite walls grimed with memories of Stamford's smokestack history. From the turnpike, the impression given was of a city trying to hide its sooty, Yankee past behind the soaring, sparkling architecture of the sunbelt.

On an overcast morning in the beginning of July, fifteen minutes early for his first day of work, Dante parked his car in the underground lot, rode the elevator to the sixth floor, and went to the men's room to give himself a final inspection. His tie, blue oxford shirt, and tan light-weight suit were the latest sartorial gifts from Greer, purchased at the same store as the other clothes, for it bore the same faint scent of new wood. He'd worn suits at his more formal gigs, but never had he gone to work anywhere looking so buttoned down. He had the same sensation as when Greer had taken his picture in the uniform—of not recognizing himself. It was partly a carryover from a gaffe she'd made an hour before, as he was walking out the door. Handing him a grocery list, she'd asked, "Could you get these for me at the Grand Union on your way back tonight, Clay?" and then, covering her mouth, grimaced and apologized. He sloughed it off, surprised only that such a lapse hadn't happened before. Still, he was unsettled. You must have a strong sense of yourself, Penny had said. But who was the self he was supposed to have a strong sense of? And what was so precious about that self that he should fear losing it? The only places it had taken him were behind a barber's chair and onto a stage with a third-rate band, whereas he now had something like a real future. And there, in an office building's men's room, a revelation fell upon him, as complete and unbidden as those the nuns in grade school had described as descending on saints and prophets. Of all the possibilities opening before him, the greatest was the chance to become someone else. He didn't yet know who that would be, only that it would be a new and more estimable self, a Dante Patrick Panetta that perhaps always had dwelled within him, waiting for the right moment to crack its shell and take wing.

He combed his hair and neatened his tie and entered his new place of employment, catching bits and pieces of his face reflected in the stainless-steel letters on the door. Beyond the reception area, brokers sat in wood-trimmed cubicles, staring at foreign stock exchange results on their computer terminals. Life in the branch office, he'd learned in last week's interview, was hierarchical. The cubicles were occupied by brokers who earned under $250,000 in yearly commissions; interior offices without windows were reserved for those who made between $250,000 and half a million; while offices with windows were for those who brought in half a million or more. The lowest of these figures was too great for Dante's comprehension—he would be earning $22,000 a year as a documents clerk in the operations room, a long, glass-girt enclosure in the back of the office. Mona Arkhan, the operations manager, had told him that a documents clerk was deep down in the entry level, only a short step above the mail room. "You're not being paid to think. Thinking is bad in this job. Don't even think about thinking," she'd said in a bombardment of adenoidal vowels and hard consonants that sounded more New York outer borough than Connecticut. "The only people who are paid to think in the back room are me and the assistant operations manager, and the only time he thinks is when I'm not here to do it for him." Bea Smith, a mocha-skinned woman who handled the stock certificates, put things to him in a still clearer light. "You look at it this way—this room is where the fi-nancial cotton gets chopped and baled, and you, boy, ain't gonna be nothin' but a field hand."

And so it was that Dante went to work in the vast plantation of capitalism. He left Fastnet each morning at eight, and with his radio tuned to WCBS for traffic and weather reports (hazy, hot, and humid was the litany that summer), he joined the daily convoys on the turnpike. His work was as menial as Bea had warned. Besides her, his fellow field hands were Vicki Corelli, the cashier, and Jarvis Traynor and Paul Hammond, the wire operators, who sent buy and sell orders to the central office in New York. While the brokers' days were marked by the dips and plunges of the market, by alternating periods of elation, gloom, and anxiety, the operations room functioned on a plane of monotony under Mona Arkhan's careful guidance. It was supposed to. The brokers could have their thrills and crises; in the back room, excitement meant that some-one had made a clerical error, and a clerical error—a mistake in the strike price on an options trade, an incorrect figure on a stop order— cost the branch money. As the documents clerk, Dante was responsible for processing new accounts applications: financial management ac-counts, joint accounts with survivorship rights, joint accounts with ten-ancy in common, IRA and Keogh accounts, margin, commodities, and trust accounts, and fifty-odd other categories, from CLU for Investment Club to UNI for Unincorporated Association. The applications with their copy pages for the branch and central offices were slipped into a slot under the glass wall each day by the brokers or their sales assistants. It took him nearly two weeks to learn all the category codes. Each re-quired its own set of supporting documents, and each of those had its transmittal code—3287-0006 for Commodity Agreement, 0008 for Hedge Agreement, on down to the ominous 0003 for Death Certificate. While Bea, in the desk behind his, stamped stock certificates with the rote movements of a European bureaucrat, the hand stamp's *thud-thump* getting on his nerves when it went on too long, Dante made sure the applications had all the required signatures and all the right blanks and boxes filled in. He then typed everything into his computer. He was nothing but a human conduit through which information was passed into the data bases of Diskant Plaice & Parsons. At first, he amused himself by trying to imagine what the new clients were like. Once he learned the codes for the types of risk tolerance—aggressive, moderate, and conservative—he would invent faces for the riverboat gamblers, the cautious old ladies, and the middle-of-the-roaders who stuck their toes in the dangerous waters of high-tech stocks and junk-bond funds while sitting firmly on a solid bank of blue chips and treasury bills. But as July burned toward its end, he found his imagination smothered by the drudgery. He couldn't picture what the people and their lives might be like; they became mere names, and then account numbers.

He got through the tensions and tedium by convincing himself that they were only temporary—a kind of purgatory he had to endure before gaining the heaven of six-figure commissions and bonuses. There were more immediate compensations, a steady paycheck not the least of them. Penny invited him to a cookout one weekend on a pretty beach in Rowayton where signs warned: "No Trespassing—For Association Members Only." Penny's and Marcia's friends were gathered around a smoking barbecue pit—an attractive crowd of confident young men and women who looked as if they'd walked out of Lands' End and L. L. Bean catalogs. As Penny introduced him, he intuited that he was being presented for inspection. His new and still unformed self smiled and chatted, was careful not to sound ignorant, and when someone asked where he worked, he tossed off that he was with Diskant Plaice & Parsons, leaving unsaid that he was a mere clerk, a chopper of the fi-nancial cotton. When the party broke up, he felt relieved, and as tired as if he'd done a full day's work. His fatigue must have showed as he walked Penny home, because she frowned with concern and asked, a little doubtfully, if he'd had a good time. Sure, a great time, he answered, for he had a hunch that she was testing his ability to trim his sails to the breezes of her native seas.

They spent the next Saturday afternoon cruising the Sound in her father's sloop. She was of course an excellent sailor, and Dante was happy that he'd absorbed enough from Greer's schooling to handle the jib competently. Afterward, pleasantly tired, their skin tingling from sun and salt spray, they sat on the point at the club, sipping cocktails under the oaks in the evening cool. The air had been scoured of haze by a northerly breeze, and they could see the tops of the Manhattan skyline, like some mystic city rising out of the earth. After he suggested that they go somewhere for dinner, she mentioned that Marcia was gone for the weekend and offered to cook for him at home. How did tuna steaks sound? That sounded fine, though he would have eaten peanut butter sandwiches for the chance to be home alone with her.

A domestic contentment settled into him as they sat in her backyard, shut off from the world by evergreen hedges and azalea bushes six feet high. A yard light made to look like a gas lamp shone with mock-antique radiance, mosquito coils scented the night with a citrus smell, while the steaks sizzling on the grill dripped fat, and flames spurted from the circle of volcanic coals. When the steaks were done, she set a mantled candle on the patio table, then brought out corn on the cob, baked potato, and a chilled Chardonnay from the kitchen. With the radio tuned to WKCR, they ate in their suburban setting to the very urban strains of Charlie Parker. Dante was almost finished before Penny had taken more than a few bites, but he noticed her refilling her wineglass and then reducing it by half in two quick gulps. She never showed the usual effects, but her drinking made him uneasy. It wasn't the amount; it was the way she drank, as greedily as a desert wanderer at a water hole, and he'd played enough late-night bar gigs to know that people who drank like that were slaking a thirst that wasn't in their throats.

The Parker hour ended as they were eating dessert—cherry pie bought with her own two little hands, Penny quipped. The station went into its jazz alternatives segment: experimental stuff, pure harmonics and abstract notes played randomly on exotic scales.

"Don't know about you, but this stuff, to me, it's not jazz. It's interesting, but jazz it ain't," Dante said. "No blues in it. Without a blues base, you don't have jazz. It all comes outa gospel and work songs and field hollers, even the way-out stuff Ornette Coleman does."

"Wow, don't you sound professorial? Positively."

Penny raised her knees to her chin, her legs as hard and golden as an idol's. Though she kept them closed, with her arms locked around her calves, a downward drift of his glance showed him a sliver of pale-blue panties peeking from under her shorts.

"Well, yeah, I . . . It was . . . What did you say?"

"Professorial."

"Okay, that wasn't me talking. It was a guy I played with in Miami. Barron Baroso. The jazz-teacher dude. I sat in on his class once. I was parroting him. I was being a phony."

"And after I told you not to be, bad boy," Penny chided, putting on a pout.

"Give me a chance to be a good one," he said, motioning at the dessert dishes. "I'll take these in and wash up."

"I'd rather you be bad."

She rose fluidly and went to him and linked her fingers behind his neck and kissed him, not as before, but wantonly and long, her tongue exploring the insides of his lips. He stood halfway, both arms around her waist, and they fell softly together onto the grass, dewy and cool, she kissing him until he ran out of breath.

"Sorry for the date rape," she whispered hoarsely. "But I've never seen a guy so shy around me. You don't give any signals."

"Till a second ago, you weren't exactly a communications satellite yourself."

"Maybe not, but I was getting the idea that you didn't want me, and I'm not used to not being wanted. So"—playfully, she nipped his ear—"I thought I'd take the initiative and find out what the hell's going on."

Was that what had ignited her? He hoped so, and not the rum and wine.

"So what makes you so shy around me, Dante Panetta? Or are you just that way?"

Before he could answer, she kissed him again, then rolled on top of him and, hemming his shoulders between her arms, looked down on him, and they were visible even in the weak light—those probing eyes that laid him bare inside and seemed to see all his flaws and cheerfully absolve him.

"You know, I wonder what you think of all this," Penny said. "I don't mean what we're doing. Greer and Julian and Fastnet and the club and my parents and me and all of this little world. Bet you think that everybody must be happier and better and smarter than where you came from, don't you?"

He didn't answer. What kind of foreplay was this?

"Well, they're not. Hungrier is what they are. Where do you think Greer's money came from? Hunger. How do you think my father got to be senior partner in one of the biggest law firms on the planet? Hunger. But not scrappy, in-your-face hunger. This is hunger that knows how to hide itself." One of her hands rose to sweep the dark wall of trimmed evergreens. "It's hunger behind the hedges, Dante Panetta. It's raw appetite in a garden. Yum."

She lowered her head and nipped his lips, and his hand worked under her shorts and then her panties to touch her already wet sex.

A fumbling at zippers, belts, buttons, was the semicomic prelude to the moment when they beheld each other's nakedness. Then came the questions about former partners—theirs a generation for whom the act of love carried the chance of a death sentence. The somber interrogations reassured them about each other but chilled their ardor. They rekindled it with kisses and touches, he sucking the rosy pinnacles of her breasts, she taking the core of him in her hands and stroking it with her cheeks, whispering, "Oh, my, my, my." He felt like a bundle of nerves there, fleshless and exposed, for in the months since his mother's death, he'd hardly been able to afford himself the sad, solitary release of masturbation. Afraid he was going to explode right then, he fell onto his back and groaned. She clamped her hand over his mouth, his smell on her fingers. "Shhhhh, the neighbors, shhhhh," she said, then straddled him, poising herself over his penis for a slice of a second before she impaled herself, drawing in a breath as she did. She brought him quickly to the moment of ecstasy, and he almost wept from the effort of stifling his outcry. Thrusting her ass forward to hold her crotch over his mouth, she asked plaintively, "Please? Please?" Darkness. Darkness. A tangle of humid black hair smelling vaguely of oyster beds, so that when he licked and pierced her with his tongue it was as though he were swimming beneath the protean mud of the marsh nearby. Penny came with a tremble and a low cry, and when she'd recovered her breath, she rolled off him and, with a wicked, barely audible little laugh, said into his ear, "Yum!"

They were a pair of healthy young beasts and made love again, and a third time, until she was dry and their faces were rubbed almost raw from kissing. They lay quietly beside each other for a time, wallowing in their exhaustion. He hoped she was going to ask him to stay the night—what a joy it would be to wake up beside her!—but then she dressed, cuing him to do the same. Pouring two more glasses of wine, she sat down again on the grass, and again half her glass was emptied in a single swallow. That subtracted from the completeness of his happiness, made him a little disagreeable.

"So now that I proved I want you, what's next? I get dropped?"

"What a thing to say after a perfectly marvelous time. At least *I* had a marvelous time."

"It's just that you said that you're not used to not being wanted, so I wondered . . ."

"I'm not a player, Dante. I like to think of myself as an honest person," she said, and highlighted the statement with a guileless look. "Wasn't kidding earlier. You're the third guy I slept with in my life, and I was—"

"You don't make love like it was only three," he said, caressing her cheek to show that he intended no skepticism.

"I'm a natural," she shot back. "I was about to tell you that I was engaged to the second one."

This disclosure restored his agreeable feelings: he was on a par with a fiancé.

"So what happened?"

"Met him in grad school. He was getting an M.A. in phys. ed. of all things. An assistant high-school football coach. He loved small towns and coaching, and I couldn't see myself as a coach's wife in a New Hampshire village. Or anywhere."

"He wasn't suitable, you're saying."

"Suitable? Funny way to put it. It's not like I'm Princess Di. . . ." She stopped herself and pulled her head back. "Oh, I get it. We're talking about you. You're thinking about Todd and my dad. Cornell and prep schools."

"Maybe," he ventured, blushing. Christ, had he come off sounding as if he wanted to give her a ring? "I was kind of . . . ," he started to add, then switched tracks and told her Greer's theory about women from her background.

"What was she doing? Warning you against Muffy, the preppie predator? Blue-blood bitch sleeps with blue-collar stud for adventure, dumps him for Brad the Third and life in the Junior League?"

"No, she—"

"I don't want anything to do with the Junior League."

"Guess what? I'm not even sure what the hell it is. Or the Colonial Dames, or any of that stuff."

"The Junior League is a middle-class nightmare and the Colonial Dames a snooty band of females descended from loyalist officers—*officers*, not sergeants or corporals—who fought against George Washington and all the blessings of freedom we hold dear."

"Okay, okay. I was going to say that Greer, she's been pushing me to get into a relationship with you," he said, and immediately wished he'd put it differently.

"Happy to hear she's pushing, not so happy that you need to be."

"You know what I'm sayin'."

"That tonight was authentic? It wasn't you giving in to Mommy's pressures?"

"Not by a light-year," he assured her, ignoring the sarcasm and the unsettling reference to Greer as his mother.

"Glad to hear that, because"—she leaned forward and pecked him on the nose, the forehead, the ear—"I find you appropriately inappropriate, Dante Panetta. Most suitably unsuitable."

"IF THAT'S HOW YOU FEEL, I'll talk to Beano and set up an interview," said Mona Arkhan, leaning on her elbows in the branch office's cramped cafeteria. With an industrial clunk, a Coke can tumbled from the soft-drink machine. Dante popped the top and sat down across from Mona, who wore her hair long today, with a thin headband that made her look like an Apache, or like Cher in her bell-bottom days. Cher was an Armenian too, he remembered.

"What'll he ask me?"

"He'll try to find out if you've got sales potential. It'll cost the firm money to put you through training. It'll be investing in you, and investing is what we're all about. Beano needs to know if you'll be a good investment."

"Hope I'm not slitting my own throat—y'know, what I said about the job."

"Forget about it!" Mona declared in perfect boroughese— Fuggedaaboudit. "The back room, it's burn-out city for anybody with an ounce of ambition. If you told me you *liked* your job, I'd wonder about you." She lowered her voice to an intriguer's whisper. "Like that mail-room dipshit or Bea, stamping those certificates day in, day out, happy as a clam to take her three-percent cost of living raise a year. Drives me nuts just thinking about how nuts it would drive me if I had to do what she does."

It was the middle of the week in mid-August, Dante's sixth week at Diskant. He'd discovered that Julian had misled him—unintentionally, he assumed—about becoming a broker. It would require more than passing a licensing exam. To take the test, he had to be sponsored by the firm, then attend a crash course to help him pass, then go through a training program; and before he could surmount those hurdles, he had to be interviewed by Ed Morel, the branch manager, who was nicknamed "Beano" for reasons no one could explain.

The next Monday, he sat tensely in Morel's corner office, with its uninspiring views of downtown Stamford, its photographs of a rifle-toting Morel kneeling beside the carcasses of moose and elk, or standing on docks in tropic countries, dwarfed by giant marlin hanging from poles. This conqueror of the animal kingdom on land and sea was only a middling-size man, with dry, light eyes, a head slender at the bottom and wide at the top, like a lightbulb, and, though he was no older than forty-five, a thatch of hair white as an albino's. He sat at a long walnut desk interred beneath reports and file reports, while several computer terminals at his back tracked every twitch in the planet's financial nervous system. Holding Dante's résumé (typed and printed by Greer on her computer at home), Morel remarked that he'd known former baseball and football pros, a couple of ex–encyclopedia salesmen, and even a Fulton Street fishmonger who'd become stockbrokers, but never a barber and part-time jazz musician. What made Dante think he could sell stocks, and why did he want to sell them?

Last night, rehearsing him, Julian and Greer had told him to anticipate a question like that.

"Because I don't see any kind of future for myself in operations," he answered.

His face a mask of neutrality, Morel waved his hand—it looked fragile and strong at the same time, like a concert pianist's—and encouraged him to go on.

"About why I think I can," Dante said, pausing momentarily to line up his thoughts. With her talent for accentuating the positive, often at the expense of the truth, Greer had shown him how to make barbering sound like a good preparation for selling stock. "The way I understand it, a broker has to know how to talk to people and like talking to people, all kinds of people. That's what I did when I was cutting hair. That's how you keep customers coming in, besides doing a good job. You listen and you talk, establish, like, a friendship. You've got to, because a barber works on commissions, just like a salesman."

"Does a man have to be *driven* to be a good *barber*?"

"Driven?"

"Fire in the belly. In this business, you've got to be driven enough and confident enough to market to some very rich people and convince 'em that you—not the next asshole, but *you*— can make 'em even richer. Listen, you hear about all these whiz kids in the business, twenty-five years old and rich as Rockefeller. For every one of them, there's a dozen casualties, guys who end up doing what they should have been doing in the first place—driving cabs or peddling lumber at Home Depot. Think I ought to dye my hair?"

"Sir?"

"I look at my head in the mirror, and it's like I'm looking at a god-damned lab rat. Maybe I oughta use that Grecian Formula. What do you think, as a hair expert?"

Was this a trick question? Then he had an inspiration, one he was sure would not have come to his old self.

"If I was a Grecian Formula salesman, I would sure try to sell you some."

An enigmatic smile flickered across Morel's lips. Maybe that hadn't been the right answer.

"Okay, besides a talent for talking to people, what other qualities do you think a broker needs?"

He was prepared for that one.

"Intelligence, Mr. Morel. And he's gotta be willing to work long, hard hours."

Morel swiveled his chair to gaze at one of his big-game triumphs— a brown bear with a head that looked a yard wide.

"Kodiak. Dressed out at eight sixty-two. See that gun? Not a modern rifle; a black-powder gun, fifty-eight caliber. One shot's all you get. Fuck it up, you're fucked. Shot that magnificent son of a bitch at thirty-five yards. Let me tell you, if I hadn't killed him clean, Papa Bear would've covered that thirty-five yards and turned me to shredded wheat faster than a Mexican farts after eating his *frijoles.*"

"Must've been something, Mr. Morel."

"Got to face the bear without pissing your pants."

"Yes, sir."

"Do you know what I'm talking about?"

"Yes . . . I mean, frankly, no."

"Balls. *Cojones.* Brass ones. Fuck intelligence. Yeah, a certain amount, but it's overrated in this business. Truly intelligent people are imaginative, and imagination is the enemy of guts. Fearlessness is what a broker needs. Listen, back in '87, I had two brokers working here. One had been a utility infielder for the Giants, who went into the minors before he finished high school; the other was a graduate of Harvard and the Wharton School. Come the crash, the ex-ballplayer rode it through, saw the big dip for what it was—a buying opportunity! Mr. Ha-vahd Whahton damn near had a nervous breakdown, and he was gone, with all the other Nervous Nellies. Now, maybe the infielder was too dumb to be scared; who cares? Stood his ground when the bear growled, and he's still around. He's right out there now." Morel's arm jabbed at his interior window, facing the honeycomb of cubicles. "Not one of our stars, but *there*. We're in one helluva bull market now, but let me tell you, it'll change species one of these days, and when it does, figure a third of those bozos out there will lose their nerve, their clients will lose confidence in them, and so will I."

"Yes, sir."

"Easy on the 'sir's. This isn't the goddamned army. Give you a riddle. Pretend I give you two free tickets to an outdoor jazz festival. What would you do with them?"

Dante's eyes bounded around the room, his underarms growing damp with the fear that his whole future depended on his answering correctly.

"With the tickets? Two of them . . . ? Okay, I would—I guess I'd take my girl, and—"

With a swift, slicing motion, Morel cut him off.

"Maybe it was unfair, coming at you from left field like that. But I want you to think this over while I think you over. Good broker material would scalp the tickets first, then go to the concert anyway by jumping the fence."

Mona reported a few days later that he'd won Beano's partial approval: the firm would put his name in to take the next quarterly exam, in early October, but Morel didn't think he was ready for a training program.

"You're going to need seasoning, a couple of years as a sales assistant for one of our better producers," she said, and then added that none of the better producers needed sales assistants at the moment; as soon as there was an opening, Dante's would be the first name on the list.

In the meantime, he should begin studying for the test. Mona handed him a thick packet of booklets from the New York Stock Exchange: *Securities Basic Study Course*.

He feigned disappointment but was in truth relieved. After Morel's speech, he wasn't confident that he would be ready to start selling anytime soon. A couple of years as a sales assistant—sales assistants were the yeomen who stood between the broker nobles and the back-room peasants—would ease him into things.

Through the last weeks of August, when cicadas shrilled in the trees and left their molted carapaces on the lawn at Fastnet, Dante's life fell into a steady routine. Weekdays in the sunless glass box, listening to the *thud-thump* of Bea's hand stamp, nights studying in his room. He felt as if he were back in high school, though the toughest subjects in high school were easier. *Open-end mortgage bonds allow a corporation to issue additional bonds under the same mortgage as bonds already outstanding. . . . In addition to Reg T requirements, in a new margin account the minimum equity requirement under NYSE/NASD rules is $2,000 or 100% of the purchase amount, whichever is less. . . .* Sometimes Greer would sit with him and quiz him with a sample question-and-answer sheet. *Name the act passed in 1934 that established the Federal Reserve Board. . . . If an investor buys 10 calls at $55 dollars on a stock trading at $50 and pays $7 per call, what is his time-premium?* She gave him other tutorials. Having almost cured Dante's bad grammatical habits, she went to work smoothing the burrs out of his blue-collar accent by presenting him with a set of elocution tapes she had bought through an ad on the radio. "Some of the people you'll be selling to might be truckdrivers, but you don't want to sound like one," she counseled. Late at night, striving to imitate the euphonious voice on the tapes (the guy sounded like a classical-music DJ), Dante would record himself on his cassette player, then play it back. If there was any change, he couldn't hear it; his natural voice kept coming through, as if his vocal cords were rebelling against the attempt to refine the sounds they made.

He saw Penny only on weekends; she was traveling a lot with her boss, scouring galleries from Boston to Washington for new talent and decorative pieces to hang on CEOs' office walls. Dante took her to the Village one Saturday night to hear Terence Blanchard at the Blue Note, and he was proud to refuse her offer to pay for half the check. The next Saturday, she took him to MOMA and trooped him around that stark shrine, lecturing him on cubism and abstract expressionism and various other artistic isms. He grew irritated; he was getting tired of being taught things—how to speak, how to act, what pictures to look at—and with his head full of facts about the investment industry, there wasn't room for all this culture-vulture stuff. They had an argument, Penny telling him that his Joe Six-Pack attitude annoyed her, he retorting that he goddamned well liked drinking six-packs and watching hockey games. The tiff left them both feeling desolate. She phoned the next morning to apologize, just as he was about to phone her. She invited him to spend the day at the beach in Rowayton. There, drinking in the sun, knowing that its heat would begin to fade within a month, they lay on the sand, watching sailboats wing past the striped lighthouse, then swam out to a raft afloat on steel drums and touched and kissed, but not too much, Penny being as restrained in public as she was abandoned in private. Dante wasn't unhappy about her reserve, because the mere sight of her pulling herself onto the raft after she'd swum out to the roped buoys that marked the swimming area, her hair sleek and shining as an otter's and her nipples outlined under her bikini top, was enough to make him suffer an exquisite torment and turn onto his stomach. He was in love, in love at that stage of a young man's life when there is no distinction between the carnal and the spiritual, when the heart sings in tune with the groin and the angel is not ashamed to dance with the beast.

In early September, that transitional time when the geese begin to muster in the skies and the days grow perceptibly shorter, though it is still summer by the calendar and in the trees, a South Norwalk real estate agent sold his mother's house to a young Hispanic couple. Shortly after Labor Day, he gathered with the agent, Greer, Ahearn, and the buyers for the closing, signed some papers, and took a check for twenty thousand seven hundred and fifty dollars. He smiled with satisfaction, but when he got up from the table, a gust of anxiety and sadness swept over him. Outside, he almost started to cry. His sentiments surprised him; he'd thought the house had lost all emotional value for him.

"I'll be goddamned—it's just like when Mom died, it feels like that," he said to Greer.

She comforted him. She'd seen this before in her real estate career. It was natural to be sad, but he would get over it in no time. She was right, as usual. The next Monday, when he deposited the check in the branch bank next to the Fair Harbor post office, the sense of loss was gone. Stepping outside and looking across the street at the boat yard, crowded with hulls pulled out of the water for the coming fall, he felt lighter and more substantial at the same time. A burden was off his hands, and he was almost twenty-one thousand dollars richer.

Modest as it was, his newfound wealth gave him a sense of independence and reminded him that he'd returned to Connecticut to open his own barbershop. Whether twenty thousand was enough, he didn't know, but he was beginning to have doubts about his new career. He seemed to be absorbing his lessons—Greer said his scores on her quizzes were over seventy percent—yet he wondered if he was cut out to peddle stocks and bonds. He'd taken Ed Morel at his word, mulled over the riddle, and come to the melancholy conclusion that he wasn't the type to scalp the tickets and jump the fence. Maybe this meant he suffered from a lack of nerve or an excess of conscience that was an enduring legacy from his mother and eight years of parochial school. In either case, the result was the same: he was likely to become one of those casualties Morel had told him about.

One night, after poring over the study booklets for an hour (*Which of the following would NOT be disclosed on an OTC confirmation? A. Odd lot differential. B. Principal cost excluding markup or markdown . . .*) and then listening to the elocution tapes, he was seized by a mutinous fit. He flung a booklet across the room, tossed the tape into the wastebasket, and picked up his Alembic to practice his music instead. Why should he try to change the way he spoke? Mona had a broker's license, she'd once sold mutual funds successfully, and she talked like a Queens pizza waitress. Morel himself had a rough tongue. Fuck this, fuck that. Dante wondered if Greer, she with that finishing-school accent, was urging him to improve his diction for his benefit or her own. Maybe his voice offended her; the way she would wince at his minor blunders, his occasional dropped endings and nasal vowels. He was beginning to feel overmanaged, molded even. Not too long before, he'd found a box of thank-you notes, embossed with his initials, on his desk. Who was he supposed to send a thank-you note to, and what for? In case the occasion arose, he would have them to send, Greer replied. Civilization was bound together by such small gestures. Jesus. Now he'd be a barbarian, a wrecker of civilization, if he didn't send thank-you notes. That on top of how to speak, what to wear, even which sports to play. She was the sculptor of his new self, Greer's work-in-progress, he thought, forgetting that he'd submitted his rough stone to her for carving and polishing.

One afternoon, on his lunch hour, he went to DeGrasso's for a haircut. When he breathed in the scents of the tonics and lotions arrayed in colors of green, gold, and rose in the stainless-steel cabinets and on the counter beneath the mirror, when he looked at the old leather chairs, each with a whisk broom hanging from its back, when he heard the barbers and the manicurist bantering with the customers to the snip of scissors, the low buzz of electric clippers, he was stabbed by a longing very much like homesickness. The owner, Dave DeGrasso, took him in his chair. Dante reminded him of who he was, and Dave said that he remembered him.

"So whatchya doing?"

Dante told him.

"Diskant? A few of our regulars work there. So you're a big shot now?"

Shaking his head, Dante replied that he was only a clerk, but he would be taking his broker's test in a few weeks.

"Oh, so you're a big-shot wannabe," said Dave with a hearty laugh.

Barbers, like bartenders, are unlicensed psychiatrists. Soon Dante was filling Dave's ear with gripes he'd been keeping to himself. He hated what he was doing. No one in the back room could talk to anyone, nor could anyone talk to any of them, because it could break their concentration. Christ, it was like working in a Trappist monastery dedicated to making money instead of to God. He finished each day tired as hell, his neck tied in knots, but feeling that he had not accomplished a thing. Because he didn't accomplish anything. All he did all day was enter data. He confessed, as if it were a sin, that he missed barbering—the smells and conversation and being able to see and touch the results of his work at the end of the day. The look on a happy customer's face. Dave understood, even if Dante didn't, that these complaints were a camouflaged attempt to find out if he had an opening.

"Like to help you out, but like I told you before, 'retire' and 'turnover,' we don't know how to spell 'em here."

"Y'know, I came back north with the idea I'd open my own place, and when I saw yours, I thought it should be that kind of place. I've got some money saved up. Nearly twenty-three thousand altogether."

Dave smiled through his salt-and-pepper beard.

"Nice nest egg for a guy your age, but let me tell you, a place this size, all this equipment and furniture, you'd need a lot more than twenty-three. Another thing, my old man started this business back in '44. We do a great business, a lotta repeat business—hell, I got fifty-year-old lawyers comin' in who got their first haircuts here—but barbershops like this, they're dying out. We're the last of the Mohicans. The business now, it's all these unisex shopping-mall joints."

"Jivey *Cosmo* girls with blow dryers."

"Yeah," said Dave, whipping off the apron and dusting Dante's neck with talc. He gave his shoulders a brief massage—"to untie those knots"—and advised Dante to think about all the money he'd be making five or six years down the road if he stuck with Diskant.

Returning to Diskant's offices, he did try to keep his mind on the future, but other thoughts intruded. As he passed down a corridor between the cubicles, with their warbling phones and flickering terminals, he listened to young brokers prospecting for new customers: *Hello . . . A few minutes of your time to acquaint you with some excellent investment opportunities . . .* and established brokers advising or calming clients: *It's a good buy, Jim . . . Consistently good earnings . . . No, Sarah, last week was just a correction . . . the market needs to blow off a little steam . . .* and could not envision himself sitting in their seats. There was an abstract quality about his ambition that made it seem more a hope than an ambition. Maybe it wasn't even a hope, for he now asked himself not if he could do what the brokers did but if he wanted to.

Such doubts and questions struck him as somehow unworthy of who he conceived himself to be, and even a little dangerous. They were the thoughts of a loser, and he tried to repress them, as, long ago, he'd tried to repress those disturbing, tantalizing images that his eighth-grade teacher, Sister Theresa, had said posed a mortal threat to his soul. He wasn't successful then, he wasn't successful now. The doubts and questions kept bubbling out of his subconscious, but he managed to keep quiet about them, until a man he never knew suffered a heart attack and made it impossible for him to maintain his silence.

It was on a Saturday morning, one week before Illumination Night, a morning of dramatic thunderstorms that had caused two power blackouts and a crisis at Fastnet. Greer was upstairs, working in the small room, off the master bedroom, that she used as a home office. Dante and Julian were reviewing test questions in the den when the lights went out the second time. Fifteen minutes after they flickered back on, Greer's footsteps could be heard thumping down the hall on the floor above, that unambiguous sign of her anger followed by a string of curses Dante couldn't imagine coming from the lips of a Colonial Dame. In a few moments, she stormed down the stairs, hollering into a portable phone.

"No, it can't wait till Monday, goddamn it. . . . You start on it today, pronto, goddamn it, do you understand? . . ." Julian and Dante went into the downstairs hall and saw her pacing there, her eyes flaring. Dante remembered Penny's warning about the way Greer could get when she heard things she didn't want to hear, and somebody, apparently, was telling her just that.

"What the hell did I just get through saying to you?" she shouted. "All it keeps saying is Disk Drive Error. I can't even get into the hard drive. . . . Of course I've got a son of a bitching surge suppressor—it must have blown right through it. . . . What? What? You think the hard drive's fried? Well, that's just great! Shit and goddamn, I've got everything on it—all my listings, phone numbers . . . What? Data retrieval? All right, then, retrieve the goddamned data. No! I need it done ASAP: I'm working on the biggest deal I've ever worked on; it's worth two hundred thousand in commissions. . . . A week! Then you'd best get to work on it right now. . . . Yes, I've got backup disks. I'll send those with . . . That's better—that's what I want to hear. I'll have it there in half an hour."

She clicked off and only then seemed to notice the two men, standing in a kind of trance.

"Dante, it seems my computer's fried, broiled, or something. It's upstairs, unplugged. Go get it and the backups and bring it to this idiot." She handed him the business card of a computer repair shop in Westport. "And right away, dear," she commanded, in a voice calmer than the one she'd inflicted on the repairman, though it still crackled with electricity, like the air outside. "I've got to get to my office computer and hope to Christ it hasn't been fried, blown, or whatever."

The trees were quaking, rain slashing past the windows at a sixty-degree angle, but Dante did not dream of asking her if his errand could wait till the weather cleared.

When he returned to Fastnet, an hour later, Julian was tying flies in his garage workshop. Someone had called, he said. The man's name and number were by the phone in the den.

It was Dave DeGrasso, who said that while "retire" and "turnover" weren't in his vocabulary, "death" was. Did Dante remember the old man who'd been working in the shop since '47? Nick Demaris? He'd died of a heart attack three days earlier, the day after Dante had come in for his haircut.

"You're still interested in working here instead of making a million," Dave said, and only half jokingly, "stop by sometime next week. Bring your license and a list of your former employers. And if you don't mind working a few hours for nothing, I'd like you to take a few customers, see how good you are. We're not barbers to the stars here, but we got a rep for doing a top job."

Haltingly, Dante said he didn't get off work till six.

"So stop by Thursday. Summers, we're open late Thursday nights. Till eight."

On that day, feeling as though he were sneaking off to an illicit rendezvous, Dante left Diskant's offices with his barber's license and his very short list of former employers. He'd been worried about Consuela reneging on her promise to give him a good recommendation and called her in Miami to sound her out. She said that she'd been plenty miffed by the way he had left, refusing her offer to let him finish out the month, but she'd gotten over it. Sure, she wouldn't say anything bad, wouldn't even say she'd fired him for cause, but no more favors after this, Dante.

After inspecting his license, Dave handed him a pale-green smock— it was the uniform at DeGrasso's—and assigned him to Nick Demaris's old chair. His first customer was a high-school football player who wanted his team's symbol, a panther's paw, cut into the back of his hair. It was a tough, unorthodox request for his debut, and he glanced uncertainly at Dave, who said, "We honor all requests." Scissors and clippers felt strange in his hands, and he was a little nervous and awkward, as if he were auditioning for a high-paying gig. But the athlete left happy. Another high school kid was next. He asked for something simpler—a buzz cut—and confided to Dante the troubles he was having with his girlfriend. By the time he finished with his third customer, an insurance agent with whom he'd discussed the Rangers' prospects for another Stanley Cup, Dante's hands and fingers had regained their old suppleness and sureness of touch. His last job was a razor cut, his specialty. How he enjoyed stropping the blade, that sound of steel on leather, and cutting and shaping with quick, deft strokes; how good it felt to use the tools of his trade again, as good as plucking full, round notes on a bass solo. Dante was bewildered by himself: he was where he thought he no longer wanted to be, behind a barber's chair, and he was happy. He rang up his final sale and took a dollar tip, feeling a brotherhood with the other barbers, with their broad, open faces, their warm voices, and their liking for the thick, hot sandwiches served by the deli around the corner on Atlantic Street, men who were experts on boxing, football, and baseball but also on the longings and sorrows of the heart, listeners and confessors, and, above all else, men who earned their living with their skilled hands. Any traveler returning to native soil from a long expatriation would understand the emotion that rushed through Dante. In a single leap of his mind, he realized that he had been looking at himself in a false light these past months; now he saw himself for what he was and should be, a work-ingman, and knew that he was where he belonged.

After closing up shop, Dave took him to the Colony Grill, another Stamford institution. It was a couple of blocks past the turnpike viaduct, no more than a twenty-minute walk from Diskant's offices; but with its noise and smoke, its smells of beer and the hot olive oil served with its pizzas, its wall behind the bar covered with family photos of servicemen from World War II right through to the Persian Gulf, it was a bowling-shirt, softball-team sort of place, and might as well have been a thousand miles from those sterile downtown towers.

Lighting a cigar, Dave said that unless Dante's references reported that he robbed the till, he had a job. When could he start?

He was thinking at the moment about Penny and how she might react to his sudden and radical change in career plans. If she'd returned the ring of a football coach, how would she feel about a barber? Buy-ing himself a little time, he said that he would have to give Diskant notice first, two weeks probably. He could do that first thing Monday morning.

"Sure. Wouldn't want a guy who'd just shove off on an employer. But wait till I talk to your references and you hear back from me. We can get along with six barbers for two, three weeks." He quaffed his beer and wiped the foam from his beard and regarded Dante with one eye nar-rowed skeptically.

"You sure you want to do that? Big bucks like that? I mean, you're good. I liked the way you took that first guy, cut that cat's paw into his hair like an artist."

Dante acknowledged the praise with a nod (no one ever congratu-lated him for a job well done at Diskant; what could he be congratulated for—hitting the right keys on a computer?) and defended his preference in jobs, pointing out that he was a long way from becoming a broker and wasn't sure he'd make a good one anyway.

"Twenty-three grand you said you got saved up?" Dave asked. After a long, thoughtful puff, he exhaled at the ceiling. "Think about some-thing. Let's say you get a clean bill of health from your former employ-ers, let's say you work for me a year or so and me and you get along okay. I wouldn't want you to quit and start your own place. You might want to consider buying into a piece of my business, like a junior partner. What d'ya say?"

He did not say anything; his face said it all.

"Hey, no promises," Dave cautioned. "Just something for you to chew on. Me too. But I need some young blood in there, and we got everything you need—the furniture, the equipment, the customers."

HE NEEDED TO TALK things over with Greer, but she was more than normally frantic the next evening, cobbling together her big real estate deal while calling her friends on the organizing committee for Illumination Night.

The chance came at breakfast on Saturday morning, when she polled Dante and Julian on whether she should color her hair or cut it. A woman at work, not known for her diplomacy, had told her that her hair was too gray to be so long or too long to be so gray. Greer had thought it over and decided she was in a mood for a change. Julian mumbled evasively that she looked fine the way she was but could do whatever she wanted. Dante voted to cut, of course.

"I'd like to introduce the new me at Illumination Night. How would you like to be my hairdresser, dear?" Greer asked, and slipping her hands over her ears, raised two broad wings of her hair and then let them fall.

"Wash your hair first, leave it wet," Dante instructed.

While Julian retired to his garage sanctuary to tie more flies—the fall run of stripers would begin soon—Dante laid out his scissors, combs, and thinning shears on the kitchen table. Wrapped in an old bedsheet, Greer sat looking into an easel mirror and said:

"You realize I'm putting all my trust in you. What's the concept?"

"That congresswoman we see on TV? Grins a lot? Has silver-gray hair?"

"Pat Schroeder."

"Like hers, with a kind of flip across the forehead. You've got a high forehead."

Clamping thin sheaves of hair between his fingers, he snipped the back of her head in one-inch increments up to the base of her neck.

"Y'know, I like doing this," he said tentatively. "Sometimes I think I ought to do it for a living again."

"Would have made sense a couple of months ago, but now?"

"Got a job offer from a barbershop in Stamford. A real cool place. If I was to open my own place, I'd want it to look like that. DeGrasso's, it's called," he said, and then told her that he'd been offered more than a job: a chance to buy into the business, a year or two down the road, if everything worked out.

"And what was your answer?" she asked, stiffening.

"That I'd give Diskant notice as soon as I heard back from Dave—the owner," he replied quickly, too quickly to sound convincing.

She snapped her head around, almost causing him to jab her with the scissors. Cupping her chin, he turned her head so she faced the mirror again.

"Don't jerk like that, Greer. I'll mess up."

"Not as badly as you would mess up. Julian went out of his way to get you that job, and he and I have taken a lot of our time getting you ready to take that exam, and now you want to throw away a chance for a real career, a real future, for a dead-end *job*? Are you nuts?"

"But it wouldn't be like that," he protested. He wanted to sound manly and firm but was coming off whiny. "I'd be in my own business. My own guy. Almost. Partners."

"*Maybe* a year or two down the road, *if* everything works out. And I'm sure this Dave person would be happy to take twenty thousand dollars from you, every dime you've got to your name, maybe to do a little redecorating."

"Look, have you ever been someplace, or in a situation, like, that you don't fit into? Makes you feel like you're wearing a shirt a size too tight in the collar. That's how I feel sometimes at Diskant. I listen to those brokers makin' cold calls, and I can't see myself doing that the rest of my life. It doesn't feel like my niche."

"And your niche is standing behind a barber chair until you've got varicose veins?"

"Yeah, all right, yeah," he answered defiantly. "A few months ago, you said you'd help me find my own place. Now . . . Why are you so bent out of shape?"

"Because I care about you and what you do with your life, you fool!" She swiped his hand aside and pushed back from the table. "You're not a boarder here, you're . . ."

She didn't need to finish, and despite himself, despite her calling him a fool, he was touched by the profession of her feelings.

"Have you discussed this brilliant notion with Penny?"

"No."

"Talk to her when you pick her up tonight."

"I'm not picking her up. I'm meeting her at the club. She's in the city all day, some gallery thing she had to go to. Can I finish now? I'm almost done."

Greer pulled the chair forward and folded her arms on the table.

"Then talk to her sometime, because I think you'll find that Penny isn't going to take you seriously if you don't take yourself seriously," she said, and something that felt like a thin, cold arrow shot through his sternum.

"You're dealing with a thoroughbred, not a draft horse. You'd have a better chance if you told her you're quitting to travel the country with a jazz band." Dante passed the blow dryer over her head, as Greer continued, with a kind of gleeful malice: "At least that has some cachet, might appeal to her artsy side. But a barbershop? Jesus, I can't think of anything more boring, more *common*."

He set the dryer down, picked up a brush, and tore through her tangled hair hard enough to yank her head backward. In the mirror, he saw her wince, but the turn of her lips had an element of victory in it. She had gotten to him.

"What about that stuff not counting anymore? What did you call them? Those old distinctions?" He combed the flip across her forehead and sprayed it in place, making an eave over her eyes with one hand. "That story about the woman lawyer and the Jehovah's Witness carpenter."

"If that influenced you, I'm sorry I told you, and sorry I didn't tell you that I thought the woman was nuts. Either that or her Kingdom Hall carpenter has something beneath his belt that should be donated to a museum when he's dead."

The mild raunchiness, so unlike her, yet tumbling so naturally off her tongue, would have made him laugh if he had been in a laughing mood.

"Anyhow, we're not talking social distinctions here, just common sense: whether a beautiful, well-educated, well-bred young woman who could have almost any man she chose would choose a man who sees himself cutting hair all his life."

Saying nothing, Dante gave Greer's hair a final spray, tidied a few unruly strands, and then raised the mirror, moving it back and forth.

"Well, my goodness, transformed!" she said, giving each side a delicate pat. "Why, I look . . ."

"Forty-three instead of fifty-three. Not bad, huh? Not bad for Mr. Common Barber."

And as she looked up at him, he had to admire his own handiwork, and her beauty. He guessed he was a sucker for that. Beauty.

"I'm sorry if I came off so harsh," she said. "It's that you're stepping into a whole new way of life, and you're probably a little afraid. I don't know if it's failure you're afraid of or success. Whatever, your instinct is to retreat to what's familiar. The one good thing about a dead end is that it tells you exactly where you are."

"Thanks," he said caustically. "I'm done—how about you?"

"Quite." She smiled her kindest, most maternal smile, but with just a touch of seduction. "And would you do me a big favor and a little one? Big—think this over a hundred times before you do something irrevocable. Little—my computer's fixed, finally, and—"

"I'll pick it up," he said before she asked.

RETURNING FROM his errand, Dante reflected on how quickly the course of anyone's life could change, how the directions people take often depend on random chance. If he had taken a plane home instead of Amtrak, he never would have met Greer. And if she had picked up her computer instead of sending him, everything would still be the same between them. Now nothing could be the same again. The computer sat on the passenger seat of his Mercury, and he almost spoke to it, as if it were a living being. In his mind, it was—a kind of witness to Greer's duplicity and arrogance. He'd read its testimony on the repairman's monitor, at first with disbelief and then with anger, especially when he thought about her sanctimonious claims that she cared about him and what he did with his life. Penny had been wrong: Greer couldn't be trusted at all. The woman probably had built her life on lies. How could he have been so blind and stupid as to put his faith in her?

He swung off the Post Road and reentered Fair Harbor, the place he'd deceived himself into thinking of as his. He had to face that— she wasn't the only one to hoodwink him; he'd hoodwinked himself. He passed between the squat stone gateposts into Fastnet's driveway. The sight of the house brought a pang of heartache and loss. He hated the thought of leaving it.

Dressed in jeans and a denim shirt, like a cowgirl, Greer was in the kitchen, packing an ice chest and a picnic basket for the festivities. What a stupid name, Illumination Night, he thought, but he was careful to smile as he sauntered in with the computer. She mustn't think anything was wrong until he was ready to show her.

"Ah, there you are," she said, looking up. For an instant, he almost didn't recognize her in her new hairstyle. Okay. If he was partly her creation, now she was partly his. "Any problems, Dante?"

He shook his head, but told her the repairman wanted her to check out a few things before he left for the day.

"Later. I'm busy." She frowned at a stain in a checkered picnic blanket. "If anything's the matter, I'll call him Monday morning."

"He's going on vacation for two weeks," Dante lied. "There's something he wanted you to look at right away. He showed me."

"Oh, for crying out loud. These damned computers are more trouble than they're worth sometimes. Well, this will just have to do." She meant the stained blanket, which she folded into the basket. "Bring it to my office; I'll be right up."

He nodded and carried the machine upstairs, his heart pounding. He passed through her bedroom, glancing at the photograph of himself in Clay's uniform. My God, how could he have allowed her to bamboozle him into posing like that?

In her office, he plugged the computer into the monitor and switched it on. He couldn't wait to see the expression on her face; at the same time, he dreaded it.

She breezed in, with her usual air of harried peppiness.

"Well?"

"Okay, the guy told me to tell you that he repaired all your damaged files and documents. And he was so nervous, after that chewing out you gave him last week, that he decided to run this data-retrieval program and restore all your deleted files too. The deleted ones are marked with an asterisk. See." Turning his back to her, he clicked the mouse, accessed her program and then her menu of files. "Take this one. 'Dante résumé.' That's a repaired document, but this one, right underneath it, 'Dante letter,' it's an old deleted file that he restored."

Clicking the mouse again, he called up the document and faced her.

"Reason I looked at it was that I didn't remember getting a letter from you. Thought maybe you'd sent one that didn't get delivered."

She took a step forward and bowed toward the screen, its blue background filled with white text, beginning with: "Dear Ms. Balbotin: My name is Eileen Kaufman. A short time ago, when I was in Miami, I stopped in your salon for a body wave. . . ."

Greer stood frozen, her face washed in the pale electronic glow.

"I was wondering if there really is an Eileen Kaufman, and where you got those photos of her head, or was that a trick shot?" Dante asked, more in weariness than in triumph. "Sure looked realistic. All those scabs, bald patches. Ugh."

She shut the machine off and fumbled for a cigarette. He was disappointed that her hand was so steady when she lit it.

"Eileen Kaufman worked in our office three, four years ago. Since moved to Phoenix or someplace. She had a problem with a salon in Westport—gave her a curly perm instead of a body wave, and her hair couldn't take it. She asked me to take pictures of her head for evidence when she sued them. I had a couple of the prints in my files."

If she felt any contrition, he couldn't hear it in her matter-of-fact explanation, or see it in the stance she'd struck, her chin raised haughtily. She took a drag and fogged the room. Dante yanked the window open, accidentally knocking the shade from its brackets. Greer flinched at the noise, the violence of his movement.

"Let's talk this out in the den," she said.

"The hell with talking it out. Just tell me why the fuck you did this. Nothing better to do that day? What?"

"I'll be in the den."

There, sitting with her arms on the arms of one of the leather wing chairs, she contrived to look both imperious and vulnerable, like a stricken queen. Dante stayed on his feet by the mantelpiece, under the gaze, at once pious and avaricious, of Captain Elliott Braithwaite.

"I sent the letter because I didn't think you'd come of your own accord, unless you had a good reason to, unless you were desperate," she confessed.

"*What?* All you had to do was invite me."

"Invitation or no, I was afraid you wouldn't come. It would have been too big a step for you. You were so lost, so, so lost and confused. I could see it in your face the night we drove you home from Penn Station."

The beginning of a movement rippled through her body; for a moment, he was afraid that she was going to cross the room and touch him.

"You got me fired. You could've fucked up my whole life."

"But I knew it was in your heart to come. I've got good intuitions when it comes to things like that. There was an empty place, a cold and empty place in your life that I could fill, and an empty place in mine you could fill. That's been our arrangement. Our quid pro quo. We haven't had to speak of it till now. It's been understood."

"Since you know so goddamned much, how did you know Connie would fire me?"

"I didn't. I took the chance that she would. I got the idea after you'd told me that you already were in hot water over . . . oh, I forget what."

There it was again—that uncontrite matter-of-factness.

"I botched a perm for a TV reporter," he said, seething. "And what you took the chance on was fucking up my life. And then that bullshit you gave me, makin' like you was—excuse me—were so worried that Consuela was trying to screw me, when it was you, Greer, you all along. I can't figure it. My mom, she hardly had a pot to piss in"—Greer blinked—"but she wouldn't have done what you did if somebody offered her a million bucks. So what is it with people like you in these fancy houses, with your trust funds and private clubs and your dusty old relatives hanging on the walls? Do you figure that gives you the right to fuck with people like me? Jerk us around like puppets? Here's Dante Panetta, Greer's little puppet."

He hopped up and down and flapped his arms spastically.

"No antics, please," she said, switching to her regal tone. "And may I remind you that you are in my house and that I'm beginning to find the four-letter words excessive."

"Yeah? Heard you when your computer got cooked. You can cuss like a longshoreman when you want to."

There was a silence, dense and oppressive, and then Greer rose and did what he had feared—laid a hand on his arm. Even through his sleeve, he could feel the chill in those bloodless fingertips.

"I'm terribly sorry for what I did. I'll be sorrier than you can imagine—I'll be devastated—if I lose you because of it. Can you forgive me? Oh, not now. I know you can't now. But someday?"

He pulled away. Her remorse sounded genuine, but who could tell?

"Deceiving you the way I did—it was a measure of how desperately I wanted you here, my darling Dante. To see your face in this house, to hear you coming down for breakfast, to have someone to care for, to . . ."

Mold, manipulate, and jerk around, thought Dante, as she, going to the desk, gently lifted one of the photographs and smiled at it gently.

". . . love," she continued. "You can't imagine what it's like to feel that you are full of love, that you have an abundance of it but no one to give it to or share it with, and you hoard it in your heart, where it goes to waste. You have given me someone I can give my gift of love to."

"Gift! Gift!" Dante practically howled. "You get my ass canned, and you call that a gift?"

"Stop it! It was, when you think about the things I've done—"

"Not for me. It wasn't for me. It wasn't me you wanted here."

"No? I never . . . The way you look, that never was anything more than an accident to me, but a special kind of accident. A sign of sorts. When I saw you that night on the train, I felt connected to you in a way that mere appearances couldn't explain. I knew I'd found someone I could give to."

"It wasn't me."

"Then who the hell is *this*? Is *this* Clay? Is it?" She wheeled and held one of the photos toward him. It was the one of him and Penny. "God-damn you, you've given me the chance to bury Clay at last, and all you can do is whine, 'It wasn't me.' "

She could shift from cold to hot, from pitiable to sweet to angry, with such nimbleness as to leave you flailing like a slugger in the ring with an artful boxer.

"Those are Clay's clothes I'm wearing, aren't they? And in the pic-ture in my room. The blazer, the trousers."

She said nothing. Okay, let's see her dance around this one.

"The smell on them. Didn't recognize it at first, but then it dawned on me—bing!—when I was driving back this morning. Cedar. They'd been stored in a cedar chest. Couldn't believe how dumb I'd been. So that isn't me in those pictures—it's me in a dead man's skin."

She closed her eyes and tilted her head back, dismissing everything he'd said as trivial.

"And you . . . You could've done what you did when you got the shot of me in the uniform—been honest about it. You could've told me that Clay's clothes were stored away, that I fit them, why not use them? Maybe I would've said okay, maybe not. But you, you can't do anything, say anything straight from the shoulder. Even if you could get somebody to do what you want by asking, you won't. You've got to trick them into it. I guess that gives you some little thrill—I don't know."

"You're saying I'm a pathological liar?"

"I'll be sure not to pack any of them."

"Ah, yes, I expected the theatrics of packing. Before you do, I would appreciate your hearing me out. Please?"

He was sure that the "please" was a feint, and yet he could not deny her.

"Do you remember, last spring, when we were driving to look at your mother's house and I told you that I wouldn't be going out of my way for you if I didn't see something in you underneath the resemblance? In *you*?"

He nodded.

"And what I saw was a smart young man who wanted to break out of his circumstances and change his life but didn't know how."

"How'd you come up with that?" he asked, disturbed by the accuracy of her perception. She and Penny were sisters on that score; to them, he was transparent. "I never said a word."

"In a way, I sized you up the way I do a client. I don't listen to what they say but to what they don't say. I watch their expressions, their gestures. I'm very good at sizing people up."

"Yeah, you told me that. After what I found out today, I don't guess that's one of my talents."

She waved the comment aside. "I don't recall when the idea came to me, but I realized that I should be the one to show you how, to act as your guide, so to speak. Maybe I was being presumptuous, but when I thought about the odds that you should look so like Clay, and then the odds that we should run into each other on a train trip—why, they were too astronomical for me to believe they were pure coincidence. There was something destined about this."

"And that's all you've got to say?"

"Oh, all right. Yes, yes, yes, I behaved irresponsibly. I could have made a mess of your life," she said sharply. "But the fact is, quite the opposite happened. Your life has been better, and you should think about that."

"I have. And the mortgage payments, the roof, loaning me your car, the job. Thanks."

"The mortgage. The roof. The car." She threw her head back and snorted. "Ah, Dante, Dante . . . I had certain hopes, the silly hopes of a lonely middle-aged woman, that things would develop between us. That I would come to love you as a son and, in time, you would come to love me as a mother. That in a way we would adopt each other—oh, not with papers and formalities, but informally. I even hoped . . . Ah, it's too silly. . . ."

She slumped onto the sofa, its tufted leather creaking, and tucked her legs under her, this posture communicating a pathos that drew him to her, against his will.

"Go ahead."

"I even had hopes that you might marry Penny someday, or a girl like her, and that you'd have children who would love me too. Do you know that sometimes I could picture your wedding taking place, right out there?" She motioned toward the window that faced the lawn in back. "My mind works that way. Jumps from A to Z. Silly, isn't it?"

He started to speak, but she silenced him when she turned to him, her eyes giving off a pearlescent, hypnotic light.

"Or is it my age? You start to think about things in your fifties. Sure, you've got life to live, but the fact is, two-thirds of your life is gone, so the thoughts are there. Who will I leave behind to remember me? And then this, all this," she said, sweeping her arm. "Who would all this go to?"

Dante felt as though breath were being drawn from his lungs, and he could not stop himself from looking around the room with a hungry, possessive gaze that seemed to penetrate the wainscot and embrace all the rooms beyond. Beauty. Grace. Surety. *His.*

"Well, now, I certainly have bared my soul, haven't I?" said Greer, swinging her feet to the floor. "Will we still see you tonight? You aren't going to break your date with Penny over this, are you?"

She reached toward him, her hand falling flat onto the cushion between them as his body stiffened. He was afraid that he would be lost for good if he allowed her to touch him again. A long time ago, when that ancestor of hers was in these parts, she might have been tried for a witch.

He gestured at the books, the brass lamp, the desk with its gold-leafed leather top.

"And all I'd have to do is dress the way you want, talk the way you want, be what you want me to be. That would be my mortgage, in a way of speaking. All I'd have to do is stop being who and what I am."

"And just who and what are you, Dante?" she asked, with a quizzical cant of her head. "Do what you want with your life, but do you honestly think you're going to walk out of here and live in some bleak little studio apartment and cut hair all day for your dear new friend and future partner and be content? Why? You weren't content before. And do you think you'll be able to give up Penny and live happily ever after with the graduate of some cosmetology school? How did you describe them to me? 'Jivey *Cosmo* girls prancing around with blow dryers'? You have walked in a different light. Whoever you were before, you're not him anymore."

These were honed and well-aimed darts.

"Whatever I am, I can tell you who I'm not, and that's Clayton Braithwaite-Rhodes come back to life. The new, improved version, better breeding stock to make those grandkids you want," he said, and saw by the way she jerked backward, as if he'd raised his hand to her, that he was not without darts of his own.

"Whatever are you talking about?"

"C'mon. No more bullshit. I know about Clay because everybody in town knows. And you know that they know, and they know you know they know, but everybody walks around pretending they don't know a goddamned thing, because that's the way you want it. Look— me, I'm no bigot. I don't care what he was, but I guess it made one helluva big difference to you, because you lied about him too. You lied about your own son—to your friends, to me, to yourself, I'll bet. Damn! You want me to forgive you? Hey, I do." He leaned toward her and made the sign of the cross in front of her face. "But I just can't believe a thing you say, Greer. That's the old bottom line. I don't trust you."

A tension pulled at the corners of her mouth and drew the skin taut over her cheekbones, giving them the edged prominence of famine.

"I want you to. I don't want you to leave here. I'll get down on my knees and beg you not to leave and to trust me again. Oh, God . . ."

Thinking she was speaking figuratively, he was appalled when she fell to her knees and spread her arms in supplication.

"There! What more do I have to do?"

"Clay . . . How . . . Tell him how Clay died. Tell him that."

Hulking and florid, Julian stood in the doorway, holding a plastic box of fishing flies.

"Get up, Greer. Get for Christ's sake up, or he'll think you're crazy."

This possibility had already occurred to Dante.

Greer didn't move. Julian lumbered across the room, shoved his arms under hers, and pulled her to her feet.

She brushed back a wisp of her hair and smoothed the front of her jeans.

"And for how long have you been eavesdropping, dear?"

"Eavesdropping in my own house? The hell with eavesdropping. Tell him."

"It's for you and me to know. You and me alone—"

"You lied to him about that, so tell him, damn you! You always get your way—well, not . . . This one time, you're not!"

Julian's cheeks darkened alarmingly to plum as he seized Greer by the shoulders and shook her. Remembering the scenes, too many of them, when his father came home fevered with whiskey, Dante instinctively grabbed the older man's arms, flabby yet hard underneath.

"Hey, c'mon. Julian. You don't have to do that."

"Certainly not," said Greer.

"You want him to be like family? All right, let him in on the family secret. Do it or I will."

"God damn you, Julian. And oh, how I mean that! Hope He damns you to hell." She hesitated, then turned to Dante and said:

"Clay was murdered."

He shook his head, not to deny the statement but to say that he was confused.

"You've got such a zeal for the truth, you shall hear it," she said. "Beaten to death in one of the heads in his aircraft carrier by a six-foot-four-inch, two-hundred-and-twenty-pound moron, one of Clay's shipmates. Nice word, that. Shipmate." Her voice caught, but she immediately regained control, and in the mastering of her emotions, she seemed almost to grow taller. "This brute, Seaman First Class Hiram Maddox, beat Clay with his fists and kicked him. Hit him so hard and often in the face that he pushed Clay's nose to one side and his mouth to the other, and one of his eyes was hanging out. That is how my beautiful boy looked afterward. Be sure to tell me if I leave anything out, dear," she said, glancing savagely at her husband. "I do so want Dante to know the whole truth and nothing but. Oh, yes, I did omit something. When Seaman First Class Hiram Maddox kicked Clay, he broke three of his ribs and ruptured his kidney, the probable cause of death, so said the navy autopsy. He quite literally kicked the shit out of Clay. The piss too. He died in his own piss and shit on a bathroom floor. Do excuse the obscenities, Dante. I certainly don't want to sound like a longshoreman again, but Clay's death was awfully obscene, don't you agree? And I do so want the truth out. And now it is."

She smiled the strangest smile Dante had ever seen.

"Flight school . . . Never went," Julian interjected, and then, in his usual stumbling fashion, beginning sentences in the middle and going straight through to the end before doubling back to the real beginning, he said that Clay had washed out of officer candidate school before he began aviation training and had to serve out his time as an enlisted man. He was on the flight deck crew of a carrier that was ordered to steam from Naples to the Persian Gulf late in 1989.

"That plane-crash story, Greer made it up. She—"

"*Lied* again," she said. "To you, Dante, and to my friends, because it's the story I prefer to tell, the story I prefer people to know. And do you know what? I'll bet it's the story they would prefer as well. How about you, darling? Do you like the image of Clay crashing into the blue, blue sea or lying dead in his own piss and shit, with his face beaten to a pulp?"

"All right, Greer."

"Please, Julian. This is the time for utter candor, isn't it?"

Almost dizzy from her candidness, Dante sat down at the desk and traced with his fingertip the filigree of gold leaf.

"The guy who killed him . . . Why?"

"Because some people don't deserve the name of human beings, I suppose. Hiram Maddox has a story he prefers to tell—the one he told the court-martial." She stood in front of the desk, as if she were testifying herself. "He claimed Clay propositioned him in the men's room of a waterfront bar in Naples while they were on liberty, that he rebuffed Clay, but that Clay persisted in his advances when they were recalled to the ship. He said that Clay *cornered* him in the head and *demanded* oral sex. And that he, Seaman First Class Hiram Maddox, due to a strict Baptist upbringing, was so repulsed and so incensed that he lost control of himself. You see, the idea was to beat a charge of first-degree murder. And it worked. Maddox was convicted of second-degree murder, sentenced to eight years, but we heard not long ago that he got out on good behavior. You can believe his story if you can believe that a slender, one-hundred-and-seventy-pound Clay Rhodes, who never did anything more violent in his life than hit a tennis ball, would corner a man built like a linebacker and demand oral sex from him—on a warship. Whatever Clay was, he wasn't insane." She tossed another glance over her shoulder at Julian. "Anything left out, dear? Oh, yes. Lying, deceitful Greer is at it again. Clay was expelled from prep school his junior year for an *alleged* homosexual encounter. You should know that, Dante, in the interests of the truth. Now to lying, deceitful Greer's version of her son's death—and she has some evidence to support it, because it's in the court-martial records. Seaman First Class Hiram Maddox indeed had a strict Baptist upbringing from the day his mother spit him out—I don't think such a creature could have been born—and he had an obsession with homosexuality. His shipmates testified that he often would tell them that he hated quote goddamned faggots unquote and that he thought the quote cocksuckers unquote had no place in the navy and if ever one of them messed with him, he would show him the wrath of God. So I believe the one with the repressed homosexual desires was Maddox himself. That he was attracted to Clay because Clay was so handsome and because he thought Clay was gay. And he propositioned Clay, that's what I think, and was turned down, but now Clay knew the truth, and, angry at the rejection and afraid of being exposed—please excuse the expression—Maddox beat my beautiful boy to death." She laid her hands on the desk and brought her face closer to Dante's, and there was something both arresting and frightening about her pain and rage. "You can pick the version you prefer or make up one of your own—I really don't give a damn, because I'm through now. Want any more truth out of me, you can hook me up to a lie detector."

Julian went to embrace her but didn't seem to know how and, instead, awkwardly squeezed her arms.

"What's that supposed to be? My reward for being a good, honest little girl? Go to hell, the both of you."

She wriggled free and took a few steps toward the door and collected herself.

"Well, now, this has been quite an afternoon, and it's not even three," she said, looking at neither Julian nor Dante. "This is what I'm going to do. I'm going to forget all this dredging up of the past. No one is ever going to know what was said here, and that is *exactly* how you two are going to behave. This conversation never took place. Now I'm going to finish packing the picnic basket, and then I'm going to the club and say so long to summer, just as I've done every year for the past twenty. I am going to have a pleasant time. Anyone who cares to join me is welcome."

THE AGED CLUBHOUSE, with pennants that spelled "Illumination Night" in signal code flapping from its eaves, looked like a fortress under siege by a cheerful horde of prosperous, fair-skinned barbarians. Out on the point, lances of summer's final sunlight fell through the oaks on scampering children and picnickers laughing and talking amid a clutter of ice chests and bottles and plastic plates, while strands of smoke from charcoal grills leaned in a soft breeze. Dante wandered among the swarms of people, looking for Penny, the only reason he had come. He'd packed his bags an hour earlier, after Julian and Greer left for the club. He would leave Fastnet the following morning and stay at a motel while he looked for an apartment. It would be bleak and lonely for a while, and he wasn't without doubts. Maybe he never would find his place; maybe his place was always to be out of place. He wondered, too, if he had changed too much to step back into his old way of life. Now that he knew what it was like to work with a net, possibly he could not bear the vertigo of working without one. But the danger of falling wasn't as grave as the peril to his very identity that would threaten and in time overwhelm him if he stayed in Greer's world, standing in for Clayton Rhodes.

Poor Clay, his accidental twin. There were few worse ways to die. And poor Greer. There weren't any worse ways for a woman to lose a son. It had taken guts for her to relive the horror and to make him, Dante, a bearer of her secret. He felt pity and admiration for her now, but pity plus admiration did not equal trust.

He spied a familiar figure, clad in a lightweight sweater and baggy shorts, stalking among the scattered blankets and tables on long, thin white legs.

"Afternoon, Mr. Cummings."

"Hello, Dante. Penny's been looking for you," Alan Cummings replied. The deep-set eyes that peered down from four inches above his own made Dante feel like a crab about to be snatched by a giant heron. "Come join us."

And this being as warm a welcome as he could expect from Penny's father, he followed him toward the picnic tables at the end of the point.

"Seen Greer and Julian?"

"Greer's helping Amanda set things up," Alan said, pointing at the beach, where half a dozen people were staking party lanterns in the sand. Something splashed a hundred feet offshore, and turning his head, Dante saw a surf caster, wading waist deep at the edge of the Sailors' Caps.

"There you are!"

In bone-white jeans and a red-and-white-striped sweater, midnight hair swept up and pinned by a red bow, Penny rose from the table, her eyes embracing him as she clasped his waist and kissed his cheek.

"I left that dreadful showing early. Upper East Siders slumming in

SoHo, talking about consciousness-raising art. Why should I listen to that when I could be with you?"

He had a feeling that this display was meant to be a declaration of sorts to her father and to everyone there: to Julian, sitting at one end of the table with Don Crandall; to her friends Beth and Todd and another couple he hadn't met before—Meredith and Schuyler Woods, Penny said, adding, with a leap of her voice, "They're just back from their honeymoon!"

"Congratulations," said Dante, shaking hands with Schuyler, who had the clear complexion of a baby.

"Italy," he said. "And call me Sky."

Dante sat down, catching Julian's lidded glance. He knew the Rhodeses' silent code now and understood: he was to mask all signs that anything unusual had happened today. And he did. Artificiality was becoming second nature to him.

"Beer?" asked Todd, baring blocky teeth. At Dante's nod, he dipped into the ice chest on the ground and then asked if Dante was still playing the sax.

"Bass. I play bass."

"Thought it was a sax."

Penny pushed her plastic cup toward Todd. "How about a little more vino bianco?"

"Actually, Dante hardly has time to play anymore. He's at Diskant now, studying like crazy at night for . . . What's it called?"

"A Series Seven. It's for a broker's license."

"Diskant?" asked Meredith, a short, perky brunette.

"Securities firm," Sky informed her.

"Hey, Beth's with Merrill Lynch. Mergers and acquisitions. She's trying to merge with and acquire me in a nonhostile takeover. Ha!"

Beth jabbed Todd's ribs.

"Oops! Hostile now!"

"Get a new joke writer," said Beth, and as everyone laughed, Dante figured he had better laugh too.

"So what do you do at Diskant?" Sky puckered his eyebrows, which were so blond they were almost invisible against his milky skin.

"Not much. I'm in operations. Entry-level stuff."

"Now don't go selling yourself short. Pun unintended." Penny tugged sweetly at the back of his head and drew closer to him, pressing her thigh to his, which excited him even as it filled him with a helpless terror, reminding him of a time, years before, when he'd waded too far onto Pennfield Reef and felt the bottom crumbling beneath him and the outgoing tide pulling at his legs. "You should tell him that you're going to go into a training program, getting set to become"—tucking her chin, squaring her shoulders, she scowled comically and dropped her voice—"a master of the universe!"

"A what?"

"Tom Wolfe? *Bonfire of the Vanities*?"

"That Tom Hanks movie?"

"It was a book first," she said curtly, but told him with her amused sparkle that she forgave his ignorance. He wanted to do two contradictory things: kiss her and rip the wineglass from her hands.

"So go on, explain to Sky," she said, motioning.

"Okay. It's a training program, but I'm not in it yet. I take this test next month, I go to work as a sales assistant to a big moneymaker in the firm, then I go into the training program. Then, someday, I'm off on my own, selling stocks and bonds."

Dante was surprised that he'd made this sound as though it could still be his future; and he was stunned when Alan Cummings clapped him warmly on the shoulder. He looked and saw a possible smile forming on the rigorous lips. Just then, Penny's mother came up from the beach and asked for help with the arrangements.

"Back soon," Penny said, giving Dante's hand a squeeze.

"Pick of our litter," said Alan as he watched the two women walk off. "You made a good move, Dante."

"Penny?"

"Sure, Penny, but I meant the securities industry." He lowered his head and said in a low, discreet voice, "One of the few industries left where a young guy without a degree but with ambition and this"—he tapped his temple—"can go somewhere." Again his hand fell on Dante's shoulder. "Mandy and I were very pleased when Penny told us what you're up to."

"Yes, thanks," he said, wondering if Greer had arranged this. He wouldn't put it past her. Whether she did or not, he realized, with a certain horror, that he was neither guest nor intruder here, but a captive in the camp of an alien tribe.

Then Don Crandall, in that booming voice of his, called to Sky, "Hey, did you and your old man get out today?" He motioned toward the greens rolling away from the shore.

Sky scooped up salmon dip with a potato chip. "Before you ask how we shot, I'll say that we were happy with double digits."

"What? On our course? It's a piece of cake," Don chided jocularly. "Say, you golf, don't you, Dante?"

"Not even to caddy."

"Got to take it up. Great game. Frustrating, but a great game."

"Me, I'm like the bumper sticker," Todd declared. "I'd rather be sailing."

And in a few moments, Dante became a silent rock lapped by two crosscurrents of conversation. Sky, Meredith, Crandall, and Julian discussed putts and drives, while Todd and Beth, who'd sailed in a club race the previous week, talked about tacking duels and rounding marks with Alan. Turning, Dante saw Penny's striped sweater at the far end of the beach, along which the lanterns made a chain of yellows, oranges, and purple. His gaze moved toward the lonely surf caster, arcing his lure into the waters beyond the shoal. With the tide almost ebbed, he was in only to his knees now, and his rod was bent and twitching.

"Hey, he's got one," Dante said. "Look, Julian. That guy's onto a fish."

"What? What's that?" Julian stood, craned his neck. "So he is. Looks . . . Yeah . . . Good one, I'd say . . ."

He sat back down as Don Crandall, looking at Todd, bellowed out, "You're kidding? During a race?"

"No. Before. When we were jockeying for the start. Sixty-three Hatteras. Big, fat guy with a cigar at the helm, cut right across our bow," Todd was saying, shaking his head in dismay. "A smaller boat would've been swamped. Not a clue about right-of-way. Zero. Ten, fifteen yards off our bow at twenty knots."

The conversation had turned, apparently, to bad boating behavior.

"Too many stinkpots on the Sound," Alan said, then sliced a glance toward Julian. "Sorry. Forgot that you're a powerboater."

"Twenty-two-foot Mako . . . Not much stink in that pot," said Julian good-naturedly. "And Greer's got a Greenwich twenty-four. Does that redeem us Rhodeses from stinkpotdom?"

"It's not the boats. It's the people in them," Alan declared, his thick brown eyebrows crawling like millipedes. "Don't know port from starboard, let alone the rules of the road."

"You're right there, Mr. Cummings," Todd assented deferentially. "It's mostly those Vinnie and Maury acts from the Long Island side."

"We've got a few on this side," said Alan, pleased to show his fair-mindedness by giving Connecticut its share of blame.

"And a few in this club too," Beth said.

Dante slipped away. Todd's and Beth's remarks, he supposed, had been unintentional, and that was the trouble. They weren't mean, just were careless. He stepped over the seawall, below which the sea bottom was exposed—gravel and weeds and snails. Beyond this narrow channel, now a dry ditch, the shoal began, its boulders a pale sandstone color on top, their wet undersides black and draped with sea lettuce and crusted with barnacles. Over the jumbled rocks he hopped, stretching his legs across tide pools in which minnows that had missed the ebb swam in trapped circles. In a few moments, he came to the tip of the shoal. The angler was sitting there, smoking a cigar. He had a dark complexion made darker by a day's growth of beard—a Vinnie or Maury act by the looks of him, possibly a Demetrius or José act. His rod and his tackle carrier nestled in a niche in the rocks, along with two fat bluefish and two beers.

"It's public here, and I come in from there," he said to Dante, and pointed toward the public beach with one hand, while with the other he popped a suspender on his rubber waders.

"I know," Dante said. "Just came out to see how you're doing."

"Last week, some yo-yo from that club there sees me walkin' from the public side, past the fence line. Now, I'm in the water, but he tells me I'm trespassin', and I told this dope, 'Hey, read your law books. Below the mean high-tide line, anybody can walk there.' "

"Nice fish."

"Big one'll go ten pounds. Was hopin' for a keeper bass, but it's been all blues. Get some of this light off the water, wait till the incomin' starts to cook, oughta get a bass then."

The sun had set only minutes before, and pale-rose and violet light banded the water to the dimming sky. A canted crescent moon shone low on the horizon.

"You wanna take a couple throws, go ahead," the fisherman offered. "Me, I been castin' an hour, and my bursitis is actin' up."

"Thanks."

Dante picked up the surf rod, with its long grip, unhooked the lure from the first guide, and, holding the rod tip at an angle behind him, made a half-step forward and cast, the lure flying out and away.

"Yo, guy! You can pitch!"

"My dad taught me. He could cast a mile. He was good at that."

Dante retrieved, giving the lure a twitch now and then, and heaved it again, out and out into the flat sea across which puffs of wind made swift, passing ruffles. There was little chance he would catch anything at slack tide, but it felt good just to cast and to be out here with this bearded fisherman who smelled of cigar smoke and bait and knew he could walk below the tide line without trespassing.

"You wanna brew, you're welcome to it," he said, and then, pointing with his cigar: "Hey, they calling you? Can't be me."

Penny and Greer were on the shore, waving their arms. Farther down the beach, a crowd was gathering, while several people, bowing and stooping, were lighting the lanterns one by one. Penny climbed onto one of the higher rocks and, cupping her hands around her mouth, called out:

"Dante! What are you doing out there? C'mon, they're starting the ceremony."

The fisherman held out his hand for the surf rod.

"Looks like you'd better go."

"Looks that way," Dante said.

PARADISE

LISSEN ME some sea talk. Waves speak me true, ain't like some pellas. Most pellas.

Uncle Elias, his knees spread wide beneath his lavalava and his hands with fingers thickened from the years of gripping tillers and raising sails and wrestling rope caskets of pearl shell up from twenty fathom (those years long past) folded in the concavity of orange cloth, gazed tiredly at the TV, his glasses low on his bulbous nose, and his green eyes, glittering in the screen's light, resembling two jade fragments stuck in a lump of caramel—jade for the same reason his complexion was brown rather than black: He was little bit white-man touched by his grandfather, Yankee Jim Nettles, the whaler who sailed these seas in the Beforetime, married a Torres Strait woman, and peopled this then unpeopled island (still called Kailag in the native tongue, though it was marked on the charts as "Nettles Is." because Yankee Jim named it for himself, the way white pellas do, Uncle Elias thought, like nothing got a name before they give it one) with a brood of children, the last of whom, Billy Nettles, was Uncle Elias's father.

He rose and, feeling the floor of his bungalow give a little on the stilts raised against the typhoons whose tidal surges periodically turned Nettles into sea bottom, padded barefoot through the translucent tunnel the

TV bored into the darkness, his bald head with its thin band of gray hair briefly illuminated as he slowly bowed and shut the video recorder off. Silly movie, sent with a dozen other tapes by his American relations as a birthday present. He had met the Nettleses of New Bedford, U.S.A., five years ago, on his first and only visit to America. This year, they'd written him, wanting to know what he would like for his seventy-fifth birthday. He asked for movies to give him a bad fright. Even at his age he enjoyed the thrill of fearful narratives, some part of him still a child trembling at the feet of Aunty Goda (who raised him after his mother died) when, on nights in the nor'wester season, thunder booming like God had his own warup, she chilled him with tales about restless ghosts, markai, and puri-puri commanded by sorcerers to kill people. His American relations, descendants of Yankee Jim's brother, for whom Elias was named, had written in their card that the videos, *Halloween,* 1 through 6, and *Nightmare on Elm Street,* 1 through 3, would give him a proper good scare, but Jason made him laugh after a while, and he couldn't quite follow *Nightmare on Elm Street.* Can't tell that Freddy Krueger pella real pella or just dream pella, silly ting, he said to himself, plucking from the bowl atop the TV a ripe wongai. More real tings to be scared of than Mister Jason, Mister Freddy, like them comin' from the department for the big meetin' day after tomorrow, Mister Tunstall, Mister Morrison.

Got to lissen some sea talk, tink what I speak them. He wiped the wongai juice from his slender mustache, giving his old eyes time to get used to the dark. Outside, the generator thumped and palm fronds rasped in the wind, the last breath of the unusual nor'wester that blew through three days before. Lissen ta them waves, they got a lot ta say, got ta lissen good, though. Don't and you be dumb to that language, like that goddamn nephew bilong me. Uncle Elias went down the steps, switched off the generator, which gave one final diesel-smelling wheeze before it went silent so that as he proceeded down the dirt street paved with seashells, his callused feet oblivious to their sharp edges, he could hear only the wind in the palms and a more distant generator—Mister MacKenzie and his missus up late again, packing fish in the factory while the packing was good. Never know when that generator get buggered up again and shut down the freezer. Kerosene lamps lit to ward off puri-puri glowed in the village windows, their light softly falling on kempt gardens of croton and bougainvillea bordered by beer bottles buried neckdown; but then the street narrowed to a footpath and there was no light save starlight, just enough of it to show him the whitened path that wound through pandanus groves, mounted the grassy knolls at the north shore of the island, then dropped down to the beach. Dark lines of wrack and weed deposited by various stages of the tide striped the pale, sloping sands. The lagoon beyond was black, like rippled satin behind the barrier reef, against which waves broke in a phosphorescent froth. Sheds of palm fronds woven over red mangrove frames and roofed by corrugated iron, in which the fishermen stored their tackle, spears, nets, and buoys, nestled in the bushes above the highest tide line, and aluminum dinghies were drawn up on the beach, anchor ropes lashed around tree trunks or the uprights of the sheds. Uncle Elias sat down beside his shed, under the rattling leaves of a Malabar almond. Though he'd quit the sea ten years before, too old to skipper his pearling lugger and the island boys, drawing the dole, too damn lazy to crew (no hard livin' for them pellas for sure), he was no more able to remain landbound than a mackerel and went fishing when the mood struck him and wind and tide let him. He also had kept his lugger, the *Teliai,* a handsome gaff-rigged boat of twelve meters, christened for the wife who'd died after the birth of their fifth child.

The *Teliai* rode at anchor in the lagoon. Once a year, he hauled her out and caulked her and cleaned her bottom in the old-time way, careening her with the help of his good nephew's son, Julius, a strong boy like his father. And when the caulking and scraping and painting were done, Uncle Elias would raise the sails, so patched now there were patches on the patches, and take her out for the day just so man and ship wouldn't forget each other, just so he could watch her canvas fill (Such a pretty ting, he would say to young Julius, who mated for him on those brief voyages. Ain't she pretty ting? Lak a bird she is) and feel her come alive when he brought her close to the wind and her lee rail would ride under a long feather of shining water, Julius always clutching the weather rail because he feared the boat would capsize, despite Uncle Elias's assurances that the full-keeled vessel couldn't roll over in anything less than a typhoon and that running aground was the only real danger, a little bit danger at that, because he was friend to all waters in those parts, every rock, reef, and shoal marked on the chart in his head, for his grandmother's father, Kebisu, last of the great head-hunting warrior chiefs, had raided from Papua south to Cape York, navigating by stars and landmarks, and had passed on his knowledge to his white son-in-law, Yan-kee Jim, who passed it on to Billy Nettles, who passed it on to Uncle Elias, who learned so well that he seldom needed the fine brass binnacle compass mounted forward of the *Teliai*'s helm. "Teachin' you this one-time, Julius, you lissen me good, you go come proper seaman, same like my youngest," he would say to his great-nephew. "How come you tink Kanese got good job pilotin' the launch on T.I. for the Torres Strait pilots theirselves? 'Cause he know the sea! Damn, Kanese be a Torres pilot himself, takin' big tankers through, them fuckan white bastard cap'ns let a nigger be one."

Uncle Elias hadn't kept the lugger only to sail her one or two times a year. He enjoyed looking at her and remembering the old days, when he was master with a crew of four hardhat divers, three tenders, an engineer, a mate, and three deckhands, Thursday Island bound with pearl shell in the holds, piled on the decks, even in the crew's cramped compartments so there was hardly room to sleep, divers and deckies not sleeping anyway thinking of the money and the grog and the women waiting on T.I. He sat and looked at the *Teliai* now, on this breezy night, and he listened to the ceaseless surf on the reef, waves coming in, drawing out, coming in. He was waiting for the sea to counsel about what he should say day after tomorrow, but instead of counsel, he heard a warning: *Watch out, look you the lagoon.* The sense that something was wrong was in his mind before it was in his sight. Scanning the lagoon, he saw an object too big to be driftwood or flotsam about a hundred yards off to his left. It was almost ashore, drifting in with the tide (the flood had started less than an hour before). He stood for a better look, but his vision was too weak for the moonless dark. The object bumped into the beach, turned sideways, and bumped again, and now its silhouette became visible: a small craft of some kind. Some pella's dinghy got broke loose, not big trouble. Uncle Elias started toward it, and was halfway down the beach when he realized that it was not a dinghy but a rubber raft, with a small outboard and only one oar, swinging freely from the lock. No one on the island owned a raft. He continued walking, out of the dry sand into the wet, and then stopped short. Something alive rolled out of the craft and began to crawl on all fours through the shallows, making funnykind noise, like a pig's grunting, only the creature was too large to be a pig. When it staggered onto its hind legs, to a height of six feet maybe, and stumbled ashore, with long hair white as surf streaming in the wind and a bare chest and legs no less white, its arms clawing at the air while it made that grunting snuffling, Uncle Elias turned, and as best as a man his age could run in sand, made for his shed and his big, iron-headed turtle harpoon. There was only one thought, one word in his head—*Markai!*—and there was only one thing to do with a markai, and that was to kill it. His years as deacon in the Anglican church, his wide travels, his wisdom and knowledge of the world gained as master of a pearling lugger for half a century—all that peeled away like coconut husk, and he was a small boy again, listening to Aunty Goda tell him that in the Beforetime all whites were considered markai because they were so pale: wandering evil spirits of dead men who were not properly dead and had not gone contented to the afterworld island of Boigu. They had to be killed proper and sent off to their proper place. But Uncle Elias came to himself in a moment. Silly old man, what wrong with you, tin-kin' all that supersishun tinkin'? White man, sure enough, but ain't no markai.

Turning, he saw that the man had fallen facedown. He approached the still, prone figure cautiously and knelt beside him. The man was strongly built and dressed only in gingham undershorts, like an islander. His long hair was blond, not white, and the skin on his back was flaking off like bark from a paperbark tree, exposing blotches of flesh the color of a fish's belly.

"Hey, you, pella, you can speak me?" said Uncle Elias, poking the man's ribs.

He didn't respond. With some effort, Uncle Elias managed to roll him over. The man's face was as blistered as his back, his lips cracked and swollen, but Uncle Elias saw that he was a young man.

"Hey, pella. You can speak me what happened? You can speak? You okay now, on Nettles Island."

Again he jabbed the man's ribs. One peeled arm rose and then fell across the man's chest, on which Uncle Elias made out the tattoo of a big bird. The man stirred, muttered something that sounded like "Ascan, Ascan."

"What say? Ascan?"

The man slipped back into unconsciousness. Tucking up the hem of his lavalava, Uncle Elias waded into shallows, grabbed the raft's painter, and pulled it ashore. There was only the one paddle. Inside was an empty plastic water bottle, floating in a couple of inches of seawater, and a five-gallon petrol tank for the outboard, also empty. Bending down, he squinted at the words stenciled in yellow on the raft's pontoons. *Winston James—Karumba.* Karumba! That port was on the Gulf of Carpentaria, six hundred miles away.

DAVID MACKENZIE was in his white rubber boots, standing there in the open-air shed beside the small cinder-block factory, a Players dangling from his lips, his rheumy eyes, above cheeks webbed with broken capillaries, fixed on the task at hand—boxing up whole mackerel, the gutted fish, with their sleek silver-blue bodies barred by darker-blue, glistening as if shellacked under the bare lightbulbs around which bugs swarmed while the generator throbbed and Dale weighed the fish and noted the weights and species in her big, clothbound ledger. Uncle Elias tolerated Mister Dave, but he genuinely liked Dale, a broad-shouldered woman with ample breasts and hips, and if she wasn't as lavishly fleshed as a proper black island woman, she was at least no rack of bones. She had a wide, strong brow and large brown eyes, slightly slanted: eyes that Uncle Elias often said spoke him true, same as her mouth, which wasn't always the case with white folks, male or female. She spotted him first as he came up, winded from his fast mile-long walk.

"Elias! What are you doing, skulking about at this hour of the night?" she asked, looking up from her ledger.

MacKenzie, long-nosed, lank-faced, his ginger hair and ginger beard speckled with a little gray, took the cigarette from his mouth and said:

"Yair, you ole bastard. You oughta be in bed. You'll catch the death, windy night like this, fair dinkum."

Funnykind ting, thought Uncle Elias. The missus was born in England and spoke like a proper good English lady; David, born in America, spoke more Aussie than most Aussies.

"You come quick, and bring medical tings, Missus Dale. White pella wash up on the nort' beach. Plenny bad sunburn, and he got no consciousness."

Both MacKenzies merely stared at him for a moment. David's eyes were red—he'd again broken his pledge to stay away from the grog. Too bad for the missus, Uncle Elias commiserated silently.

"Em prawner pella, I tink. Maybe shipwreck, maybe castaway, I don't know. He come in one them rubber rafts, got the name of a boat on it, *Winston James,* home port Karumba. Plenny prawners sailin' outa Karumba."

"They got prawn beds within a day's sail o' Karumba," said David. "But you go up a ways on the Cape York peninsula and you got marijuana farms and blokes lookin' to ship it out. Bloody 'ell." David quickly banded the insulated fish carton and stowed it in the freezer. "Righty-o. Let's go 'ave a look at this bloke."

BEHIND THE WHEEL of the only motor vehicle on the island, the tractor owned by Joseph Nettles, chairman of the Nettles Island Group and Uncle Elias's eldest nephew, David MacKenzie wondered if he'd been too long in this forsaken world of treacherous reefs and deceptively beautiful seas, too long isolated from modern civilization and his own kind, among people only a little more than a century removed from head-hunting and cannibalism, their minds bloody spook houses populated by puri-puri and demonic spirits. After seventeen months of dealing with them, with only a weekend off now and then in Cairns or Brisbane and one month's leave each year, maybe their superstitious nonsense was leaking into his brain. For no sensible reason, the stranger lying unconscious in the baggage cart bouncing behind the tractor on the rutted road made him uneasy; more than uneasy. It wasn't only because he was a rough-looking bloke, with his nasty tattoos of serpents and birds of prey, together with his broken nose and the scar that blazed jaggedly down the left side of his face, no doubt mementos of bar fights; nor was it only the possibility that he'd been sailing on a prawner out of Karumba, that haven for thugs, disbarred lawyers, contrabanders, and bail jumpers from all over Queensland and the Northern Territory. There was something else about the muscular man with the blond mane sun-bleached to platinum, something whose presence MacKenzie sensed from the moment he looked down on his young, partly ruined face: the aura of an evil more complex and menacing than the evil of a simple roughneck. How he could have come to such a notion was perplexing. He was a public official, an employee of the Island Industries Board, a pragmatic man with a pragmatic mission of teaching subsistence fishermen the rudiments of running a modern economy. The demons he believed in were the real demons of this world, like the kind that came distilled in bottles, not the occult devils of the islanders. But maybe he was changing without being aware of it until now. Going troppo, and him with two and half a years left on his contract. A lot could happen to a man's mind in two and a half years out here, little of it good. MacKenzie's predecessor had been sent home sedated on Thorazine after he'd drunk a native concoction of methylated spirits and food coloring, donned a mask and joined the local men in a warriors' dance to welcome a visiting delegation from the Queensland government, and then shot an arrow at an MP, narrowly missing him.

"Em speak me again," said Uncle Elias, riding in the cart with Dale and her patient. "Same ting speak me when I been find em. Ascan. You been got the meanin' of that, David, my boy?"

"Nope. Might be some foreign word. Got all kinds fetch up in a place like Karumba." He threw a glance over his shoulder. " 'Ow's he doin', luv?"

"Second-degree sunburn in places, exposure, some dehydration," said Dale, rubbing ointment onto the man's chest by flashlight. He felt a twinge of jealousy, her hands on another man's body. There was no more sensible reason for this than for the foreboding the unknown survivor roused in him.

"We'll need to pack him in ice, try to get some water into him," Dale added. She had learned bush doctoring at her ex-husband's cattle station in the N.T., and was the island's nurse as well as its schoolteacher. Dale was a good one to have around in medical emergencies that didn't require surgery. She was a good one to have around in any kind of crisis. It was when things were going smoothly, when there wasn't enough to engage her energies, that she got flaky, took to dancing by herself, after school let out in the afternoons, in the stand of wongai and ghost gums that she called her "sacred grove."

"Once we get his temperature down and rehydrate him, and then a long rest, he'll be up and about in no time. I'd say he was on the raft at least two days, probably three. Another couple of days and he would have been for it. Wonder who he is?"

"Wasn't no wallet, no identification in the raft; just the water bottle and the petrol tank." MacKenzie paused. "Say, Uncle, wonder if he was tryin' to say 'gas can.' "

"Maybe. But only Yankee pella been sayin' 'gas' for 'petrol,' and he don't speak me like Yank. Like proper Aussie."

"Well, whatever he is, bloke musta left his boat in a hurry," MacKenzie said, trying to formulate a likely scenario. "Either he was given the heave-ho or she went down fast, and at night, I'd judge; otherwise, he'd have been dressed. No time to put clothes on, enough water to survive on. 'Ell, that liter jug would get 'im through a couple of days at best. Fire at sea, explosion maybe. Well, he's 'ere now. Old tradition, these seas. People just fetchin' up ashore. If this had happened in the Beforetime and you was that big chief great-granddad of yours, you woulda wrapped this bloke in banana leaves and put 'im on the coals, right, Uncle?"

"That ain't how you eat pella," the old man replied indignantly. "You take small part, like skin from the forehead, eat that, em a smart pella, or you cut out his heart, eat that, em a brave pella. Don't eat the whole ting. You know that, David, my boy."

"Apologies for forgettin' me cannibal etiquette. And you needn't get upset, Uncle. Just givin' you a poke, one Yank to another."

"Only little bit Yank me."

"Me too. No Yank atall, after fourteen years. A dinky-di Aussie now," MacKenzie said, a brief, blurred snapshot of a drab clapboard house flickering in his memory. Vietnam had plucked him, a lobster-man's son, out of Gloucester, Mass., in 1969, a week's R & R in Sydney had brought an enchantment with Australia, a bullet in the leg had taken him out of the army a year into his two-year hitch, and an absolutely dreadful homecoming—antiwar activists pelted him with rocks as he limped down the street one day, and not a job to be found except pulling traps for the old man—sent him back to Australia for good. He thought it would be the way America had been a hundred years ago: a last frontier where an ordinary man could fulfill extraordinary dreams. By the time he realized that that was a fantasy, he'd acquired a job, Dale, and his Aussie accent; it was too late to go back to the U.S.

In the village, Uncle Elias roused his nephew Julius to help carry the stranger (a fair-size bloke, fourteen stone at least, MacKenzie judged) to the factory. There, MacKenzie took a stubby of Fosters out of the freezer, drawing the inevitable censuring glance from Dale, and then helped Julius lay the stranger facedown on the cool concrete floor by the stainless-steel cleaning tables. Not that Julius needed much help, he a star prop-forward on the Nettles Island rugby team, with a footballer's palm-trunk legs and an immense chest, muscles layered under fat from a diet of dugong and cassava so that his body resembled a statue of mud-black marble. He gave off a muscular sexuality, and it still drove MacKenzie half crazy, knowing that Julius had seen Dale without a stitch on months before, that he had wanted her. MacKenzie studied him, checking if he was even now undressing her with his eyes, but Julius and his great-uncle were looking at the blond man with the blank expression that was considered polite among the islanders: a mask so impenetrable it was impossible to guess what they were thinking or feeling. Put 'em at a poker table, they'd clean house, MacKenzie thought.

He was feeling better himself, thanks to the stubby and to the lights, whose glare seemed to lift the menacing aura from the man. What he saw now was a sun-savaged, pitiful survivor of some as yet unknown minor maritime disaster, maybe a buggered-up drug deal. He was probably some waterfront drongo no more dangerous than any of the deadbeats MacKenzie had encountered, pissed up and pissed off, in the pubs in Cairns and Cooktown, hoping for a berth from a prawner skipper who paid in cash, didn't ask questions, and was more interested in your strong back than in your history.

He watched Dale, with a professional's absence of shame or squeamishness, pull the shipwreck's drawers down and insert a rectal thermometer.

"If he's a poofta, he'll love that," MacKenzie said, and sucked the dregs from the Fosters and tossed it in the rubbish barrel. "Poofta was used to gettin' buggered by blokes with sliver dicks."

"You usually don't get disgusting until you've had at least four of those," said Dale. She pulled out the thermometer quick as a needle and wiped it. "One-oh-four on the Fahrenheit. Not good, but not catastrophic, either. Another day and it would have been. Been a poor raving lunatic out there, blood bubbling in his brain. All right. Let us get a tarp and pack him in ice."

"Why not stash the bugger in the freezer?"

"Because we want to bring his temperature down gradually, not kill him. Come along, now."

Julius helped him chop up the blocks in the freezer, and they dumped the chunks, smelling vaguely of fish, into the tarp and wrapped the man in it, while Dale held up his head and tried to force some water down his throat. Most of it dribbled out between his swollen, salt-whitened lips. She said she wished she had an IV; she then could administer a saline solution and rehydrate him in no time. "Perhaps you should radio the flying doctor, see if he can come in tomorrow."

"He's that bad?" The coconut palms made a sound like sandpaper in the wind; it got on MacKenzie's nerves.

"No. I should think he'll be all right in another twenty-four hours, but it would be a good idea to have it on record that we called. Never know. This chappie could be Rupert Murdoch's black-sheep son." Her mahogany-brown eyes, tilted at their corners like a Scandinavian's, lowered toward the stranger's face. "You know, if it wasn't for that smashed-up nose and that scar, he'd be awfully good-looking."

Again the pang of unreasoning jealousy.

"That's like sayin' that Frankenstein would be handsome if he wasn't so g'damn fuckin' ugly. While I'm at it, think I'll buzz up the coppers on T.I. They might have an interest in this bloke. He washed up a good long way from home. And if he's a foreigner, the immigration blokes will have to deal with him."

Three hours and that many beers later, the flying doctor service and the police on T.I. notified, MacKenzie and Julius loaded the Robinson Crusoe of Nettles Island back onto the baggage cart and brought him to the guest cottage across the lane from Mrs. Billy's bungalow. His temperature had fallen, and he had regained consciousness briefly, just long enough to give a bewildered look around with eyes as blue-green as the waters on the reef, to ask where he was, and to answer "Barlow" when MacKenzie asked his name. Then he swooned off again. He spoke like an Australian; if he was, then contacting immigration would be unnecessary.

Mrs. Billy, a chocolate-skinned woman said to be half Papuan, was instructed to look in on the stranger during the rest of the night and to notify Dale and David immediately if anything went wrong. MacKenzie would not have imposed on anyone else at this hour; Mrs. Billy was the most devout Christian of Nettles Island's one hundred sixty-seven souls, ever willing to show her faith through good works.

All that could be done for the unfortunate seaman, prawner, or contrabander—whatever he was—had been done. MacKenzie walked back to the factory with a worried, preoccupied expression. Dale had classes to teach tomorrow and had gone to bed in their own cozy bungalow, pleasantly situated in a mango orchard at the edge of the village. He still had a mess of fish to clean, package, and stow in the freezer, but he was afraid of working without Dale there to help him resist the urge crying in his very nerves. But he had to do both—work and resist. The *Merlin,* the refrigerated factory ship, was calling day after tomorrow. He made a box over the Styrofoam form and stapled its bottom, then gutted enough mackerel to fill it, scooped in a layer of ice, and banded the box shut. Over a brightly colored logo—a generic fish, a lobster, an oyster, and a turtle—were the words "Nettles Is. Fish & Seafood Ltd." and, below that, "Whole Mackerel." Fancying up the packaging had been one of his innovations—not that it had done much good. He did a second box and then, with a bleary stare at the mound of guts in the basin, asked himself, "What the fucking hell am I doing this for at one in the morning? I'm the bloody manager." He gave in, pulled another stubby from his cache in the packing house, and drank it down, hoping to regain the agreeable feelings granted by the first bottle, though he knew quite the opposite would happen if he kept it up, that his mood would alternate between belligerence and moroseness before it settled into an unrelieved gloom in which he would perceive himself and all that he was struggling to achieve here as pointless.

Dale called this "alcohol-induced depression," implying that it was a pathological state; yet every day of frustration and failure confirmed that the sense of black hopelessness was the opposite. After all, he wasn't imagining things when he saw two dozen dinghies drawn up on the beach when the tide was right and the winds fair; the young men lolling around the village when they should have been fishing were not hallucinations. Nor were the stark figures in Dale's meticulous account books, showing that the factory had processed and shipped 12,000 kilos of fish last year for total sales of $65,000 while incurring expenses of $69,500. Off the grog, MacKenzie wasn't dejected by the red ink, the idle fishing boats and fishermen. You might say he knew the facts but did not feel them. But he did when the beer or rum or whiskey—whatever he could cadge off the prawners who occasionally anchored up off the reef—flooded the channels of his brain: His predecessor had failed, he was failing, and his successor, if there was to be one, would also fail. It was as though alcohol liberated him from the illusions that veiled and colored his vision when he was sober, and allowed him to apprehend the full truth of his situation. This led him to draw two conclusions: that drinking, far from falsifying one's perceptions, actually sharpened them; and that the temperate were generally more content than the alcoholic because they didn't see things for what they were.

"THINK OF YOURSELVES as economic missionaries," Morrison, the chubby, bald department head at the Industries Board, had told MacKenzie and Dale a few days before they boarded the Sunbird Airways Cessna for Nettles. In 1988, the Torres Strait islands were to be granted greater autonomy, the islanders to be weaned off the dole of a beneficent welfare state, and the Council of Island Chairmen to become more than mere native figureheads for the mostly white Queensland administration. But for that lofty goal to be realized, the islands had to have a self-sustaining, self-managed market economy. Morrison spoke of small, flourishing enterprises based on local resources—commercial fishing and lobstering, tourism, and so on. People like the MacKenzies were to lay the foundations. The bureaucrat (who seldom left the mainland) was sometimes given to extravagant language, and he speculated that 1988 would one day be seen as the second Coming of the Light (the first having shone in 1871, when the London Missionary Society's ship, the *Surprise,* landed those resourceful apostles, the Reverends MacFarlane and Murray, on Darnley Island to begin the holy task of persuading the Torres Strait natives to embrace the cross and cease lopping off each other's heads and eating one another's flesh). As the MacFarlanes and Murrays and all those who followed had converted the islanders to Anglicanism, so would the MacKenzies and other disciples convert them to market capitalism. Of course, they had to be mindful of their congregation's customs and traditions, not try to impose things on them— "Y'know, get them to adapt their way of doing things to our way; you've got to be understanding," Morrison said and then paused, his upturned nose twitching like a rabbit's. "But not too understanding," he went on, explaining that one of the pitfalls of missionary work—religious, economic, or otherwise—was being converted by those whom one seeks to convert. This was when MacKenzie learned about Holbrooke, his hapless predecessor, who in despair of persuading, cajoling, or bribing the fishermen to fish often and hard enough to make the Nettles factory profitable, spent his last six months as a beach bum, collecting seashells and bêche-de-mer, or lazing in the shade with the fishermen, guzzling their local poison (a means of respecting native customs, MacKenzie supposed), while the factory fell into ruins. This was the prelude to his final surrender, when he donned native mask, fell in with the men dancing to the throb of the warup, and attempted to put an arrow through one John Talbott, member of the Queensland parliament.

The MacKenzies landed at Nettles' grass airstrip on a sparkling morning during the Dry. They were dazzled by what they'd seen from the air. A transparent world of light and water. Countless islands that looked like green periods and commas, dashes and accent marks, inscribed on a vast sheet of shimmering turquoise, through which shallow reefs showed darkly, their edges marked by surf. And then their new home had come into view: a horn-shaped island, not quite four miles long by a mile wide at its widest point, with white beaches on its two long shores, a palm-fringed lagoon, and clumps of low, wooded hills at its western and eastern tips. There was a smaller island offshore, connected to the main one at low tide by sandy flats. As the plane dropped for a landing, they saw roofs of palm thatch or corrugated iron peeking through fruit trees and blazes of bougainvillea shrubs. Stilt bungalows lined two narrow streets that, crossing each other and paved with shells and crushed coral rock, resembled a bleached crucifix from above. A wooden crucifix topped the steeple of a small church built of limestone blocks and shaded by two huge ficus.

"Christ, it's paradise!" MacKenzie said when he and Dale stepped off the Cessna, into a gentle trade wind.

"Yeah? Wyte till y'been 'ere six fuckan months," Stan Stone replied to this appallingly trite observation. He had met them at the airstrip, along with Joseph and Uncle Elias Nettles. A man so weathered that he looked fifty-five instead of his thirty-five, Stone was a mechanic and all-around handyman who had been banished to the island by his employer, the Department of Community Services, for various sins.

If MacKenzie's observation was trite, so were his and Dale's aspirations. After laboring for seven years as a fisheries inspector, he was going to have a chance to make his mark. He would quit drinking, if for no other reason than that booze was hard to come by in the islands (though he knew that the determined drunk could find a drink in a Shiite's desert). His and Dale's marriage, foundering because of his habit and her two miscarriages, would right itself; they would be working together, toward a common goal. Dale would teach at the village school and help him in her spare time to get the factory onto a paying basis.

They were too busy during the first six months to become disillusioned. They replaced the factory's old tin walls with cinder block, put on a new roof, and, with Stone's help (the man's sour disposition had to be endured; he was a wizard with engines and all things mechanical), got the generator into working order. Then came the far more difficult task of convincing the island's two dozen able-bodied fishermen to abandon their subsistence ways. There could be no more going out when the mood struck them; the commercial fishing industry was an industry, which required industriousness. MacKenzie set production quotas, made inspiring speeches about the work ethic and enterprise and self-reliance. He sounded awfully like a Thatcherite, Dale kidded him, though that production quota business smacked a bit of Soviet collectivism. His sermons were politely listened to and ignored; his quotas never met. There would have been no production whatsoever if it hadn't been for the five or six fishermen who fished regularly. The others put to sea for two or three days, then took two weeks off, pleading one excuse or another—the tide was wrong, and if the tide was right, the wind was wrong, if tide and wind were favorable, the moon was in the wrong phase, and in the rare instances when tide, wind, and moon were in conjunction, the outboards were buggered, and by the time Stone fixed them, tide, wind, or moon was wrong again. In the meantime, there were expenses for fuel and tackle to meet; a dinghy and its outboard, lost when a careless boy of seventeen failed to secure it properly during a nor'wester, had to be replaced at a cost of five thousand dollars, which was charged to the factory account because the fishermen didn't own their vessels—the Island Industries Board did. MacKenzie continued to prod and preach. In khaki shorts and stained singlet a size too large for his bony frame, his gold-red locks leaping in the breezes as if flames were shooting from his head, he stalked the village and the beaches, searching for the lazy with the hawkish eye of a truant officer. *C'mon, mates, the weather's good, there's fish to be caught, money to be made. . . . Weather been comin' around to bad by 'n' by, MacKenzie; be a bad ting, get caught one of them dinghies in the nor'east channel. . . .* When his promises of a heaven of profits failed to have their desired effect, he resorted to threatening a hell of deprivation. *The government's going to get stingy in just a few years, you're not going to be getting unemployment checks like it's your due, any bloke who can work and isn't will find himself shit out of luck!* Still, they refused to be redeemed. MacKenzie was sure the missionaries of the cross had had an easier time of it. He suspected that his gospel of self-sufficiency wasn't being heeded because the islanders believed in their hearts that the largesse flowing to them from Canberra through Brisbane and the Department of Community Affairs and Northern Development would not be cut off under any circumstances; it *was* their due, their wages for allowing an alien government to rule them.

This wasn't exactly the case, but it was close. MacKenzie learned from Uncle Elias that he had a rival—a priest of an opposing religion, so to speak—and that was Elias's nephew Joseph: Joseph, stocky and square-faced, who would sit in his DCS chairman's office with stony impassiveness, adjudicating petty disputes, but who would Uncle Tom it when the head of the DCS, Tunstall, visited to hand out lollipops to the kids and money to the adults, Joseph breaking into a piercing laugh when he wasn't saying "Yes, boss."

"Em the department's man here Nettles, same the other chairmens their islands there, em toe the department line and them pellas back in Brisbane, they don't want tings to change, 'cause then they don't got jobs no more. Same with Joseph. Em want tings to stay like they are, David, my boy. Em sign his name to those checks, em got the say who gets what, who can do this, who can do that. Em don't want that factory start makin' money, 'cause then nobody be unemployed, nobody got any need of Joseph and no use for his office."

Uncle Elias professed that he and MacKenzie were of one accord. He was nearing the end of his life, he had aspirations for his people. Onetime, Nettles was the center of the Torres Strait, not Thursday Island, not Badu or Moa or any them other places, and onetime, all Torres Strait islanders the highest colored race in the world, said Uncle Elias, but now, David, my boy, we half one ting, half the other, half island people, half European. He wanted them restored to their preeminence and their pride, and claimed to be the real power on the island. Joseph might say that he gave the orders and cracked the whip, but he was a disgrace to the Nettles name, fawning the way he did in front of Tunstall. "But I speak you true now, David, my boy. Joseph been sayin' 'Yeah, boss' to Tunstall, but he don't do nothin' here Nettles I don't tell him."

"Then why don't you tell him to tell these lazy buggers to get off their bums and start fishin'?" asked David at one of their impromptu conferences.

And Uncle Elias, showing a fine understanding of how to fight bureaucratic wars (for a bureaucratic war was what it was, with the DCS on one side and its own subsidiary, the Industries Board, on the other), said that confrontation was not the way to go about things. "You been runnin' around, tryin' to change tings all onetime, yellin' at these pellas to get to work, they ain't gonna lissen you. They got no discipline, one ting, not like the old days on my lugger. You been seein' discipline then. Diver or deckie not gettin' up in the mornin', you can bet Elias is down there plenny quick, toss a bucket of cold seawater that pella's face. But that the old times, these the new times. Got to lay low, like Br'er Fox," said Elias, whose regular reading included Joel Chandler Harris, Aesop, *Reader's Digest,* and the New Testament. "You let me speak them fishermen, quiet. You me lay low, we work quiet underneath tings, or Joseph been gettin' together with his boss man and they cut us down."

MacKenzie called it the Uncle Remus method, and it worked for a while. Uncle Elias doubled the number of dependable fishermen. That still left a dozen-odd idlers and wasn't enough to put the factory in the black; but the numbers in MacKenzie's monthly reports to Morrison looked better. He and Dale allowed themselves to relax. They visited other islands in the group in the "company car"—a fiberglass launch that came with his title of General (and only) Director, Nettles Is. Fish & Seafood Ltd. They took rigidly regular walks on Nettles—only half the island each day, so they would have something to look forward to the next. On one of the strolls, Dale discovered her "sacred grove" of wongai and ghost gum in the clump of low hills at the eastern tip of the island, and there she began to dance in the afternoons after school was out. She had studied dance as a girl in England. Once, MacKenzie sneaked up on her and watched her. She was not a beautiful woman, with her bovine body and her face weathered from five years on an outback cattle station, yet she possessed a breasty, country-girl allure as, naked as Eve, she spun and leaped in the febrile light piercing the spectral branches of the ghost gums. He wanted to rush in and ravish her, there on the ground covered with ripe, crushed fruits, but he was inhibited: she didn't look like the woman who'd shared his bed for five years; it was as if he'd intruded upon some mad stranger performing a private ritual. But that night, remembering her full buttocks and lush breasts quivering in the grove, he made love to her for the first time in weeks, and then confessed that he had spied on her. Did she mind? Not if it inspired him to do what he'd just done, she answered.

"Or is it that you've stopped drinking?" she then asked, in an oblique reference to the most unfortunate effect of his habit.

"Maybe a little of both," he said. "By Christ, you looked like a mad English milkmaid out there. Felt like giving you a jump right on the spot."

"Rather wish you would have."

"What were you up to? It really is a bloody mad thing to do, when I think about it."

"My way of working off excess energy, I suppose. Tensions, I suppose. It's damned difficult, you know, trying to get these kids who hear nothing but pidgin all day to start speaking standard English."

About a week later, Uncle Elias asked to have a talk with him. They went to the old man's fishing shed and sat under the Malabar almond—the usual site for their conferences.

"Y'know, island can be funnykind place for folks ain't used to it," Uncle Elias began, peering at MacKenzie professorially through his steel-rimmed spectacles while he wound new line onto his trolling rig—a grooved plastic wheel. "Folks do funnykind tings sometimes. Julius been onetime go to harvest some wongai por me, down the other end, been seein' wife bilong you, got no clothes on, makin' lak a dance, all alone herself. Now, Julius good Christian pella. His fadda, my other nephew, onetime Canon Nettles at the church before he die of the diabetes. Now Elias his fadda, and em me come, tellin' me what em been seein' and that lookin' at the missus—she ain't no skinny ting like that wife bilong Tunstall—mak Julius want give her one. Lissen me good, David, my boy. I lak the missus—she been teachin' those kids proper good, makin' 'em so they ain't dummies—but she got to stop that funnykind business."

The thought that Julius had already possessed Dale with his eyes and desired to possess her fully made MacKenzie wild. And though he liked to think of himself as open-minded, he supposed that Julius's race had a lot to do with the depth of his jealousy.

"Bloody well right she'll stop," he said.

Dale protested at first—it was so *innocent,* for Christ's sake—and that little grove was so hidden, so remote. There was nothing remote on a four-square-mile island, MacKenzie said, and nothing innocent about a twenty-two-year-old man looking at a naked woman dancing. And so she stopped, but she wasn't happy about being deprived of her release, and MacKenzie for weeks afterward kept a wary eye on Julius.

Then came the nor'wester season, a strange time when the transparent world of light and water became an opaque world of clouds and thick, violent squalls that could be seen hanging over the horizon like immense black curtains before they swept down on the island with tremendous claps of thunder and buckshot bursts of rain, the sky split by lesions of lightning. The dinghies were beached almost every day, and as Christmas approached, MacKenzie surrendered all hope of achieving his goal—reducing the factory's losses by half.

Christmas was the time when he always grew nostalgic for the America he'd abandoned. In the upside-down world of Australia, December was summer, and sentimental memories of skating ponds, snowy Massachusetts streets, and Christmas lights shining through the frost would tease him and remind him of his expatriation. That sense of displacement was never more powerful than on Nettles. Weird how the island had seemed more familiar and comfortable the first day he saw it than it did after months of living on it; perhaps that was so because it had looked like every travel poster and brochure he'd seen in Air Queensland terminals. The longer he stayed, the odder the place became, as if its essential, hidden strangeness were bleeding through its superficial appearances. The bougainvillea and hibiscus looked garishly exotic, the palms and ficus out of phase with the season, the southern constellations glimmered like the stars above some alien planet. And on Christmas morning, when he and Dale joined the congregation in the small church, with its mildewed limestone walls and the air so still and thick before the afternoon rains that he felt as if a wet gunnysack had been put over his head, he barely recognized the hymns of his childhood, sung in pidgin to pagan rhythms. With Stan gone back to Brisbane for the holidays—"damned if I'll spend Christmas with savages," he'd declared—the MacKenzies were the only whites within a couple of hundred square miles of coral reef and water. They were painfully conscious of themselves in the church; though they'd been bronzed by the sun, their legs and arms seemed as pallid among the worshipers as the limbs of ghost gums.

After services, most of the population gathered in the community hall behind Joseph Nettles' office for a children's Christmas party. Dale had sewn a Santa Claus suit (it looked as absurd in this setting as a lavalava would have in Norway) for the fattest man on the island, Reggie Timao, whose curly black beard had been dusted with talcum powder and sprayed with hair spray. Reggie sat down beside the stack of presents, and the children lined up, dressed in their starched, ironed Sunday best, their mothers wearing loose-fitting Mary dresses, their fathers lavalavas or white shirts and cotton trousers. The kids waited to see Santa, exactly the way kids did back home, and then everything changed. An older woman, for no reason MacKenzie could discern, produced a totem mask of the Crocodile clan—a hideous thing with seashell eyes, orange carved teeth, and a green snout with nostrils rimmed in red—and put it over Reggie's face. When a child approached, Reggie would hold out a present then pull it back, then hold it out and snatch it away again, snarling. The game went on until the kid succeeded in grabbing the gift from Reggie's huge hands, or ran away in terror. Some kids were too frightened to get near him. A quaking girl of four or five, Phoebe Crossman, clung to Dale and MacKenzie until her father, Moses—one of Nettles' most industrious fishermen—picked her up and pulled her screeching and kicking toward the menacing Santa Claus.

"This is bloody disgusting!" MacKenzie bellowed, and jerked the little girl from her father's arms. "What the hell are you people doing? This is Christmas, it's a happy time, and look what you're doing to these kids, you ignorant bastards!"

A hundred faces stared at him silently. He stared back, with the baffled concentration of a man trying to read a message written in a foreign language.

"Take that damned thing off!" he shouted at Reggie. Reggie didn't move; the crocodile mask turned toward MacKenzie, the shell eyes staring opaquely, the orange teeth grinning.

"Take it off or by Christ I'll rip it off!"

And as he grabbed the mask, Reggie rose, all six feet and three hundred pounds of him, the great vertical mound of chest and belly knocking MacKenzie backward as Reggie seized his wrist and squeezed, numbing his entire arm.

"Now, Mah-Kinzie . . ." he said, his voice muffled. His power demonstrated, he let go.

MacKenzie flew outside, enraged and humiliated, Dale beside him, scolding. "You shouldn't have, Dave—oh, it was disgusting, but you shouldn't have."

"Fucking niggers!" he sputtered. "Morrison and his respect for their customs and traditions. Ha! That kid was about to dirty her knickers, and at Christmas! Christmas, for Christ's sake!"

"You shouldn't have challenged him like that. It's their respect you've lost, Dave."

And he had. Two days later, when there was a break in the squally weather, Moses Crossman and three of his mates caught two hundred fifty kilos of mackerel and coral trout but did not bring their catch to the factory. To save fuel, they made sails by tying their lavalavas to fishing spears, and voyaged all the way to Badu, where they bartered their catches for videotapes, cigarettes, and sacks of rice. "Don't need no factory, been to get along fine, tradin', like in the Beforetime," Crossman declared when his party returned on New Year's Eve.

MacKenzie was brooding on the deck of his bungalow (the veranda, as he and Dale sometimes called it in jest) when he heard about Crossman's apostasy. So it was away from market capitalism and back to stone-age barter—well, good, let the barbarians make their idiot bargains. Two hundred fifty kilos at market prices would have fetched them a thousand bucks. Their videos, smokes, and rice might have been worth one-fifth that, he thought as he sat in a wicker chair, a .22-caliber revolver loaded with rat shot on his lap; he was planning to ring in the New Year with a bang and perhaps knock off a tree rat while he was at it. Scanning the mangoes for a target, he saw the long, rust-spotted hull of the *Melbidir,* the barge that provisioned the prawn fleet, in the distance. She was anchored off the reef line, with prawners nuzzled up to her like kittens to a mother cat's belly. "Can do a bit of bartering of me own," he said aloud. Setting the revolver down, he walked to the factory with the stride and expression of a resolved man, snatched a carton of lobster from the freezer, and shoved off in the launch.

For the carton of bugs, he received a carton of Foster's and a bottle of Johnnie Walker. The whiskey was soon emptied, MacKenzie, the *Melbidir*'s skipper, and a couple of prawn-boat captains toasting one another's health for the new year. Two hours later, a full moon and the providence that looks out for fools and little children guided him back without his running aground. He staggered in knee-deep water, puffing as he attempted to pull the heavy launch ashore. The hell with it. He took the anchor, walked it up the beach, and wrapped it around a tree, trusting that the same providence would hold it there. Transferring the carton of tinnies from the launch to the factory's ice bin became a feat of endurance and coordination. It also made him throw up. The inevitable remorse set in. He plopped down on the factory floor—Factory! What a pretense! The structure was hardly bigger than a cottage—and felt immensely sorry for himself.

Dale was short on pity when, partly sobered, he trudged up the stairs. Is this your New Year's resolution? she shrieked. To get yourself potted? They had quite a fight, a real knock-down-drag-out, which could be heard at the other end of the village. I'm not allowed to let off steam in my way because maybe I'll incite rape! But you, you can get yourself pissed to your eyeballs and that's quite all right! Rape! Don't flatter yourself, you bloody cow! he roared back. Their candid exchanges ended with her locking herself in the bedroom. He retreated to the veranda, where he resumed his former perch in the wicker chair. Picking up the revolver, he wondered if he could do himself in with rat shot; no, he'd probably live through it and succeed only in making a mess of his face. In no time at all, his self-destructiveness metamorphosed into belligerence, and a rat that made the mistake of leaping from a mango branch onto the veranda rail became the victim of it. The shot was still echoing when Dale screamed and ran out of the bedroom.

"Donchya worry, luv," MacKenzie said with a cackle. He held the dead rat up by its tail. "Shot this, is all. You still got me to put up with the rest of your life."

Five minutes later, he was visited by a delegation consisting of Uncle Elias, Julius, Joseph, and Reggie Timao, all breathless from running up the street.

"Oh, no, David, you must not shoot the missus!" Joseph cried.

MacKenzie waved the .22 and laughed at the four men, clustered at the foot of the stairs.

"The missus is alive an' well! But there's a rat that ain't. Ha!" Then he stared drunkenly at Julius. "Tell me there, if I 'ad shot the missus, would it have broke your heart? Would you have mourned her untimely passing?"

Ridges formed on Julius's brow.

"Don't got your meanin', Mah-Kinzie," he said.

"Oh, yair y'do. You got it, all right."

And then Uncle Elias, with one hand on the stair rail, climbed slowly to stand a step or two below MacKenzie.

"I tink you go come drunk, David, my boy. You be careful," he said softly, his lips twitching so that his mustache wriggled like a thin silver minnow. "You up there very lightly, and it's me the one keepin' you there."

WELL, HE REFLECTED with some self-congratulation, at least he'd been abstinent since then—six whole months; and he'd had only five beers tonight. He finished the last carton, switched off the generator, and went home. All he could see in the bedroom was the faint glint of the huge lacquered hawksbill turtle shell hanging on the wall, yet he knew Dale was awake. With the generator off, there was no sound now save that constant sawing of palm fronds in the wind, the wind he would pray for in the stifling interludes between blows during the Wet, as he now wished it would stop for just a few minutes and silence the scraping trees. Her breathing, that's how he knew she wasn't asleep; he would have heard her deep, slow breathing if she were.

He undressed and lay beside her, she on her back, looking up at the motionless paddle fan.

"You might as well know I 'ad one more when I was finishin' up."

She turned over, her back to him.

"Thought I'd tell you that, so you don't think I'm sneakin'. No secrets between us, eh, luv?"

"I don't want to hear about it. You've been good since New Year's, and I don't want to hear about it, David."

David. There was the tip-off that she was stewing. Not Dave, but David.

"Got 'em off a prawner the other day."

"I really don't want to hear about it. How is our visitor?"

"Snoozin' like a baby, I expect. A copper's flyin' in from T.I. to-morrow. Wants to have a chat with him. Seems there's no record of a Mayday from any vessel called the *Winston James.* I'll bet she was a drug-runner. Some blue on the high seas, and this bloke survived." His eyes had adjusted now, and he traced the curve of her buttocks, that broad British bum of hers, under the sheets. "Ask you somethin'?"

"What?"

"What did you mean, 'e was good-lookin'? Bloke looked pretty rough to me."

She rolled over to face him.

"Please don't try to tell me that caused you to . . ."

"It ain't that. I'm not jealous of some scruffy—whatever he is." He let out a breath, flapping his lips. "Got it all packed up. We'll be shippin' a thousand Ks. Wish Tunstall and Morrison would stick around ta see it, but they're just here for the meeting and then the tombstone unveiling. It's Amos Nettles'. Whole year the family saved up to buy the thing. So our two bureaucrats will get to watch a little native dancing, and that'll be that. See the colorful savages. But I want them to see them blokes shippin' stuff out, see that we're accomplishing something here."

"Is that what's got to you? The meeting?" she asked, and signaled her forgiveness of his fall from grace by running her hands through his hair.

"Yair. Think I'm goin' to get the facts of life told to me. Think they're wonderin' about me what I been wonderin' about myself—if I oughta be a public official. Maybe I reached my limit as a fish inspector."

"Well, I hope you give them some what for. Precious little support you've been getting from the department. Especially that they haven't sent somebody to replace Stan, now that he's quit on us. They can't expect you to run things and fix outboard engines and do God knows what else. I hope you speak your mind. No more lay low like Br'er Fox."

"That's what old Uncle himself said. 'Tink them pellas gonna need tellin' off.' Elias is worried they're thinking of bringing tourists in here. 'Tourists, they come, go makin' more dummies on my island,' is the way he put it."

Her hand fell to his chest and rubbed his hairs in a passionless, matrimonial way. A cool ribbon of wind streamed in through the jalousies.

"Well, at least you've got Uncle in your corner."

"I hope. Times I think the old man is tellin' me what I want to hear. Or what he thinks I want to hear. Like the old boy's got some secret agenda all his own. By Christ, I want to see this thing go. I want to leave here and look back at that little factory and say to myself, 'We built that, you an' me, Dale, and we made it go.' That's what's keepin' me 'ere, y'know. That picture."

Turning on his side to face her, he rested his palm on her hip, as dispassionately as she had touched his chest. There was no sense in arousing her when he knew he could do nothing about it.

"Well, at least y'know I'm not drunk, luv."

"Why is that?"

"Because I wouldn't see that pretty picture if I was."

WAITING WITH JULIUS on the tractor, Uncle Elias saw the plane break out of the gray bristles of rain brushing the sea beyond the airstrip, its bright-green avenue slashing through the dark green of the trees in the middle of the island. He remembered the bulldozers and the sinewy engineers who'd built it long ago, in the war in which his lugger had been impressed as a supply ship for the Torres Strait Light Infantry, guarding their archipelago against the Japanese. Nineteen forty-two. The year Joseph was born: Joseph, who was returning with his missus and two young kids from his Brisbane holiday. Uncle Elias was going to have little bit talk with Joseph before tomorrow's meeting, remind him to behave like a man and not disgrace the Nettles name and go grinning and laughing like a nigger and saying "Yes, boss."

The plane bounced along the runway and rolled to a stop before the stacks of blue petrol drums. The little door swung open; out came

Joseph's missus in her flower-print dress, a casserole dish and a bag of potato chips under one arm; then the two small kids; then Joseph, wearing his white man clothes; and, last, a broad-shouldered islander in a police sergeant's uniform—cap, creased khaki shorts, shiny pistol belt. Plenty smart-looking. Uncle Elias greeted the missus, shook hands with his nephew, tweaked the kids on the noses.

"Must been cold there Brisbane," he said, gesturing at the children's sweaters and windbreakers.

"Wa! Lak winter it is. Very tame, very tame," Joseph said, and gave out the screeching laugh that Uncle Elias despised.

"It *is* winter, Joseph, my boy."

"Wa! That it is!"

The policeman, transferring his briefcase to his left hand, extended his right and introduced himself as Sergeant Mosby.

"You must be the fella found that bloke washed up here last night, that's right?"

"Uncle Elias Nettles my name me, ain't no pella, onetime master the pearlin' lugger *Teliai,* you don't mind, sergeant there."

He had a dislike of official authority, regardless of what complexion it came in.

Mosby raised two fingers to his cap in a lazy, somewhat disdainful salute.

"My apologies, Captain. Where this bloke is?"

"Tak you to him," Uncle Elias said, motioning the sergeant to climb into the baggage cart. "This Nettles Island taxi, come free."

Joseph, riding in the cart with the bearing of a returning prince, looked with approval at the boys filling potholes in the street, the women sweeping their pathways and tidying their gardens for tomorrow's visit, but he scowled when he saw two men sawing a branch from the ficus that shaded the little monument and flagstaff at the intersection of the village's two streets.

"Who them give authority cut that tree?"

"I do," Uncle Elias replied. "Branch got cracked in a blow three days past. Can't call you there Brisbane ask you okay to cut it, ain't that right?"

Joseph made a gesture of dispensation and said to the sergeant:

"Chairman me here Nettles. I give the orders, crack the whip."

"You tell me that in the plane," said Sergeant Mosby. "This bloke, the doctor been to see him?"

Uncle Elias informed him that the doctor had conferred with Missus MacKenzie on the radio this morning and had determined that he could do nothing more for the man than she had. He had little bit sunstroke, but he was conscious now, able to talk. His identity also had been discovered, MacKenzie having gone to the raft only an hour ago and found, jammed under its floorboard, a ditty bag containing a pack of cigarettes, a lighter, and a wallet.

"Name him Anson Barlow, twenty-seven years old. This bloke got him trouble with the law?"

"Nothing like that. This is just routine," the sergeant said, as Julius parked in front of the guest cottage. MacKenzie and his missus were waiting outside.

"Pella washes up on a beach, middle o' the night, that ain't no routine," Uncle Elias said, and climbed out. He turned to Joseph.

"When you done unpackin' me, you gone ta have a talk."

"Mind if the three of us sit in when you talk to Barlow?" MacKenzie asked Sergeant Mosby.

"All right with me. By the way, we found out the *Winston James* was a prawner, home ported in Karumba, just like you think. She sailed out of there little over a week ago, called at Bamaga to refuel and take on ice. Last time she was heard from. The Coast Guard said there's no record of a Mayday from a vessel of that name. Is he awake?"

"Dozin' on and off. 'E's a bit groggy. Probably hadn't slept for two or three days, besides gettin' burned to a crisp and damned near dead of thirst. But we told him where he is and 'ow we come to find him. And that you want to talk to him."

They passed through the parlor of the two-room cottage into the bedroom, where in the hazy, ribbed sunlight admitted by the shutters, his skin glistening with burn ointment, Anson Barlow sat up in bed and held to his fissured lips a glass of water. He inhaled it rather than drank it.

"Christ, never thought that'd be so good," he croaked. He was in a pair of shorts and a singlet loaned by Julius—MacKenzie's were too small for him—the singlet spotted from the ointment and the excretions of his blisters. "Must 'ave a guardian angel, drift ashore on an island with people like you on it." His eyes, clear and youthful and open, moved across MacKenzie's, Uncle Elias's, and Dale's faces. "You saved me life, you did, thanks, mates."

"Luck did. If you got caught in one of the currents we've got out here, Christ knows where you would've wound up."

"Dead is where," Barlow said. "Thought for sure I was. . . . When was it? Yesterday, I reckon. When I lost me oar. Fuel run out for the outboard, and then a sea knocks me oar outa the lock. 'That's it for you, Anson,' I said to myself. 'You're buggered but good now.' "

"This is Sergeant Mosby, he flew in from Thursday Island," MacKenzie said.

"G'day, Sergeant. You'll excuse me if I don't get up and shake hands. Hurts like 'ell to move. Like somebody went over me skin with a wood file."

"Don't go worryin' about formalities," the sergeant said pleasantly, and pulled up a stool to the battered rattan table on which Barlow's wallet lay, still damp from its voyage. Opening his briefcase, he squinted at the driver's license and copied the information from it onto a form.

"So you're Anson Timothy Barlow, born April sixteenth, nineteen fifty-eight, correct?"

"You see it there."

"Where were you born, Anson?"

"Sydney. Redfern."

"Redfern? Never been there, but I heard that's rough."

A crooked smile, but with a little pride in it.

"First thing I learned in life was to run from coppers, but reckon I can't run now. Second thing, the old Redfern uppercut."

Mosby looked at him, puzzled.

"That's a swift kick in the nuts, Sergeant," Anson explained, and then shot a glance at Dale. "Sorry, ma'am."

"I have heard far, far worse," Dale said.

Mosby asked, "So prawning's your trade?"

"Nah. Fixin' marine engines is, all kinds, and not bad at it. But I got the sack about a year ago. Got inta the piss once too often—excuse me again, ma'am. Went to work on the boats; just a deckie is all."

"Anyone you want notified that you're safe and sound?"

"Who you got in mind?"

"Wife, parents . . ."

"There's me sister, Lucy. Livin' in the U.K. somewheres—Manchester, I think—with her old man. That's about it in the way of family."

This was said so plainly, and with such absence of bitterness or self-pity, that it evoked an "Oh, dear!" from Dale. Her maternal instincts were showing themselves, or big-sisterly instincts—Barlow was only ten years younger than she. MacKenzie himself wasn't ready to feel sorry for him, not until he'd heard his story, but Barlow's trade interested him.

"Well, then, how about your employer? Maybe he'd like to know," Mosby said.

"You're jokin', ain't you? My employer's Willy Wharton, captain of the *Winston James,* and I reckon he's in a tiger shark's belly about now. 'Im and the second deckie, Norgate."

With a small nod and a flip of his ballpoint, Mosby invited him to describe how the captain and the deckhand had come to such an end.

Grimacing, Barlow turned onto his side and reached for the water pitcher with an arm from which layers of dead skin curled and flaked. Dale went quickly to his bedside and poured for him. He asked for a smoke. MacKenzie gave him a Players, and he grimaced again when the filter touched his lips.

"Y'know that sayin', if somethin' can go wrong it will, and at the worst possible time?"

"Murphy's law," MacKenzie said.

"Well, it goes double when you're at sea, goes triple if you're at sea in a blow in a prawner whose captain ain't too particular about maintenance," Barlow said.

The *Winston James* had departed Karumba on the sixth, bound for the fishing grounds southeast of the Nettles Group, because Captain Wharton had been disappointed with their meager catches in the Gulf of Carpentaria. He intended to trawl the beds south of Darnley Island, which made Barlow and his shipmate, Norgate, somewhat nervous: those waters were marked "unsurveyed" on the charts. After four days of uneventful steaming, with a refueling stop at Bamaga, they were preparing for a night drag when they picked up a weather report on the marine radio: a line of severe thunderstorms, with high winds and lightning strikes, was coming out of the northwest; small-craft warnings had been issued. The three prawners could see the storm low on the horizon, a black streak blacker than the rest of the sky, tongues of lightning spitting from its rim. The captain decided to cancel the night's fishing and make for Darnley, which, near as Barlow could figure, was about twenty miles to the northeast. The plan was to anchor in the lee, ride out the storm, and begin trawling the next day.

"The *James,* she wasn't no fast boat—she was a hog even for a prawner—and we wasn't halfway there when that nor'wester come down on us. A nor'wester, this time of year—freaky thing. You musta got hit by it here."

MacKenzie nodded.

"Me and Norgate was below, tryin' to get in a snooze, when it hit. I reckon we 'ad gusts up to half gale, and that water in there so bloody shallow we 'ad these bloody great rollers and groundswells whackin' us damn near dead on the beam, and what was worse, seas runnin' against current so some of them waves was peaked up like mountaintops. There ain't nothin' worse than a prawner in a beam sea, them outriggers up there goin' back and forth, y'know, like a pendulum on a clock, only upside down."

There were between them and Darnley those uncharted waters: a treacherous maze of reefs and shoals and banks. Barlow and Norgate, going to the wheelhouse, pleaded with the captain to bring the vessel head-on, drop the anchor, and ride out the blow where they were, Wharton cursing them, the sea, and the weather, as his glance flew from his compass to his loran to his depth sounder. But he saw the wisdom in his crew's advice and was bringing the helm hard over to put the bow into the seas, when there came a sound Barlow said was the worst he'd heard in his life, a shrieking and groaning of splitting planks and braces. The vessel gave a violent jerk, knocking them all back against the bulkhead, but the *Winston James* plowed on—they had struck not a reef or bank but a coral peak, or so Barlow surmised. *Got no steerageway! Lost the rudder!* Wharton cried as the boat spun stern to the seas and drifted off the peak. Barlow and Norgate ran below to survey the damage: there was a hole in the bottom in the engine room, "like somebody shot a cannonball through it." Green water poured in, rising toward the engine, the worst sight in his life, all that boiling seawater, like it was alive, like it *wanted* to drown them.

"That was it. We'd lose power and the generator in no time, so I yells to Norgate that we gotta go topside and get the life raft, and then I guess we turned beam on again because she rolled, and when she did, Norgate—he's standing up to his knees in water—grabs for somethin' to steady himself, and the next thing I see, just before the water got the generator, is him lookin' at me bug-eye like and twitchin'. Thought he'd gone bongo, but what he'd done was grab a cable to the generator, y'see, and like I told you, Willy Wharton wasn't much on maintenance, and the insulation had wore through and Norgate got electrocuted."

"Oh, my God! It must've been horrible!" Dale said.

Delicately, Barlow put the cigarette in his mouth, blew out a cloud of smoke.

"Reckon it was; didn't have time to think about it then. He was a bad bloke, Norgate. Me and 'im didn't get along too well, but that was a helluva way to go for anybody."

"What do you mean, a bad bloke?" Mosby asked.

"Wouldn't hold up his end. Tell 'im to do somethin', he's as likely to tell you to get fu—to go bugger yourself as do it. Kinda quiet in a bad sort of way. I don't know, I just didn't trust 'im."

"So go ahead."

And puffing on the cigarette, drinking water as though he never could get enough, Barlow related how he'd gone topside, to find that the captain had already broken out the life raft. He was up on the bow, wrestling the outboard onto the raft's transom. The stern deck awash, the *Winston James* began to bump bottom—they had drifted onto a reef or bank. A burst of lightning revealed for an instant ten-to-twelve-foot waves, tumbling and frothing.

"Looked like a pack of snarling mad dogs, that's what. If we didn't sink first, we was goin' to capsize in them rollers," he continued. "So I run into the crew's compartment, grab a couple of life vests. I was damned scared, Sergeant. I can't swim. Not a stroke. Not that there was anything to swim to out there. I wanted to get in me clothes and foul-weather gear—I'm still in me knickers, for Christ's sake—but—"

"You remembered your wallet, though," interrupted Mosby. "And your smokes."

"Yeah; they was in me ditty bag. I was sayin', Wharton's yellin' at me, 'The petrol tank, get the fucking petrol'—he meant for the outboard—so I run back into the wheelhouse and get it. Wharton asks me where Norgate is, I tell 'im 'e's in heaven or hell, most likely hell, and then we lower the raft, best we can. Wharton pitches in a liter of water, and then 'e goes back into the wheelhouse and picks up the radio and starts givin' our position and callin' 'Mayday! Mayday!' Musta been off his nut, because there wasn't no power, what with the generator out and the twelve-volts all underwater by now. I'm yellin' at 'im to get in the fucking raft, that he might as well yell fucking Mayday inta that bloody great wind. . . . Excuse me, ma'am, but I get all worked up just thinkin' about, much less tellin', it. Now, this next part . . . I don't know. It's really mixed up in me mind. First off, I feels the *James* give a kinda lurch. She ain't bumping bottom no more; we're pushed right off that shoal or bank into a channel, where she commences to go down, hard by the stern. Next . . ." His hand quaked a little, setting down the water glass. "This bloody great crash and flash, and I'm knocked ass over the gunwale into the raft, and it's lashed to the *James,* so it's goin' down with her. What I figure is that lightnin' hit one of them outriggers—they're stickin' thirty feet in the air, and all steel, y'know. Now, I'll tell you, Sergeant, I ain't gonna try to dress things up pretty, but I didn't think nothin' at all about Willy Wharton then. I figured he had to be electrocuted too, but I can't say he was for sure. I cut the raft loose and drifted off. Last I seen of the *James,* she went down stern first. I just started to row, no idea where I was goin', just rowed day and night till I lost me oar, and then I reckon I passed out. Drank up all that water the first day, like a fool, I was so thirsty, rowin' in the heat."

MacKenzie, Dale, and Uncle Elias stood silent, rapt by Barlow's tale. Of a less romantic temperament, Sergeant Mosby studiously finished his notes, then removed a nautical chart from his case and, pulling his chair to Barlow's bedside, asked if he could point to about where the vessel went down. MacKenzie peered over Mosby's shoulder, watched Barlow's finger move uncertainly over the vast white swath, specked with the green of nameless shoals, that lay beyond the reassuring depth soundings, the contour lines and recommended course headings, inked on the charted waters. The blank spot bore this ominous warning: "UNSURVEYED (Unexamined coral reefs and sand banks . . . Strong tidal currents constantly shift sandbanks and may expose coral pinnacles . . . Extreme caution must be exercised)."

"Somewheres in there," Barlow said. "Never got a look at the loran, so I can't say exactly."

"The coasties'll want to search for wreckage, bodies."

"Ain't likely to find either."

"The effort's got to be made. For the families, y'know. Speakin' of that, we got the captain's address. What about Norgate? Did he tell you where he's from?"

Barlow shrugged and said he knew next to nothing about him except his first name—Jack. It was his first voyage with Wharton, and the same for Barlow, both hired off the Karumba docks by the captain because his last crew had quit on him, an action that Barlow now fully understood and wished he'd taken the moment after he signed on. Some skipper. Sailing off into unsurveyed waters, charts warning that extreme caution must be exercised. The bastard didn't exercise no kind of caution.

"But Norgate," Mosby persisted, ridges forming across his dark forehead. "You were aboard a prawner with him near one week, and all you know is his first name?"

"Like I said, he didn't talk much, except to tell you to bugger yourself when you told him to do something. And you know 'ow it is on the docks. Bloke shows up, you don't ask 'im a lot of questions. Lotta blokes are up in a place like Karumba to get away from people askin' questions."

"What did he look like? Any idea about his age?"

Barlow looked off, into a slat of sunlight, frowning as if he were trying to recall a face seen long ago.

"My age, give or take a year. About my height, but thinner. Blond hair, about like mine, but he cut 'is short. Blue eyes, I think. And no tattoos. Oh, yeah—he 'ad a scar on his chest, kinda diagonal like, right about 'ere," said Barlow, pointing at the fierce blue-and-red hawk that covered his chest. "Kinda faint; you 'ad to look hard to see it. That's about it." He paused and, with an arching of his eyebrows and an uplifted finger, said that he'd recalled something else: Norgate spoke strangely, a little like a foreigner.

"What kind of foreigner, mate?" asked Mosby, smiling amiably.

"Don't know exactly. Sounded Aussie most o' the time, but he'd say 'aboot' sometimes, like a Canadian. Worked with a Canadian bloke once, and he'd say 'aboot' instead of 'about.' "

"Could've been a Scot," Mosby said, and then closed his notebook. "Got a story to tell your grandchildren, Anson."

Barlow gazed at the sergeant, and the battered face took on the expression of a lost, confused boy.

"What now? All the money I got is in me wallet. Nice little spot, this, but I'd like to get back to the mainland."

"Not for another twenty-four hours," said Dale, with a kind of cheerful sternness. "Doctor's orders. I spoke by radio with him, and he said you're to rest up until tomorrow, wait till your temperature's down to normal. He'll be flying in to give you a check. Once you've got a clean bill of health . . ."

She stopped, looked to MacKenzie.

"The Island Industries Board will see that you get to Cairns, free o' charge. On your own after that."

"Been on me own since I was fourteen. Well, reckon there's worse places I could be locked up for a day."

"Been in any of those, have you, Anson?" Sergeant Mosby asked, moving toward the door.

Again, the crooked, prideful smile.

"Only overnight, Sergeant. For a couple o' pub blues I got into," he said, a hand going to his prizefighter's nose.

Outside, Uncle Elias said goodbye to the policeman and went to Joseph's office. He'd decided to lay low and keep his misgivings about Barlow's story to himself, at least for the time being. That young pella did not speak true. Maybe he spoke some tings true, but there were other tings that perhaps made sense to a policeman who'd never walked a wet deck but did not make sense to an old seaman.

MacKenzie meanwhile walked Sergeant Mosby back toward the airstrip. He'd been strangely touched by Barlow's admission that he'd abandoned ship without attempting to rescue his captain; under those circumstances, MacKenzie would have done the same—and he might have lied about his actions afterward. Still, there was the one question nagging him.

"What did you think, Sergeant?" he asked.

"About all that?" said Mosby, twitching his head indifferently. "I suppose it was like he said. Why?"

They stepped to the side of the street as a loose pig came running toward them, two boys chasing it.

"Seems they come a long way to go prawning. Prawners in these waters, they're outa Cairns, T.I., not all the way from down there."

Mosby responded with a thick basso laugh.

"Thinkin' drug-runner, are you? You been readin' too many magazines, I think, MacKenzie." His speech, now that he was off official business, was reverting to the islanders' patois. "Drug-runnin' bloke would stick to the coast, where there's a market, maybe off-load to some blokes with a truck near a highway. Wouldn't be floatin' around here, middle o' nowhere, where nobody's got the money to buy them more than a tin of beef."

"Yair, reckon that makes sense."

"But we'll be gettin' in touch with the big boys down there in Brisbane. See if this Barlow bloke got him a sheet for somethin' more than a blue. Let you know if we find anything."

IN THE SERRATED shadows of the coconut palms, showing no sign of his years beyond a slight stoop and his band of gray hair, Uncle Elias trod on the broken pearl shells and coral gravel that led toward the community hall, his rose lavalava swishing around his ankles, his feet sandaled now, in keeping with the official nature of the day's affairs, and his medium-size frame flanked by the mud mountain that was Reggie Timao and by the leaner, shorter Moses Crossman, while in front of them walked side by side Joseph, MacKenzie, Morrison, and Tunstall, whose white shirt, white hair, and blanched complexion made him look truly like one of those fugitive and bloodless spirits who wandered the islands to trouble the living. Tunstall, having bestowed gifts on Joseph's family—a new dress for the missus, a gold ballpoint for Joseph, and plastic hobbyhorses for the children—was now dispensing, as he always did, lollipops to the other island children, who laughed as they ran out from behind bougainvillea and hibiscus shrubs to snatch their prizes from his long, pale fingers. As a devout reader of the New and Old Testaments, Uncle Elias understood the nature of biblical allegory and parable—they were fictions that told truths—and he had applied that understanding to his Aunty Goda's tales that white people were markai. Whites had roved about the islands—not their natural place—and had caused trouble. Europeans had been the blackbirders who swooped down in the Beforetime, enslaving islanders for the Queensland sugarcane plantations; white pearlers took native women by force, impressed the men as divers, and if they got the bends and could no longer dive, often murdered them. The one good thing whites had done was to bring the Light, effecting a conversion so swift and complete that to this day anthropologists roved the Torres Strait, trying to figure out what had made it possible (Uncle Elias had himself been interviewed by a few of these itinerant scholars, for he had heard firsthand from his grandmother the tales of her father, the warrior chief Kebisu); but in gaining the gospels, the islanders had lost their language, recalled now in only a few phrases, had lost their ancient rituals and customs, commemorated now only in dances full of ceremony but empty of spiritual meaning.

Easy to see why Aunty wanted to warn him about whites, though her own sister had married one. She, like many islanders, made an exception of Yankee Jim, because he had become one of them. Something about this world had enchanted him, so that, on his third whaling voyage out of New Bedford, U.S.A., he jumped ship in Sydney, eventually got himself a pearling lugger, sailed it northward, and never saw his homeland again. Uncle Elias's deepest regret—his only regret, in fact—was that he had not been alive in those days. He was sure he could have influenced the change to European ways, married the two cultures as Yankee Jim had married Kebisu's youngest daughter, and helped create a people who were whole and complete and not as they were now—half one thing, half the other, submitting to laws imposed from afar and taking handouts from the white man. And now, having learned to live on handouts, the islanders were supposed to change course and learn self-sufficiency (like we wasn't self-sufficient in the Beforetime, he murmured to himself), were to learn to manage a modern economy, but only in the ways the whites wanted: the whites were still in charge. Well, now, no European had taught him how to be a pearling captain; his own father had, and what he hadn't learned from his father he'd learned on his own. Too bad he couldn't run this little island as he had the *Teliai*.

No longer master me, he thought as he entered the community hall, his sandals slapping on the rubber-tile floor. He was losing his powers to make things happen, a diminishment he felt almost physically yet managed to conceal behind his dignified bearing, his look of blank solemnity not unlike the expression worn by Her Majesty in the photograph that hung with those of the prime minister and the governor of Queensland above the long cafeteria table, at which Uncle Elias took his seat. Very well, he was losing his powers, but they were not yet lost. If he could influence the changes here, if he could make a beginning here . . . He foresaw the day when the Torres Strait islands would be an independent state within the Australian union, equal in status to Queensland or New South Wales. The islanders would be as they were in the Beforetime, without reverting to the savagery of old: one high, proud people united and tempered by the gospels of Jesus Christ and in full command of their own affairs. There would be no Joseph Nettles cracking the whip for any Mr. George Tunstall, because Mr. George Tunstall's authority would end at the coast. But for the moment, as a telescope's field of vision is reduced when it is zoomed on an object, Uncle Elias's was reduced to the banality of Nettles Island Fish & Seafood Ltd. He didn't think its general manager should be David MacKenzie, or any other white; its general manager should be an islander. He would have nominated himself, since he had the experience, both at sea and in commerce, but he was too old. Instead, he had Julius in mind. Julius would hold the title while he, Uncle Elias, had breath and strength to teach him the business. The center of power on the island would be Joseph's office no longer but the company, and that center would be a beacon and an example for the other islands. He wasn't going to declare his intentions today; his keen political instincts told him it was too early for that. He needed David for the time being and would lay low like Br'er Fox. But on some other matters he would not lay low.

There were the usual preliminaries and pleasantries, the usual routine matters to be dispensed with. Those he left to Joseph, Mr. Yes-Boss. Tunstall and Morrison mentioned that they'd heard Nettles had had some excitement the other day—a shipwrecked sailor cast ashore. Rare event these days. When the meeting was over, they would like to see the survivor and hear his story.

"Well, gentlemen, we've got a lot to discuss and not a great deal of time." Tunstall spread some papers on the table. "So I'll come to the point without the customary niceties. It appears that our little experiment here isn't working out. The factory showed a loss of"—he glanced at the papers—"of sixteen percent in the last reporting period: half the projected losses made at the beginning of the year, and far, far short of our hopes eighteen months ago that it would be breaking even by now. Comments? Explanations? Questions?"

MacKenzie looked with loathing at the sharp-chinned, pallid face, the ecclesiastical hands, the tiny, oyster-gray eyes twinkling with vicious amusement because his prophecies of failure were being fulfilled, in no small measure because Old Turnstile had done all in his power to make sure they were.

"Since you come to the point without the niceties, so will I," MacKenzie said. "We're losin' money because of an almost complete lack of departmental support."

Morrison *tsk*ed almost inaudibly. Tunstall, still looking on with cold merriment, gestured for elaboration.

MacKenzie ticked off his litany: New generator, to replace the current museum piece, requested eight months ago . . . A full five hundred kilos of fish lost to spoilage because of generator problems . . . Can't show a profit that way . . . Replacement for Stan Stone promised five weeks ago, but still no mechanic and maintenance man on island . . . Engines have to be sent to T.I. for repair; very expensive . . . Fishermen who want to put to sea cannot until the engines are returned . . .

Tunstall replied that he would take up the personnel problem with subdepartment heads. As for the generator—that had been budgeted for on the premise of lower projected losses.

"If the factory were a private business, you would have to pay for your own equipment, wouldn't you? And if you didn't have the cash, you couldn't expect the government to pick that up for you, could you?" he added. "As a matter of fact, if the factory were a private business, it would now be up for liquidation and bankruptcy proceedings, wouldn't it?"

"Now, George, that's beside the point and bloody well unfair," Morrison interjected in his high voice which sounded as if he were speaking with his nostrils pinched. His pudgy hand wiped sweat from his sleek skull. "This is a government-financed, government-sponsored project."

"Quite. And the government supplies the boats and engines, it supplies maintenance and support personnel, so the department would like to see some evidence that a self-sustaining economy is being created. The fact is, if these enterprises cannot sustain themselves—and believe me, I'm not singling out Nettles; the same problems exist elsewhere—it would be more economical and efficient for the government to keep everyone on the dole and on unemployment."

Which is exactly what you'd like, MacKenzie thought. *Let's care for and protect our colored brethren, because they can't do it themselves—and in the meantime insure employment for ourselves as their protectors and caretakers.*

"You speakin' proper good there, Tunstall," Joseph said. "Wastin' public funds here Nettles. If a pella wants ta fish one day, let em fish that day, don't want ta, don't make em. People here Nettles content with that."

"Thank you for your input, Joseph."

Tunstall bestowed a sidelong glance of recognition on the chairman, while Uncle Elias dropped his eyes in shame. The lecture he'd given yesterday had done no good. He should have gotten to Joseph long ago, taken him as he had his own sons to the distant, secret islet where Kebisu's bones lay in a cave beside the bones of his wife-woman; there he would have made Joseph touch the skull and ribs, and told him: *Here Kebisu, great-great-grandfadda you, seafarin' man with discipline and skill to sail him two hundred mile by star and sun alone, warrior who took his enemies' heads and fought the blackbirder devils, his bow and arm so strong one arrow prom him go halfway to the feathers inta the oak hulls them slavetraders' ships. This who you come prom, boy.*

"On Joseph's point," Tunstall went on. "How many able-bodied fishermen have you got here, Dave?"

"Twenty-seven. And to answer your next question, ninety percent of our production comes out of twelve of those."

"I see. So why don't those others pitch in? Oh, you know my feelings on this; there are no secrets here. It's simply not their way of doing things out here. I have repeatedly said that attempting to impose a twentieth-century, time-clock, market-driven system on an aboriginal culture is an exercise in futility."

Uncle Elias had heard his fill, and he felt an anger like the quick, hot-blooded temper of his youth.

"Lissen me one time you there, Tunstall. We ain't no ab'riginals. Them abo pellas there the mainland don't compare with us and never did!"

With a slight smile, Tunstall raised the elongated wafer that was his palm.

"I am sorry, Uncle Elias. I should have said 'native cultures.' "

"One ting, gov'ment supply us the boats and motors, sure, but the wrong kind por these waters here. Them tin dinghies no good in any kinda sea, any kinda wind. Lak toys they are go come a big blow. Needin' wood boats or fiberglass."

"Much more expensive, Uncle."

" 'Nother ting, stop *givin'* the boats and motors. You let fisherman *buy* the boat, motor. He tak a loan, pay it off outa what he catches. Then you see some fishin' then! No pellas layin' about the beach, sayin' 'By 'n' by, that'll do, that's near enough.' He got his own vessel, got him some pride, same lak me when I buy the *Teliai."*

"All suggestions are welcome, but you can't ask the department to become a maritime mortgage lender." Tunstall groaned. "What would we do if a bloke couldn't or wouldn't make his payments? Hire debt collectors? Foreclose on a bloody *dinghy?* Be reasonable, man."

But Uncle Elias wasn't in the mood for reasonableness.

" 'Nother ting more, Tunstall. Gov'ment tells us we got to sell fish to wholesale house gov'ment approves. Why not let us sell fish where we want, direct? No middle pella then. We sell cheaper, sell more. That's business."

"Uncle, we appear to be partially successful in our experiment. You, at any rate, have caught the free-enterprise spirit. Even to the point of wishing to see your fellow islanders in debt. I will be sure to take up your ideas in Brisbane. I assure you, all this will be discussed and studied." He began to gather up his papers, with the air of a busy man. "I don't have anything else, unless someone else does?"

"Yair," MacKenzie said. "You want us to make money, here's how. Even if we had all twenty-seven blokes workin' their bums off, we would just be breakin' even because of the vessels. These little dinghies, bloke goes out with a tide, comes back on the next. Sometimes a bloke will burn up three to four twenty-liter drums of petrol in a day, at fourteen dollars a drum. We get two dollars seventy for a mackerel fillet from them wholesalers. So he's got to catch twenty to thirty mackerel every day, no matter what, just to come even."

"Thank you for the arithmetic, Dave."

"No problem, George. Now look, if we had a diesel-powered, sail-assisted mother ship, say nine or more meters long, with a two-ton capacity, here's what we could do. Tow two dinghies out to the fishin' grounds, two fishermen per dinghy. They don't have to travel far to start fishin' and don't have to worry about comin' back on the tide because the mother ship stays out, say, two days. You save petrol costs. And with the diesel mother ship, you save too. Diesel's more economical than petrol, and if you've got a fair wind, you don't need power at all. Okay, while the four blokes are on the dinghies, you've got, say, six more fishin' from the big boat. You stay out till you fill your holds, ice up your catch on board, bring it ashore for final processing. We'd double our output and halve our costs."

"An enterprising idea, Dave. Must be that Yank blood in you."

"It was Uncle's idea, maybe on account he's got Yank in him too, fair dinkum. The old days, the pearlin' luggers would bring their haul to a schooner, off-load, sail right out to the beds again, instead of all the way back to harbor."

"And where is this wondrous vessel to come from?" asked Tunstall.

"Here Nettles," answered Uncle Elias. His glasses slipped down his large nose, and he pushed them back. "Old lugger bilong me. She's still seaworthy, but needin' refittin', new sails. Old diesel her all buggered up, needs proper good overhaul, maybe new engine. And the holds got to be insulated to keep the ice."

Tunstall lowered an eyelid, as if in a sly wink. "All this refitting, new sails, overhauling, and so forth is to come out of the department?"

"Well, since the department ain't done—" MacKenzie started to say, but stopped when Morrison laid a hand on his wrist and subtly shook his head. "We were hopin' the department would help."

"You have my blessing, but not any department funds. We are stretched past our limit as it is. But . . . no ruckin' furries, as my wife says. Since all of you here appear to have read your Adam Smith, I feel assured you'll find a way to finance your scheme." He stashed his papers into his case and stood—a pale taper of a man. "Enough of all this. Perhaps we'd better get on with the unveiling."

Men in rose and orange and yellow lavalavas, women in their Mary dresses, kids in shorts and singlets—the procession moved solemnly through the village, with no sound but their feet crunching on the gravel. MacKenzie, Morrison, and Tunstall walked at the rear. The line of people wound itself into a semicircle around the covered tombstone in the small cemetery in the ficus grove beside the church. New, white-washed grave markers stood straight in the ground, ancient ones leaned, the names and dates weathered almost to illegibility. In the center stood the six-foot stone cross that read:

JAMES CHARLES NETTLES—"YANKEE JIM."
BORN NEW BEDFORD, MASS., U.S.A, 1843.
DEPARTED THIS EARTH, NETTLES IS., QSLD., AUS., 1915.
GONE BUT NEVER FORGOTTEN.

The sheet over Amos Nettles' stone was pulled off, Uncle Elias read a passage from the Psalms and then reminded all that though this was a Christian ceremony, it was also a ritual from the Beforetime—a confirmation that the deceased's soul had taken on its final, proper form in its final, proper place, the afterworld island of Boigu. It would not be drifting about in the shape of a clan totem, shark or croc or bird, to trouble the living. Then "Amazing Grace" was sung to a swaying rhythm, and when the hymn was finished, Moses Crossman began to beat the warup.

Four long lines of men in palm-leaf skirts came out from behind the trees, shaking rattles in time with the drumming, their feet with white rings around the ankles rising and moving side to side together, so the white bands looked like a wraith or ghost slithering just above the ground—the spirit dance that kept the souls of the dead in their proper place.

When it was over, nearly half an hour later, Tunstall turned to MacKenzie and said:

"Well, now that *that's* over, how about a chat with your remarkable survivor."

"Let me check in on him first, see how's he feelin'," said MacKenzie, and walked out, his head lowered, his sneakers, stomping heel first into the shell and coral, making a sound like someone walking over broken glass, and his fists balled so the veins popped out on his forearms, swinging so vigorously it was as though he were propelling himself on their power alone.

At the guest cottage, he found Barlow stripped to the waist and lying facedown on the bed, while Dale smeared across his back the antibacterial lotion the doctor from the Flying Doctor Service had left that morning.

"Looks like a bloody massage parlor in here," MacKenzie muttered.

"I can see things didn't go very well," Dale said.

"Don't even ask. Hey, you, Anson . . ."

Barlow cricked his neck, raising toward MacKenzie those aquamarine boyish eyes.

"Havin' a good time?"

"I've had worse, mate. You don't look like you are. Look like a billy on the boil."

"Sit up a sec. Want to talk to you. You as good as you say with marine engines? Straight now. I'm in no fuckin' mood for fairy tales."

Barlow arranged himself on the side of the bed and peeled off a strip of skin from one arm.

"Keep me off the piss, and I can fix most anything made for small craft."

"Then I've got a proposition. Thirty days room and board, maybe a few bucks on the side for smokes and a stubby now and then. I need a right old Cummins diesel put to rights and somebody to look after the outboards here. Month is up, I promise you a ticket anywhere you want to go on the mainland, Sydney to Perth. What do you say?"

"Room and board? A few dollars for smokes and a beer? Sounds a bit like lockup to me."

"Not many lockups with beaches and palm trees, but it's your call. I'll get on the radio, see there's a plane for you to Cairns in the mornin'."

"Now hang on and give me a minute, for Christ's sake." He lowered his head in a show of pondering—possibly he really was pondering—and then looked up.

"Deal. But engines is all. No sweepin' and cleanin' and fetchin'. Engines." Barlow held out his large callused hand.

"Deal. Couple of blokes from my department want to hear your story."

"Well, ain't I the celebrity? Bring 'em on." Barlow paused, and for an instant, just long enough to make MacKenzie feel a twinge of that first night's disquiet, his expression took on a dead cold implacability reminiscent of a bull staring at an intruder in its paddock. "I'll be holding you to that ticket, mate," he said.

11

MACKENZIE AND UNCLE ELIAS stood over the open hatch aft the *Teliai*'s helm. Wedged into the engine room—an exaggeration if ever there was one for that cramped space—cursing every time his tender skin was scraped by a stringer or rib or some protruding metal piece, Barlow inspected the four-cylinder diesel early the next morning, his flashlight occasionally illuminating rotted hoses, rusted mounting bolts, a battery floured by corrosion and condensed salt, and an engine block oxidizing toward a shapelessness that would soon make its original function a mystery to anyone who looked upon it, like the blighted shards of obsolete implements that puzzle visitors to ghost-town mines. MacKenzie's slender store of hope that the Cummins was salvageable diminished with each "Goddamn!" or "Jesus Christ!" that drifted up from below with the noxious stench of bilge water (Barlow called upon the Creator when commenting on the engine's condition and used Anglo-Saxon epithets when he bumped into something).

"Hey, old man, when was the last time you turned this thing over?" he called.

"Uncle Elias my name me. Master this vessel."

"La-ti-da. If I'd known you was royalty, I would've put on clean drawers. So when did you last start it, Uncle Elias?"

"Maybe five years past."

Sweating, his T-shirt stained with rust and grease, Barlow pulled himself back on deck and wiped his hands on a bandanna.

"Mates, gettin' that bugger goin' again would be like raisin' the dead. You need a new engine, or a rebuilt."

MacKenzie contemplated the thin, bleached planks, then gazed aft, past the mizzen boom, toward an infinity of flat bright-green water mottled with pale greens and blues.

"Either way, it would cost thousands. You're sure this would be hopeless?"

"Tell you what it would involve, MacKenzie. That engine's gotta come outa there, number one. You see them mounting bolts? Take King bloody Kong to get them loose, and then I expect they'll bust off. Then the engine's gotta be disassembled, see what can be salvaged, what can't. Expect you'll need new injectors, new starter motor, new raw-water pump. And if she ain't seized up, I'll start goin' to church. That means her cylinders got to be rebored, pistons machined, and I'm talkin' fine work here. Compression's what's diesel's all about—don't have that, might as well get out and swim. I could go on till they take sleigh rides on this island. Only good news I saw is that your shaft, what I seen of it, and your gearbox look okay, and your throttle and transmission cables ain't buggered. How far is T.I. from 'ere?"

"Little over a hundred miles. Why?"

"You sail her there. Put into a boatyard, where they got tools, facilities. You'll have to pay dockage and haul-out fees and whatnot, but your labor's free, righty-o? I'll sleep on the boat. I'll need cash for tucker, though. So how long would it take to sail her, Uncle Elias?"

The old man looked doubtful—one of the few times MacKenzie had seen him that way. He took off his glasses, wiped them with his lavalava, and sat leaning against the cabin bulkhead, one hand on the greened brass of the binnacle compass.

"Her sails buggered. Last time with Julius, got to haul down the mizzen, she's so rotted up. Sail T.I., go come to a blow lak last one Barlow here see with his own eyes, we get ourselves in a proper good fix."

It rose in MacKenzie then, from somewhere below his navel: that tyrannical craving for white rum or brown whiskey, hot and satiny and sedating, and it made him lick his lips and squeeze his hands. He felt that something was expected of him, that the old man's eyes were on him, measuring him, that here now was the chance to win back the respect lost last Christmas. He'd gone and signed Barlow on just to show that papery-fleshed bureaucrat that he didn't need any bloody departmental support. Barlow could talk the talk, but could he walk the walk? Like the now blessedly dim memories of automatic weapons and grenades, that old phrase came back to him from Vietnam. If Barlow was incompetent, then the whole plan would fail; he would fail. It all hinged on this tattooed stranger. There was something fantastic about him; he had just appeared on the beach, as if he'd been spawned by the sea itself. Maybe he, MacKenzie, should abandon this crazy scheme. Dammit, though—he could see with imagination's eye the *Teliai* coming in with her hold bumper-full, the money flowing in to the islanders, the pride and—yes—gratitude on their faces; they would be slaves to the tide no longer. Splendid progress reports going out to Morrison, and MacKenzie could hear with imagination's ear the talk that would go around the board's offices in Brisbane. *Dave MacKenzie out there on Nettles, he's a man to watch.*

"We do it here, then," he said, with a turn so sudden he narrowly missed cracking his head on the mizzenmast. "We've got a maintenance shed and a small machine shop the last bloke here used. And tools—they belong to the department, not him. Whatever else you need, Barlow, we'll get out of T.I. If I have to row there, we'll get it."

FIRST THERE WAS the problem of freeing up the engine mounts, which Barlow sprayed with WD-40 and bathed in penetrating oil, let sit overnight, and when they still would not come loose, sprayed and bathed and let sit another day and night, and still they wouldn't budge. He couldn't get any leverage in the tight enclosure, not with ratchet, open-end, or socket wrench, so he rammed a long, solid-steel rod he'd found in the maintenance shed through the hatch and into one end of a socket wrench whose other end was affixed to a bolt, and pulled the lever with all his strength, his lateral muscles flaring. Nothing happened. Then he and MacKenzie both pulled, and still the bolt did not budge. Barlow admitted defeat. The bolt heads would have to be sawed off, the shafts drilled or pounded out of the holes in the four tropical-oak braces that formed the engine bed. MacKenzie told him to wait, hopped in the dinghy tied off to the lugger, and went ashore to fetch Reggie Timao.

The giant stood over the hatch, gripped the rod, and, spreading his enormous legs, gave one steady pull. The bolt turned as smoothly as a door handle. And the next and the next, until all six were freed. For a brief time, they all three stood there in the heat and light, Reggie with his frizzy coal-black beard sprinkled with sweat, MacKenzie and Barlow looking at him as they might look at a phenomenon of nature.

"Case I forget, remind me never to get on the wrong side o' that bloke," Barlow murmured.

Later that afternoon, a block and tackle was jury-rigged with the lugger's main halyard, sheets, and pulleys. The ropes were tied off through the holes in the mounting brackets where the bolts had been, two more lines were looped around the engine block to prevent it from tipping. While Barlow and MacKenzie, with their heads poking above the hatchway, stood in the compartment to guide the engine through the opening, Reggie, Julius, and Moses Crossman hauled away as if they were hoisting the main, and the engine slowly ascended into a daylight that it probably had not seen since it was first installed, God and Uncle Elias knew how many years before. Ever so gently, MacKenzie and Barlow swung it over the gunwale, ever so gently the three islanders lowered it into the company launch to be ferried ashore, where half a dozen other strong men waited with a platform built of scrap lumber and bamboo logs. On this and on the islanders' shoulders the engine was borne up the beach and through the village like some strange, rust-scaled mechanical Ark of the Covenant, into the metal-sided maintenance shed, and set on a bench cluttered with tools.

There Barlow remained for five days, day and night, working with the concentration of some mad, obsessed composer or scientist, emerging only to take the meals—fried eggs in the morning, pork or beef and damper for dinner—brought to his cottage by Mrs. Billy, and to have his burns treated by Dale. Then he would return to the shed and the tortuous disassembly of the engine, part by part. During darkness, the clang of tools punctuated the steady throb of the generator, often till past midnight, which moved Dale to suggest that they pay Barlow something beyond room and board and pocket change, even if it had to come out of their own pockets. She'd never seen anybody work twelve, fourteen hours a day, even for top scale and overtime. And MacKenzie, exhausted himself from preparing the next shipment for the factory ship, as well as anxious about Barlow's professed skills (what he'd seen in the shed looked not like precision repair work but like wanton demolition, a wreckage of rotted gaskets, valves, rocker arms, and injectors littering the floor while Barlow tried to free a seized piston by whacking it with a mallet, and with all the precision of a carnival roustabout driving a tent stake): "You gettin' sweet on him, with all them muscles he's got?"

Dale sighed and said she wouldn't quarrel, but not before she'd told him that she found his jealousy his second-worst trait.

The *Merlin* dropped anchor at the end of the week, unfortunately at low tide, so the dinghies in which the crated fish were to be transported to the ship had to be dragged over a plain of mudflats and the crates passed down a human chain to the dinghies. Half the village was at it. MacKenzie stuck his head into the shed and asked Barlow if he could lend a hand.

"Fuckin' kiddin', are you, mate?" he asked, in a surly voice. "Have a look at this."

He held up by their connecting rods two pistons, one in each hand, the sides scratched and streaked, though otherwise they were intact.

"Got 'em out all by meself without wreckin' him, and I'm about to get the third, and you want me to play stevedore?"

"Thought you might want to take a break from this. You've been—"

"Engines—that's the deal, mate!" he snarled. "You got fifty fuckin' niggers out there!"

Barlow's hands milked the connecting rods, causing the muscles in his arms to jump under his still-blistered skin, and his face went cold and mean again, his soft-colored irises intransigent. MacKenzie wasn't at that moment reassured by the courteous message he'd received the day before from Sergeant Mosby on T.I.—Barlow did not have a criminal record.

"I know the deal," he said, careful not to show weakness. "Wasn't givin' orders, just askin' civil like. Been no trouble for you to give me a civil answer."

And the killer's look vanished in an instant. He was all rough, boyish charm again, with his flattened nose and a cocky grin.

"Sorry, MacKenzie. Been workin' me bum off. Little uptight is all." He set down the pistons, picked up a piece of brown wrapping paper. "Me shoppin' list. Somebody's gonna haveta go to Cairns or T.I. We need new head gaskets, new rings, injectors, valves. And if I can't get these other two pistons out without bustin' 'em in two, we'll need them too. Once I got that stuff, I can start puttin' her back together again."

IT WAS THE DAY after David had left for Cairns, and Uncle Elias was steering his dinghy over the sandy flats that protruded like a spear point from the western end of Nettles, where the low hills forested with ghost gums and wongai rose away from a shoreline to which mangroves clung by their arching roots and where, Uncle Elias was sure, Joseph hoped one day to see a small hotel built for snorkelers and scuba divers and sport fishermen, because at thirty, maybe forty feet, it was the highest point on the island and had the prettiest view. That would be Nettles' industry, and the sons of fishermen who were the sons of pearlers who were the sons of warrior chiefs would wait on tourist tables and bring drinks to half-naked white women sunning themselves beside a pool. Might be problems with those mangroves, though—saltwater crocodiles hid in them. Uncle Elias had seen a twelve-footer there once—plenty big enough to eat three or four tourists.

It was a fine day today for hunting rays, almost windless. In the bow, the brown boulder that was his belly hanging over his belt, to which a sheath knife was attached, and a three-pronged spear in one hand, Julius turned his head methodically side to side, looking for muds or the winged shadow of a cruising ray.

"Lak this way pishin' better'n line pishin'. More lak huntin' it is," he said. Sunlight and that little bit white man's blood had tinted the tips of his black hair a reddish gold.

"Wa! That hook 'n' line, for old men and the ladies it is," Uncle Elias said. "But hook 'n' line, that's what brings in the money."

"Wa."

The forty-horsepower Mariner sputtering at near idle, they came to the edge of the flat, the bottom slanting away into a channel in which crabs and small prawns and mangrove shoots swirled in a tide rushing in at two knots or more. A fathom down, a blacktip shark cruised, with slow sweeps of its tail. Uncle Elias turned the boat and started shoreward to make another pass at the flat.

"Been wantin' speak you sometime now, Julius. You been through high school there T.I. You got most schoolin' any Nettles man, and you proper good rugby player. Pellas respect you. Tink maybe time is comin' we see that schoolin' do you some good."

"Got to go mainland there. Nothin' here por a pella to do 'cept pishin'."

"You lissen me good, Julius, my boy. There plenny here. We get the *Teliai* goin' again, Nettles company been makin' some money. One day David been gone prom here, and I don't want ta see one more white pella come here Nettles to be manager that factory. Tink you can do it."

Julius turned to look at him.

"Askin' me you I tink I can be *manager? Lak* David me?"

"Sayin' tink me you can onetime. When em come him back Nettles, I speak with em. You be lak his deputy till em gone prom here. Em show you what to do in the proper way. You watch, lissen good, tak a notebook, same lak you do in school there T.I. Uncle show you a few tings too. Tak you out the *Teliai* when she back to sea, show you how to handle a crew. No by 'n' by, that'll do, that's near enough—none o' that. The proper way. And when David gone prom here, God willin' still livin' me, I help you out you got problems with the bus'ness."

Julius ran a hand through his auburn-tinged curls and smiled uncertainly.

"Got to tink about that. Big job, runnin' that fact'ry, runnin' a ship."

"Do it proper, you onetime top pella here Nettles, top pella maybe all islands. Same lak me when young pella me, master o' the *Teliai*. Got respect from captains, divers, all over, white, black, Japanese."

The engine coughed, exhaling a puff of blue smoke, and threatened to quit. Uncle Elias felt the prick of fear he always did when machinery malfunctioned. Suddenly, the engine throttled up all by itself, and Julius, knocked off balance, grabbed at the gunwale.

"What you got against white people?" he asked. "You little bit white man touched, same me, Uncle."

"Got nothin' against 'em. 'Em wanna live Nettles same lak us, got no problem with that. Tak 'em island gal por wife-woman, give her white pella baby, okay too. Yankee Jim live that way. But when white people come tellin' us what we gotta do, and how, and when, that got a big problem with me. Tak this Mariner engine here. Gettin' buggered up again. Ain't as good lak Japanese engine—Yamaha, Suzuki. But islanders no can go buy Yamaha, Suzuki. Gotta take what pellas there Brisbane send us. Little tings lak that, that's what Uncle don't lak."

Then all at once Julius's body went immobile with tension. He was looking toward the shallows close in to shore.

"Look you there, Uncle," he said, raising the spear by its bamboo shaft.

"Tupmul?"

"Wa. Goin' for deeper. Speed it up."

Only then did Uncle Elias spot the milky cloud where the ray, startled by the sound of the engine, had burst out of its hiding place in the sand. But his old eyes could not see the creature itself, and he had to steer by the directions Julius gave with the spear, its shadow moving with the boat over the plain of tide-rippled sand, white as sugar. At last he saw the ray, a little bit off to the starboard side, its wingtips flapping with slow, powerful strokes, its long tail tapering off to a point so that the ray itself looked like the gliding shadow of some huge, oval-bodied bird. He throttled up, knowing which course the ray would swim, got ahead of it, and then told Julius to hold on as he brought the dinghy hard over into the ray's path, Julius vaulting out an instant later and then running through the flats, his muscular legs pumping as they did when he ran down a football pitch, and the old, old thrill of the pursuit, half forgotten, pumped through Uncle Elias anew. Julius raised the spear and thrust it, with such power that the shaft quivered when it struck, Julius grasping it with both hands now, pinning his quarry to the sand.

"Got em! Em a big one, Uncle! Plenny tucker here!"

Uncle Elias idled up and then passed the turtle hook to Julius, who slipped the hook through the ray's nostrils and hoisted it, its brown body textured and glistening like wet sandpaper. Julius drew his knife and slit the pale belly, folding back the skin to reveal a thick, pearl-gray layer of fat that Uncle Elias even now could hear sizzling in a saucepan.

"Em a good one, all right, Julius, my boy!"

Julius pulled himself into the dinghy, and then the ray, laying it flat amidships, its wings wide enough to spread across the beam and bend with the curve of the hull.

"Em king tucker, Uncle!" he said, and, his face sparkling with sweat and salt water against the backdrop of the mangroves, he grinned into the bright perfect grin of Uncle Elias's false teeth.

While Mrs. Billy and a couple of other women cleaned and cut up the ray for cooking, the chunks of wing meat and fat to simmer in water to make the meat tender, Julius carried the Mariner on his shoulders to the maintenance shed. Barlow was outside, with his long hair in a pony-tail to keep it out of his way as he worked on two other outboards (he could do nothing more with the diesel until David returned), fastened by their mounting screws to a bench. Laid on a table or on the tops of empty fuel drums were screwdrivers and wrenches and lubricants and various parts—a flywheel with broken teeth, a carburetor, spark plugs. Uncle Elias was pleased to see Moses Crossman observing and lending a hand; when Stan Stone was on island, he wouldn't let anyone near his workbench, snarling that the woolly-headed savages would only bugger things up worse. The islanders would need to be able to do their own repairs one day, and the more Moses learned, the better.

"Yavoh!" Uncle Elias said.

"Yavoh!" Moses replied, and then, looking at Julius: "What trouble got you that engine there?"

"Dunno. She start to gettin' buggered up."

"Couldn't be more specific, could you, mate . . . I mean, Uncle," said Barlow, squinting as he slipped a thin metal strip into a spark plug.

"She sometimes almost stoppin', then goin' again, no reason."

Barlow nodded and told Julius to mount the engine next to the others.

"Could be the same as this one. Bad points and plugs. More likely the fuel filter. Okay, Moses, pop the cowling off that un and we'll 'ave a look."

Barlow gapped the plugs and then screwed them back into an engine, its exposed innards an almost total puzzle to Uncle Elias, who'd always had an engineer to operate and maintain the engine and the air compressor on his lugger and so never had a reason to learn what made mechanical things tick. Moses had meanwhile removed the fuel filter from the Mariner, held the small plastic bottle up to the light coming in thin golden arrows through the motionless palms, and then took the cap off and pulled out a small, circular piece of fabric speckled with brown grains and smelling of petrol.

"Wa. Filter. See them, Uncle?" he said, pointing at the granules. "Them gettin' in the lines, bugger up the engine."

"We got a couple spares inside. Put a new one on for him. Be good practice for you," Barlow said. He wiped sweat from his eyes with the back of his hand, his new skin there paler than the old skin.

"Been tinkin', Barlow, my boy, maybe when you peenish with the diesel, you been startin' a school for Moses, other pellas, teachin' 'em to fix engines."

"No chance. Month is up 'ere, I'm for Sydney side or Adelaide or Brisbane. And I won't 'ave nothin' more to do with boats. Seen me last boat. Stay ashore. Drive a truck before—" he said, and then stopped himself and abruptly picked up the broken flywheel. "Look at this bloody thing—scrap . . ."

"You was sayin'?"

"Said I'd sooner drive a lorry than get on a boat again."

And though there was no sound from the unmoving sea, no roar of surf or whisper of running tide, he heard it speak to him quietly. *Somethin' wrong . . .*

"You had bad time that last boat, all right. Been tinkin', that cap'n, em a bad one, lettin' his crew take their clothes off, get them little bit snooze with a nor'wester comin' down on 'em and 'em in dangerous waters 'em don't know."

Barlow lit a cigarette. "What's your drift, Uncle?"

You be berry, berry careful now. Lay low, like Br'er Fox.

"When master lugger bilong me, storm comin', the whole crew ready, got foul-weather slickers on, divers, deckies, engineer, everybody. Ain't lettin' nobody take a snooze. But that the old time on the sea. This the new time. Now ain't no one boss, now everybody in the crew boss man."

The cigarette clamped between his teeth, Barlow, winking against the smoke, picked up a wrench and jerked the nut on the flywheel of the next engine.

"Yeah, I reckon it's that way," he said.

" 'Nother ting that cap'n do—runnin' a prawner in a beam sea with his outriggers up. Now, a prawner one roly kinda vessel. You run one o' them in a heavy beam sea, you gotta have them outriggers spread out, lak this. . . ." Uncle Elias stretched out his arms. "Mak your vessel steady. Top o' that, he got 'em up with lightnin' all around. . . ."

With a clang that startled Uncle Elias, Barlow slammed the wrench on the bench and turned on him, his light eyes gone dark some way and narrowed down.

"Old man, just what in the fuck are you tryin' to say?"

Somethin' wrong, for certain, but you not bein' careful, Uncle, you not layin' low, better to now.

The sea always spoke him true.

"I myself am sayin' you lucky pella, come out o' that livin', bad cap'n like that, em better off where he now is, bottom o' the sea."

"Fair dinkum he is," Barlow said, and then looked at Moses and asked sharply when the bloody hell he was going to get the filter on. Simple job like that should take two minutes.

Then Missus MacKenzie came up in her schoolteacher's clothes—a faded denim dress and white blouse—and her brown eyes laughing and her hair the color of ficus bark but shining in the sunlight. She was carrying sponges and two plastic bottles of medicine, and her presence changed Barlow, taking the dark out of his eyes and the angry look from his face.

"I figured I'd find you here, the workaholic," she said.

"Better'n the other kind of 'holic," said Barlow, and the missus' smile faded for a moment.

A brief silence.

"School's out?" Barlow went on.

"It is. Time for me to play nurse. Off with the singlet."

"That bloody soap burns," said Barlow, pulling his singlet over his head, and the twined serpents on his upper arms and the great winged creature on his chest moved as living things with the movement of his muscles.

"It's supposed to. Antibacterial. Those burns get infected, it would be off to a hospital with you," she said, and squirted the soap on a sponge and began to scrub Barlow's back as he sat on a bench. "How's that feel?"

"With you doin' it, it don't hurt at all."

She did not say anything at first, and then, with a look at the scattered tools and parts, asked where he had learned so much about marine engines.

"Picked it up, y'know. No formal trainin'. Picked it up 'ere and there."

She dried his back with another sponge and then rubbed it with ointment. Uncle Elias watched Barlow incline his head backward a little, close his eyes.

"You could talk to Dave about getting you on the payroll. We need a good mechanic out here."

"Been sayin' the same em me," said Uncle Elias. "Em could teach island pellas how to fix."

"Never 'ad so many people wantin' to give me a job," said Barlow. "It's an unusual experience."

"So you'd have a job, and we'd have a mechanic. Turn around and lift your arms."

"I'd want a fringe benefit," said Barlow as Dale scrubbed his chest and stomach. "You'd haveta give me a rubdown like this twice a day every day."

"Behave yourself, Anson," she said, and then dried the front of his body.

"Sorry. I'm used to sheilas, not to a real lady."

The missus smiled, in a funnykind way that troubled Uncle Elias; he was troubled, too, by the way Barlow had spoken to her.

"I'm hardly a lady. Lived five years on a cattle station. My ex-husband was the manager there. No real lady could last more than a few months in the outback."

She moved around behind him again and, squatting, washed the backs of his legs, her hands moving up and down his thighs, for longer than Uncle Elias thought was proper. Everyone on the island knew there was trouble between MacKenzie and his missus, and he foresaw the chance of more coming.

"And now you're 'ere in paradise, righty-o?" said Barlow.

"It's paradise for a while, and then you go a bit buggy if you don't get off once in a while. Island fever. There's all this space, all this light, and yet you feel trapped. It was the same in the bush. Out there, we called it 'the tyranny of distance.' Here it's the tyranny of the sea."

"So that's 'ow you feel? Trapped?"

"Sometimes." She handed him the two bottles and the sponges. "You do the front of your legs. . . .

"Dave and I visit other islands, or we take walks to keep the fever at bay," she went on. "One day we'll do half the north side—that's a round trip of four miles—then half the southern side the next day. Then we'll take the boat to the far end and walk the other half, and if we've got the time and are feeling ambitious, we'll walk round the whole thing." She laughed softly. "Good for the figure too. If I didn't do that, I'd be fatter than I am now."

"Oh, 'ell, Dale, you ain't fat. You look just fine."

"Well, thank you, Anson. Even if you don't mean it."

"So when's the next time you take one o' these treks?"

"This afternoon. It's the southern side this afternoon."

"Mind I go along? Like to explore this place a bit, take a break from internal combustion engines."

She hesitated and frowned, and then, wiping her hands, looked quickly toward Uncle Elias, Julius, and Moses Crossman.

"Perhaps tomorrow, when Dave comes back. Or Monday. But I'll tell you what let's do for some recreation. Uncle and Julius speared a big ray this morning, I heard. Ray is quite good, properly done. Perhaps we could have a barbie on the beach."

"A ray? You mean like a stingray? You'd eat a bloody *ray?*" he asked, with a grimace.

"Island funnykind place, as the locals say, and you eat funnykind things. It would be you, me, Uncle, Julius, Moses and his missus. Would that be all right, Uncle?"

Uncle Elias raised his eyebrows.

"That means yes," she said to Barlow.

MACKENZIE WAS three days longer in Cairns than expected; spare parts for a diesel as old as the *Teliai*'s were hard to come by, but he'd managed to find gaskets and injectors by scouring marine repair shops, and he was lucky enough to come across the skipper of a sport-fishing vessel who had once run the six-cylinder version of the exact same engine and still had a complete set of rings and pistons from it. That captain had put him onto a local sailmaker, whom MacKenzie contracted to make a new set of sails, and the sailmaker referred him to a ship's carpenter, who agreed to refit and insulate the vessel's cargo hold for a thousand dollars and a round-trip ticket to Nettles. The engine parts had come cheaply enough, and MacKenzie intended to charge them off to the department, concealing them as general and miscellaneous expenses, but there would be no way to camouflage the costs for the new sails and carpentry. He had a plan for that but would need Uncle Elias's help. All in all, it had been a successful expedition, except for his last night.

Because returning to Cairns after six months' absence had been a strange experience. Even the rain-forested hills embracing the town looked strange. He was so used to living in a world barely above sea level that any land much higher than fifty feet struck him as alpine, and distant Mount Bartle-Frere, its mist-cloaked peak rising five thousand feet, became a snowless Everest. In the town itself, it took him two full days to get used to automobiles, phones, high-rise hotels, and TV news. Walking the Esplanade along Trinity Bay, among the crowds of tourists, the millionaire sportsmen out to kill a black marlin on the barrier reef, the bronzed women flowing into and out of boutiques, he must have looked like a castaway in his floppy, sweat-stained hat, his cracked leather sandals, shorts, and grubby T-shirt. He felt like a castaway, a temporal one, washed onto a late-twentieth-century shore from a place hardly changed since the nineteenth. A peculiar loneliness overcame him in his few leisure moments, and once, he almost embraced a pair of stocky Torres Strait islanders because their faces were a relief from the somehow foreign, Caucasian complexions surrounding him.

He was in just such a lonely mood on his last night. Eating dinner in Hides Hotel, where he was staying, he heard American voices at the table behind his, one speaking in a distinctly Boston accent. The bloke sounded like one of the Kennedys. Ambushed by a powerful homesickness, MacKenzie struck up a conversation with the two forty-something couples and disclosed his American birth. Could've fooled me, one of the women said. He told her that the transition from a Yankee accent to an Australian one wasn't difficult—they were both rooted in cockney. At first, the Americans were wary of this sloppy, sun-cracked character with a curly beard that looked as if a mass of maplewood shavings had been pasted to his jaw, but they relaxed and became fascinated when he told them what he did for a living. One thing led to another, that is, led to the pub, where he shouted them to a round, they shouted him to another, and the self-discipline he'd shown the previous five days was washed away by a torrent of beer.

Now, with a terrible headache and full of guilt and self-recrimination, his eyes doused with Murine so Dale wouldn't see the telltale redness, he gazed down from the single-engine Cessna at the brush strokes of aquamarine and emerald, and at the more distant sea merging seamlessly into sky, as if air and water had become one, and at islands so pitifully small that it seemed the ocean had only to take a gentle breath to inundate them all and make earth one with water and air. This aqueous world was home, he guessed.

At the tiny cinder-block structure they grandly called the "terminal," Dale waited for him, appareled and made up as if for a date in the city: a flowing print dress that showed her full figure to its best advantage, a necklace, earrings, dark-red lipstick. Standing on tiptoe, she embraced him and kissed him as she hadn't since they were dating, what seemed a lifetime ago.

"Holy shit, old girl, what brought that on?"

"I'm just glad to see you," she replied, but with a serious, somewhat troubled look. Had his mouthwash failed to erase all traces of alcohol on his breath?

"Everything's okay?"

"Oh, yes. It's that . . ."

And now a disquiet crept into him, one that had been lurking in the back of his mind ever since he'd left. He'd wanted to take her with him, but couldn't because of her teaching duties.

"Been a good girl, haven't you?"

She gave him a look of shock and reproach.

"Just kiddin', luv," he said.

"It's that you've never left me longer than overnight, and this place, five days alone, oh . . ."

"Well, home is the sailor and all that, and with everything we need to get that diesel cranked up again. And," he said, patting his carry-on, "a bottle of perfume for you."

"Oh, good! I'll wear it today! It's Saturday, Dave, so take the day off and let's have a picnic down at the west end. Only the two of us. Please?"

"Sure, luv. Just let me get a few things squared away first."

He and the pilot—a bloke who looked almost too young to drive—lugged the two wooden crates of parts to the tractor's cart, along with his suitcase, which contained a contraband bottle of champagne. MacKenzie had persuaded himself that it was for ceremonial purposes rather than personal consumption—Dale would break it over the *Teliai*'s bow when the boat was ready to sail again.

With his bare feet up on his workbench and a stubby in his hand, Barlow was lounging in a lawn chair under the trees by the maintenance shed.

"Takin' a holiday, are you?" MacKenzie said cheerfully.

"Been busy, real busy," Barlow answered with a kind of insolent smile. There was something different about him—a proprietary air, as if he'd taken possession of the island in MacKenzie's absence.

"I know it ain't in our terms that you fetch and carry, but give me a hand with these crates. Got everything you'll need and more."

"Good on ya, mate," Barlow said, and swung his legs off the bench. "So 'ow was Cairns? Some nice-lookin' sheilas in Cairns."

MacKenzie didn't like this familiarity and said, "That's for you single blokes. Be a good idea if you got to it straight away. Half your month is up."

"You really got what I need, that engine'll be ready in three to four days. Another day or two to install, a day to test-run her and get the bugs out, and then I'll be lookin' for that ticket to Anywheres, Australia," Barlow said, and leaned his head back to drain the stubby, but his eyes never left MacKenzie's face.

MacKenzie next tracked down Uncle Elias, who was standing beside his dinghy in the ankle-deep shallows of the lagoon, a wide straw hat on and his shoulders bare and the top of his lavalava tucked around his waist. He was putting new fishing line on his handline rigs.

"Yavoh, Uncle!" said MacKenzie, coming down the beach.

"Yavoh, David, my boy," replied the old man, but with a distant, distracted air. Everybody seemed a little off the mark.

"Things been goin' all right?" he asked, shaking hands.

"Sure. Been goin' fine," said Uncle Elias, but in that same far-off, indifferent way, and his gaze, usually so direct, glided off to the side. "One ting want me ta speak you about."

"Makes two of us." MacKenzie sat down on a flat rock sticking up out of the sand and slapped the ground beside it. "Have a seat, Uncle. Let's powwow, one Yank to another."

He then told about his contract with the sailmaker and the carpenter and about what it would cost.

"Been doin' good you, David, my boy. But where the money come prom?"

"I'm going to chip in half my month's salary, that's how bad I want to see this thing go. And I want you to talk to the boys, ask 'em if they'll kick in half what they earn off this month's catch. If we do a thousand kilos, which we been averagin', that'll do it."

The old man looked pensively at his feet, then raised his eyes toward a pair of white Straits pigeons, flying along the shoreline.

"Be hard ting to ask 'em, but give it a try. Joseph, em gonna make noise about it."

"Let the bloody lackey make noise. Tunstall said for us to figure out a way—well, here it is."

"Now I myself want you do one ting por me. You take on Julius deputy manager you. You show em how to run that factory proper good, so when you gone prom here, Julius can run that ting."

So long in command, or thinking of himself as in command, Uncle Elias was incapable of making a request sound like one; it always sounded like an order.

"You know I can't do that," MacKenzie said, a little taken aback, and, the old man giving him a look of interrogation, he added with stiff formality:

"The manager's job is a government position, and I'm a public official, appointed by the board. I don't have the authority to appoint anyone as deputy manager."

"You got aut'ority to mak that Barlow mechanic."

"He's here temporarily to fix an engine. It ain't the same thing. Julius would have to take the exam for government service, same as I did. He'd have to be hired by the Industries Board, same as I was, and they'd be the ones to say he can be my deputy or take over when I'm gone."

And still the look of interrogation.

"Look here. I'd be happy if Julius would help me and Dale when we've got a shipment ready to go. We could show him how to keep the books. Hell, we'd love it if *somebody* on this bloody island gave us a hand with the dirty work."

"Julius, em know how to do dirty work. Want em to learn how to *manage.*"

"Uncle, I know how to manage and I ain't too proud for the dirty work," MacKenzie said, growing angry. "Maybe if I see a little sign that Julius is willin' to work up to his elbows in fish guts till one or two in the morning, I'd be willin' to put in a good word for him."

"Know how it come to go wi' that board. See Julius island pella, they themselves say to themselves, 'Can't have no island pella be manager.' 'Y'know, us here Nettles, them Badu, Moa there, all these islands, we sorta been canceled out. We sorta in a box like, wi' a foot on top it. We never been released."

"I know that, and I'm doin' what I can to get that foot off. But only what I can."

"Now, how come I gonna do this ting por you, talk to the pellas, but you no can do one ting por me? Y'know, up there lightly you. Just tacked on, David, my boy. All people here Nettles layin' low about your drinkin', so bad word don't get back to the mainland. Even Joseph layin' low, cuz it's me tellin' him to."

MacKenzie bowed his head and drew breath deep into his lungs to force back a quick, hot flash of temper.

"Listen, Uncle, about your talkin' to the boys—you're doin' that for them and for yourself; it ain't no favor to me," he said, aware that that wasn't the entire truth. He stood up. "And don't go threatenin' me, Uncle."

The conversation made him a disagreeable picnic companion, as did the weather. The sky had taken on the same metallic shade as the dinghies, and though the haze softened the sun's brightness, it did not relieve the heat. Island and sea were cloaked in a sullen oppressiveness, and the almost unbreathable air and the absence of horizon only heightened the impression MacKenzie had had earlier—that air and water were becoming one, devolving to the elemental unity, hostile to life, they had possessed before Genesis. He and Dale sat under royal palms, some leaning, some as straight as pillars, and indolently munched the sandwiches and sipped the sodas she'd packed in the ice chest. The launch was drawn up on the beach, sandy high up, muddy lower down, the muddy part widening slowly as the tide fell out. MacKenzie was brooding silently, and Dale told him to cheer up. She never would understand the masculine mind, as compartmentalized as a ship. Either/or, black or white. All he had to do to humor Uncle Elias was *say* Julius was his assistant and then show him the ropes.

"I pretty much suggested that already. Anyways, what happens after? He starts to think he'll manage it when we leave? The board wouldn't go for it, so all I'd be doing is raisin' hopes that can't be fulfilled."

"Then let the damned board deal with that," she said irritably. "We've got to get this thing off the ground and ourselves through the next couple of years as smoothly as we can."

"Ah, me sensible Pommy," he said, and patted her thigh. "And I think it'd be sensible for us to shove off soon. Once that tide falls, we'll have a hundred yards of muck to drag the launch through."

"Oh, the tide, the damned bloody tide," she said, with an exasperated swat at the shore. "Uncle Elias and the tide and the factory and the tide and that diesel engine and the tide. I'm sick of it."

"We're slaves to it."

"We don't have to be. Come, let's take a walk." She stood in her shorts, brushed sand from her knees and her bottom, and, reaching down, took his hands in hers. "Come on now, and I'll help free you from the tide."

They went through the palm grove, past a mangrove swamp where fox bats hung obscenely from the branches, then into a stifling swale of long, pale-green grasses, over a knoll into a shallow bowl, stepped around a dead ghost gum, its trunk and branches as bare and white as the skeleton of some prehistoric beast, and at last entered a stand of wongai ornamented with reddening fruits. Beyond stood a few more ghost gums.

"Recognize this spot, don't you?" Dale asked flirtatiously. She picked one of the ripe, plum-purple fruits from the ground and offered it to him. "Thought I'd play Eve. You know the legend of the wongai."

"Yeah. If you eat one, you'll be sure to return to the islands. Not sure I'll want to once I'm off."

"Whatever you wish, but I'm going to dance for you, David MacKenzie. I can't dance here alone, but I can with you here."

"Dale . . . ," he began, but had no idea what to say.

She unbuttoned her blouse, with a kind of fetching shyness, and pulled off her shorts, her panties, and then, without hesitancy and in milk-skinned nakedness, did a turn on her toes, kicked one leg high, made another turn, her breasts flopping lushly, the flesh on her buttocks and thighs quivering like pudding. She spun and kicked before him until her soles were darkened by crushed fruits and her body was glistening with sweat. After one of her slow pirouettes, she looked at him with a willed lasciviousness that made him cringe, embarrassed for her. A helpless panic rose in him. That first time had aroused him because of its secrecy and mystery; he'd stolen a glimpse of her. Now there was neither secrecy nor mystery, only a kind of daftness, and there was no desire, only the desire for desire. He cursed himself, and the deadness within himself, and the inner governor that restrained him from abandoning himself to the lunacy of this moment.

She danced away from him, and then up to him, and put her arms around his waist and said:

"Make love to me. Here. Now."

Her hands moved to his belt, fumbled with the buckle. He was as ashamed for himself as for her, and a host of questions passed through his mind all at once. Was it his drinking that had turned him from ardent lover into this husk of a husband? Didn't he love or want her anymore? Had he lost his manhood? Damn his own soul to hell, but half his mind was on the launch and the danger of missing the tide.

"Please don't humiliate me by making me . . . ," she began to say, and then kissed him as she had when she met him that morning. He didn't think he was humiliating her, but he was disappointing her. He seemed to be very good at disappointing people: Uncle Elias this morning, himself last night in Cairns . . .

She backed away, giving him space within which he could come to her.

"Dale, it isn't you . . . it's me. . . . Got so much on my mind, and—"

"You've got to, Dave."

And when he heard the urgency in this appeal or imperative or whatever it was, he understood that nothing had happened in his absence but that the possibility had presented itself, and it had frightened her. He pulled off his shirt, stripped his shorts, and went to her, without zeal or passion but with the resolve of a warrior about to enter some desperate struggle, knowing he would lose, yet compelled to try. Maybe she would give him points for that. God, he could use a drink.

I I I

WORK COULD BE a lot of things—easy or hard, frustrating or fulfilling—but it was not unfathomable, like the depths of the heart or the abysses of the mind, and so he immersed himself in it. Joe Barrett, the wirily built, short-tempered carpenter, landed in the middle of the week, with his tools and glues and fiberglass compounds, and flew into a foul-mouthed wrath when he discovered that there was neither jetty nor dry dock on Nettles. How in the name of Jesus was he supposed to operate his power tools when the goddamned fuckan boat was out there on the lagoon, a quarter mile from any electrical source? He was ready to fly back to Cairns straightaway, when Uncle Elias suggested that they careen the vessel, as he did when he scraped and painted the bottom. The carpenter could meanwhile build a cradle from scrap lumber on the island; the *Teliai* could be raised onto it and held in jury-rigged dry dock on the beach, above the high-tide line, and a generator could be brought up to supply power.

With the help of the tractor, all the able-bodied men on island, including MacKenzie, hauled the dismasted lugger up the beach as far they could. "Looks like somethin' outa one of them Bible movies, ya know, where the slaves is draggin' the fuckan great stone blocks for the pyramids," said the carpenter, pronouncing "Bible" as "Boyble" and "slaves" as "slives," in his thick drawl. The *Teliai* lay on her side. Hawsers were lashed to her hull—bow, midships, and stern—the midships line hooked to the tractor, and then the vessel was raised by machine and human muscle, slowly and ever so carefully onto her keel. As soon as she was right, men leaped in and jammed the cross-braces of the cradle against her sides and held them there by hand until others, up on ladders dragged from maintenance shed and houses alike, could drive the pilings deep into the sand. For extra stability, empty petrol drums were rolled under her, turned upright, and filled with sand. The job took all of a day, but there she was, raised up against an orange-and-peach sky, her dented prop six feet in the air. MacKenzie was ecstatic. He was the missionary again, preaching to his flock. "See what we can do when we put our minds and our backs to it?" he said to the assembled islanders. "We can do this, we can catch every fish in these seas and make a bloody million, you'll see!"

For a week thereafter he scuttled from the factory to the boat, to lend Barrett a hand as he lined the hold with plywood and laid fiberglass over the plywood, fashioning a kind of huge fish box that he guaranteed would keep block ice for up to three days. Emerging with his head swimming from glue fumes and his arms itching from embedded strands of fiberglass, MacKenzie would then make for the shed, where, under a caged lamp hung from a beam by an orange power cord, Barlow and Moses Crossman rebuilt the engine bolt by bolt, Barlow calling now for a crescent or socket wrench, now for a Phillips or slot screwdriver. There were maddening delays—once, the generator quit, so Barlow had to take an entire afternoon to get it running again—and the expenses were running far higher than MacKenzie had anticipated. Barrett had to order more plywood and fiberglass—fortunately there was some on T.I., so flying it to the island wasn't as pricey as from Cairns—but the carpenter had put in a full week instead of three days. Filled with a reckless exuberance, MacKenzie paid his extra wages out of the factory's operating funds, trusting that he could repay the amount from the sale of the past two weeks' catch.

While Barrett refurbished the *Teliai's* innards, Uncle Elias and several men stripped and revarnished her masts and repainted her exterior. The day after Barrett flew back to the mainland, the lugger was refloated and towed to her anchorage, and a fine sight she made, her graceful hull as white as a heron's wing, her mahogany masts gleaming. The new Dacron sails arrived a couple of days later, delivered by the *Merlin* on her monthly call. The captain presented MacKenzie with the sailmaker's bill. Because everyone had been so busy helping to refurbish the *Teliai,* the shipment was considerably under the thousand kilos anticipated; that is, even with the donation of half his salary and half the fishermen's wages, MacKenzie could not cover the cost of the sails. Again he broke out the factory's checkbook and made up the difference.

He reboarded his launch with a pensive frown, half his brain a calculator, the other half devising creative accounting schemes for the month's report to Morrison.

This was what he was thinking about when he heard a sound that never failed to remind him of the day when, with his right leg bloodied and his mind a blissful fog of morphine, he experienced the nearest thing he would ever know to an ascension into heaven: the hard, rapid slapping of a helicopter. It was hovering over the airstrip, a white bubble-cockpit craft with the emblem of the Queensland police on its fuselage.

Ashore a quarter of an hour later, he found Uncle Elias and Joseph pacing outside Joseph's office.

"What's goin' on?" MacKenzie asked, peeking through the window to see Barlow, smoking a cigarette and drinking a soda while he sat at a table with Sergeant Mosby and two other people—a heavyset man wearing a loosened tie and a thin, dark-haired woman.

" 'Em police, wantin' ask Barlow there 'bout the sinkin'. 'Em tell us to wait outside, but no worries, 'em say. Very tame," Joseph explained.

"Always sayin' that you," said Uncle Elias. " 'Very tame.' No matter what, you say 'very tame.' Don't make no sense that."

"Askin' him what?"

Joseph shrugged, managing to look officious and obsequious at the same time.

MacKenzie barged inside, drawing a look of rebuke from the woman. With her prim, scrawny face, severe hairstyle, and fierce gaze, she reminded him of nothing so much as a vengeful nun. Nautical charts, legal tablets, a tape recorder, and a case file were spread on the table. MacKenzie introduced himself and, pointing at Barlow, said that the man they were questioning worked for him and he would like to know what it was about.

Barlow took a swig from his tinny of Coke and grinned his crooked bad-boy grin.

"No worries, mate. I'm a celebrity," he said, jerking a thumb at the file, which contained a photograph of a slender, brown-haired, very young man with a thin nose and a military haircut.

"What kinda celebrity? Don't look like you exactly," MacKenzie said uneasily.

"Damned right it don't," Barlow said.

The bulky man told the woman to explain things. With a stab of her head, she instructed MacKenzie to come outside.

She was Detective Tessa Phelan of the Queensland police, her colleague Detective Malcolm Brent, and she apologized for the inconvenience; they wouldn't be but another hour at the longest.

"We believe Mr. Barlow's shipmate was this man," she said. Her lips barely moved, making it difficult to understand her. "John Northfield, also known as Jack Norgate."

"Oh, yeah. Norgate. The bloke he said he didn't like."

"Perhaps with good reason. Sergeant Mosby pitched his report down to Brisbane, asking if Barlow had a criminal record."

"Yair, I asked him to."

Good thing you did. Malcolm handled Mosby's request. That name Norgate rang a bell. Malcolm recalled it from unsolved case files. He fetched them, and noticed Barlow's description of Norgate matched the one in the files—five-ten to six feet, slender build, light-brown hair, blue eyes, a vague semicircular scar on his chest. Above all, Barlow's mention that Norgate spoke with an Australian accent most of the time, but sometimes lapsed into what sounded like North American English. Northfield, alias Norgate, is—we hope *was*—an American. From the state of Virginia."

"Bloody hell, that's right!" MacKenzie said in a loud, startling voice. "Barlow said he sometimes said 'aboot' instead of 'about,' like a Canadian, but people from Virginia, parts of it anyways, got the same pronunciation. I was in Vietnam with a bloke from Virginia, and that's how he'd say 'about.' "

She looked at him quizzically.

"I'm a Yank originally, and I make lapses now and then myself," he said.

"Lucky we found you. Your information's interesting. I'll pass it to Malcolm."

"So this Northfield did what?"

"He deserted the American armed forces toward the end of the Vietnam War, '73, but not out of antiwar principles. He murdered a prostitute in Saigon in some squabble over money. The crime wasn't discovered until he was over here, in Sydney on R & R. The U.S. military authorities issued a warrant and asked our Commonwealth police to execute it, but Northfield got warned somehow and eluded them. There was still an active antiwar radical network in Sydney, and he found them. He was only twenty at the time, but no scared kid in serious trouble. Apparently a clever, streetwise bloke. Been in scrapes with the law before he went into service."

"Yair, we was gettin' all kinds in uniform toward the end," MacKenzie said, and looked over at Joseph and Uncle Elias. He lit a Players, offered one to Phelan. She shook her head. "So I'll bet he convinced those bleedin' hearts that he'd gone over the hill so's he didn't have to——"

"Exactly," she interrupted. "They had a nice little setup, well organized, a few old-line Reds in their ranks who knew the ropes. They got him a forged Aussie passport under an assumed name, a forged driver's license, the lot. There was even word they'd helped him change his appearance, dyed his hair, perhaps put him onto a sympathetic plastic surgeon. Compol got that from one of their snitches—they had the group pretty well infiltrated—but they never could confirm. All they had to go on were his prints and his army ID photo, which they got from the American military police. Truth is, that's all we've got now. So Compol was about to snatch him up and turn him over to the Americans when"—she snapped her fingers—"he vanished. The underground spirited him off to Brisbane, or so the snitch said. At all events, Compol made sure the radicals found out they were dealing with a murderer, not some pacifist, to cut him off from their further services."

"And that's it, for *twelve* years?" asked MacKenzie, incredulous.

"Not quite. Five years later, in Sydney, a man got into a dispute with a prostitute over her fee and bludgeoned her to death with a club or pipe. New South Wales police lifted prints from her room, checked them out, and what do you know? Up comes Northfield's name and an outstanding warrant. Bloke seemed to have problems with the economics of paid sex. But by that time he was gone again. He was quite itinerant and hard to keep track of. Australia's an easy country to disappear in. Especially then, before we went to photo IDs. And let's face it, an American deserter from years past, a dead whore way off in Saigon, another dead whore in Sydney—not what you'd call top priority. But when Malcolm read Sergeant Mosby's report, he contacted the Feds and they asked us to have a chat with Barlow. Tie up loose ends."

"Ain't had this much excitement on Nettles since, I reckon, the last head-hunting raid, just two weeks ago," MacKenzie said, trying to draw a smile from the gaunt, grim detective. "What do you hope to find?"

"The wreck. The waters around here aren't terribly deep, even in the channels. Thirty meters or so. If we can get divers down, there's a chance we'll recover the bodies. Use dental records for positive ID. And if it's Northfield . . ." She made a cleansing motion with her hands.

"Good luck. There's barracudas, blacktips, tigers, and great whites out there. Reckon your fugitive's dental records have been digested by now."

"Yes. But Barlow says he got electrocuted in the engine room. Could be his body's trapped there, where the sharks can't get at it. We'll give it a try. But if we can get enough concrete information out of Mr. Barlow, possibly we can close the books based on his testimony," she said blandly, and with a glance inside.

"SO HOW LONG you here for?" asked Detective Brent as he and Sergeant Mosby and Detective Phelan came out with Barlow.

"I get that engine turnin' over this afternoon, I'll be on me way tomorrow, day after."

"Thought this would be the sort of place nobody would want to leave." Brent, a white pella fat like island pella but in the wrong way fat, wiped his brow and wrinkled his nose as he looked at the sweat spots in his shirt. "Bit hot, though." Then he reached into the side pocket of the rumpled tan jacket slung over his shoulder and pulled out business cards, passing one to Joseph, one to Barlow, one to David. "Anson, let us know your whereabouts, in case we need to have another chat. You others, if any wreckage or bodies wash ashore, ring us up. Got a phone out here?"

"Marine radio; we can patch into a phone," said David, and then Barlow clasped the detective's hand.

"Never thought I'd say this to a copper, but glad if I 'elped out some. Y'know, I knew that Norgate was a bad bloke."

"Ah! My purse is inside," said Phelan. She went back into the office. Uncle Elias, standing alongside the doorway, caught her doing a funnykind thing—she pulled out a handkerchief and with it grasped the soda can Barlow had been drinking from, dropped it in her purse, and snapped the purse shut and then came out. He recalled what the sea had told him that afternoon not long ago: *Somethin' wrong*. Why? What? And then, as Julius pulled up in the tractor to drive Sergeant Mosby and the detectives to the airfield, Uncle Elias felt a gecko lizard crawling up his spine, only no lizard was there. *Truck!* Em say "truck" for "lorry," same lak David sometimes when em forget himself. *Truck*.

Uncle Elias counseled himself to lay low. They needed Barlow for one more day, and then he'd be off the island, one less white pella to deal with, and a bad one too.

WITH ITS RUST scraped off with a wire brush and its pitted block spray-painted battleship gray, the mechanical Ark of the Covenant was carried through the village the next morning, on the same shoulders that had borne it over a month earlier, laid into the launch, ferried to the lugger, lowered once again into its dank, bilge-reeking compartment, and bolted down. Barlow had test-started the engine late the previous night, with a hose in a rain barrel connected to the raw-water pump and a jury-rigged fuel line to a drum of diesel, and half the village had heard the cough, the sputter, and then the rattling thump as it ran steadily.

Now Uncle Elias, Julius, and Reggie Timao looked on impassively while Moses Crossman laid out tools and, with the sureness of a surgeon's assistant, passed them below as they were called for. Cables were connected from a new twenty-four-volt battery to the starter motor, the shaft was reconnected to the shaft housing, throttle cable to throttle, transmission cable to gearbox, fuel line to tank, Barlow and MacKenzie working by turns, MacKenzie more than Barlow because his thinner frame could slip into the tight space more easily. The sun was past the meridian when Barlow pushed the starter button on the helm post. There was a click, a straining sound, and then nothing. He wriggled the throttle lever on the dulled chrome control box beside the helm, punched the starter again. Another click, groan, and then nothing. Sweat dripped through the bandanna around his forehead.

"What the . . . She turned like a bloody top last night."

He tried again, with the same results.

"Engine, how come she no go?" Uncle Elias asked.

In an explosion no less unexpected and stunning than if a grenade had gone off, Barlow flung a wrench and cried out, "How the fuck do I know, you flamin' black bastard!" The wrench struck the deckhouse bulkhead, close enough to Uncle Elias to give the impression that the miss hadn't been deliberate.

"Hey, Barlow, watch yourself, for Christ's sake."

"Go to hell, you bastard!" he snapped, turning on MacKenzie. "She ain't gettin' any gas, and you installed the fuel pump, the throttle cable . . . you buggered somethin' up—she was runnin' like a goddamned top last night!"

"I didn't bugger anything. She's right, mate."

Barlow leaned against the deckhouse, staring down at the deck, his back rising and falling, and then he gave MacKenzie that chill stare he seemed to be able to switch on at will.

"Okay, *mate*. She ain't right, but I'll get her right, and then you'll owe me a little overtime. Been 'ere two days over the thirty. I'll need some walkin'-around cash with that ticket. Two fifty should do it."

"Jesus Christ, Barlow . . ."

"Two fifty," he repeated, and lowered himself into the compartment.

In less than half an hour, the problem was found—a frozen impeller in the fuel pump. The thick plastic blades, which had fit to a fine tolerance in the cool night air, must have expanded in the day's heat and jammed against the housing. With an ordinary razor-scraper, Barlow shaved a microthin slice off each blade, sanded them all with emory paper, and reinstalled the pump.

He climbed back out on deck, wild-eyed, and jabbed the starter button with his thumb. The straining, groaning sound came again, but then a muffled explosion, and a blue-black puff of smoke flew from the exhaust pipe at the transom waterline. Barlow cranked the throttle to prime the pump, held the lever forward, and tried starting again. The engine caught, almost died, caught again, and then came a continuous rattling and tapping, and a shuddering that made the afterdeck vibrate underfoot. He revved her up, and she rumbled like the diesel in a Mercedes lorry, steady, full-throated, beautiful. Everyone stood breathless, poised for something to go wrong. Barlow throttled back to idle and engaged the gears—the *Teliai* had only one, forward—and the lugger crept up on her anchor rope. Putting her in neutral, he asked for the anchor to be weighed. Reggie and Julius did this without a word, they and MacKenzie and Uncle Elias respectful and silent and anxious in the manner of a courtroom audience awaiting a jury's verdict. The gears were engaged once more; the *Teliai* nudged forward. Uncle Elias, going quietly to the helm, swung the bow out toward the notch in the reef, marked even on the calmest days by a constant line of surf. Barlow muttered that none of the gauges worked, "but if you buggers can't fix those, you don't deserve to run this boat," and then he bumped the throttle by degrees with the heel of his hand; the vessel picked up speed—two knots, they guessed, then three, four—and now her bow was throwing a wake.

"She's goin'! The old whore is goin'!" And Barlow let out a warbling cowboy yell as unexpected and in its way as stunning as his rage had been an hour earlier.

"All right, now let's see how she looks under sail—how about it, Uncle?" MacKenzie asked.

The old man regarded him with that standard islander expression, hostile in its vacancy, like the stare of a crocodile. Things had been cool between him and MacKenzie, whose refusal had opened a breach in their relations that wasn't going to be closed by anything but the elevation of his great-nephew to the post of deputy manager.

"Okay, we raise sail," he finally said.

Reggie and Julius hauled them out of the sail locker. Very much the captain now, Uncle Elias supervised the rigging—the main and mizzen gaffs fitted to the masts by gooseneck and gaff jaws, the sails' luffs to masts, heads to gaffs, feet to booms. The jib was clipped to the forestay, and then a bewildering tangle of sheets and halyards had to be sorted out and run through blocks, lead blocks, and cleats. Even with the old man showing them what to do, the rigging took an hour. When all was done to Uncle Elias's satisfaction, he stood by the helm and told them to get ready to make sail: Reggie and Julius to the main, MacKenzie and Barlow the mizzen.

"Haul away!" he said, and they all four grasped the halyards, the two sails creaking up the masts by the wooden mast hoops, to flap listlessly.

"David, raise the jib when the anchor free."

MacKenzie noted the absence of the affectionate "my boy" after his name and went forward. The *Teliai* fell off a little. Uncle Elias brought her bow into the wind so MacKenzie could raise the jib. He made it fast. The slap of luffing sails ceased as all sails filled, and what had been a construction of wood and fiberglass, brass and Dacron, became one living being that seemed to leap ahead for joy, her rigging humming faintly, her bow wave hissing, and her wake cutting a path of light froth in the green seas as the shoreline fell away.

At the helm, his lavalava rippled by the breeze, Uncle Elias checked the set of the sails, had them sheeted in as he pointed up.

"I feel her under my feet me," he said, more to himself than to anyone else. The impassive look fell from his face, and he blinked two or three times, gazing aloft.

"Ain't seen her lak this in twenny-five years. Ain't she pretty? Lak a bird she is."

Coming back in, with a proclamatory air, he said that *Teliai's* rebirth would be officially christened after church tomorrow. There would be a big feast and big dancing, just like for a tombstone unveiling—roast pig and rice, turtle and yams and cassava, dancing.

THE MORNING BEGAN with the customary island sounds of crowing cocks and laughing children, then church bells and venerable Protestant hymns sung in the lilt of pidgin. Dale slept through those, but she was startled awake by a hideous, almost supernatural shriek that rose in intensity for a full minute. MacKenzie, sitting by the marine radio with the headset over his ears, was attempting to conduct a patched-in phone conversation with Sergeant Mosby on Thursday Island. Difficult enough to have to say "Over" after every sentence without being half deafened by the screams of a pig being slaughtered.

"I hate that sound!" said Dale, shuffling into the kitchen in one of MacKenzie's old shirts and her cotton panties. She poured a cup of coffee. "I've seen it, I know it's necessary, and I hate it."

MacKenzie waved to her to be quiet. He'd seen it too and could see it now, two or three men holding the struggling animal down while Reggie Timao slashed its throat and then, squeezing its artery like the neck of a plastic ketchup bottle, squirted the blood into a bowl, the children looking on in silent excitement until the creature gave its last squeal.

He finished with Mosby, giving a farewell "Over and out" and then gazed vacantly at a pair of aboriginal spears hung crosswise on the bamboo-and-rattan wall above the radio.

"What was all that about?" Dale was in her robe now, sitting in a butterfly chair.

"Funnykind ting, like the old man would say. Mosby. Asked if Barlow was still in residence and could I make sure he doesn't leave for another twenty-four. Seems the coppers have more questions about the wreck."

"Well, you couldn't possibly get him on a plane before then anyway."

"Yair. Told him so, and then he says I ain't supposed to tell Barlow. That they want to talk to him some more. Just make sure he stays put."

She looked straight at him, with a brief flicker of . . . was it fear, or something else?

"He said not to worry, Barlow's no killer like his shipmate, but he wouldn't explain why the secrecy. I'll bet there was drugs on that boat."

He idly tapped the radio microphone. "Y'know, there's always been somethin' about that bloke that set me off. Got a flamin' violent temper sometimes, and a way of lookin' . . . Be glad when he's gone. How about you, luv?"

She fiddled with the knot in her robe and said, "To cut to the chase and set your mind at ease, I didn't fuck him while you were gone. Or while you're here."

"Wish I could say I'd blame you if you did."

"What a talent you've got for saying the wrong thing."

They didn't speak a word to each other during breakfast—a light one of toast and marmalade, because they knew they would be required to stuff themselves later on.

He was slipping into his cleanest pair of shorts when the marine radio operator summoned him again: another phone call. It was Morrison this time, ringing up from Cairns. He was coming in on the Industry Board's Cessna that afternoon. But it's Sunday, said MacKenzie, you ought to be back in Brisbane with the missus and the kids. Been in Cairns on business, thought I'd pop over for a friendly visit, check on how things are going, replied Morrison. MacKenzie did not believe that for a second. It couldn't be about his monthly report—he hadn't submitted it yet. Glad to have you. Wait till you see what we've done here— the impossible, he said, trying his best to sound carefree and enthused.

Down the shell-and-coral cobbled street he went, preoccupied, fretful, and irritable all at once, past a mango orchard where chopped turtle meat and guts steamed on a huge shell laid atop hot embers in an open-pit oven, while two men shoveled earth into another, the smell rising from it telling MacKenzie that it contained the butchered pig. Farther on, near Barlow's cottage, a band of ample women kneaded dough for fresh damper on a canvas tarpaulin.

He found Barlow bathing in the outdoor shower in the back, wearing a crown of shampoo lather. He made a startled hop, knocking a brown plastic bottle off the pallet beneath the shower.

"Christ, mate, don't you believe in knockin' first?"

There was something almost charming about the modest way he turned his back. MacKenzie picked up the bottle. Hydrogen peroxide. For disinfecting his burns, he supposed.

"Sorry. Was goin' to find out if you picked a destination yet."

"Lemme rinse off and get dressed first, for fuck's sake. And wait out front, unless you're some flamin' poofta."

Though it was said in a not entirely humorous way, MacKenzie laughed, then went around to the front.

Barlow came out in thongs and shorts, a towel draped over his head like an Arab's kaffiyeh.

"Auckland," he said, and with no suggestion that he was kidding.

Why didn't I realize that this guy was going to be an asshole about this? thought MacKenzie, his inner voice reverting to American idiom.

"Anywhere, Australia. That's the deal. Last look I had at the atlas, Auckland's in New Zealand."

"Figures it this way, Dave. Let's say I wanted to go to Perth. So it's here to Cairns, Cairns to Perth. More'n three thousand miles. Here to Brisbane, there to Auckland, it's about the same. Won't cost you no more."

"That's international, and it might. We'll see. Might take a little extra time to arrange, y'know."

He shrugged to say that that was all right.

"You're sure, now? All the way to New Zealand with the shirt on your back?"

The smile again. "And two fifty cash in me wallet. Wouldn't mind seein' that check before the day's over. I did one helluva job for you and these niggers."

"Save that kinda talk for Auckland, and don't use it in front of a Maori. Deal's a deal. Tell you what—I can spare fifty for your overtime, out of my own pocket."

Barlow leaned against the stone wall, tipped with the green of Spanish bayonet, and shook his head.

"Look—let's you and me get along for the next day or two. I want off this fuckin' rock, and I know you want me off."

MacKenzie questioned him with a look, and Barlow sidled up beside him, assuming a confidential, sincere, brotherly manner.

"It's Dale. You oughta take better care of her. I can bloody well smell a hungry woman, and she's sweet on me, I can tell by the way she'd give me them skin treatments. And me, out here, it ain't been easy, but I've behaved meself, respectin' you as a man. So"—and now the threatening glare—"it's two fifty, Dave."

MacKenzie normally would have reacted with fear or rage or a little of both; but instead, there poured into him that absolute, sure, tranquil murderousness he could not recall feeling in his veins since the war.

He put his right foot up on the wall, raising his shorts, and pointed to the four-inch ragged scar on his upper thigh.

"Y'know, I look at you, and I see a boy who's spent some time liftin' weights, a boy who's won him a couple of pub blues with drongos so inta the piss they can't stand on two legs, but one thing I learned in Vietnam is how to fight till one or the other's dead."

Barlow backed away a foot, smirking. "I'm in a flamin' fright, I am."

But MacKenzie closed the distance again. "You wanta have at it, we'll have at it here and now, and it'll be me dead or you, and if it's me, you're dead anyway, because my mates here, like Reggie, will get hold of you and . . . You heard that pig squealin' when it got its throat cut? Well, you oughta know that in the old days these island blokes called their human victims 'long pig.' " He saw that he had Barlow's full attention now. His hand darted like a snake and tweaked the broken nose. "Oink-oink. There'll be a fifty-dollar check waitin' for you at my place. See ya around, mate."

MORRISON'S PLANE landed at eleven-thirty. Flushed from his shining moment of glory in the face-off with Barlow, MacKenzie strode out onto the airstrip and grasped Morrison's hand and threw an arm over his shoulder and nudged him toward the waiting tractor.

"I want you ta see this. We got that old lugger shipshape, ready to go. We're gonna be in business."

Morrison irritably pulled MacKenzie's arm off and said stiffly, "I don't think I've got the time, Dave."

"What! You fly all the way out here on a Sunday and you ain't got the time?" MacKenzie jerked his thumb at the Cessna, which the pilot was refueling from the petrol drums with a hand pump. He figured it would help him, when the bean counters took a look at the books, if Morrison was impressed with all he'd accomplished. "C'mon, mate, think of the government funds you've spent gettin' out here. Got to make it worth taxpayers' money."

"The seriousness of this is indicated by the fact that I *have* flown all the way out here to talk to you in person—on a Sunday."

MacKenzie looked down on the small, hairless head, the cherubic face dappled with sweat, and wondered how Morrison could have discovered he'd diverted department funds against Tunstall's instructions.

"Okay, look. If it's about the money we've spent . . . We've done it, dammit! We've got a mother ship, a motor sailer, all fitted out and ready to go—"

"I don't know what you're talking about. Listen to me, Dave. You are in serious trouble if you don't have some good answers," Morrison said, nervously wiping his neck with a handkerchief. "I couldn't discuss any of this over a marine-band radio. I . . . Tunstall has gotten word that there've been repeated instances of you getting publicly drunk on this island. Is that true or not?"

"For Christ's sake . . ."

"These islanders are prohibited from buying so much as a stubby without a chit from their chairman, so what sort of example does it set if the board's representative here is into the piss? Now, is that true or not?"

The small man pursed his lips and stared straight up at MacKenzie.

"I've had a nip or two in the bungalow. That's private, but on an island this small, everything you do is public."

"To be specific, Dave: This past New Year's, you got quite drunk, you had a quarrel with Dale, and then you fired a revolver in the middle of the night, causing the islanders to think you had shot her. You claimed that you had fired at a rat. Did that happen or didn't it?"

Heat waves and petrol fumes came off the drum, veiling the pilot in swaying waves, and MacKenzie felt a little sick, realizing what had happened.

"This comes from Joseph, right?"

"Dammit, Dave . . ."

"Yair! All right, it happened! Seven months ago, and after—"

"Yes, yes," said Morrison, with an impatient wave. "After you had disrupted a Christmas party, I understand. Were you drunk then too?"

"I was bloody disgusted is what I was."

"What did I say about respecting their ways of doing things?"

"Don't talk to me like I'm a schoolboy."

"I think I'll speak to you as I see fit. Have you been drunk on island since then?"

"If I was, I was too drunk to remember," he said, too tired and used up to offer a defense—he'd overdrawn himself as well as the company's accounts this past month.

"Try not to self-destruct, Dave. Tunstall wants to give you the sack, but he asked me to talk to you to see if there's a reason not to. You haven't given me one so far."

MacKenzie moved out of the direct sunlight and leaned against one of the trees bordering the runway.

"You wanta know why Joseph told Tunstall this, seven months late? Because Uncle Elias told him to. And Uncle told him to because I wouldn't appoint his great-nephew, that Julius bloke, deputy manager of the factory. He wants Julius to be the boss when I leave, and I told him that's impossible, so out comes the knife in my back."

Morrison mopped his throat again and then the ripe, glimmering peach that was his skull.

"I'm not interested in petty island politics. Give me a reason to tell Tunstall that you should be kept on. I don't mean just here, either. I mean in government service."

"If you'd come with me, I'd show you one. In two months' time, we'll be shippin' twice as much outa here as we did. We'll be showin' a profit, you'll see, for the first time since this operation started."

"I'll pass that on to Tunstall. But I don't think it'll cut much ice with him. It barely does with me. Goodbye, Dave."

A few minutes later, MacKenzie watched the plane until it disappeared into the immense and desolate sky. He shuffled back toward the village, where smoke from the *kapmowrie* ovens rose. Drummers were practicing on their warups for the big dancing. How in Christ's name he was to take part in all that feasting with an untroubled face was beyond him. Also beyond him was how to tell Dale that he was as good as sacked, and that unless a way could be devised to conceal what he'd done with the funds, he could be more than sacked. He stopped suddenly, turned, and headed for the north beach, afraid that if he ran into Uncle Elias he would do or say something for which he would pay more than he was paying now. Punch the old bugger's lights out.

Quite a dressing-down, he thought, shambling between the greenish-black rows of tide wrack, and looked out toward the reach of sea, the foreign, glinting sea that offered no consolation. *Teliai* rode on the slow and silent swells that came in over the reef. All he'd wanted from this speck of coral and mangrove and sand was the chance to do something, to feel that he could make a difference. Perhaps he had made a little. It would be nice to think the islanders would remember him when they heard the lugger's diesel throb and saw her coming in under full sail, her hold bumper full. Damned nice, but not bloody likely. She'll probably be buggered up within a year, and the next bloke out will be battling with red ink and poor catches and all these impenetrable faces. He sat down with a cigarette and concentrated on summoning his powers of fakery.

A FLOTILLA of dinghies, each packed with fishermen and their families and riding low in the water, accompanied the launch out to the *Teliai*. The launch carried MacKenzie and Dale, a quiet, chastened Barlow, Uncle Elias and Joseph and Julius and Reggie Timao. MacKenzie eased up to the lugger's bow and shut off the engine. Julius hopped aboard and tied the launch's painter to the *Teliai*'s anchor winch.

"You'll do the honors, luv, but if you don't mind . . . it's a special occasion, right?"

He tipped the champagne bottle to his mouth and took a good long satisfying pull, rationalizing that it would help him maintain his untroubled front, and then he recorked the bottle and passed it to her. She swung hard but failed to break it, swung again, and again it didn't break.

"Too much still in it, I reckon," he said, and indulged himself another belt.

"Damn you." She snatched it from his hand and shattered it with one swift blow, throwing bubbly over herself and Barlow and Uncle Elias.

The sails were raised, the engine was started, the anchor weighed, and the *Teliai* made a triumphant tour of the lagoon, attended by the fleet of dinghies, whose passengers banged oars and harpoons rhythmically on the gunwales. Uncle Elias brought the lugger in as close to the shore as he dared, presenting her to the rest of the population, who cheered and whistled and stamped their feet to songs their ancestors must have sung, welcoming home a triumphant party of war canoes.

Ashore, the official dancing began in the mango orchard. The men danced first in their lavalavas and palm-leaf skirts, and then the women, and the men again, the slow, hollow notes of the warup accompanied by the faster thudding of empty petrol drums, the insistent clacking of bamboo palaga sticks, the dancers' bodies wreathed in the smoke from the *kapmowrie* ovens. It went on all afternoon and into the evening, under the glare of a floodlight hooked to a generator and in the flicker of small bonfires. The warup beat on and on, steady as a heart.

The young women began a dance in honor of the sea; they in their pale-blue dresses moved like waves, rose and fell like swells, while the fans of white heron feathers in their hands imitated the roll and leap of surf, the warup beaten by Moses Crossman never ceasing its measured *thud-thud-ta-thud*. It created a hypnotic intoxication, and sitting cross-legged in the front row between Dale and Barlow, MacKenzie watched his wife begin to sway her head in time with the waving fans. He was more conventionally intoxicated, or nearly so, from clandestine nips of the methylated spirits that had been his predecessor's downfall. Bottles of the illegal hooch were hidden in the bushes, their location kindly pointed out to him by one of Moses' children. It helped him to pretend that he was having a good time.

When the dance stopped, great bowls of turtle and pig and dugong were brought out to a long plywood table supported on sawhorses and petrol drums. There was a rush at the table, a mad yet somehow orderly thrusting of hands and arms at the meat and cassava, the coconut and yams, the spirals of baked turtle guts. MacKenzie thought he should eat something, before the effects of the alcohol became apparent, but he found, as he moved away from the press with Dale, that he had very little appetite. And she, sitting down on a bench and attacking the heaping plate in her lap, asked him what was wrong.

"Think the gut's a bit off," he said, with a fake wince and a palm on his belt.

"Too bad. Ain't had tucker like this in an age," Barlow said, diving in.

"Fact is, I'd better take a quick trip to the loo."

He walked off and ducked into the darkness behind the bushes, where two other reprobates were sharing swigs.

"Thanks, mates, don't mind if I do."

He took the pint bottle, and the brew scalded down his windpipe; another shot made something pop in his brain like a camera flash. Clarity. He walked unsteadily back into the orchard, a tingling in his toes.

"Ain't no good ting, goin' back there, David, my boy."

He stared red-eyed into the old face that was the color of maple syrup.

"Lissen me. Been tinkin'. That Barlow pella . . ."

"Fuck Barlow. Y'know Morrison paid me a call today," he said, forcing his speech.

"Sure know."

"You're about the most ungrateful son of a bitch I've ever known,

Uncle. And a back-stabbing bastard to boot." The warup had started again. The men were lining up for a bow-and-arrow dance. "We'll have us a talk tomorrow. Don't wanta spoil the party."

The men had taken up their long bows, each with its painted arrow, and now the warup was joined by the clacking of palaga sticks, the clacks timed to simulate the shooting of an arrow as the bows were drawn in mock combat. Rejoining Dale and Barlow to watch, MacKenzie speared a chunk of cold turtle meat, and nearly choked on it.

"David, are you all right? Maybe you've got—" Her hand rose to touch his forehead; he brushed it away.

"Just a touch o' the runs, luv. It's good, purges the system," he said, loudly, over the drumming, the dancers' grunts. "Helps you to think clearer. That's all I'm tryin' to do, y'know. See things clear. And I have had an insight. Care to hear it?"

She looked alarmed.

"How about you, Anson?"

Barlow made some indeterminate motion. Warup and palaga pounded and clicked; sweat-slicked bodies advanced, turned in rhythm, advanced again; arrows were drawn.

"Here it is. The heart—I mean the art—the art of livin' is the art of not seein' things too clear. If everybody shaw—saw—things for what they are, I . . . it is my firm belief that . . ."

The choreography was so perfect that bodies before him seemed to merge into one single body.

"What the hell ish—is—my firm belief? Oh, yeah, if everybody saw things the way they are, nobody could get through a single day . . ."

He swayed slightly, caught his balance.

"Shplendid sh—sight, eh? A barbaric sh—sple—ndor. Think I'll join in. . . ."

Dale grabbed his sleeve as he lurched toward the dancers. He shoved her aside, hard, and was vaguely aware that she would have fallen if Barlow hadn't caught her. He leaped in at the end of the first line of dancers, the biggest men in the village, anchored by Reggie Timao, the biggest of all and a fearsome sight in his crocodile mask, brandishing his six-foot bow. MacKenzie tried to mimic the intricate steps, tried to open himself to the warup and allow its beat to become one with his own heart and command his feet and legs to move in cadence—but such syncopation would have been difficult if he were sober and was impossible in his current state. Some of the children in the audience were laughing at his ridiculous movements, but the adults were not—he saw their blank, unintelligible faces staring at him. The dancers, all as one except for him, crossed their ankles and made a quick turn; MacKenzie tripped over himself and fell on his side. Someone grabbed his arms, someone else his ankles, and he watched a cloud of sparks from one of the fires twinkle overhead as he was roughly carried off and dumped under a tree. A bucket of cold salty water was tossed in his face, and then another. He sat up, sputtering.

"That's what I do onetime my crew when they drunk and making fools theirselves," Uncle Elias said. "You go home now, David, my boy. Missus plenny angry her wi' you."

The water hadn't done much to sober him. He sat there alone for some minutes, then embraced the tree trunk and pulled himself to his feet and vomited. That did him some good. Through the trees and in the ring of electric and firelight, the audience sat enraptured by the dancers, who moved backward, turning their heads one side to the other, then drew their bows and advanced, with the precision of a marching band, to warup and palaga. Not ten yards away, MacKenzie felt as distant as if he were watching a *National Geographic Special,* filmed by some intrepid cameraman. Yankee Jim had come to know them and to become one with them. What was his secret? he wondered. Shouldn't have left the mainland. Now that I think of it, shouldn't have left Massachusetts. Coming slowly to himself, he looked around for Dale but couldn't find her. Barlow wasn't around, either, and that absence had the effect the cold water should have had.

He hurried to the cottage, found it empty, and then went on to his bungalow, climbed the steps, and called for her. There was no answer, no sound of any kind from within. He was slightly relieved to find the bedroom unoccupied—at least she had the decency not to betray him in their own bed. He could let this go, like everything else, until tomorrow, but the lurid pictures that leaped in his imagination wouldn't allow it. Nor would the conviction that he'd suffered enough indignities for one day. Reaching into the drawer of his bedside table, he pulled out the Ruger .22, loaded five chambers with rat shot—the only ammunition he had—and shoved the gun into his back pocket with a penlight.

In a few minutes, he was walking quickly down the south beach toward the wongai grove. A long way to go for a tryst, and a bit dangerous, what with the chance of stumbling across a croc, but certainly private. The flashlight showed him their footprints, and while he was no expert tracker, he judged that Dale had gone ahead and Barlow had followed her. Had they arranged it that way to make sure no one saw them together? Why bother, when they knew everyone was at the feast? No matter. He wouldn't touch Dale, for he truly could not blame her. He'd been awful tonight. Barlow was a different matter. Damned if he was going to be cuckolded by a drongo off a prawn boat.

He'd gone another hundred yards or so when he began to wonder if he ought to suspect Dale at all: Barlow's footprints became wider-spaced, the toes digging in, the heels barely leaving a mark. The bastard was chasing her!

As he came around a point marked by the skeleton of a dead-fallen tree, he saw Dale, alone, stumbling toward him. He ran to her. Her hair was disheveled, her blouse ripped, and a mark of some kind was on her shoulder, another on her right cheek. He grabbed her by both arms.

"Let go of me!"

She tried to spin away, but he held on with one hand and with the other shone the light on her face, the mark there showing as a purple bruise about the span of a man's fist.

"What the hell did he do to you?"

"Nothing! Let go of me!" she said, sobbing.

"What did the bastard do, goddamn it!"

She pushed his chest, clutched at his fingers, digging into his palm with her nails.

"I'll kill the bastard, swear I will—"

"Go ahead! I hope you both kill each other!"

She stomped his foot as hard as she could and then ran off, toward the bungalow. He didn't pursue but stood watching her figure recede into the darkness. Switching off the light, he continued on down the beach, following the footprints now by starlight, not hurriedly but at a curious calm, deliberate pace. After a quarter of a mile, he spotted Barlow, sitting atop a rock at the sea's edge and tossing pebbles into the water. Just the thing to do after assaulting another man's wife. With rat shot he would have to shoot point-blank, so he quickly dodged up the beach to conceal his movements in the shadows of the trees—that rank of romantic, rustling palms. He was in the war again, an armed man stalking in the humid night. When he came even with the rock, he cut back into the open, coming up on Barlow from behind, but then Barlow leaped off and began walking along the shoreline, toward the village. No element of surprise now.

"Barlow!"

Barlow stopped and, leaning his head forward, looked toward him.

"That you, Dave?"

"Who'd you think?" he said, hoping his voice did not betray his intentions. "Thought I'd walk it off."

He approached with what he hoped looked like a normal, casual gait. Six feet would do it, no farther than that.

"Ain't seen Dale, have you?"

"Nah. She was in a flamin' snit at you, y'know."

Barlow wasn't bad at feigning, either, MacKenzie thought, and when he figured he was close enough, he reached into his back pocket for the Ruger's grip and pulled. The front sight caught on his pocket. With a jerk, he freed it, but the hesitation had been just long enough to alert Barlow, who instead of running, as MacKenzie would have expected, lunged and tackled him. Falling against a small rock that jolted his spine and took his wind, MacKenzie realized what a mistake he'd made earlier in the day. Until then, Barlow had been contemptuous of him. He should have left him to his contempt, for Barlow wasn't the type who ran from a serious threat—he eliminated it.

Barlow pressed flat against him, grasping for the revolver, which MacKenzie had somehow hung on to.

"Jesus Christ, MacKenzie! You fuckin' nuts?"

With both hands, Barlow clasped the wrist of MacKenzie's gun hand. The Ruger went off, the shot splattering sand beyond his head somewhere, and then Barlow stunned him with a punch to the forehead. He arched his back, trying to throw the bigger man off. Barlow's fist rose again. MacKenzie somehow sensed that it held a rock, just before it came down full onto his mouth, and he began choking on blood and broken teeth.

"Me dead or you dead, huh?" Barlow grunted.

He struck MacKenzie again with the rock, this time above his right eye. His muscles relaxed, all resistance draining out of him, and a dreamy, morphine-like lassitude came over him.

"Didn't do a thing ta her she didn't ask for—I want you to know that, you bastard."

Barlow's voice sounded far off. He couldn't see anything, could only feel the pressure of Barlow's knees pinning his arms and then the bite of the Ruger's muzzle against his temple.

LISSEN ME some sea talk. Always speak me true.

Uncle Elias sat by his shed, under the Malabar almond, and kept his inner ear open to the sea that at the fullness of the tide reached to within a few yards of his feet, the small waves on the lagoon multiplying the sparkle of the stars. The ears in his head were filled with the sounds of the dancing, half a mile away. It would go on all night, and some would be dancing and drumming into the morning, their spirits carried away so that their bodies would not feel tired. Warup and palaga made a fine sound, a sound of joy, which he didn't share at the moment, bothered as he was about David. Possibly he had overstepped his bounds, hoping to get David replaced by someone who would be more tractable to his plans, and he waited to hear if the mother who had nurtured and sustained him and his people since before the Beforetime had any counsel to offer. As he waited, he became aware of someone nearby. A man was running up the beach, beyond the reach of his vision, but he sensed the presence as he always sensed things in these meditative moments, without hearing or seeing or smelling. In a few moments, the man appeared, pale in the darkness, with long hair that streamed from his head like moonlight. Just like a markai he looked, but this ghost carried over his shoulder a plastic sack like a tucker bag and in one hand a plastic jug. He tossed jug and sack into a dinghy, which he began to pull toward the water. Uncle Elias stood up and called:

"Hey, Barlow there, what doin' you? That ain't dinghy bilong you."

He saw that his voice startled Barlow, and he did not need the sea to tell him that there was some very big trouble. He reached into his shed for his turtle harpoon, the one with the detachable iron head that had been invented by Yankee Jim himself. Thus armed, he walked cautiously toward the dinghy.

"What doin' you, Barlow?" he asked again.

"Hullo there, Uncle. The engine . . . I was just goin' to take a run out to the lugger. . . . See, there's somethin' I want to check out in that engine, and . . . Figured it would be okay if I borrowed a dinghy for a little while. . . ."

"Ain't okay. Dinghy there bilong me."

Things were not clear to his old eyes in the darkness, but he saw stains all over Barlow's singlet.

"Well, good, then. You can come on out with me. Fact is, you was just the man I was hopin' to see."

"What for?"

Barlow came slowly around from the bow, lit a cigarette, and in the flare of his lighter Uncle Elias saw the nature of the stains, and he backed away a foot or two, giving himself room to throw—if he still could.

"Was wonderin' how long it might take that lugger to get to Thursday, now that she's runnin' good."

"Full sail, with her engine helpin'—full day, full night."

"And you know these waters pretty damn well, I hear."

"Friend to all waters me."

He backed off another foot, but Barlow was much too young and fast for him. In an instant, he had Uncle Elias from behind, one arm around his throat while he held a revolver to his head. There was only one Uncle Elias knew of on the island, so this trouble was much bigger than any he'd thought.

"And I'll take that," said Barlow, ripping the harpoon from his hand. "You and me're goin' on a little cruise, Uncle. Get in the dinghy, face the bow, and keep your hands behind your head."

"You need full crew, tucker, water—"

"Already seen to the tucker and the water. We'll just have to make do, the two of us."

"David, the missus . . ."

Barlow jabbed him in the back with the harpoon.

" 'Ope you're too old to be scared of dyin', 'cause dead is what you'll be you don't get your black ass in that fuckin' boat."

He climbed in, surprised to discover that he was afraid of death—at least of death at this man's hands—and sat as he'd been instructed. Maybe he feared dying because he wanted to live to see if things would turn out as he hoped for his island. Barlow shoved them off, cranked the outboard, and they cut across the lagoon toward the barely visible silhouette of the *Teliai*.

THEY CLEARED THE REEF outside the lagoon, under power; then Barlow tied Uncle Elias to the wheel and raised the sails himself—a strong young man to be able to haul the main without help. Some five or six hours later, as the last stars were losing light and the sky was turning the color of pearl shell, the lugger was making four or five knots in a moderate breeze. Astern, the dinghy slewed a little in the wake, drawn as a line is drawn across the dark-green passage between the Warrior Reefs.

Uncle Elias had persuaded Barlow to free his hands; these were treacherous waters, and he couldn't steer tied up. He'd hoped Barlow would fall asleep, but the young man had stayed vigilant throughout the night, leaning against the taffrail with the point of the harpoon pressed into Uncle Elias's spine. It was there now.

"Don't need that harpoon, y'know," said Uncle Elias. "Old pella lak me ain't gonna try anything with young pella got a gun."

"This suits me okay. You just keep steady on, mate. How far we come, you reckon?"

"Thirty mile maybe. After midnight, we there."

"How the fuck you know where you're goin'? Ain't even taken the cover off the compass."

"Don't need it. Friend to all these waters."

Perhaps something in his voice had betrayed him, perhaps Barlow was enough of a seaman to see that the brightest part of the slowly brightening sky was abaft their starboard beam instead of to port, where it should have been for a run to Thursday. Uncle Elias felt the sharp pressure on his back relieved as Barlow pulled the cover off the binnacle and looked.

"You got lousy friends, old man. Thursday's west by south o' Nettles. You're bearing west by north, y'know that?"

Well, Barlow would have discovered the trick sooner or later.

"Sure know," said Uncle Elias.

"What the fuck're you up to?"

"Tink me you mean to shoot me soon as we raise T.I., so I sail inta these waters. You kill me here, Barlow my boy, no time you wreck up steerin' you yourself." He gestured at the surf boiling on the reefs to the north and south. "And this time, you ain't gone ta be rescued, 'cause all these reefs, these islands here, ain't got nobody on 'em."

"Ain't you the clever nigger, though." Barlow flung down the harpoon and, still holding the revolver, grabbed at the wheel with his free hand. "You turn this boat around, you black bastard, or I'll blow you away!"

Uncle Elias didn't move.

"I said, turn the fuckin' thing around!"

Barlow pressed the revolver under his ear. Uncle Elias wondered if he'd miscalculated. Barlow might be desperate enough to try anything, even take the lugger through the Strait single-handed.

"Lissen me now. Doin' good ting by you, not takin' you Thursday. I tink coppers waitin' there por you por sure," said Uncle Elias, playing his other, and even riskier, card.

"What're you sayin'?"

"You the pella they lookin' por. The Yank pella. Norgate, ain't you? Pella got two names, but no Anson Barlow you. I know that, coppers know that by now. Lissen me good, Norgate, Northfield, whatever name you got. See me that woman detective, goin' back inside, take the soda you drinkin' prom, put inta purse bilong her. Wonderin' what por. Ask Julius me, em smart boy, tells me that por fingerprints, tell 'em coppers por sure who a pella is, who he ain't. Maybe coppers on Nettles right now. I myself hear myself, what we call coconut telegraph, that they comin' back talk ta you some more. Lissen me good, Uncle speak you true."

"Fingerprints? Off the Coke I was drinkin'?"

"Speak you true."

"What makes you think I'm Northfield?"

Uncle Elias thought the young man sounded scared.

"I myself hear you say 'truck' 'stead of 'lorry.' Same lak David do sometime, same lak my relations in U.S.A. Know Yankee you. Maybe you change the way you look, maybe you change your name, lak woman detective says, but you Northfield por true."

"You oughtta been a detective yourself, old man. Worked on this accent so bloody long and hard I couldn't talk like a Yank now if I wanted to, but I reckon I slip up sometimes. That bitch didn't decide to get me prints because of somethin' you said, did she, Uncle?"

"No. I lay low."

"Good on ya." Northfield withdrew the muzzle and resumed his post at the taffrail. "Where you headin'?"

"Boigu."

"What the fuck is Boigu?"

"Plenny big island over by Saibai, over by Papua, same distance Nettles lak Thursday, but the other way and better place por you. No coppers. Boigu island where spirits o' dead pellas go when they proper dead, but don't you worry. Won't bother you them spirits there. Proper dead."

Northfield grabbed the back of his lavalava and jerked his head back. The lugger veered two points off course, and the sails began to luff.

"What the hell mumbo-jumbo are you givin' me? You got charts on this piece-o'-shit boat, or don't you need *them,* either?"

Uncle Elias told him there were charts in the deckhouse. Northfield started toward the hatch, remembered he'd left the harpoon on deck, retrieved it, and then went in.

"This is it?" he asked, unrolling a chart stained with mildew. He held it in front of Uncle Elias's face, his thumb on the island that almost corked the mouth of the Mai River in Papua.

"Boigu that. Bilong Australia. Ain't just spirits there. Live pellas too, 'em know Uncle Elias. Trade with 'em sometimes in the old times. Pearl shell, bêche-de-mer. Pellas there Boigu don't lak gov'ment much, hide you good and proper, but I myself got ta go ashore wi' you, speak them me por you."

This was almost a total lie, but Uncle Elias knew he might need to buy time once they reached their destination.

"That all right wi' you, Northfield, my boy?" he asked, keeping his line of vision on the bowsprit, gently dipping and rising in the swells.

"Reckon it'll have to be," came the voice from behind him.

"So who this Anson Barlow pella? I tink myself maybe other deckie em on that prawner. One name you Norgate."

"You're a smart old black bugger, you are."

"How you mak your picture that driver's license wi' name him?"

"Just keep steerin', Uncle."

Northfield was silent for a time. Uncle Elias held the wheel steady, listening to the bow wash, the wind sounds in the masts and stays.

"Me and Barlow was in on somethin' together, but he didn't know I was in on somethin' all by meself," Northfield said suddenly. "It was like this. Yeah, I changed my looks. Way back when, some mates of mine put me onto this quack who fixed up me face. Ha! Give me this pretty nose I got now. And I kept me hair bleached and had this put on to hide me scar." He pointed to the tattoo under his singlet. "But I was always lookin' over me shoulder, waitin' to get snatched up, and I was damned tired of it. There ain't no statute of limitations for murder, even of a 'hore. And I'm still wanted Stateside by the FBI for desertin' and murder. 'Johnny, boy, time you get a fresh start in life,' I said to meself. So when I run inta Barlow in Karumba and I see the bloke's about the same height as me and only four, five years younger, I figure, shit, all I gotta do is get hold of his license and get somebody to paste me picture on it, nice and realistic like, and then find some way to get rid of 'im, but make it so the cops will think he's me. Nicked his wallet after I got 'im good and drunk one night. Knew a bloke who makes forgeries of licenses and that other stuff. Lotta blokes in Karumba need those services. Did it for me in a night, by the time Barlow wakes up and is sober, he's got his license back, none the wiser. Me and him, we was gonna take off Cap'n Wharton. Runnin' a drug deal, he was, off Cape York. Gettin' fifty thousand on delivery. So after the stuff was loaded, we killed him, weighted 'im down and sent 'im to the bottom and hijacked the prawner . . ."

"David, em tink first time you pellas runnin' drugs."

"Yeah? Good on 'im. So we was headin' south for Cairns when that nor'wester hit. Lost our engine when a bilge pump blew, flooded the engine room. We got it pumped out, most of it, but drifted for a couple of days. Got caught in one of these currents, I reckon. Threw the bales overboard in case we did get rescued and towed in. Broke me heart to see 'em floatin' out there—fifty thousand dollars floatin' away. Well, we never did see another vessel. Driftin' around like that gave me plenty of time to figure out what to do and to come up with a good story. Y'know, Uncle, livin' the way I 'ave the last twelve years, you learn to think ahead. So I reckoned to do Barlow and fake a shipwreck and get meself ashore somewhere where there was people. I wasn't goin' to say that Barlow was Northfield and that I knew everything about him. No. That wouldn't sound realistic. I figured to just let on that he 'ad a scar on his chest and that he talked kinda funny sometimes and that he went by the name of Norgate. I knew that somebody would notify the coppers when I come driftin' in with me story and that they'd check things out and that that name and the description would set off an alarm somewheres. I'd let the coppers think that they'd figured out who Norgate was all by themselves. And that's just about what happened, wasn't it, old man?"

"Just about, but that only near enough—and near enough, that ain't enough," said Uncle Elias. "'Em detectives suspectin' you straight away. So they get your fingerprints."

Northfield waved his hand, as if to say that those suspicions had been only a minor glitch in his brilliant plan.

"Anyways, after we been driftin' for almost three days, I checked our loran coordinates on the chart, and seen we're about twenty miles off

Darnley. I knew there was a settlement on Darnley. Figured it was time to make me move. Gave Barlow a nice tap on the head with a pipe wrench when he wasn't lookin'. Took his driver's license out of his wallet, put my old one in. First, I thought I'd just toss 'im overboard, let him wash up somewheres, but, always thinkin' ahead . . ." With a proud smile, Barlow raised a forefinger to his temple. "I figured, what if he washes up before his body's had time to rot or the sharks and the barracudas 'ave taken a few big chunks out of him? He'd be too easy to identify, and if some doctor did an autopsy, he'd see straight away that Barlow died of a blow to the head. So I dragged him down to the engine room because I was goin' to say he got electrocuted there. Now I figured that once my story was out, the coppers would ask the Coast Guard to try to raise that vessel, or send divers down to it, and I *wanted* them to find me shipmate in it. By the time they got around to that, he'd be such a mess that his own mother wouldn't be able to identify him. And if somebody took the trouble to find the crack in his skull, well, they'd probably think he got that when he fell after gettin' electrocuted. So what they'd 'ave is this six-foot dead bloke with Jack Norgate's driver's license on him, and that would be that. Case closed. Was goin' to start fresh, I was."

"I chopped a hole in the bottom of the prawner and got in the life raft and watched her sink. I hung around out there for a day, goin' over in me mind everything Barlow told me about himself. He was a great talker, Barlow was. Besides, I wanted to look like a shipwrecked bloke, good and sunburned, half dead of thirst. Wouldn't let meself drink any water. Makes me thirsty just thinkin' about it." Northfield paused to drink now from the water bottle. "When I couldn't stand it no more, I cranked up the outboard, but ha! There wasn't enough petrol in the bloody can to get me twenty miles. Not even ten. Had to row and then lost the oar, and then—these goddamned currents you've got out 'ere—I couldn't paddle against 'em with one oar. I was adrift again. Don't know 'ow long. Reckon that made things look more realistic than I'd planned."

One question now was fully settled in Uncle Elias's mind. Northfield was going to kill him no matter where they made landfall; he would not have told him that story if he didn't mean to.

"David, em dead em?"

"Tried to kill me with this in my hand 'ere. Thought I'd fucked his old lady."

"David, em plenny jealous pella. Tink onetime Julius givin' his missus a good one."

"Well, he ain't jealous no more. Steer, Uncle. Steer and shut up."

He steered on, beset by a bewildering mix of emotions. He was sorry for David, though he knew that David had been killed by his jealous temper as much as by Northfield. He was especially sorry for the missus, all alone now, and a desire to avenge her loss rose in him like a flame. And yet—Uncle Elias had to admit to this feeling—he was glad things had come to this. That Holbrooke pella going crazy, David murdered—maybe now he could convince Tunstall and Morrison not to send another white pella but to let Julius take David's place. There was a good reason to live! He had to think of a way to save himself.

Lay low, like Br'er Fox, the sea counseled him. But don't lay low too long.

By midmorning, the breeze freshened to perhaps fifteen knots, a nor'easter that sent the *Teliai* clipping on a beam reach, and the sails taut and the bow tossing spray—Uncle Elias figured they were at her maximum hull speed, six to seven knots. By sundown he had Adrian Reef off his port bow.

His old body couldn't take the standing and steering any longer—a young man would have been exhausted by such a trip without sleep—and indeed Northfield was fighting to stay awake. Uncle Elias gave him a course—north by west till he saw a big island rising to starboard: that would be Mount Cornwallis.

"When you see that, you come wake me, Northfield, my boy. I got to be full awake bring her inta Boigu. Plenny shoals there."

Northfield tied his hands again. He fell into his old bunk inside the deckhouse, thinking he would not be able to sleep, but he was unconscious almost immediately. Only a few minutes seemed to have passed when he heard Northfield thumping on the deckhouse bulkhead with the butt of the harpoon. He rose, shook the sleep from his head, and went on deck. Under the arch of stars, the dark hump of Cornwallis was slipping past their starboard beam. Northfield untied him and asked, in a voice drugged with exhaustion:

"How much farther?"

"Twenny mile. Three hours maybe."

Tinkin' the right way that first night, Uncle Elias said to himself as he checked the constellations, in their slow, slow wheeling across the sky.

Em markai, em tak name o' pella not proper dead, Barlow. Em lak ghost he is, wanderin' around, and only one ting to do wi' markai so it don't go wanderin' and makin' trouble. For the first time since leaving Nettles, Uncle Elias felt he had at least a chance. The nap had refreshed his mind, and he'd remembered something Northfield had told Sergeant Mosby—he couldn't swim.

The Southern Cross was high when Boigu showed dead ahead, a low lump of blackness blacker than the surrounding waters, and froth boiling over one of the shoals that guarded the south side of the island. He sailed on, keeping the island to starboard, watching for the far western tip of the island to appear, if he could see it. Low tide now. The wide shoals called the Red Sands would be visible, marked by surf and heaving groundswells. He would have to run in just right, run it as well as he'd ever run anything in his life. He would make a quick tack and sail her in as close to the wind as he could bring her, straight into the wind at the last moment, so she wouldn't grind into the shoal and bury her keel and make it impossible to float off when the tide filled.

David em gone prom Nettles now, missus she ain't gonna stay, this pella em soon gone too, I hope.

"Hey, you, Barlow, you can see that island good?"

"Yeah."

"You speak me when you don't see it no more. That when we got ta anchor up. We gone ta land in the dinghy."

They sailed on another half hour or so. Barlow craned his neck, peering into the night.

"Think that's it. Think it's past."

"Okay, got ta tack now us," said Uncle Elias, and instructed him how to handle the jib.

"Hard alee!"

The jib flew free, the sail backed a little, began to fill, and Barlow sheeted it home, and now they were bearing almost due north on a close reach. Not close enough, though. Uncle Elias brought the *Teliai* up another point and told Northfield to trim jib and main for close-hauled.

"Now lissen me good, my boy. You go up forward, get set to drop anchor. You see big groundswells, any surf, you call out loud, y'hear?"

"Wha . . . wha . . . ?"

He was practically asleep on his feet.

"Up forward. The anchor! Drop it when you hear me say so!"

"You drop it . . . Old bugger, don't try anything with me—"

"Quick, damn you, my boy! Or we gone run aground! Quickly now!"

Northfield, bent over to grasp the handrails atop the deckhouse, staggered toward the foredeck. Uncle Elias started the engine and sheeted in the jib a little more. He hoped he wouldn't shear the prop or bend the shaft; he would need the engine to make the voyage home single-handed. He could not see Northfield any longer through the sails and rigging. The lugger was hauling in as fast as she could go, heeling hard to lee, and then he heard the cry:

"Shoal ahead! Dead ahead!"

He held firm to the wheel, bent his knees to brace himself.

"Shoal!" Barlow shouted.

And then a sharp, jolting thud as her prow knifed into the sands, Uncle Elias falling against the wheel, and the lugger driving on, grinding, groaning, cracking. Oh, pretty bird, hate to hurt lak this. He shoved the throttle forward for a moment, pulled it back, then brought her dead into the wind while she still had a little water under her. The sails flapped wildly, like huge and ghostly wings in the darkness. As suddenly as if she'd struck a wall, the vessel stopped with a shuddering that went through her whole length. Knocked backwards, Uncle Elias heard a cry from the foredeck but did not hear a splash. The swells bumped into the *Teliai's* weather side, rocking her as she grounded. Sails, and loose rigging, and swinging booms and gaffs made a racket. Northfield was hollering and cursing, but still from up forward, not from overboard.

Picking up the harpoon, Uncle Elias crept along the deck between the gunwale and the deckhouse, crouching low, summoning up the spirit of Kebisu, he whose arrows could pierce the hulls of the blackbirders' ships, he whose bones his own hands had touched. He had fought in his share of blues when he was young, but he'd never killed a man, never had even tried.

Northfield was hanging from the bowsprit by both hands, frantically kicking his legs in an attempt to swing himself back aboard. Dragging the harpoon, the old man went up on his hands and knees, past the capstan, and then stood, spreading his legs to keep his balance. Northfield wasn't more than six feet away and a yard below, his feet flailing comically at the air, his hair streaming back in the breeze. Got to be with me now, Uncle Elias thought, raising the harpoon with both hands. Northfield looked up, but Uncle Elias could not hear the sound coming from his throat or see the expression on his face. He rose onto his toes and thrust, with all the strength left in him, and watched the harpoon bury itself in Northfield's chest. Northfield gave one last, spastic kick, then let go of the bowsprit, the harpoon's shaft sticking straight in the air before his body rolled over in the swells and drifted away.

Markai. Proper dead now. At the turn, he would be carried into Boigu, proper place of the dead.

Uncle Elias sat down on the foredeck and waited for the tide to rise.

IN THE FOREST OF
THE LAUGHING
ELEPHANT

THEY HAD BEEN SIX, now they were five, and none of them could see the sun. Three of the men, standing on one side of a deep, fast river, were looking up at the forest canopy, thick as thatch but green and wet and higher overhead than any thatch roof could be. A hundred feet at least, maybe two. Above it hung a dense ceiling of monsoon clouds. Turning their heads quickly side to side, like bird-watchers trying to spot some rare and elusive parrot, the men looked for the sun, the guiding light. They had no idea where they were.

Neither did the fourth man, who was on the other side of the river; but he was not trying to find the sun. Sitting naked at one end of the rope-and-plank bridge from which he'd jumped, attempting to rescue the radioman, he was wringing out his wet clothes. His rifle and his rucksack, lumpy with rations and coiled rope and other gear, lay on the grass where he'd tossed them before he'd leaped after his radioman, who had fallen from the bridge and went twirling and tumbling down the river like a broken branch.

The fifth man squatted nearby. He was the smallest and dressed only in shorts, sandals, and a cork helmet that had once been green but was now faded almost to white. It was difficult to tell his age, because his skin, the color of slightly overdone toast, was deeply creased on his face but as smooth and taut as a youth's on his arms and torso. He himself did not know how old he was in years; he had no idea what a year was. He measured his life by the rises and falls of the sun, the phases of the moon, the rhythms of the two seasons, wet and dry. His name was Han, and he was a hill tribesman and a hunter, a very good one. A quiver bristling with arrows hung from his belt, a leather pouch filled with krait poison from his neck, and a crossbow lay in his lap. It had been his father's—a beautiful weapon carved from mahogany, its stock bearing his father's talisman: three rings cut with a tiger's tooth and inlaid with mother-of-pearl. The three rings held the tiger's power. Han had killed more deer and birds with the crossbow than he could remember; with it and its arrows tipped in the venom of the krait, he had killed Tiger three times and Panther five. He rubbed the mother-of-pearl as he squatted, waiting for the tall *trung-si* to finish drying his clothes. Like him, Han was not looking for the sun; unlike him, he knew where he was.

The tall man stood and gave his trousers a last twist before putting them on. His black hair was cut very short—it looked as if a three-day growth of beard had migrated from his face to his skull—and the sooty wings of a luxuriant mustache swooped under his long, narrow nose. From the waist up, his body appeared to have been painted, so sharp were the lines between his browned arms, face, and neck and the white of his shoulders and chest. It was a sickly white, a pallor suggesting malaria or dengue, but Lincoln Coombes was far from sickly. The muscles in his abdomen were as ribbed as beach sand after a tide's run out, while those in his arms were long and tightly braided. He'd killed several men in hand-to-hand combat; he'd strangled them or broken their necks or crushed their skulls with blows from a rifle butt.

He tucked in his shirt, aligning the buttons with the buckle of his web belt, his movements slow and mechanical, as though he were just learning to dress himself. *Don't rush things,* he said silently as he looked into the forest, where vines hung in the shadowy, twisting corridors between the trees like electrical conduit in some unfinished construction project. He was not gazing idly but in a way meditating upon the forest's infinite patience, and trying to draw with each breath some of that patience into himself, for in that fecund world, time wasn't measured by man's petty instruments of gears and jewels, but by nature's clocks. The forest did things at its own slow, inexorable pace; some of its great trees had been saplings when Columbus sailed from Spain. *Don't rush things; be like the forest.*

He had been. Until last night, he had learned to live outside time, like the tiger, like Han. Yes, his military calling required him to keep a watch and maintain certain schedules, but he had freed himself from *caring* what day or month or even year it was. This land of jungles old as the earth had been the ally of his liberation. Its temporal landscape was barren of prominent features, its weeks unmarked by Sabbaths; its numberless years had names like Pig, Snake, and Monkey, the names repeating themselves in an endless cycle, and its two seasons joined like the halves of a circle, each day of the Dry fusing into the next without seam or weld, the nights of the Wet flowing smoothly into one another. And the war. The war, too, had helped Coombes unshackle himself. Monday or Friday, January or June, it was all the same to him because the war was all the same: a stalemate without advances or retreats, triumphs or defeats. It just went on, the events of one month or year near-perfect copies of those from the month or year before. By his own choice, he'd been in it for so long even he'd forgotten how long, or thought he had. The firefights and pitched battles had become laminated in his mind into one continuous battle, as the seasons and the hot days and wet nights had merged into a constant, dateless *now*. And there was this too, this above all: Coombes' indifference to time had made him indifferent to death—the end of time for each human being—and that indifference had given him mastery over fear . . . until last night. Now he had but one aim—to return to that calm space where no clocks ticked, no calendars turned, and he was not afraid.

Be patient; be like the forest, he said to himself once again. Impatience had caused Gauthier's death. He'd hurried Gauthier across the rickety bridge, and now he was drowned and the radio drowned with him, although, Coombes realized, the radio's loss was not the disaster it had seemed at first.

THE MEN ON the other side of the river, finding no break in the canopy or clouds, gave up their quest for the sun. For a few moments, they stood silently and listened to the far-off rumble of the war. It was a sound they had heard for so many days and nights they could not recall a day or night when they had not heard it. It was part of their lives, as traffic noise is to a city dweller. For all its menace, they found it comforting on this day; without it, they would have thought they were the only human beings in a kingdom ruled by trees.

They listened and watched Coombes, waiting to hear what orders he would give.

"What's he doin', standin' there?" asked Eric Swenson, called Eric the Red because he never tanned, only burned.

"After making a thorough study, I'd say he's standing there," answered Thomas Pearce Bledsoe, Teepee for short. He turned to Jimmy Neville, who had sat down, wedging himself between the buttress roots of a ma- hogany tree. "What do you say?"

"Agreed," replied Neville, who did not have a nickname. In a soci- ety where most men were known only by their nicknames, that was tantamount to not having an identity. "Coombes is standing there. Definitely."

"There it is, Red. The incontrovertible evidence of our senses has told us that Coombes is indeed standing there. Now what?"

"You're always tryin' to prove you're not a dumb nigger with them fifty-cent words, but you don't impress me."

"Careful. I'm African as a Zulu, African as the tsetse fly." Teepee's fingers fluttered in Eric the Red's face. "Buzz buzz buzz."

"You be careful. I just might swat you."

"You're not fast enough. Tsetse Fly put you to sleep before you know what hit you."

"That don't impress me, neither."

Teepee flashed an amiable grin, showing teeth so straight they looked false. "Coombes," he reminded.

"This here's the point, here it is." Eric the Red puffed out his chest, like a politician about to deliver an important address. "The Goat is dead. The radio's gone with him. Sunk and gone. The map and compass— sunk and gone. We got no idea where we are. We oughta be makin' our hat for home, y'know? But Coombes is standin' there, lookin' into the big green like he's thinkin' we're gonna ruck up and go on. That ain't . . . acceptable. There's a half-dollar word for you. Acceptable."

"More like a nickel. More like a farthing, my good man."

"C'mon, Teepee," said Jimmy Neville, who was short and slight and young enough to still have acne problems. Nestled between the sloping buttress roots, he looked like a pimply toddler in his father's armchair. "He's, like, standin' there and lookin' into the big bad green like he's fig- urin' which way we should go. Right?"

"Why don't you ask him." Teepee grinned again, fixing his eyes on Neville's.

Jimmy Neville turned his gaze to contemplate the toes of his boots.

"Didn't think so."

"So what d'you s'pose he's gonna do?"

Teepee looked across the rope bridge, seeing in his mind's eye Gauthier slipping through the ropes like a fish through a net, then falling into the rushing water.

"Damned if I know."

HAN THOUGHT the *trung-si* was, in his motionless silence, mourning the man taken by the river. It was bad luck to disturb someone mourning the dead, so Han said nothing about the pawprint. He had spotted it as soon as he'd crossed the bridge, and had been about to yell to the *trung-si* when the man with the talkingbox fell into the river. Since then, Han had been squatting beside the print, not moving an inch, as if he were afraid it would walk away if he let it out of his sight. He had seen only faint sign since leaving the soldiercamp, but this print was fresh and clear. Twice now he'd measured its depth with his thumb, its width with the span of his hand, and both times his heart rolled over from an excitement mingled with fear, but more from excitement than fear. A male, bigger than the one he and his father had killed long ago, when Han was no longer a boy but not yet a man, and that one was huge. Spread out, its coat had made a blanket four people could sleep under shoulder-to-shoulder.

Out of the corner of his eye, Han caught the flare of a match. The *trung-si* was smoking a cigarette; his mourning must be over. Han hissed to gain his attention.

He came over, rifle flat on one shoulder, his hand on the barrel. Han pointed to the pawprint.

"Jesus."

"This is the one," said Han, speaking in his tribal tongue, which the *trung-si* understood. "A big male, moving fast."

"Jesus."

The smoke from the *trung-si*'s cigarette hung like campsmoke in the hotwetquiet air.

"He isn't running. Walking, but fast."

"Jesus Christ."

All the *My* said that all the time. The white *My*, the black *My*. A word from their tongue. Han had no idea what it meant, had never asked. Jesus. Jesus Christ.

The *trung-si* bent down and, spreading his fingers wide, laid his hand in the print.

"How can you tell it's walking?"

"If running, tracks would be more far apart."

"What else?"

"He's carrying his kill. In his teeth. Look." Han pointed to the long, shallow drag marks in the mud. "Those are made by the kill's feet. Tiger is carrying him in his teeth. I don't know why. Tiger kills, Tiger eats close to where he kills, but now Tiger is carrying his kill to someplace far, walking, but fast."

"How big?"

"Very big."

"I mean, how much weight do you think it has?"

Han turned to him with truth in his small, earthbrown eyes. "In all my hunting, *trung-si,* I've never tracked one this big."

That wasn't much help. Coombes already knew that the cat was very big, for he was the only one of the five to have seen it. What he needed now was its weight and length, its speed of travel, the number of its teeth and claws and stripes, every last little concrete fact that could be ascertained. Coombes always made it a point to know his enemy; the more he knew, the more likely he was to win, but in this case, knowledge had a value beyond the practical. He hoped that facts would help dispel the mythic power of the awesome phantom that now stalked his memory with eyes glowing like the eyes in a jack-o'-lantern, only they were yellow-green instead of orange. He could see them still, as he'd seen them the night before, burning with no expression in them except serenity. Yes, serene, and malignant in their serenity, looking at him as *he* might at an ant or a worm. He'd never seen anything so terrible, for he could not believe there was anything in creation capable of looking upon him as if he were an ant or a worm.

A numbness began to spread through his legs. He stood to restore feeling in their nerves, strength to their sinews; he was afraid they would crumple the way they had last night, when the tiger, after staring at him impassively for a few seconds, padded off with Valesquez in its jaws, as effortlessly as a house cat with a mouse.

He needed facts.

"Han, how did it cross the river?"

"It swam. Tiger can swim. Or it jumped. Tiger can jump very far."

"Nothing could swim that river, and it's thirty meters across. He's carrying a man weighing one hundred kilos."

Han was silent, irritated by all the talk about meters and kilos. The

My always spoke about kilos and meters and the time on their watches. Kilos. Meters. Hours. Jesus.

"Answer me, Han. What tiger could jump thirty meters with a big man in its jaws?"

"This tiger, *trung-si.*"

"What are you saying?" asked Coombes with a sardonic laugh. "That it flew?"

"If it is Ghostiger, yes."

"What?"

Han explained. Sometimes, when Tiger turned man-eater, it ate a man's soul as well as his flesh. If the soul was angry, it possessed Tiger, giving it extraordinary powers. Powers to fly. To be in two places at once. Ghostiger sustained itself by devouring other souls.

"And that's what you think this is?" Coombes asked, rolling his eyes.

"I hope not. If it's Ghostiger, then we must not kill it."

"We're going to kill it, all right."

"Not if Ghost. The angry spirit will find a new Tiger to make its home in, and the new Ghostiger will kill the man who killed its brother. In revenge, it will devour his body and his soul, and the bodies and souls of his wife, his children, his children's children. So Ghostiger must be left alone." Han traced the outline of the pawprint with his finger. "That is why I hope Tiger is not Ghost. If we leave it alone, you will not pay me."

"I'll do worse than that," Coombes muttered in English.

He looked at his watch. Eleven o'clock. They'd been tracking for almost six hours and had another six or seven hours of daylight left. Hightower had given them until noon tomorrow to find Valesquez, or whatever was left of him, and bring him back. *Be patient; be like the forest.* Tomorrow noon. What was so magical about that hour? Coombes unbuckled the watch and, with a casual movement, flipped it into the river. Instantly, he felt lighter, and he rubbed the band's impression on his wrist like a prisoner when the cuffs are taken off. He waved to the others to come across.

"WHAT DID I TELL YOU, what did I say?" Eric the Red flung an arm out to the side. "Wants us to do it. Right into the big bad green. Teepee, talk sense to him, use them half-dollar words on him. No map, no compass, no radio, the Goat's dead, we don't know where we are. God's tryin' to tell us somethin'."

Teepee knew that was no mere figure of speech; Red was a Bible-bouncer, always the first to pick up his well-thumbed prayer book and fall to his knees when the chaplain flew into base camp on Sunday mornings. Teepee was a skeptic, despite his Catholic education, yet this spooky wilderness inclined him to entertain the notion that Gauthier's death and the loss of the radio and instruments of navigation had been a divine warning.

He walked up to the bridge. At its far end, towering like a tree, long, hard muscles like roots, Coombes pumped his arm up and down in a signal to move out on the double.

"Yo!" Teepee shouted above the river's roar. "Think we should make our hat for home!"

Coombes must not have heard, because he kept signaling. *Big boss man, don't you hear me when I call?* Teepee remembered his uncle Elmond singing the old work song and strumming a bottleneck slide on the front porch of his house in Gretna.

He cupped his hands into a megaphone and hollered again.

"Yo! Coombes! No map, no radio, no compass, no nothing!"

Coombes dropped his arm. He'd expected something like this—Gauthier had spooked them—and still he felt disappointed. He always did when men failed to live up to his expectations, when they failed the best in themselves and surrendered to fear, to caution, to the need for safety and comfort. It was human nature. Last night, he'd disappointed himself far more than Bledsoe was letting him down now, more than any man ever had.

"Han's found a fresh track!" he shouted back. "Fresh as a brand-new egg! Biggest track he's seen! It's still got Valesquez!"

Though he was a hundred feet away, Teepee swore he could see Coombes' eyes, burning as blue as pilot lights. *There* was one white boy with a fully functional mojo, and he had it working now. Teepee could feel it, entrancing him into acting against his own common sense. *It still had Valesquez.* But how could Coombes know that? Because he always knew. He knew everything in the way of useful knowledge: where the ambushes would be laid, where the booby traps would be placed, where the trails went. He could name every tree, flower, and fern, identify every screech, roar, and howl the flying, creeping, crawling things made in the jungle. He knew when to fight and when to run. Everyone in the company wanted to be in Coombes' squad, because no one under his command ever died. Gauthier had been the first in living memory, and he had been killed not by the enemy or through a mistake on Coombes' part but because of his own clumsiness. Coombes had knowledge, and knowledge was power. That was the secret of his mojo. *It still had Valesquez.* Knew which emotional buttons to push too.

"We don't know where the hell we are!" Teepee yelled, making one last attempt to deter him. Yeah, let's see if he knows that.

"Han does!" came the reply. "Let's go before that cat dies of old age!"

"Where does Han say we are?"

Coombes' disappointment grew. They needed to know where they were. Prisoners of maps because they were prisoners of clocks, slaves of time and space. All right, he would humor them.

"Han, they want to know where we are."

"Cigarette me, *trung-si.*"

He gave the hillman a cigarette and lit it for him.

Han took a drag and exhaled, the smoke like breath on the highest mountain on the coldest monsoon dawn.

"This river is called the River of the Virgin's Tears, and on this side of it is the Forest of the Laughing Elephant. Tiger is heading toward Black Grandfather Mountain."

Coombes shouted this information to T. P. Bledsoe, who laughed a bitter laugh when he heard it.

"Got that?" he said to the others. "Now we know. Got ourselves pin-pointed. Located right to the inch. We're in the Forest of the Laughing Elephant."

"What kinda craziness is that?" an outraged Eric the Red asked no one in particular. He wanted map coordinates and grid lines, latitude and longitude—anything to give him at least a half-assed idea of where he stood in this world where he could not see the sun and the giant trees made him as blind to landmarks as a beetle in a cornfield. "The Forest of the Laughing Elephant?"

"Yeah; elephants can't laugh, can they, Teepee?" said a bemused Jimmy Neville.

He's even dumber than I thought, Teepee said to himself, then Eric the Red pointed across the river.

"Hey! They're takin' off on us!"

Teepee turned to see Coombes and Han vanish behind a mass of vines whose oval leaves, large as serving platters, reminded him of philodendron. They were strangler vines. Coombes had taught him that. Philodendron meant loving trees. Coombes had not taught him that;

Father Aloysius LeClerc had, in Greek class at St. Martin's Catholic Preparatory School in New Orleans. Teepee thought of Father LeClerc's lesson because the vines seemed to clutch Coombes and Han, not violently but with the gentleness of some green, tentacled mother drawing lost children to her breast.

Philos (love) + dendron (tree) = loving tree.

What good does knowing Greek do me now? Teepee gripped the handropes of the bridge and stepped onto the first of the split-bamboo planks. Knowing Greek won't help me get across this bridge.

"Teepee, don't, man," pleaded Eric the Red, who dreaded crossing the river. For reasons he could not even guess, the jungle on the far side looked scarier than on this side. "Coombes has lost it, man. We can find our own way back. Follow the river."

"Learn that in Boy Scouts?"

"Bilged outa Boy Scouts, but I know damn well, you follow a river, you're bound to come to somethin'."

"We stick with Coombes and the Yard. At least the Yard knows where he's at."

"Right. The fuckin' forest of the laughin' fuckin' elephant."

Red uses some awful language for a Bible-thumper, Teepee thought. The planks swaying under him, he held tight to the handropes as he gingerly turned his head to yell over his shoulder.

"Wait till I'm on the other side, then come on. One at a time and slow!"

Below, the white-brown river spewed like chocolate milk out of some gigantic hydrant. You let me down, Father Aloysius LeClerc. None of what you taught me has done me any good over here. Never did much good back home, either. Down in Louisiana, a nigger who can speak Greek is still a nigger who'll end up in a place like this because he can't go college tuition, unless he can run the forty in four-two or shoot hoops from the outside. You should have taught me that and how to cross a river on a rope-and-plank bridge instead of philos (love) + dendron (tree) = loving tree.

Teepee reached the last plank and jumped onto the blessedly solid earth. He signaled Eric the Red, who stepped onto the bridge, as Teepee had known he would.

Red was not agile or athletic, just big. Once, he'd tried to convince everyone that he'd been a football star, but a headquarters clerk discovered that he'd only played tuba in his high-school marching band. Now, watching him cross the bridge as if he were coming down the field at halftime, his knees lifted high, his feet stomping, Teepee tried to picture him in a colorful bandsman's uniform on a bright autumn Saturday, swinging his tuba to the beat of a big bass drum. The image was blurred and fleeting. He could no more picture Eric the Red in a colorful bandsman's uniform than he could picture himself in the green-and-gold blazer of St. Martin's, learning Greek in Father LeClerc's classroom. It was impossible to imagine himself or his companions as anything other than the soldiers they now were. They had lost their pasts here. They knew each other more by the nicknames they'd given each other than by the names their parents had given them and had consecrated over baptismal fonts. It was as if they had died and been reborn: infants without memory, children of the forest. They were not its legitimate children, like Han, but its bastards, lacking all claim to its inheritance. Except for Coombes. The jungle had adopted him.

Eric the Red took one long, final stride and planted his oversize feet on the bank.

"We shunta done this." His eyes had a funny light in them, one Teepee hadn't seen before. "We shunta crossed this river, Teepee."

"Coombes'll get us back. A man who's been here for nobody knows how long *without being scratched* has a charm big as the Goodyear blimp."

"Crap. He ain't got no charm."

"Stop using so many double negatives."

"Aw, the hell with you!" Eric the Red tossed his hat down, stomped on it, then picked it up and jammed it back on his head. "The hell with all this shit!"

The funny light burned more brightly in his eyes.

When Jimmy Neville was safely over the bridge, T. P. Bledsoe's next problem was tracking down Coombes and Han. Fast as they moved, they could be a mile away by now. He looked at the wall of great trees, silent and still, but could not find the maze of vines the two men had vanished into. He'd seen them clearly enough from across the river, but now vines seemed to be everywhere, vines thin as tendrils and thick as a man's arm, vines with leaves and without leaves, light-green vines and dark-green vines and vines of every shade of green in between. He had to find the ones with leaves like giant philodendron, but there were a dozen of those, and he couldn't tell which was which.

"Hey, dintja see where they *went?*" asked Red in a panic.

Teepee, looking for footprints, moved this way and that, like a bird dog sniffing for lost scent.

"Here!" He picked a spot at random. "They went in here!"

He plunged into a tangle of wait-a-minute vines. One coiled around his canteen, and as he turned to free it, another caught his rifle sling, and as he turned to free the sling, another knocked his hat off, and as he bent down to pick up his hat, another cuffed his wrist, and as he tugged to free his wrist, another looped over his magazine pouch, and as he lunged to snap it, another gripped his ankle and tripped him, and he fell face-down, crying out, "You bitch!"

Eric the Red and Jimmy Neville were within five yards of him, cursing and thrashing, but he could not see them. He got to his knees, pulling at the vines twined round him like yarn around a kitten.

"Goddamned wait-a-minutes!"

"That's Cambodian mimosa."

It was Coombes, standing not six feet away. Where had he come from? Or had he been there all along?

HE BROUGHT the three men to the place where he and Han had been waiting, the trees there like pillars and everything so dim and quiet that Eric the Red felt as if he'd entered a cathedral at vespers, though this cathedral did not bring a sense of calm or peace or greater nearness to God.

Coombes told them to sit down, and they did. He did not speak a word at first, just looked at them with blue eyes burning steady and direct yet without heat.

"This isn't some sporting holiday we're on, this isn't a hunting trip," he began. "It's a rescue mission, it's search and destroy."

He paused, allowing his scornful glance to sweep over their faces once again.

"You people need to be reminded of a couple of things. Number one, we *never* leave our dead. That's our code. Number two, the tiger got Valesquez. That makes the tiger our enemy, and we are here—this is number three—to kill the enemy, two legs or four. We are going to kill that tiger and bring Valesquez back, no matter what." He extended one long arm and slowly pivoted until he made a full circle, as if to encompass the entire jungle. "Isn't that why you volunteered for this mission?"

Eric the Red started to speak, but Coombes silenced him with a look.

"Listen up, people. From now on, 'going back' isn't part of our vocabulary. Am I clear on that?"

The three men shifted uncomfortably. None of them could look Coombes in the face, as if they'd done or thought something shameful. Off to one side, Han waited with immeasurable patience.

"I said, am I clear?"

His voice was angry but under control, suggesting teams of rage he could let loose if he chose to slacken the reins. Teepee and Jimmy Neville each muttered a "yes." Eric the Red gave a nod that could have been mistaken for a twitch.

"Good," said Coombes. "Now forget about Gauthier. It happened, it's done, nothing we can do about it now."

Teepee saw the wisdom in that; and under Coombes' glare, he decided that Gauthier's death had not been a divine warning after all. Just a stupid accident.

"Today, or tomorrow, or the day after, something might happen to one of you," Coombes continued. "Might happen to me. That doesn't mean the rest should get spooked and quit. It would mean our mission has been sanctified by the sacrifice of life. It's already sanctified. Gauthier gave his life to bring Valesquez back. If we quit, we'd be betraying the both of them. It's payback time for that tiger. We're going to go on, until we've cornered that son of a bitch and killed it. Any questions?"

Eric the Red found the nerve to ask one.

"Cap'n told us the mission's to get Valesquez. Didn't say nothin' about killin' the tiger. And he give us till noon tomorrow. What's this about goin' on and on?"

Coombes' laugh was dry and mirthless.

"Right. Hightower's curfew. Listen up: Hightower's a clock-puncher, and all this out here doesn't give a snake's fart about a clock-puncher's curfew. For damn sure that tiger doesn't."

"But Hightower does," Eric the Red persisted. "We disobey his orders, that's court-martial."

With a smile mirthless as his laugh, Coombes shook his head.

"You're a hoot, Swenson. You've got the smarts of a tree snail with a brain tumor. We lost our radio, remember? Lost our map. Our compass. We're *lost*. We're the lost expedition." He sounded delighted by their predicament. "But we're going to come back with that tiger's skin and

Valesquez wrapped up in it. Don't care if all that's left of him is his little finger. We'll bring that back. And when we do, the last thing that clock-puncher's going to do is court-martial us. Over here."

They rose and followed Coombes a few yards farther into the forest.

Han watched the *My*, wondering what they were doing now. Tiger was moving fast, the trail growing cold.

Coombes pointed at the ground.

"Jesus," said T. P. Bledsoe, sucking in a breath as he looked down.

"Jesus," said Eric the Red.

"Jesus," said Jimmy Neville.

First chance he got, Han decided, he would ask the *trung-si* what a Jesus was.

"Han thinks it's the biggest he's ever tracked," Coombes said.

"So how big is that?" Teepee asked.

"Only guessing, but figure five to six hundred pounds. Maybe more."

In the wet, black earth, the print looked as broad and deep as a mess kit, its front edge scalloped by the toes that sheathed the claws. As the three men stared at it, a dry, metallic taste entered their mouths. They felt a pinching in their lower guts, a quick, hot rush of blood in their limbs, and a tingling in their scalps. Reflexively, they flicked the bolts of their rifles. The 5.56-millimeter cartridges, adequate for killing a man, appeared now as puny and impotent as darts. *Five to six hundred pounds.* That would make it bigger than two middle linebackers put together, with jackknives for fingernails and railroad spikes for eyeteeth. The tiger had been only a word, an abstraction. Now the track allowed them to give it form and substance in their minds, and each of them was flooded with a consciousness of his smallness and frailty in this soaring wilderness, of whose might and majesty the great cat seemed the incarnation.

"Han thinks they were made this morning," Coombes told them. "So the tiger isn't too far ahead of us. You can be easy for a while, Swenson. Might make the clock-puncher's curfew after all. Give me your watch."

Eric the Red knit his pale-blond brows.

"Lost mine with the map and compass," Coombes explained, rubbing his wrist.

Eric the Red hesitated.

"Let's see it, Swenson."

Eric the Red handed him the watch. Coombes held it to his ear and shook it.

"Doesn't seem to be working."

"Workin' fine . . ."

"Bledsoe, Neville, yours."

They turned their watches over. Teepee knew what was going to happen, yet felt powerless to stop it.

"You're nuts!" shrieked Eric the Red when Coombes dropped the watches and stomped on them.

Teepee realized then how the map and compass had been lost, but he didn't think Coombes was nuts. The blue-eyed bastard knew what he was doing. Smashing the watches was logical, perhaps necessary. Like Cortés burning his ships on the beach.

"You crazy son of a . . ." On his hands and knees, Eric the Red picked up the shattered dials, scratched in the mud for tiny gears and bearings and shafts.

"Let's go."

"You crazy bastard!"

"Let's go, Swenson."

Eric the Red looked up at the forest canopy. For a moment, his lips quivering, it looked as if he was going to sob. Instead, he cracked a peculiar grin that combined with his feverish eyes to make him look like a tortured saint finding rapture in his martyrdom.

"Can God see me anymore?"

"Don't know, but I can," said Coombes, and grabbed his collar and jerked him to his feet. "And I'm telling you to get moving."

He and Han took the lead, walking side by side, the top of the hillman's head reaching only halfway between Coombes' waist and chest. The other three fell into single file. Teepee watched the left and Jimmy Neville the right, while Eric the Red, cursing Coombes under his breath, watched the rear. All three were warier than usual; they almost missed the familiar dangers of snipers and booby traps. Better to die that way than to be pounced on by a cat that could crush a man's skull like an eggshell and shred him into a bloody slaw.

Ahead, Coombes and Han tracked with painful care. Move a few yards. Stop, look, listen. Move again. At this pace, we'll be out here for the next year, Teepee thought, peering into the verdant twilight. Could be noon. Could be dawn. Could be sundown. Out of habit, he went to look at his watch, the unexpected nakedness of his wrist causing him to feel the panic of a heavy smoker who reaches for his cigarettes, only to find that he's misplaced them. In the many bad moments he'd known in battle, moments when, as now, time stood still and it seemed he never would see home again, Teepee relied on his watch to tell him that time was in motion after all and he with it. He would imagine himself riding on the hands as on a carousel, circling yet moving forward through temporal space toward the hour, the minute, the second when the mythic Freedom Bird would fly him out of this hot and alien land forever. He would have to find a good strong stick and notch it every evening; out here, to lose track of time was to lose hope. Coombes had robbed them of hope! And that must have been his intention. Maybe it was ridiculous to compare him to Cortés, but the principle was the same. The way back is the way forward, the way out the way in.

They tracked all afternoon through the Forest of the Laughing Elephant. Teepee made sure not to let Coombes and Han out of his sight. They were the map and compass now. Besides, he liked watching the two men, so different in size and in other ways, yet so similar in their movements, walking toe to heel without a sound, spinning lightly around clumps of fern or underbrush, bowing under low-hanging vines without missing a step, circling around big trees, Coombes on one side, Han on the other, dancers dancing to some silent tune. Teepee tried to imitate them, but he couldn't hear the music. If there was a root to stumble over or a twig to crack, his feet, like those of Red and Jimmy Neville, would find it. His eyes always seemed to miss a vine or branch that would slap him in the face, as if to reproach him for the oversight.

The day was utterly still, except for the patter of rain and the thunder of the war, growing fainter. Eric the Red's ears clung to the sound. He recalled the deer-hunting trip, three years before, when he and his father had got lost in the Cascade Mountains. They'd walked for hours before they heard a whisper that sounded like a soft wind in the trees but wasn't. "Follow that sound," his father had said. "Don't lose it, now. Those are cars on a highway; that's our salvation." Eric the Red felt the same about the far-off booming. It was odd to think of war as salvation, but there it was. *I hear the rolling thunder . . .* In his memory, he heard his father, a baritone in the church choir, singing the hymn to keep up their spirits as they walked out of the Cascades. *As through the woods and forest glades I wander, And hear the birds sing sweetly in the trees . . . I see the stars,*

I hear the rolling thunder . . . Then sings my soul, my savior God, to Thee, How great Thou art, how great Thou art . . . Singing it now to himself, Eric the Red made a decision: If this hunt or rescue mission or whatever it was went past the captain's deadline, he would listen for the rolling thunder and head straight for it. Where there was war, there were men. He would keep his head down, make sure the men were friendlies, and then go to them and give them his name, rank, and serial number and tell them he'd been missing in action, lost in the jungle. They would take him back to Hightower's company. He would be home again, safe in the arms of the war.

The land rose toward Black Grandfather Mountain. The trees stood wide apart, as in a park. The shortest looked as high to Eric the Red as the highest buildings in Spokane, but not as high as the giant redwoods in California. He'd visited those trees on a family trip when he was thirteen. One of them was so big the highway had been cut right through it. His father told him that the redwood had started growing before Jesus was born. How old were the trees in this forest? He couldn't tell, but he had the smarts to know that they hadn't started growing before Jesus was born. They hadn't started growing when Jesus was born, either, or after. These trees had nothing to do with Jesus, because Jesus was not here, in the Forest of the Laughing Elephant. Eric the Red could feel His absence, just as he'd felt His presence in the Lutheran church during Sunday services.

In front of him, Teepee, then Jimmy Neville, raised their hands in a signal to halt. Eric the Red dropped to one knee and looked to the rear to make sure nothing was sneaking up on them. Suddenly, a loud shriek came from the branches far above. He leaped up, rifle in his shoulder, and caught a rainbow flash of fleeting color over the front sight. He turned and lowered his rifle and saw Teepee and Jimmy Neville doing the same thing.

"Just a goddamned parrot," Jimmy Neville said. His small, acne-marked face wrinkled into a quizzical frown. "Hey, I just thought of somethin'. Whole time I been here, I never seen a parrot. What about you, Teepee? You seen a parrot since you been here?"

Teepee shook his head.

"What about you, Red? You seen a parrot ever?"

"Uh-uh."

"So how come none of us seen a parrot before but now we seen one?"

"Maybe we weren't looking," said Teepee. "Had our mind on other things."

"Or maybe there wasn't none where we were," Eric the Red offered, looking toward the understory for the flicker of green and bright-yellow wings. "What spooked that one?"

"The tiger?" asked Jimmy Neville in a whisper.

"Probably us. Not like crowds of people come walking through here every day," Teepee said, and then got down, cradling his rifle in his lap. He looked to the left and imagined the beast watching him as it crouched in a thicket; then a lunge of lethal grace, and T. P. Bledsoe would be on his way to becoming cat shit. He tried to push the image from his mind, picturing instead the short-timer's calendar in his foot-locker back at camp. It was a drawing of a naked woman, her body divided into three hundred ninety-five pieces, like a jigsaw puzzle. Each piece symbolized a day in his tour of duty, the final one marked in red over the woman's vagina. Pussy, poontang, snatch, mons veneris. Home. When he made an "X" across that delectable triangle, he could go home and reclaim his lost past—and his future as well. One hundred seventy-one and a wake-up. Or was it a hundred and seventy-two? These dark woods were fouling up his mental chronometer. He had to find a stick and notch it every night.

Eric the Red had resumed his watch on the rear. Once, his eyes roamed upward, again seeking the parrot. He looked hard but saw only leaves and branches intertwined so thickly he was sure the laughing elephant could walk on them without falling through. A deep uneasiness crept into him; if he couldn't see out, then nothing could see in—not helicopter pilots, not satellite cameras, not even God Himself. Reverend Berger had often preached from his pulpit in Grace Lutheran that the smallest sparrow doesn't fall without God's seeing it, but Eric the Red sensed that even the eye of heaven couldn't penetrate the dense roof of the Forest of the Laughing Elephant. He had vanished from the eye of God, and that had happened to him only once before.

He turned to glance at Teepee and Jimmy Neville. Their nearness reassured him a little, but beyond them stood Coombes, talking to Han beside a fern that sprayed like a gigantic household plant. Uninvited, a thought barged into his head. *I could kill him.* He could fire over the heads of the other two men and put a bullet through the crazy man's back. *Maybe I should, before he kills us or gets us court-martialed.* The thought was mother to a desire. His palms grew damp as they gripped the rifle. He had to talk to his arms to stop them from raising the weapon. At that moment, he heard a rustling behind him and snapped his head around, crisply bringing the rifle to his shoulder. Nothing was there, only trees, yet a chill crept up his neck.

"WHAT IS IT?"

"He knows we are tracking him." Squatting, Han pointed at the thicket of ferns. "Do you see that?"

"What?"

Coombes squinted, annoyed that his eyes, so sharp and practiced they could spot a trip wire thin as lightbulb filament, couldn't see what Han's did.

Han duck-walked to the ferns and made a circular movement with his hand. It came clear then—a slight depression, no deeper in the humus than a vaccination mark in a man's arm.

"He lies down here. He lays down his kill. See . . ." Han broke off a fern, spotted with dark fluids. "He lies down to listen, to smell, then I think he hears us, smells us, and runs away with his kill." Han stood and walked around the thicket and pointed at the tracks, leading deeper into the forest. "Tracks more far apart, more deep in back than front. He is running with his kill."

"Valesquez," said Coombes.

"Tiger is strange. When Tiger knows he is being tracked, he runs one way, then the other way. Sometimes he makes a circle and attacks his trackers from behind, but Tiger is not doing that now. He is running straight and away."

"What does that tell you?"

"He is going to some secret place, I think. Some place he feels safe. There he will eat."

Eyes bright as a jack-o'-lantern's, serenely staring at him as if he were an ant or a worm.

"So how far do you think this hiding place is?"

Han shrugged. "I am not Tiger, *trung-si.*"

LATE IN THE AFTERNOON, they began to climb the mountain. It rose up against them, steeper and steeper, resisting as if by conscious will their every step and forcing them to bend forward to the slope so that, in places, their noses were only an arm's length from the ground. Their empty bellies rumbled, but they had time only to take a quick gulp from their canteens.

The tiger's track led into a ravine, cobbled with mossy rocks. Shrubs and bushes grew along both sides and made an arch overhead. The faint light struggling through the leaves was now a bottle green, now the black green of a dead fly's thorax. The men could hardly breathe the air, dense, motionless, smelling of dead things and live things growing out of the dead things. Teepee felt as if they were in the rank arbor of some garden abandoned to the wild, but Eric the Red could think only of the tunnel. His breath grew short. A fetal panic rose in his chest. He thought he was going to scream, as he had in the tunnel months before, the last time he had fallen out of God's redeeming sight.

In front, Han followed sign. He was glad that the *trung-si* was quiet and not pushing him, as he had when they'd left soldiercamp. Hurry, Han. What's taking so long, Han? He'd had little chance to study the ground and learn its messages. The *trung-si* was more patient now, and Han was happy about that because the bottom of the ravine was hard and the only signs he could see were the small, bent branches Tiger had brushed against and, splashed on the rocks, blood spots like dark-red coins. He'd learned about coins from the *My,* who paid him money to track men.

Long ago, in the camp Han and his family had fled to after the Sky-fire fell on their village, the *My* had asked him to help them hunt their enemies because they'd heard he was a great hunter. Of course, he agreed. There was nothing to hunt in the camp. He had to buy rice to feed his wife and five children. Besides, the *My* were powerful. It was they who made fire fall from the sky, they who brought the Medicine Rain that browned the trees. With the money they paid him for hunting men, he could buy more rice for his family. And so he learned about coins.

Now he followed the spots. It was good to be hunting Tiger again, but Tiger puzzled him, and because it did, it also frightened him. Tiger was not behaving as in the past—running straight instead of crooked, not eating its kill but carrying it far away. He'd never tracked Tiger so far in less than one sun, and this also was odd and made him wonder again how it had crossed the river. The *trung-si* was right: it could not have jumped or swum with a man in its jaws. Things, as Han had once understood them, were ceasing to make sense, and the forest, always full of mysteries, seemed to have more than ever. Then, as he paused to look and listen, he saw something that made him forget about the things he did not understand and start thinking about the things he did.

WAS THE SUN SETTING? Or was the tangle overhead growing thicker? Eric the Red didn't know, knew only that the light was growing fainter and fainter. The embryo of terror in his chest sprouted arms and legs. Its little hands squeezed his lungs. Its little feet kicked at his breastbone as it struggled to be born.

WHEN HAN POINTED to the big, flat rock three paces ahead, he caught a vague, fleeting scent on a puff of wind blowing down from the mountaintop. He breathed a little easier; the scent was one of the things he understood.

"Smell it?" he asked softly.

"That?" the *trung-si* said, pointing at the rock.

"Do you smell Tiger?"

"No."

"I do. The smell Tiger makes to tell everyone where his country begins. We are in his country now. We must be quiet. He is not far away."

Coombes thought of sacrificial altars as he walked up to the bloodstained rock with its aura of bloated, buzzing flies. Kneeling, he touched the bloodstain with his fingertip. Still sticky. Holding his breath, he undid the laces of the canvas-and-leather boot that seemed ready to burst from the swollen foot still in it. He rolled down the boot top to check the name tag sewn inside. All the letters but two had been blotted out: a *V* and a *Q*. The beginning and the middle, enough to tell him the end.

"Tiger was going to eat here, but again he heard us, smelled us, and now he goes farther away with his kill."

"Valesquez," Coombes whispered through clenched teeth. "His name was Angel Valesquez. He is not a 'kill.'"

"He is now, *trung-si.*"

There was a short, sharp scream from behind.

Coombes seemed to cover the fifteen yards to the rear in a single stride.

Eric the Red lay gasping on his back, each pore in his flushed face a tiny spring of sweat. He was trying to say something: "Dove . . . dove . . ."

Coombes looked at Teepee, who shrugged. "He just screamed and hit the deck. Must be heatstroke."

"He's wet and redder than usual. Been heatstroke, he'd be white and hot as an ironing board."

"Ville . . . Dove . . . Ville," Eric the Red mumbled; then his eyes flicked up into his head, like a doll's eyes, and he lay quiet.

"Ain't the first time I seen this. He done it before, in the tunnel."

Coombes turned to Jimmy Neville. "What tunnel?"

"Happened before him and me was shipped to Hightower's outfit. We come to a ville, find a tunnel. Red volunteers to search it, even though he's too big to be a tunnel rat. Sure enough, he got stuck down there. Screamin' his ass off. Me and another guy got him out. Red's flipped out, like he is now, mumblin' about doves bein' in the ville. Passes out, comes to, he's okay. Couple weeks later, we're back in the boonies, just strollin' through the tulips, and Red starts to freak again. Doves, the ville. Passes out. Eltee says it's the heat, same as Teepee's sayin', but we knowed different. We knowed Red was back down in that tunnel. He, like, seen somethin' down there."

Jimmy Neville reached into his pocket for the soap dish in which he kept his cigarettes dry and asked with a gesture if it was all right to smoke. Coombes nodded, and Jimmy Neville lit up and said:

"We just gotta wait a minute or two. Red'll snap out of it again, good as new."

"Aren't you forgetting something?" asked Teepee.

"Don't think so."

"The end of the story. What did he see in the tunnel?"

"Doves, I guess. Little doves in the ville."

"Why the hell should that make him flip?"

"He never did say."

"Didn't you ask him?"

Jimmy Neville drew his head back and, half closing one eye, looked askance with the other, as if Teepee's suggestion for solving the mystery were the most outlandish thing he'd ever heard.

Eric the Red's eyes, meanwhile, had rolled down from inside his head. The funny light still shone in them, purple as a bruise, purple as Lent.

"You all right?" Teepee asked.

Red sat up and nodded.

"Must've been some kind of anxiety attack. Like claustrophobia. This gully's kind of like a tunnel," Teepee said to Coombes.

"Thanks, Dr. Bledsoe. I ask for volunteers, guys who fired expert on the range, who did some hunting back in The World. I get that, but what else do I get? A clumsy bastard who drowns himself and a black-assed Sigmund Freud."

Teepee wanted to remind Coombes of the many white boys the Tsetse Fly had put to sleep in the Golden Gloves; but he heard the fury mounting in Coombes' voice and knew he was not to be messed with. *I'm scared of him,* he thought. *That's why I'm here, why we volunteered. We were too scared not to.*

"Yessiree, that's what I get. And a moron who goes crazy on me and faints." Coombes pulled Eric the Red to his feet and shook him, the big man's body so limp he seemed to have lost his skeleton. "Anxiety attack, is that what you had, Dolores? C'mere, I'll show you something that'll give you all a full-bore nervous breakdown."

His thumb pressing a nerve behind Eric the Red's ear, Coombes forced him to look at what lay on the rock. He didn't have to force Teepee and Jimmy Neville. The severed foot held their glances like a magnet.

"There it is, Swenson. A little piece of our late mess sergeant. The tiger that did that was in the neighborhood when you let out that scream. Now I figure he's in the next time zone. Get the picture?"

Eric the Red twisted his neck against the grip of Coombes' hand, but as he did, pain shot through his inner ear.

"Because of your little fit, it might take us a week to get this close again. We're not going to make the clock-puncher's curfew. Get the picture?"

Eric the Red heard a ringing deep inside his ear, underneath the pain.

"Christ almighty," said Coombes, and slapped him twice with the back of his hand, and tears flooded his eyes as the ringing filled both ears.

"See the picture now?"

He did not see any sort of picture, though he heard the ringing compose itself into the brassy blare of his high-school band playing the fight song. There were horns and trombones, and his own tuba going oompah-pah, and voices shouting from the stands: "Do it! Do it! It's okay!" It was the cheering section, telling him that anything he did here in the Forest of the Laughing Elephant would be all right, because God could not see him. He nodded to tell the cheerleaders that he understood.

"Well, good; so glad you've got the picture," Coombes replied to the nod, then he turned around and moved ahead.

Do it! Do it! It's okay!

Eric the Red raised his rifle to his hip, resting the flat of the stock against his thigh.

Suddenly, Teepee blocked his line of fire and gave him the signal to take his place as tail-end Charlie. He held fast. He was confused. Why had Teepee stepped in front of him just as he was about to do it?

"Yo, Red! You still freaked or are you cool? Point the muzzle to the flank and watch our ass."

Teepee showed his back and commenced to climb the ravine. Thin as a card, Jimmy Neville slipped into his place in the middle. Eric the Red waited until the proper interval opened, then he began to climb. Maybe it wasn't okay to kill Coombes. Maybe God could see him after all and had made Teepee step in front of him to save him from committing a terrible sin. Maybe. He didn't know what to do or what was expected of him, and he silently prayed for a sign.

THE PULL IN his hamstrings told T. P. Bledsoe they were nearing the top of the mountain. Another five hundred feet would do it, but he was ready to climb a thousand, two thousand if he had to. And if they had to chase the tiger into the next time zone, he was ready to do that too. He'd been worn out only a quarter of an hour earlier, but a strange emotion, a kind of exhilarating anger, had restored strength and suppleness to his legs.

At least he knew now why he was here, and it had nothing to do with fear of Coombes. He had looked upon sights more terrible than the one on the blood-darkened rock, but those had been caused by bullets and bombs and grenades and land mines. A living creature had torn off Valesquez's foot, and that fact somehow made the sight worse than all the other sights he'd seen. He had been wounded once, shot through the fleshy part of his thigh. He hadn't felt a thing when the bullet struck, which had led him to conclude that he would've died without suffering, without even an awareness that death had come, if the round had pierced his brain or heart. The tiger had granted no such mercy to Valesquez, who must have felt excruciating pain when its fangs sank into him, who must have felt an anguish beyond imagining.

Teepee saw himself and all his comrades as more than mere men; they were warriors, the proudest and bravest of men. Yet the tiger had shown no fear of them, sneaking into the camp right under their noses, snatching their mess sergeant as easily as any one of them might crash a kid's birthday party and steal a piece of cake. A bite, a swipe of a paw, was all it had taken to convert Angel Valesquez into cat food. Pretty soon he would be cat shit, if he wasn't already. The tiger could do the same to one of them anytime it chose, and that was intolerable. The beast's very existence was an affront to their dignity. It had to be shown who ruled this jungle.

THEY REACHED the mountaintop at what they guessed was dusk.

"We will camp here," Han said. "Too dark for tracking."

"What's your plan?" asked Coombes, looking at the tracks that vanished into the undergrowth.

"Cigarette me."

Coombes gave him a smoke.

"Tiger will finish with his kill tonight."

"Valesquez."

"Tomorrow he will rest for maybe two suns before he hunts again. But we will not let him rest. I will scout you a good place down the mountain. You stay there, then me, the three soldiers, will track Tiger, making noise to chase him from his hiding place. We will chase him into you. You will have one, maybe two shots. No more. You must not miss, *trung-si.*"

"I never do," Coombes said, then turned to the others and told them to set up camp.

Teepee began to string his hammock between two trees, but Eric the Red and Jimmy Neville fell onto the wet ground, too tired even to spread their ponchos, much less string hammocks. They were asleep in a minute, and would have slept till dawn if Coombes hadn't nudged them each in the ribs with his size-twelve boot.

"Off your backs and on your feet, ladies. String your hammocks. When you're done with that, I want Neville and Bledsoe to go with Han for some firewood. Swenson, you dig a slit trench."

Eric the Red looked up at his tormentor.

"We ain't got no E-tools. What'm I sposta dig it with?"

Coombes tossed him a survival knife.

"What do you need a slit trench for? It ain't like we're in base camp."

"Because when we leave here, I don't want a sign that we've been here. There's still people out here who want to kill us. Number two, just because we're hunting an animal doesn't mean we have to live like animals. Number three—this is the most important one—because I *told* you to dig one."

While Eric the Red dug, Teepee foraged with Han and Jimmy Neville. He was amazed by Han's ability to find dry wood in the dripping jungle. Little dude could probably find it at the bottom of a lake, he thought, as he hacked branches off deadfalls and windfalls with a machete. He kept one of the sticks for himself, then cut a notch into it and put it in his rucksack. One day down. How many more to go? As many as it would take.

With their armloads of wood, the three returned to the campsite, passing Eric the Red, who had not made much progress on the slit trench. Teepee set his bundle down and handed him the machete.

"Use this. It'll go—"

He was interrupted by a noise that almost made him jump out of his skin, a single noise composed of many noises—caws, warbles, whistles, howls, and shrieks. Deafened by the shrill chorus, goose bumps rising on the backs of their necks, Teepee, Eric the Red, and Jimmy Neville stared up at the canopy, where dark wings beat among the leaves and a troop of monkeys swung madly between the branches.

"Jesus!"

"Where'd they come from?"

"What the hell set them off?"

Although he did not comprehend the words, Han sensed what the *My*'s questions were.

"They are talking to Sun, telling Sun it is time for him to sleep," he explained, but the three men did not understand him.

It stopped as it had begun, all at once and for no reason, or for no reason apparent to the Americans. Night fell instantly, as if an immense shroud had dropped on the jungle.

Eric the Red stood up slowly, the dirt-caked knife hanging loosely in his hand, and stood turning his head side to side.

"Listen," he said in a near whisper. The forest was quiet yet seemed to be awaiting something, something whose advent would be awful and without annunciation, like a tiger's pounce.

"Don't hear a thing," Teepee said.

"Exactly," replied Eric the Red.

Teepee grasped his meaning. They couldn't hear the war! It came to him that they hadn't heard it for the past three or four hours but had been too absorbed in the hunt to notice. Now the absence of the familiar rumble thundered in their ears, disorienting them, making them feel lost in a sea of primeval silence.

"It's probably just a lull."

"Lull? When was there ever a lull?" said Jimmy Neville nervously. "Ain't no lull. Man, where the hell are we?"

"Maybe it's over. Maybe the fuckin' war ended," Eric the Red wondered aloud, imagining statesmen signing treaties beneath sparkling chandeliers, troops striking tents, packing up duffel bags, and marching to airfields and seaports.

"Are you shitting me? It'll never end," Teepee said. "C'mon, Neville, let's get a fire built and think about this."

Han put a match to a pile of tinder, then knelt to blow life into the fire. The flames spurted, casting a jittery light on the hammocks, which hung like empty cocoons.

Teepee said: "I got it."

"Whajagot?"

"Why it's so quiet. Have you seen one bomb crater since we crossed the river? One shell crater? Seen even one defoliated tree?"

Jimmy Neville shook his head.

"The war isn't over, and there's no lull. We're out of the war—for now anyway."

"What d'you mean? Like we crossed the border? Like we ain't in country no more?"

"We couldn't have reached the border in only a day. We're in country, all right. What it is, the war never touched this place. Bypassed it."

"What! Hey, we got, like, hundred-percent coverage, I heard. Spy planes flyin' over the country all day, all night, and what they don't see, these satellites do. I heard they can get a picture of the mole on a guy's nose from a hundred miles up. That's how they run the bombing strikes. From the pictures. There ain't one part of this country that ain't been bombed or sprayed or both."

"Supposedly. Somehow, some way, they missed this part."

"That ain't possible!" Jimmy Neville said, and Teepee understood his shock and outrage. With such technology, you would've thought that someone would have noticed that an entire forest had gone untouched. What the hell was this place? Some kind of wildlife sanctuary? He wished they hadn't lost the radio; with it, he could report the blunder to higher headquarters and request immediate air strikes. Bombers and spray planes would scramble, lovely chemical clouds would roll from beneath their silver wings, bombs tumble from their silver bellies and cut through the Forest of the Laughing Elephant like titanic chain saws. He saw acre upon acre of leafless trees and blackened stumps, and the tiger running through them. Plenty of room to run, but no place to hide. Killing him would be a piece of cake.

The fire was a frail levee of light, struggling to hold back the tide of darkness that lapped at the edges of the campsite. Eric the Red came back from his work, sat down, and stared across the flames at Coombes, who'd begun to chop an onion and some garlic on a strip of bark. Teepee didn't like the expression on Red's face. What was wrong with him anyway? There was a riddle he had no answer for: Red had started looking and acting weird from the moment he'd crossed the bridge. Stomping on his hat all of a sudden. Asking Coombes if God could see him anymore. Screaming and fainting, thinking he was in that tunnel where he saw something but nobody knew what. Doves in a village. It was as if he'd been bitten by some snake or spider whose venom had addled his brain; but there had been no snake or spider, no reason at all for the change in his behavior, none that Teepee could see.

"Hey, what's for chow?"

It was Jimmy Neville.

"My own five-alarm chili," Coombes said, not looking up from his preparations. "It'll take a while, but it'll be worth the wait."

"Can't we just heat up our freeze-dried? Man, I'm, like, hungry."

"We're going to eat like civilized human beings. We're going to do that in honor of Valesquez."

"He's dead."

Coombes poured water from his canteen into a small pot, which he hung over the fire on a stout stick crotched in two forked sticks. After he scraped the onion and garlic into the pot, he reached into his rucksack, took out plastic bags of ketchup and dried chili peppers, and added those to the mixture.

"Don't know who's dumber, Neville—you or Dolores. That's the point: Valesquez is dead. He was the best mess sergeant in this or any man's army. We always ate better than anybody in this war, and if he were alive now, he'd want us to eat like civilized human beings. What was supposed to happen tomorrow?"

"Memorial Day. A Memorial Day cookout."

"Right, so that's why we'll honor him tonight."

"The Fat Angel's Memorial Day surf 'n' turf spectacular. Man, where'd he come up with enough steaks and lobsters for, like, eighty men?"

"Trade and barter, Neville. He was a genius at that."

Teepee's glance moved to Coombes. "Funny, isn't it? Ironic, I mean. The steaks are what did him in. The smell must've been all over him. The tiger must've gotten all mixed up. . . ."

Teepee wanted to believe what he was suggesting. It made the tiger seem less awesomely malign to think that it had not gone after Valesquez himself but had merely been misled by its nose into confusing him with a T-bone.

"The smell drew it in, all right, but you can bet that when it saw two hundred and twenty pounds of warm, fat, living meat, it forgot all about a few frozen steaks," Coombes said.

"How do you know?"

"Ever known me to be wrong?" Coombes answered, even as a voice yelled in his head, *Because I saw it take him!* But that was a secret he intended to die with.

He added a package of shredded beef to the pot, boiled the chili for a minute or two, then, gloving his hand with his bush hat, took the pot off the fire.

"Now we let it burn down to coals. Chili's got to simmer."

"Man, how long will that take?" Jimmy Neville whined.

"Got somewhere to go?"

The flames fell slowly, allowing the blackness of the forest to engulf the campsite, except for the islet of embers and the faint halo it cast outward for a foot or two. Sounds returned to the night—the hoots and screeches of night birds, slitherings and rustlings in the undergrowth, twigs cracking—not the sounds Teepee, Eric the Red, and Jimmy Neville particularly wanted to hear. Each threw furtive glances over his shoulder, each tried to wedge himself into the hazy corona surrounding the coals, as if that wan light could protect him from whatever dangers the darkness held.

"Hey, Coombes . . . ," said Jimmy Neville.

"What is it now?"

"Teepee thinks the war passed up this Laughin' Elephant place."

"Yeah, I heard."

"Think that's true?"

"Mistakes are made," Coombes said.

"Ask the Yard how come this mountain's called Black Grandfather Mountain."

Teepee could tell Jimmy Neville merely wanted to keep the conversation going, wanted to fill the fearful night with the sound of human voices.

Smirking beneath his mustache, Coombes translated the question for Han, who answered that the mountain was called Black Grandfather because that was its name.

A befuddled frown creased Jimmy Neville's brow. He picked at an acne pimple.

"What I mean is, how could this grandfather be black, because there ain't no black people in this country. Ain't that right, Teepee?"

Teepee shoved his face in Jimmy Neville's and gave his best imitation of a *Gone With the Wind* house nigger's grin. "Sho nuff ain't, marse Jimmy! Nohow, no way. Less black folk in dis heah country den dey is in de Klan!"

"Hey, cool it, man. I didn't mean no insult. Just wonderin' where this black grandfather come from."

"It's the grammatical construction of the language," Coombes explained as he stirred the chili. 'Black' modifies the mountain, not the grandfather. Literally translated, it would be the 'Black Mountain of the Grandfather.' "

Jimmy Neville's puzzled frown deepened. He picked at the pimple on his nose.

"So what about this Forest of the Laughing Elephant?" he persisted. "How does Han explain that?"

"You're from Pensacola, right?" answered Coombes. "If Han asked you why Pensacola is called Pensacola, what would you say?"

"That's different. Pensacola makes sense. Laughin' Elephant don't. Elephants, like, can't laugh."

"Never mind," said Coombes as he dipped a spoon into the chili to sample it. "Five-alarm, all right. Dig in, troopers."

"Jesus, is it ever," Teepee said, gasping at the first scalding bite.

"Jee-sus!" Jimmy Neville stuck out his tongue and fanned it with his hand. "Jee-sus Kee-rist!"

Han could not bear wondering another moment. He nudged the *trung-si.*

"I have question. What is Jesus?"

Coombes' laugh was short and sharp, like a bark.

"Need you on this one, Swenson. Han wants to know what a Jesus is. C'mon, Bible-thumper. Here's your chance to do some missionary work."

"Tell him Jesus was the son of God."

Coombes translated the answer, then Han's next question: "Which god?"

"Only God there is. Tell him that and that Jesus died to save all men from sin and death."

This Coombes did.

"But, *trung-si,* all men must die. Nothing can save them from that," replied a bemused Han.

Turning again to Eric the Red, Coombes said, "Looks like you've got your work cut out for you, Bible-thumper. Han doesn't get it."

"That's because he's an ignorant little heathen."

"Yeah. And you'd best remember that this ignorant little heathen is all you've got to get your Christian ass through this jungle."

"Guess you seen to that," said Eric the Red in a flat voice.

Coombes glared. *Man is cranking up his mojo,* thought Teepee, but he noticed that Red was glaring right back.

"How come you smashed our watches?"

"I hope, Swenson, that you don't think I owe you an explanation."

"No, so why dontja just *give* us one, like a present."

Coombes said nothing for a long moment as he pondered whether to let his men in on his secret. Were they worthy of the knowledge he had gained through painful experience, through years of thought? Would they understand? Possibly Bledsoe would, but trying to impart the lesson to those other two would be like teaching integral calculus to someone who'd flunked consumer math. Still, he'd give it a try. At least for Bledsoe's benefit.

"I'll give you a parable, just like Jesus," he began. "My old man was like ninety-nine percent of the people back in the world. Running scared against the clock. Humped slabs of beef all his life back in Water-loo, Iowa. The Rath meat-packing plant. Alarm told him when to get up. Noon whistle when to eat lunch. Shift whistle when to quit. Scared to death he'd get canned if he missed a day. It got so he didn't need an alarm anymore. One went off right in his head at six every morning. He was trapped inside time, like one of those little wooden men who come out of a Swiss cuckoo clock and go *bong-bong-bong* with a little hammer, except he went *bong-bong-bong* on his own head. Get the picture?"

"How come you smashed the watches is what I asked."

"Don't interrupt Jesus in the middle of a parable. Listen up. My first tour, I was the same as you. Scared I wouldn't live through it, counting the days. But when it ended, I figured something out. I'd get a job and end up like my old man. *Tick-tock, bong-bong.* So I extended for another tour, but then I kept thinking about when that one would end. Must have been halfway through it when we ran a patrol up a mountain, higher than this one, highest mountain around. Far as I could see there were mountains and jungles, and mists coming up out of the trees. It all looked old, old, but it looked young at the same time, like the world did when dinosaurs were around. And that's when I saw it, like a vision. I was in a place that was very old and very young, where time didn't make any difference. Soon as I got back to base, I signed up for an indefinite extension. Here for the duration, and if this war ever ends, I'll still be here."

"Why'd you smash the watches?"

"You want the moral of my parable? Here it is. The clock-punchers send you here, tell you, 'Do your tour of duty,' and give you the date when you can leave. From day one, you start keeping score of the months, then the weeks, then the days, and you wake up one morning with more jewels inside your heads than a storeful of Bulovas. *Tick-tock, bong-bong.* You'll do anything to live to that second when you can go home, and pretty soon you're ready to crawl on your bare knees over ten miles of broken glass just to kiss the ass of the man who can get you there. I didn't smash your watches—I broke your chains."

"I never heard such shit."

"Then try this. If you had those damned things, you wouldn't have your minds on killing the tiger. You'd be wondering what time it is, what day it is. You'd be thinking how long before you can go home. Thinking about Hightower's curfew. Fact is, you still are."

His long arm reached sideways into Teepee's rucksack and pulled out the notched stick.

How the hell did he know what it was and where I put it? . . . Because he knows everything.

"See this, Swenson? Your buddy has a few more smarts than you, so he figured to make himself a kind of calendar out of this stick."

Teepee felt slightly nauseous when Coombes cracked the stick over his knee and tossed the pieces into the jungle.

"You were slaves, now you're free, but you're too goddamned dumb to know it—you especially, Swenson."

Eric the Red leaped to his feet, lips quivering, eyes damp.

He wants to break the mojo's grip, but he knows he can't, so now he's crying.

"Dumb, am I? Smarts of a tree snail? Listen, what about the map and compass? You dint lose 'em, didja? I got the smarts to figure that out. You got rid of them, same as you done the watches, maybe same as you done the radio, dintja?"

"The radio got drenched. Would've been useless even if I did get it back."

"Gimme an answer, damn you!" Eric the Red pitched slightly forward, as if he were about to lunge across the fire, but was stopped when Coombes rose, rose and rose so far above the coals' feeble glow that everything from his shaved skull to his chest vanished into darkness. Without a head to go with them, his words seemed to come down out of the night itself.

"You goddamned idiot! Do you think that tiger's following a compass bearing? Can't you see that if we're going to kill it, we can't stand outside all of . . ." His hand, describing an arc, reached down from his headless body and flickered whitely in the blackness. "All of this. We have to get *inside* all of this. Radios, watches, compasses . . . they get in the way."

Han, sitting cross-legged at Coombes' feet, tugged at his trouser leg.

"Trung-si. No more talk."

Han cocked an ear, his still, lined face like a mahogany mask carved with a dull chisel. There—he heard it again. Sambar, Deer, giving its warning bark.

"Tiger," he said almost inaudibly. "Very near."

Coombes squatted down and breathlessly picked up his rifle.

"What is it? What's the Yard saying?" Teepee asked in a whisper.

"Visitor. Guess who."

Coombes motioned to the others to form a tight perimeter and face toward the jungle. This they did, easing the safeties off their rifles.

Teepee strained to see, but the firelight had ruined his night vision. He could not have been more blind if a sack had been tied over his head.

Here we are, he thought, circled up like the wagon train in Indian country, but that thing could be on us before we know it.

Eric the Red, his heart pounding, felt himself slipping back into the tunnel's eternal night.

Jimmy Neville, trying to muster courage, silently sang the theme song to the old TV series *Davy Crockett*.

Every muscle tensed, Coombes listened. He listened with his ears, listened with his skin, pores opening to receive the slightest vibration in the air. He could sense the big cat's presence, and if it came at him, he would be ready this time. Things would go differently than they had last night, when he'd gone to relieve Valesquez on watch.

Afraid of theft, the mess sergeant had decided to guard the steaks and lobsters for his Memorial Day surf 'n' turf spectacular and had asked Coombes to take the night watch, for as everyone knew, no one had sharper eyes or keener ears.

Coombes had risen instinctively at midnight; he didn't need an alarm to tell him that it was time to take his turn on guard. He had slung his rifle, walked across camp to the mess shack, and pushed back the flap. It was dark as a cellar inside, but he made out a huge form at the far end and smelled a powerful, musky odor. Something moved. "Hey, Angel," he called, but Valesquez didn't answer. Something moved again, a sound like a man dragging himself across the plywood floor. Coombes flicked on his flashlight, and two eyes glowed back at him, eyes slanted like the eyes in a jack-o'-lantern, and as big, and they were set in the head of a tiger, its jaws clamped around the neck and shoulder of Angel Valesquez. His first thought was that he was hallucinating. He hadn't heard a growl or any noise at all, but that strong, wild-animal smell was not a hallucination, nor was the blood smeared on the cat's whiskers and lips. He went to drop the flashlight and unsling his rifle, but couldn't move. He couldn't blink. His lungs stopped working; it was a wonder his heart did not go into immediate arrest. For a moment, mesmerized by the flashlight, the tiger stood still and stared. It did not snarl or gather itself to spring, just stared with that dreadful serenity. It seemed to know that Coombes posed no danger. Never in his life had he seen a living thing so big and so obviously deadly; never in his life had he felt more frail and mortal. Then the tiger raised its enormous head, lifting Valesquez with absurd ease, and walked toward the door, bumping Coombes aside, its mounded shoulder muscles reaching past his waist, its whole bristling length brushing against him. Even in that light touch, he could feel its mass and strength; it was as if he were being brushed by a fur-covered pickup truck. As it padded noiselessly outside, its switching tail smacked the backs of his knees, and his legs went out from under him. He fell on his ass and caught the disgraceful stench of his voided bowels.

While he sat in his own waste, his flashlight illuminating saucers of Valesquez's blood on the plywood floor, he had a sudden and overwhelming urge to know what time it was. He couldn't explain why. Maybe it was because hours had seemed to pass as he and the great cat stared at each other, but the whole encounter could not have lasted thirty seconds. *What the hell time is it?* he asked himself. *How long have I been in here?* Outside, he heard the hiss and pop of a hand-held flare and sentries calling to each other. . . . *What's goin' on there? . . . Thought I seen somethin' . . . ,* but all Lincoln Coombes could think about was the time. He looked at his army-issue watch, and it told him that it was 12:07 in the morning, May 25, a Friday. Those temporal facts drew others out of the deepest recesses of his memory: he'd been in this country six years, one month, and eleven days. How he knew that baffled him; he was sure he had forgotten, but some built-in chronometer must have gone on ticking in the back of his mind, faithfully recording the hours, the dates.

Another flare burst outside, followed by three or four panicky shots, then yells. *Jesus Christ! It's a tiger! A tiger! I think I seen a tiger! . . . A what? . . . A tiger! . . . You hit it? . . . I don't know. . . . Holy Christ, I think it's got somebody! . . .* Officers were shouting at sergeants to assemble their squads to see who was missing. Any minute now, someone would come in and discover him like this, literally scared shitless. He peeked out the back door to make sure the coast was clear, then ran to the sergeants' tent to change his clothes.

The tent was empty, thank God. He quickly undressed, went outside, and tossed his foul drawers into the four-holer latrine. Returning to the tent, he cleaned himself, put on fresh clothes, and sat on his cot, lighting a cigarette to settle his nerves. His watch now told him it was 12:24. To think about time was to think about death. To think about death was to know fear, and Coombes loathed fear. He loathed its coppery taste, its fecal musk, its touch like the touch of bloodless fingertips.

He had not told his three men the entire truth of what had happened during his first tour of duty, so long ago that it now seemed in another lifetime. Yes, he had been counting the minutes as it drew to a close, and the closer he got to the minute of deliverance, the more frightened he became, as if he feared the irony of dying at the last minute as much as death itself. He had only a week to go when he froze in the middle of a firefight. The first spattering of gunfire sent everyone in his patrol diving behind a rice-paddy dike. It wasn't heavy fire, and the lieutenant stood and yelled, "Charge!" and all but Coombes got up and charged. He stayed behind the dike, curled up in a ball, he, Lincoln Coombes, who had won two decorations for valor. The worst part came after his comrades returned. They didn't scorn or censure him. They all knew he had only a week left, and someone helped him to his feet and someone else patted him patronizingly on the shoulder. Even the lieutenant was kind. "That's okay, Linc. You're short; I should've let you stay back," he had said. The charity in those words only heightened Coombes' sense of disgrace. He had discovered something about himself he had not wanted to know, and what was more, it was a discovery he could not live with. His collapse of nerve had to have been an aberration, one born of fear, and the fear had been born of hope, and the hope had been a child of his acute consciousness that he had had only one week left. As soon as the platoon returned to headquarters, he volunteered for another tour. The lieutenant thought he was crazy. "Nobody's talking, nobody thinks you're yellow," the lieutenant assured him. "There's no reason for you to do this." And Coombes answered, "The hell there isn't."

He remembered that episode as he sat smoking in the tent. He had been all right, had conquered time and fear, right up until the instant he stood face-to-face with a creature he had never expected to see. Twelve-thirty. Strength began to return to his limbs, pumped into them by anger as he realized the full extent of what the encounter with the tiger had done to him. He knew then that he would have no choice about what to do.

Now, atop Black Grandfather Mountain, he stood in a half-crouch, his rifle at the ready. He could hear each cricket's chirp, each drop of slow rain falling on the canopy far above, but his eyes couldn't pierce the darkness. Suddenly, the crickets fell silent, and nothing made a sound but the rain. For all he knew, the tiger was only a few yards away, poised to spring. If he could see just a few feet farther, he would have a split-second edge; but the night wouldn't yield an inch. All right, then, let the cat spring straight at him out of that blackness. He would kill it point-blank in the middle of its leap. It would be a pleasure to see it bleeding at his feet, to watch the serene light go out of its amber eyes.

Its roar, dreadful and unearthly, blew the silence into fragments.

Teepee hit the deck with his rifle aimed, though he could see nothing to shoot at.

Eric the Red went flat and covered the back of his head with his hands, as if he were under mortar fire.

Jimmy Neville fell backward into the embers, then, howling, tried to climb the tree to which his hammock was tied, but its mossy trunk was as slick as a greased pole, and he slid into a crevasse between its buttress roots and curled up in a ball.

Coombes stayed on his feet, turning this way and that to get a fix on the tiger. It seemed to be circling the camp, its roars echoing, the echoes echoing until he couldn't distinguish roar from echo, echo from reecho. They came from all sides and merged into one sound that seemed the voice not of one but of all the beasts in the jungle.

"Let's see you! Let's have a look at you, you big son of a bitch!" he shouted, sending out his voice to wrestle with the tiger's: a contest as unequal as a hand-to-claw fight would have been. He raised his rifle.

"*Trung-si!* Don't shoot! There is no danger!"

His glance fell on Han, squatting with the crossbow on his lap.

"Tiger will not attack. Tiger does not make sounds before it attacks. He talks to us. He is telling us we are in his country, warning us not to go farther."

"*Warning* us?"

"Yes."

The roaring went on without pause. Even Han was amazed; never had he heard Tiger speak so loud for so long.

Eric the Red passed beyond terror into a dreamy lassitude he'd experienced only once before, under a sustained artillery barrage. He yawned and rested his head on his arms, yearning for sleep.

Jimmy Neville, wincing from the blisters on his back, reached up and pulled his hammock over himself, trusting, as does the child hiding under the sheets from the bogeyman, that he could not be harmed by what he could not see.

T. P. Bledsoe let his rifle fall from his hands and pressed his hands tightly over his ears; but the sound entered him through his nostrils and shook his brain; it bored into his guts and made them quiver. A million years of human evolution fell away. He felt naked and diminished, a puny half-ape, shuddering through the predator's night without weapons or fire or the intelligence to invent a god to call on for deliverance.

Lincoln Coombes looked at his men with loathing.

"Get up! On your feet!"

None of them moved.

"That son of a bitch is telling us that this, all this, is his turf!"

He grabbed Teepee and Eric the Red by their belts, one in each hand, and yanked them to their knees, then strode to the tree beneath which Jimmy Neville cowered, and pulled the hammock off.

"Stand up or I'll kick the life out of you!"

All three men stood. The tiger went on bellowing.

"Sing!" Coombes commanded. "You, Bible-thumper! Give us a hymn!"

Eric the Red opened his lips to sing "How Great Thou Art," but his tongue stuck to the roof of his dry mouth.

"Useless bastard! Somebody sing!"

Jimmy Neville began in a small, cracking voice, " 'Davee! Davee Crockett, king of the wild frontier,' " but the tiger drowned out his faltering attempt. Though it didn't seem possible, the roars grew louder, pummeling the Americans into a state of awed stupefaction. Songless, speechless, they could only stand and listen, as they might to an avalanche or a thunderstorm.

Then a puff of wind found an opening in the canopy and blew on the coals. A small flame rose from under a charred log, fluttered, and rose higher. Teepee kicked a dry branch into the flame. It caught, and he picked up the torch and held it in one hand, his rifle in the other. He was *not* some puny half-ape without weapons and fire. Leveling the rifle, he fired blindly into the jungle on full automatic. *Rock 'n' roll.*

"You got something to say, cat? Listen to this!"

He let go another burst. The tiger roared again, off to his left. Teepee swung, aiming from the hip.

"I've got the floor, kitty . . . I'm talking now!"

Rock 'n' roll.

The bullets snapped over Han's head. The foolish soldier was ruining his plan for tomorrow.

"Trung-si! Tell him stop!"

"Bledsoe, cease firing!"

"Here, kitty, kitty . . ." Teepee felt exalted with the rifle barking and jumping in his hand. Not a puny half-ape, but a man, not cat food, but a man with weapons and fire . . . "Come get yours, kitty . . ." He swept the rifle in an arc until the last round sprang smoking from the ejection port.

In the silence that followed, his senses heightened by the adrenaline surging through him, he could hear the tiger panting, the twigs cracking under its feet as it fled. Dropping the torch, he popped the spent magazine and reached to load another, but Coombes snatched the weapon from him.

"You made your point."

Teepee's chest heaved. His narrowed eyes gleamed like slivers of bleached oyster shells set in onyx.

"Yeah, I did. Guess he knows whose turf this is now."

From far off, another sound rose, deep and hollow, half growl, half groan.

Han turned toward the forest.

"The shooting, *trung-si*. He will run very far now."

"We'll track him down," Coombes said. "We'll kill him yet."

IF TEEPEE HAD spent a worse night in his life, he couldn't remember it. After he got into his hammock, the fury that had given him the courage to drive off the tiger leaked out of him, and he lay awake, clutching his rifle. Every branch that cracked became the tread of the big cat, and all through the long hours of the night, he heard its roar in his memory.

Once, he managed to raise his head and look around. Near the fire, Han slept soundly on the bare ground. Coombes sat beside him, on watch, relaxed but alert. That made Teepee feel a little better; with Coombes on guard, the tiger couldn't stage any surprise attacks.

Or could it? After all, forty-two men—half the company—had been guarding the perimeter when the cat abducted Valesquez. It had crept past them, through a minefield and a double row of concertina wire, and then snatched the mess sergeant and run off with him without being seen until the last second. It was a feat of infiltration the slickest, sneakiest enemy sapper could not have equaled, Teepee thought as he lay in his hammock, too frightened even to swat the mosquitoes whining in his ears. What was the matter with him? Wasn't he a brave man? Hadn't he proved his valor over and over, in the boxing ring and on the battlefield? Possibly he hadn't been brave all those times. Possibly his deeds had been nothing more than glandular reactions—unconscious explosions of adrenaline. What was courage anyway? The capacity to overcome fear and do the proper thing in the face of danger or death. Had this strange rigor come to his body because he didn't know the proper thing to do under these circumstances? Maybe Red was right: the proper action would be to obey orders, ruck up and hat for home by noon tomorrow, Valesquez or no Valesquez, tiger or no tiger.

Yet Teepee could not picture himself doing that. He wouldn't be able to look himself in the mirror if he failed to bring Valesquez out of here. Okay, that would be a proper action. Never leave your dead. The code. But what about killing the tiger? If it did take another week to track it down, Coombes would have some fast and fancy talking to do to get them out of a court-martial. And yet . . .

Man-eater . . .

If the cat got away with what it had done, it would surely try again. It would regard their camp as a kind of pantry it could raid whenever it got hunger pangs. No one would feel safe, no one would be able to sleep, no one would dare to venture beyond the perimeter. They'd be prisoners, tyrannized by the Lord of the Jungle.

Bullshit. He's no lord of anything, only an overgrown cat. Slowly, the muscles in Teepee's arms and legs relaxed. His congealed blood began to flow again, and the darkness grew more annoying than fearful. He was anxious for daylight, eager to get on the tiger's trail again.

But was that courage?

THERE WAS NO DAWN, only a slow diffusion of crepuscular light through the forest.

Coombes gave Eric the Red's hammock a shove.

"Reveille, Dolores. Off your ass and on your feet. Neville! Bledsoe! Reveille, reveille! Wake up and smell the coffee."

"I don't smell no coffee," muttered Jimmy Neville in a voice woolly with sleep.

"It's a figure of speech, you goddamned moron," Teepee snarled.

The three men rolled out and started to pack their rucksacks, but Coombes made them put on dry socks first; he didn't want to be slowed down because someone got blisters or immersion foot.

"S'pose next he'll tell us to shine our boots and put on ties," Eric the

Red mumbled sullenly to himself. He turned to Teepee. "Noon. I ain't followin' that crazy man past noon."

"How will you know?" asked Teepee, pointing up at the fragments of sky that looked like countless bits of gray flannel patching the holes between the leaves. "Then you got the problem of getting back. What are you going to do? Ask directions at a gas station?"

God will show me the way, and His grace will lead me home.

"Red, your telling me you're going to hat out at high noon is like a man on a life raft in the middle of the ocean saying he's going to jump out and swim for shore."

Smart-ass nigger.

AT FIRST, the hunters walked around and around the mountaintop, following Han as he followed the crisscrossing tracks the tiger had made in its circuits of the camp. Two or three times, he set off on what he thought was the right trail, only to have it loop back to where it started. Finally, he found a line of pawprints that headed straight down the mountain, the prints spaced wide apart.

"This way, *trung-si*. Running."

An electric current raced up Coombes' legs, into his groin.

"*Di-di,*" he said. "*Di-di, maulen.* Go, go."

EVERYTHING in this damned place is out of whack, Teepee thought as he trailed Coombes. The morning was growing darker instead of lighter. What he could see of the sky took on a leaden color; the air, thick with a sticky green heat, seemed to be changing from gas to liquid. Going to need scuba tanks to breathe pretty soon. In places, lianas hung in such profusion they were like gargantuan versions of the bamboo reeds that curtained the doorways of villagers' huts. Some sprouted leaves that scraped like sandpaper. Strangler vines coiled up the trunks of many trees, patiently throttling the life out of them. Philos (love) + dendron (tree) = loving tree. No love here. Each shrub and tree seemed to be battling the other in a slow, remorseless struggle for light, water, and air. Dog eat dog, vine eat tree, cat eat man, kill or be killed, no love at all.

Coombes stopped, then silently signaled for Teepee, Neville, and Eric the Red to wait while he and Han scouted ahead.

"It's almost noon," whispered Eric the Red, sitting down with his rifle in his lap.

"Big Ben," said Teepee. "Bong-bong-bong."

"I'm keeping track." Red produced a stick and explained: Counting "thousand-one, thousand-two" each time his heels hit the ground, he had calculated that it took a hundred seconds to walk a hundred paces. So thirty-six hundred paces equaled one hour. To avoid losing count, he borrowed a page from Teepee's book and notched the stick with his knife at the end of each hour. There were now five notches. "So we don't need watches," he said proudly. "And we don't need him. He's crazy. You heard that crazy shit about extending indefinitely, about his old man, the meat packer in Iowa. The guy extends indefinitely just so's he doesn't have to go into a meat-packing plant, like his old man? Nuts."

"Why did he say he was from Iowa?" asked Jimmy Neville. "He ain't from Iowa. He's from out West somewheres. Montana. Colorado."

"How do you know where he's from?" Teepee asked.

"That's what I heard."

"You heard wrong. Because I heard he was from up north. Minnesota or Michigan."

"So okay. Now we got it from the horse's ass's mouth," said Eric the Red. "He's from Iowa."

"Maybe," Teepee said. "Maybe he just said that."

"But, like, so what?" Jimmy Neville popped another acne pimple. "So what if he's from Iowa or Montana or wherever. He's aces in the boonies. You talk to dudes in his squad, and they'll tell you. He can get us through. Like he done that recon patrol he led. They was twelve days in the boonies, and the bad guys got onto 'em and chased 'em for twelve days, and Coombes gave 'em the slip. The patrol ran outa chow. They ate leaves and bugs and shit, and y'know, when they gave the bad guys the slip, Coombes turned to 'em and said, 'Okay, now let's continue the mission,' or somethin' like that."

"Who told you that? The guys in his squad were never on no recon where they had to eat bugs for twelve days," Eric the Red declared resentfully.

"I heard it around. It's what you, like, call common knowledge."

"The one thing you can say for common knowledge is that it's common. The fact is, nobody knows anything for sure about Coombes," said Teepee, recalling the times he had seen Coombes in the sergeants' mess tent, sitting alone and aloof from the other NCOs in the company. He had nothing to do with them, nor they with him.

"Well, then, how come you said a while ago that he had a charm like a blimp because he'd never been hit all the time he's been here? How'd you find out that he ain't been hit, never?"

"Look at him when he's taking a shower, Neville. There's not a mark on him. Not a scratch."

"I heard that Valesquez knew everything about him." Eric the Red scowled. "That they was tight. That's why I figure he's gone nuts over this tiger."

"Coombes isn't tight with anybody," Teepee said, and they all three fell silent, as if wondering why they were following a man who had no certain date or place of birth, nor verifiable history of any kind, a man who was not a man so much as the sum of the stories that were told about him. A shadow.

And now he reappeared, and with a slow wave signaled them to get up and get a move on.

BRIGHT BIRDS darted to and fro. Monkeys squatted on branches or hung by their tails, gazing down on the five human beings gathered in a circle around the remains of a sixth, lying in a thicket beside a stream bed and beneath a lofty banyan that stood on aerial roots arrayed like organ pipes. Not much left, so little that to call it a corpse, let alone to call it by a name, seemed to T. P. Bledsoe to be an example of wishful thinking. Angel Valesquez, beloved mess sergeant, and all that remained of him now were his head and shoulders, half of one arm, a few fragments of ribs and thighbones. Consumed. Devoured. As Teepee stood staring, a stream of water splashed into Valesquez's face. One of the monkeys was relieving itself. Of course, it intended no irreverence, but Teepee could not help but see its act as deliberate—untamed nature's final insult. He killed the monkey with one shot. Its bristly little body tumbled through the canopy and bounced on the ground. Its colleagues howled as they swung off in panic. Then Teepee, joined by Jimmy Neville, went off to be sick.

"How about you, Dolores?" Coombes asked Eric the Red. "If you're going to toss your cookies, do it now. I'll be wanting you to pray over the Fat Angel in a minute."

"I'm okay."

He was in fact overjoyed. A sign had been shown to him. They had found Valesquez at what he estimated to be between high noon and two in the afternoon—close enough to Hightower's deadline to save themselves from court-martial. Eric the Red knew it was between noon and two because he'd put the sixth notch in his stick shortly before Han pushed into the thicket and practically tripped over Valesquez's body. And now, as Eric the Red stood over it, another sign was shown to him: he heard again that familiar intermittent rumble, the rolling thunder of the war. God could see them after all, for wasn't it God who had led them to accomplish the mission on time, and wasn't it God who now brought that sound to their ears, the sound that would lead them home, even if they lost Han? *Follow it, son, that's our salvation.*

These reflections were interrupted by Coombes' brusque orders: Bledsoe and Neville to dig a grave, Eric the Red to make a cross and think of an appropriate eulogy.

"You mean we're gonna bury him? You said we was gonna bring him out. Even if all that was left was his little finger was what you said."

"Want to carry this mess back in your ruck? It's ripe now and getting riper by the minute. Get to it, Swenson."

He laid his rucksack and rifle beside the others on the stream bank. He saw the practical sense in burying Valesquez here; still, it didn't seem right. What about the Fat Angel's family? Wouldn't they want his remains? He found two sticks and bound them into a crucifix with strips of liana. This thing'll last maybe one good rain, and then there won't be anything to tell anybody that someone's buried here. Didn't seem fitting, the Fat Angel interred in an unmarked grave in wild, unconsecrated earth. Eric the Red sat down, took out his dog-eared Book of Common Prayer, and searched for an appropriate passage. What could be appropriate for someone who had died this way?

While Teepee shoveled with the flat of his machete and Jimmy Neville, with his hands, piled the loose soil stinking of primeval microbes and fossil insects, leaves and twigs dead a million years, Coombes turned to Han.

"What do you think he'll do now?"

"Rest."

"Near? Far?"

"Far. He's heard your guns. He smells you your guns. He won't rest until he cannot hear you smell you your guns anymore."

"The smell of guns didn't bother him when he killed this man. He walked in past eighty rifles."

"He was hungry then. He was hunting then. The hunger and the hunting made him bold. Now he wants only to rest." Han's eyes turned into slits, curved and white like pared fingernails. "Listen to me, *trung-si:* if we track slowly, so he gets away from the gunsmell, and if we track quietly, then maybe we can catch him when he's sleeping and kill him then."

"I don't want that. I want him to see me when I kill him."

This made no sense to Han, but he didn't say so, having learned that very little of what the *My* said and did made sense. They were a mysterious people, but strong, with powers to make the skies rain fire and to blow the dust that turned the forests brown.

"Very well, *trung-si,*" he said. "But be sure to shoot quick, or it will be you who sees him before he kills you."

"We'll bury this good man now."

"Good?" asked Han. "He must have done a wrong thing."

"Now it's I who don't understand you."

"My people believe that Tiger kills only those who have done a bad thing."

"He wasn't one of your people."

Coombes tore the dog tags from Valesquez's neck and with the toe of his boot nudged the partial corpse into the small hole. Jimmy Neville covered it up, and Eric the Red planted the cross.

"Okay, speak your piece, sky pilot."

Eric the Red cleared his throat and bowed his head.

"O Lord, we commit our buddy and mess sergeant, Angel Valesquez, to your care. Forgive his sins and let him into your kingdom, and be sure to bless his surf 'n' turf spectacular and our brothers who are eating it today. And forgive us, Lord, for burying him in un-Christian ground, but we don't have no radio and can't call a chopper to take him out of here. And bless us, O Lord, as we—"

"No long speeches. Wind it up, Swenson."

"Sure. This here's from the Twenty-second Psalm." He opened the Book of Common Prayer. " 'Be not thou far from me, O Lord: O my strength, haste thee to help me. Deliver my soul from the sword, my darling from the power of the dog. Save me from the lion's mouth.' " Closing the book, he looked upon his comrades and composed his lips into the smile the Reverend Berger used to bestow on the congregation after a sermon. A smile wise and kind. "That's it. I tried to find somethin' about a tiger, but I couldn't and figured a lion was close enough."

"Shouldn't we fire, like, a salute?" asked Jimmy Neville. "Ain't that what sojers do for sojers?"

Coombes shook his head. "The tiger might still be close enough to hear the shots. Don't want him scared off any more than he already is."

"So what? So what if he runs his striped ass all the way to China?" asked Eric the Red. "I figure it's noon or not much after. See, Coombes? I kept time." He brandished the notched stick. "Each one of those is a hour. Mission accomplished."

"Half, Swenson. Ruck up. We're moving out."

Coombes took a long step toward the row of rucksacks and rifles, but Eric the Red was a yard or two closer and got to them first. He snatched his weapon and, falling into a half-crouch, pointed it at Coombes, who, with his hands on his hips, stood looking down and shaking his head. Then he sighed long and loud and looked up again at the rifle leveled on his chest from six feet away.

"This another fit, Swenson, or is it mutiny?"

Eric the Red had feared this moment would come, had hoped against his fears that it wouldn't, but now that it was here, he felt calm and spoke with the tranquillity of a man sure of his moral ground.

"Ain't no mutiny. I don't gotta obey no order I know is wrong."

"Wrong? Wrong?" A smile, almost sad, played across Coombes' lips. "That's a good one. Wrong. Everybody's talking wrong." He sighed again, like a parent resigned to an incorrigible child's disobedience. "Okay, Swenson. For you, mission accomplished. Take off."

Neither Teepee nor Jimmy Neville could believe what he'd heard. Coombes had to be running a bluff; he wouldn't allow his authority to be defied so blatantly.

Eric the Red hesitated; he, too, doubted his ears, was looking for the bluff, the sneak attack.

"Go on, Dolores. Hat for home. I asked for volunteers because I wanted people who wanted to be here."

"I wanted to find Valesquez."

"And you did! Mission accomplished." He tossed the dog tags at Eric the Red's feet. "Take those with you, show 'em to the clock-puncher when you get back, if you do." He faced Teepee and Jimmy Neville. "Same—same you two. Don't want to be here, go with Swenson. Want to, with me. One condition—you go now, you stay gone. Anybody leaves, then changes his mind, tries to throw back in with me, I'll kill him."

Without taking his eyes off Coombes or moving the rifle an inch, Eric the Red squatted low and picked up the dog tags and put them in his pocket.

"Fair enough. C'mon, Teepee, Jimmy. Let's go."

"Go where? Which way?" asked Jimmy Neville in a nervous voice.

"Hear that? We head straight for that. The war. We got a war to fight."

"That's thunder," Teepee pointed out. "Only thing that'll lead you to is rain."

"Orders, the cap'n's orders," Eric the Red argued plaintively. "What else we got to go by but orders? Gotta follow 'em, gotta try."

"No more time for these long conversations." Coombes stepped forward, brushed Eric the Red's barrel aside as if it held no more threat than a broomstick, shouldered his rucksack, and slung his rifle. "I'm crossing the stream with Han. Whoever's with us on the other side is with us the rest of the way. Who stays on this side is on his own with Swenson."

"Hey, give Red a chance to change his mind. We can't leave him here alone, wandering around like—"

Coombes interrupted with a loud snort, and Teepee, realizing he'd used the plural, fell silent. Then he hefted his pack by one of its webbed straps, holding his head down so he would not have to look into Eric the Red's face.

"Don't follow," he warned. "You know the man's serious about what he'll do."

"And you know I'm gonna make it back and you know I can't lie to Hightower and you know I won't lie at no investigation or a court-martial."

Teepee nodded to say that he accepted the risk, and then he advised Red not to cut cross-country, chasing after noises.

"Follow this stream down. It must empty into the river. Then you follow that till you come to the bridge. From there, you should be able to pick up our tracks, follow them back to base camp. Do anything else, you'll be lost."

"Not as lost as you're gonna be."

With Jimmy Neville, Teepee splashed across the stream.

"Not as lost as you are!"

That cry seemed not to have been formed in any human throat but to have composed itself spontaneously out of nothing, for Red could not be seen behind the veil of bamboo and liana and aerial roots. Not ten yards away, and it was as if he'd ceased to exist—a dust mote sucked into the jungle by some vast inhalation of its moist green lungs. All that was left of him were the words "Not as lost as you are!" hovering in the paralyzed air.

ERIC THE RED wasn't scared, at least not as much as he thought he would be, left alone in this dominion of plant life. He was worried about his finding his way back, but beneath the crust of that apprehensiveness lay a reservoir of excitement and confidence. Rather than abandoned, he felt liberated. From the tyranny of Lincoln Coombes, from everyone who would direct his life. For the first time in his twenty years, there was no one—not father, mother, minister, teacher, sergeant, or captain—to tell him where to go or what to do. His only ruler was his own conscience, and it decreed he was doing the right thing, and that knowledge was the source of his confidence. The only question now was how to do the right thing. Following the stream was the surer thing, but also the slower; it would loop and bend and triple the distance he had to travel. But fixing his internal compass on that distant booming would give him a more direct route. A beeline. A straight shot. The trouble was, Teepee had planted a doubt in his mind. What if it *was* only thunder, weather instead of war? He listened carefully through the silence surrounding him, a silence profound yet untranquil, and turned his head slowly to one side, slowly to the other. The sound was like an ore car rolling through a tunnel, and it seemed to be coming from behind the mountain Han called Black Grandfather—the direction they'd started out from. Had to be the war. He pushed through a tangle of vines and tendrils, and followed his ears.

NOW THEY WERE FOUR. They tracked all day through galleries tapestried in green and never saw the sun. They camped that night in a hollow scooped out of a mountainside and didn't see the stars. They went on the next morning and into the afternoon, descending to a valley where the trees, dripping with wild orchids, suggested temple pillars festooned for a rite of sacrifice, one whose meaning they could not fathom. They didn't speak, their glances darted side to side, they moved through the jungle's dim, breathless halls with an anxious reverence, as if they were trespassing in a precinct both sacred and evil.

Teepee, following Coombes, watched the forest close in behind him with each step, even as, ahead, it cloaked where he was going. He felt shut off from his past, barred from any vision of his future, trapped in a present in which he'd become a stranger to himself. He couldn't be doing this, abandoning a fellow soldier, disobeying his commanding officer's orders, going over the hill on a renegade mission. He wondered if he would have returned with Red if he'd not seen what the tiger had done to Valesquez. But he had seen, so now it would not be enough merely to kill the animal. He intended to annihilate it, make it disappear, boil its heart and liver and organs in a stew, give its meat to Han's tribesmen for a feast, leave its guts to the vultures, grind its teeth, claws, and bones into powder and scatter the powder to the four winds so there would be no sign remaining on earth that the tiger ever had drawn a breath. He wondered if it might have been this way half a million years ago, when those puny half-apes discovered weapons and banded together to hunt, with spear and club, some saber-toothed beast, not for meat or hide but to teach a lesson: we are not to be trifled with, we are not to be picked off and devoured with impunity.

The next day, they passed through a gap in the mountains. They found the places where the tiger buried its scat, just like a house cat, Valesquez transformed by digestive chemistry into cat shit.

Later on, they found a tree branch on which the tiger had sharpened its claws. The branch was over seven feet from the ground.

They went on.

T. P. Bledsoe had begun to feel that they were not pursuing the tiger but being pulled by it, Coombes leashed to it and he, Han, and Neville shackled to Coombes by immaterial chains.

The land rose gradually to a plateau. They didn't realize it was a plateau until they'd walked a long time without climbing up or down. A while later, Teepee noticed that the trees had become shorter and their placement more regular, that orderliness and the scrub jungle growing between the trees suggesting a long-neglected orchard. Still another while later (he'd begun to measure time in such imprecise increments), he smelled a tangy odor tinged with rancidness and heard soft, plopping noises on all sides. Then something fell in front of him, and he stepped into a pulpy, yellowish mass. Raising his eyes, he saw golden fruits hanging from the branches. The same fruits, more red than gold, littered the ground in varying stages of ripeness and rot.

With a low whistle, he tried to get Coombes' attention, but Coombes kept walking beside Han, his eyes and mind fixated on the scalloped circles printed in the earth.

"Yo!" Teepee whispered. Coombes kept walking. *Big boss man, don't you hear me when I call?*

"Yo! Coombes!"

Finally, he stopped, throwing back his head and raising, then dropping, his long arms to gesture his exasperation.

"This is an orchard, or it used to be," said Teepee softly.

"Great powers of observation, Bledsoe."

"A mango orchard. Somebody's living out here. Or used to."

"Incredible powers of deduction."

"So who the hell would be growing mangoes way the hell out here?"

"Make a difference who?"

"If it's the bad guys, yeah."

Coombes conferred with Han, his bass voice straining to sound the falsetto tones of the language.

"Ready for this, Bledsoe? Good news, bad news. Good news is, it's not the bad guys. It's the People with No Noses. We're in the Valley of the People with No Noses, and Han doesn't know this country real well. Says it's a bad place and no one comes here."

"No noses?"

"It might be the People Who Can't Smell—I'm not sure how to translate it exactly into English. Han says this orchard belonged to them. He's pretty sure they're long gone from here, but in case they're not, we shouldn't get too close to them because we'll lose our noses if we do. Or lose our sense of smell. Something like that. Satisfied?"

"More bush mumbo-jumbo."

"There it is. People with no noses who grow mangoes. You've been here long enough to know that everything's possible in the big green. Shit, you see Joan of Arc riding by in full armor, you don't ask what she's doing here, you salute and move on with whatever mission you've got. So let's get on with ours."

The mango orchard gave way to pineapple groves, which the jungle was patiently throttling to death; thick yellow vines reticulated like bamboo and brown vines plaited like hawser coiled up the trunks and around the broad, feathery leaves. Pineapples lay all around, and Jimmy Neville picked one up and asked to borrow Teepee's machete so he could split it open and eat it.

"It's rotten, you moron. You'll get the runs."

"Then how 'bout I shinny up one of these vines and get us a fresh one?"

"No, Neville. No Tarzan shit."

"It'd be like shinnying up the rope at boot camp."

"No."

"But I'm, like, hungry," Jimmy Neville whined while Teepee thought: *Pineapples are bromeliads and bromeliads are epiphytes and epiphytes are plants that grow on plants.*

Had he, Thomas Pearce Bledsoe, become a human epiphyte, an outgrowth of Lincoln Coombes? They drank the sap of the same obsession, their purpose was the same, but while Coombes did not need him, he needed Coombes to sustain him in these many-storied jungles.

Epiphyesthai. Epi + phyesthai = to grow on.

No help whatsoever, Father Aloysius LeClerc.

They passed beyond the ruined pineapple groves into a tea plantation, where none of the trees grew higher than twenty feet and where they saw, for the first time in what seemed a year, the unbroken arch of the sky. A wind sprang up, the thick monsoon clouds dissipated, and the plantation and the steep, dark-green mountains surrounding it were inundated in a dazzling, sudden light. In a short time it was hot beyond measure, but despite the heat and the steam that rose from the sodden ground to prickle his nostrils and throat, Teepee rejoiced. He could tell the time of day and the direction they were traveling in: high noon and west. Not that that temporal and geographic information meant a great deal. It might have at the bridge, but now, so what? West toward where, from where?

A stick in front of him exploded into motion, shooting between him and Coombes in a series of swift S's. Off to one side, something lay in tight coils and glowed a bright red-orange, like an electric burner turned on high, except it was striated with thin black and yellow bands. There were rustling sounds all around. Nothing to be alarmed about, Coombes explained soothingly. The tea plantation offered the most light, and that light had summoned the snakes from their nests and lairs in the encompassing forests. They needed to balance their body temperatures, soak up a few rays after so long a time in the gloom. A little serpentine sunbathing, that was all. Just be careful where you step.

More than careful, Teepee walked with the fearful caution of a man crossing a minefield. Behind him, Jimmy Neville grasped the back of Teepee's rucksack and planted his feet in his tracks. Coombes tried to calm them by naming the snakes he spotted, as if he were a zookeeper leading kids on a tour of a herpetarium. Over there, a bamboo viper. There a krait. There a spitting cobra—watch out for him—and there— look at that monster—an amethyst python. Could swallow a small deer whole. We overcome our fears by naming them, Teepee thought, but all of Coombes' zoological information could not pluck from Teepee's heart the primeval terror of a sudden injection from venomous fangs. Might as well try to keep a man cool during an attack by naming the calibers of the guns and shells being fired at him.

On they went, with such slow and tentative care that it took them an hour—or what they would have known was an hour if they'd had watches—to cover half a mile—or what they would have known was half a mile if they'd had maps. At last they returned to the forest, a scrubby, second-growth forest amid whose tangle, as big as tabletops, rose the mossy stumps of teak and mahogany and tropical oak cut down in some forgotten time. In this twilit place, Coombes called a break. Teepee sat alongside Jimmy Neville against one of the giant stumps, grateful for the absence of snakes. He hated them, had hated them ever since he'd seen a cottonmouth open its whitened jaws as it hung from a tupelo in the swamp where Uncle Elmond used to take him hunting. A couple of yards away, Coombes and Han were conferring again, plotting some strategy. Lulled by their voices, Teepee closed his eyes and dozed. In a half-slumber, he dreamed he heard a choir singing in the distance. Jimmy Neville nudged him. He opened his eyes and realized the hymning had not been a dream. He still heard it, though barely, fading in and out.

"What the hell is that?" Jimmy Neville asked in a hushed tone.

Teepee shook his head, too embarrassed to say what he thought: ghosts. He hadn't believed in ghosts until he'd come to this land, where ghosts were almost as common as mosquitoes, where even the most educated and enlightened people spoke, as casually as people back home spoke about their neighbors, of restless spirits haunting village graveyards, of visitations from ancestors dead a hundred years. He'd never seen an apparition, but he'd heard one one rainy, flare-lit night, when his squad was holed up in an abandoned schoolhouse, drying off after a long patrol in the monsoon. There was a banging at the door. At first, Teepee and his squad leader thought it was one of the sentries posted outside, but when they issued the challenge, there was no response except a more violent banging, as if someone were trying to tear the door off its hinges. "Password!" the squad leader shouted, his rifle and Teepee's and the rifles of the others leveling on the door. It banged and banged, and then one of the planks sprang loose, and they heard someone or something moaning outside. The five soldiers inside blew the door to splinters, but when they went outside to check, they found neither blood nor footprints nor sign of any kind that anything living had been there. And nothing living had, the villagers told them next morning. It was the teacher who had been assassinated in the school for refusing to join the guerrillas. He returned frequently to the scene of his terrible death— the terrorists had slit his throat, then disemboweled him; that was why the school had been abandoned long ago. The Americans accepted this supernatural explanation. Why not? They were in the Big Green, where all things were possible, where if you saw Joan of Arc riding by in full armor, you saluted and carried on.

Now, listening to the far-off singing, Teepee seemed to be hearing a whole chorus of spirits. A lamentation of male and female voices, as if the souls of men and boys slaughtered in this place of endless dying were crying out against their fate, as if the souls of the women who'd mourned them were crying out their sorrow. It was coming from somewhere off to the left. How far, he couldn't tell. Then, through some trick of acoustics, the chant grew louder and more distinct for a few moments before fading again. But in those moments, he realized the chant was no plaint of troubled souls; it was coming from living throats, and it was stranger than all the ghosts in the world.

Coombes stood, rising up and up, cocking one ear toward the sound.

"Han says it's them," he said.

"Who?"

"The people with no noses. He says they sing like that. A language he never heard before. Me neither. Don't recognize it."

Teepee licked his dry lips. The sweat on his neck and back had begun to feel like ice.

"Latin."

"Say again?"

"Latin. They're singing in Latin."

Coombes stared at him. The white-boy mojo—was it strong enough to deal with this?

"You know Latin when you hear it, Bledsoe?"

"Roger. Greek too. That's either an evening mass or vespers. Too weird. Even for the Big Green, it's too weird."

Weird, but not too, thought Coombes. Nothing's too weird for this place. He squatted and looked into the hillman's fissured, frightened face.

"Han, maybe they've seen the tiger. The tracks lead that way."

"I won't go near them. Everyone who goes near them, their noses fall off, their fingers, their feet. They're cursed. They make people fall apart. I thought they were gone from here—"

"Now listen to me, Han. It's only a foolish story. Like ghost tigers."

Han looked at him angrily.

"I won't go near them."

"Did you not tell me a little while ago that you don't know this country?"

"No one knows this country. No one comes here, because—"

"Well, *they* must know it. They live here. They can guide us—"

"No, *trung-si*. I value my nose, my fingers, my feet."

In the face of this mulish superstition, Coombes felt a rush of violent intolerance, an urge to slap the ignorance out of the hillman's benighted brain. He drew in a breath.

"I'll make you a bargain. You stay here with one man. I'll go with the other and talk to them. If we come back with our noses still on our faces, will you believe then that it's all foolishness? Will you go near them then and convince them to help us?"

Han said nothing. He needed to think for a moment. Perhaps the *My*, with their extraordinary powers, would not be affected by the curse. Perhaps they could protect him from it.

"Answer me, Han. Will you?"

"Yes, *trung-si*. I hope you'll be all right."

THEY FOUND the remnants of a road: a corridor of younger, shorter trees hemmed by tall trees, patches of red laterite showing through the tangled ground cover. They followed it less than a quarter of a mile before they saw a clearing and then a steeple, its stern Gothic lines rising incongruously above clumped palm and breadfruit, its belfry with no bell in it and crowned by a leaning crucifix. The mud-brick church was as small as the clapboard country churches in Coombes' Iowa and Teepee's Louisiana, yet it possessed, in that brooding Asian wilderness, the fantastic quality of a fairy castle. It was surrounded by stilt houses with thatch roofs and walls of woven reed, some in ruins, and there were vegetable gardens, some tended and some not, a stone well, and beaten paths covered with footprints and pocked by small, shallow holes. The singing had stopped and no one was in sight.

"Lot of cripples, that's what it looks like," Coombes said, inspecting the holes and footprints. "Canes, crutches."

Teepee licked again his dry lips. "Hospital? Think the bad guys turned this into a field hospital?"

"Would the bad guys be singing a mass? In Latin?"

"Nobody anywhere sings the Latin mass anymore. Last time I heard one, I was ten."

They moved cautiously past the well, rifles at the ready, toward a long, mud-walled bungalow with four wooden doors and a faded sign over each door. Teepee peered at one, and the ice crystals on the back of his neck spilled down his spine and up over his skull at the same time.

"This is a mission, Coombes. A Maryknoll mission."

"A what?"

"Maryknoll priests. Missionaries."

"Too bad Swenson isn't here. Feel right at home."

"French. See this? It says: 'Father Pascal Tourane, director.' *Directeur* in French. And those initials after his name, those are for the Maryknoll order."

"You know French too?"

"Loozeanna French. Coon-ass French."

Coombes nudged the door open with his shoulder, crouching with rifle pointed in case the occupant was not a missionary, and entered a small room, the dirt floor, smooth and hard as concrete, striped by the light slashing through the rattan blinds drawn over the single window. The air was stifling and held an odor at once disgusting and sweet. A picture of Christ laying healing hands upon a sick man hung on one wall. There was a small trunk at the foot of a straw-mat bed, a table on which some boxlike object sat shrouded by a canvas case so thinned by dry rot that the slatted light fell through it as through a sheet of wax paper. Coombes pulled it off, the canvas falling into shreds. Underneath was a two-way radio, a communications period piece with cracked dials and switches corroded to a pale green and a battery crank rusted shut. A message tablet lay in front of the radio. The top page was written on. Coombes told Teepee to read the faded script. He made out a couple of words but couldn't decipher them.

"Sorry. This is real French. It's different than Cajun French, and . . ." He paused, noticing a set of smudged numerals at the top left-hand corner.

"What is it?"

He put his eye almost on the paper, then raised it to the window. The paper crumbled and fell through his fingers.

"This is too goddamned spooky."

"What is it, Bledsoe?"

"That was a date."

"Yeah? Yeah?"

"June second, nineteen fifty-four. Way too spooky for this nigger."

"Don't lose it. Don't you lose it on me now." Coombes stared out the door. "They're in there." He motioned at the church with his rifle. "They saw or heard us coming and they're scared and they've barricaded themselves in there. Man, they must be *way* out of touch. They think that still exists."

"What does?"

"Sanctuary."

They went outside and toward the church, its steeple's shadow drawing a skewed rectangle on the earth. They weren't two yards from the door when it was flung open and filled by a figure almost as tall as Coombes and as insubstantial as a windblown reed, with a long, white, yellow-streaked beard and long white hair. His nose was missing and his skin was blotched and almost transparent, like stained butcher's paper. His shirt was a mosaic of patches, his trousers had shrunk to his kneecaps, and sandals cut from a rubber tire covered feet missing half their toes. This being stood motionless for a few moments, his head cocked slightly forward as he squinted at the two soldiers; then he raised a hand red with suppurating sores, but Teepee and Coombes couldn't tell what this gesture signified. Was he greeting them? Blessing them? Asking them to lower their rifles? They were too astonished to do or say anything. The being took a couple of steps toward them, steps too short to be called steps or even to constitute a shuffle, as the bruise-colored knobs beneath his ankles were too truncated to be called feet, as the legs above them were too thin to be called legs. He tottered, then shuffled backward a few inches and reached with one arm into the church doorway. Somehow a pair of crutches appeared. On these, he propelled himself forward, the ribbons of his legs flapping. His mouth opened wide, its cavity joining the cavity where his nose had been, so that the entire center of his face was a penumbral maw, from which came a sound at once sibilant and hollow, like a whisper through a tube. A voice, yes, the being had a voice, and he was speaking two words as he swung toward the soldiers.

"Mon Dieu!"

They backed away from his approach and the stench that wafted from him: the same stench as in the room—a distilled essence of rot and decay.

"Vous arrivez!"

Teepee struggled to remember the patois he'd heard spoken on Uncle Elmond's porch back in Gretna.

The being paused and stared at him, baring scarlet gums and a couple of nubby teeth in something like a smile.

"Sénégal? Vous êtes sénégalais?"

"Oui, oui," Teepee answered, deciding it would be better to answer in the affirmative until he could collect his wits and figure how to communicate with the wraith.

"Vous êtes de la Légion Étrangère?"

Le jeune étranger? The young stranger? Okay, he was young, a stranger.

"Oui, oui."

"Incroyable! Vous êtes vraiment ici!"

"Oui. Uh . . . me . . . I . . . *Je . . . Je comprehend,"* Teepee said, although in fact he did not comprehend. He paused. "Uh . . . parlay-voo . . . English—I mean *anglais? Parlez-vous anglais?"*

"Anglais?" The priest looked at him. *"Pourquoi?"*

Pourquoi. Right. Why English? Okay. Because . . . How the hell did you say 'because' in French? *Parce que . . .* Okay. *Étranger.* That also meant foreigner. Right. English because we're foreigners.

"Étranger," he said. *"Oui."*

"Je comprends! D'accord! Bien sûr!"

"Oui, oui. Ah, you—I mean *vous . . . Vous* Father—I mean *Père—* Pascal Tourane?"

"Oui. Je m'appelle Père Pascal . . ."

"Translate," muttered Coombes. "What the fuck's he saying?"

"He's Father Pascal. Something about foreigners arriving. All I got so far."

The priest gestured at Coombes.

"*Et il . . . anglais?*"

"*Oui, oui.*"

"*Ah, la Légion Étrangère. C'est romantique. Anglais. Sénégalais. Tout le monde.*"

"*Oui, oui.*"

"*Alors, c'est vrai? Vous êtes arrivé pour nous?*"

"*Oui, oui.*"

The priest managed to hold his crutches steady with his elbows as he brought his ruined hands together in a gesture of thanksgiving.

"*Merci Dieu.*" He began to cry. "*Merci Dieu.*"

Father Pascal turned and hobbled back toward the church, calling in no tongue Teepee ever had heard before, flailing with one withered arm while with the other he held himself upright on the crutches. A figure appeared in the doorway: an old man short enough to be a child and dressed, like the priest, in harlequin rags. He stepped out into the light. His skin, what little unscarred skin remained on his face, was as brown as Han's, and his left arm ended at the elbow; his right hand, wrapped in filthy gauze, clutched a walking stick. He hesitated, fluttering his eyes as if he had not seen daylight for hours or days, until the priest pointed toward a hut and uttered more words in the unknown tongue. The little man went toward the hut, hopping like a one-legged bird. Others followed, men and women, though it was hard to see any difference between sexes. There was about them all a suggestion of maimed corpses abandoning a crypt as they emerged blinking from the church, the corpses of the damned risen on Judgment Day, souls reunited to repulsive bodies beyond all hope of restoration to the full glory of their youth and beauty. Yet they moved about the compound with a sense of urgency, hobbling and scuttling to the insistent voice and wild gestures of Father Pascal—the animator of those living dead, the zombiemaster. Amazingly, they scaled the ladders into their stilt houses. In a few minutes, small bundles were being pitched out the doors, and the living dead were climbing back down the ladders. Then two men—two of the perhaps five or six with limbs still intact—came up, whipping the mud-stained flanks of yoked water buffalo that pulled a pair of big, two-wheeled carts, hitched together. The drivers halted the team, then with those others still capable of unaided motion went about the compound, gathering bundles of clothes, metal urns, statues of household gods, and began to load them in the lead cart. All this went on in an atmosphere of excitement, even of gaiety. A rapid chatter filled the dead hot afternoon air. As he watched them, Teepee realized what they were, but he couldn't utter the word or even think it, freighted as it was with a biblical dread.

The priest had meanwhile vanished into his room, yet his voice could be heard above the other voices, hollow and sepulchral, the voice of one already speaking from beyond the grave. He droned a repetitive chant. Though Coombes and Teepee couldn't understand the French, the rhythms and the timing of the pauses told them it was neither prayer nor incantation but the repetitions of a radio call sign. They walked over and peeked through the door. A few things became clear to Teepee as he looked at him, sitting on fleshless buttocks in that harsh, slashing light, speaking into a dead radio to people who had fled this land twenty years before.

"He's not exactly crazy," he said.

"You being a black-assed shrink again?" Coombes shook his head, communicating in that brief jerking movement more contempt than pity for the diseased, deluded priest. "Think you can remember enough of that coon-ass French to talk to the sky pilot?"

"Coombes, this is a leper colony! We ought to get out of here."

"I know what it is. No sweat. You've got to be around lepers for years to catch it, and even then you might not. Okay, can you talk to him?"

"You talk to him. Sounds like he speaks the local lingo."

"That's some montagnard tribal dialect. Different tribe than Han's. Can you get through to him? That's what I need to know."

"Sure, but . . . Don't you get it, don't you get why those people are packing up their stuff? The buffalo carts? Why he's in there, talking into the radio?"

"He's nuts."

"Lost is what he is. Lost in time. Lost *to* time. That message on the tablet. Way back when, when the French pulled out of here, somebody radioed him. He and these folks were going to be pulled out. Maybe taken to a sanitarium somewhere. Soldiers would come for him, and he thinks we're—"

Coombes crooked his rifle in his elbow and moved away from Father Pascal's door.

"French."

"The foreign legion. He thinks I'm from Senegal and that you're British and that we're foreign fucking legionnaires, finally coming to the rescue. And now he's on the radio, making an announcement. Telling headquarters or whatever that we're here."

Coombes said nothing, staring coldly into the distance, through and past the bustling people. The healthy ones—those lucky few who'd acquired an immunity to the disease—were helping the most crippled onto the carts for the ride out, down the road that didn't exist anymore. A woman—maybe a woman—came up to them, cackling in her tongue, making movements with her ulcerated hands as if she were shooing a dog or a bothersome child. There was a huge lesion on her cheek, flies lapping at its edges, and her nose was an oozing stump. She cackled some more, waving at them, and they realized they were standing in her vegetable patch and that she wished to pick some of whatever was growing there. Something to take with her on the journey.

"You can see how it happened," Teepee continued. "Man, I've lost track of the days since the bridge. Stay out here long enough, you lose track of the months, then the years, and then one day you don't even know what decade you're in."

"That's interesting, Bledsoe. Make a great yarn, but get this. You tell the sky pilot what we're here for and that we want those five or six people who are still healthy to guide for us."

"You're something," Teepee said, apalled. "You're really something."

LOOKING MONKLIKE in his hooded poncho, Eric the Red sat in the rain beside a bomb crater so big his parents' house back in Spokane could have fit inside it. There were craters for a mile around, single craters, double craters linked into figure eights, quadruple craters shaped like rosettes, craters within craters. Eric the Red sat against a blackened tree stump, shivering and sweating simultaneously under his poncho, his eyes nearly closed from mosquito bites. He was dizzy with hunger. He had run out of rations two days before and subsisted on bark and leaves until this morning, when he feasted on cooked rice balls he'd found on a dead enemy soldier a few hundred yards from the swath of craters. It was weird: the soldier didn't have a mark on him, but he was dead—killed, Eric the Red figured, by a bomb's shock wave. The rice balls were wrapped in wax paper inside the soldier's pack. Showed you how backward the enemy was—they still used wax paper instead of cling wrap. The rice balls had filled the hollow in Eric the Red's belly for a little while, but now the hollow was back. Just like everybody said about gook food—stuff yourself, and you're hungry an hour later. But for all the ache in his stomach and the welts around his eyes and the rain, he was happy. He had survived three days in the jungle alone. Or maybe it was four . . . no, five . . . no, maybe it was three. No matter, he had survived a long time, wandering alone through the Forest of the Laughing Elephant, following his ears, and now he was back in the war. He was home, and it was beautiful. Who ever would have thought that he'd consider a landscape like this as beautiful? It wasn't as if this part of the jungle had been bombed by planes; it was as if it had been struck by meteors, the Almighty's very own thunderbolts. Still, it was beautiful, beautiful to be able to see, not three or four or six feet, but for a whole mile, to look up, not at an impenetrable weave of branches, but at the open sky. For sure, God could see him now.

And so would the soldiers who were coming to assess the damage. He knew they would be here soon. The bombers bombed, then the infantry landed to tally up the arms and legs and make a body count. That was the pattern. Eric the Red had taken part in several such operations himself—not real soldiering; janitorial work, in a way. Groundskeeping. Yeah, if this war was like the football games at which he marched in his colorful bandsman's uniform, then soldiers like himself were the groundskeepers, cleaning up for the next game. Groundskeepers and scorekeepers. Count the arms and legs, divide by two. The soldiers would come as soon as the rain let up. It was raining and blowing too hard to land helicopters safely. Eric the Red hadn't realized how hard it was raining and how strong the wind was blowing until he stepped out of the jungle, into the place of the craters. A driving rain that pelted his poncho, a wind that chilled even though he was hot under the heavy rubber. This was the unbeautiful part, this rain, this moaning monsoon wind, but he would wait here. He was out of rations. He wasn't going to tramp any longer in the forests that made him feel like a beetle crawling through a cornfield, not without rations, a map, or a compass.

He pulled the drawstrings of his poncho to shield his face and head from the rain, pulled them tighter and tighter until all that showed through the hood were his mouth and nose. Maybe he ought to wait at the edge of the bombed area, beneath the sheltering trees. No, not a good idea. A helicopter or an observation plane might fly over on a scouting mission before the infantry came in. The pilot wouldn't see him if he was under the trees. Better to tough it out in the open. He looked up. Man, the clouds were low, their long, swirling gray arms reaching down almost to the ground. The rain blasted into his eyes, and he bowed his head again, then remembered the souvenir he'd taken from the dead soldier. It was in his rucksack. He stood up, raised his poncho, and slipped the ruck off his back. Inside was an olive-green pith helmet. Its hard brim would keep some of the rain out of his face. He tore out the leather band inside, so the helmet would fit, jammed it over the poncho hood, and sat down again. Sure enough, the rain sluiced off the brim as off the eaves of a little roof. He had a little roof for his head, but now he was colder than ever. The rain had soaked him to the skin in the few seconds it had taken to lift the poncho and pull off his rucksack. He was not sweating at all now, only shivering. This was ridiculous and unreasonable—to be in the tropics and shivering. Everything about this country was unreasonable, immoderate, intemperate. Hey! Weren't those half-dollar words! Teepee words. Unreasonable, immoderate, intemperate. Well, that was this country. When it rained, it rained twice as hard and twice as long as it did back home in Washington, and that was the rainiest state in the Union. When the sun came out, it got hotter than the doorknobs in hell.

A gust swept across the craters and slipped up through the bottom of his poncho and made him shudder. He began to feel disconsolate, not like a soldier awaiting rescue by his fellow soldiers but like the last living human being on an earth blasted and scourged by an angry God. Alone. Deserted. Too bad he couldn't take out his Book of Common Prayer. That would keep his spirits up. Got to think happy thoughts. No sense in getting gloomy. You're doing the right thing, and you're in God's sight now, he said to himself. The big CO in the sky is looking at you with binoculars. Not a single sparrow falls. Think about that. Think about how it'll be when the grunts show up and find you here. He would say something cool and casual, words that would become legend. *Hey, guys, what's happenin'?* No. Something cooler than that. *Hey, guys, what took you so long?* That would be good. Even better if the grunts were from his own company. He would become a legend. *Man, we land in this bomb zone, not a fuckin' tree standin' inside of a mile, craters like the moon, and who's sittin' there like he's in a park but Red Swenson? And what's he say? "Hey, guys, what took you so long?"* What a reunion that would be. Back with the old company, then the chopper ride back to base camp. Think about how great that's gonna be. Hot coffee, hot chow, hot showers. Dry clothes, dry socks, a dry cot. Three hots and a cot.

He shuddered again. Better get up and move around, keep the blood flowing. As he stood, water guttered through his sleeve as through a downspout. Some poncho. He paced along a muddy ridge between two craters, blowing into his hands, fanning his arms. Ridiculous. The equator was spitting distance from this country, and he felt like he was in the Cascades in December. Well, the grunts would be here soon. The water in the craters didn't look very deep, and the dead soldier's body hadn't begun to decompose. Meaning that the air strike had been very recent, meaning further that the damage assessment could not have been made yet. Meaning the grunts would be on their way as soon as the rain let up. Eric the Red walked along, his rucksack and rifle butt making twin humps under his poncho.

I hear Thy voice, I hear the rolling thunder . . . Then sings my soul, my savior God, to Thee . . . He sang, first to himself, and then aloud. "I hear Thy voice, I hear the rolling thunder . . . How great Thou art! How great Thou art!"

HAN SQUATTED with his crossbow in his lap. He was nervous. The *trung-si* was taking too long. Perhaps, even though he was *My,* he did not have powers against the curse, and his nose had fallen off. And his fingers and feet. The *trung-si* should have listened to him! What if the *trung-si* and the blackface soldier had fallen apart? He wished the *trung-si* had left him with some cigarettes. He looked at the young spotface soldier.

"You, you," he said in the only *My* talk he knew. "Cigarette me."

The spotface soldier turned to him. "You wanna cigarette?"

Han nodded, and the spotface soldier got up from where he sat and took out a little plastic box with cigarettes in it.

"There you go. Ever think of buying your own, Han?"

Han did not comprehend a word of that, but he smiled and nodded, as he always did when the *My* spoke to him and he didn't understand what they were saying. He lit up, inhaled. Ah! So good. Cigarettes so good when you were nervous. He squatted and smoked and tried not to think about the possibility that the *trung-si* and the blackface soldier had lost their noses and fingers. That would be the end of the hunt and all chances of being paid. He thought about Tiger. A strange one. Tiger always did things this way—hunt, kill, eat for twothree suns, rest for twothree suns, hunt and kill again. But this Tiger, why, it was like he didn't need to rest . . .

COOMBES SAID, "I'm going back for Neville and Han. You talk to the sky pilot. Bring him up-to-date, fill him in on recent history. We're not French, we're Americans, and we need to borrow a few of his congregation."

Teepee never would understand the military mind that fixes on the task at hand to the exclusion of all else, that is as devoid of compassion as it is of curiosity and wonder and imagination. Tunnel vision in the extreme. Mole vision. All Coombes saw in this bizarre place of disease and exile were a few people who might help him track the tiger.

"I can't do that!" he said. "For Christ's sake, these people are sick."

"Hard of hearing, are you? I said just the healthy ones."

"I still can't. These people, the priest, they think we're here to . . ."

It came down on him, that look Coombes could get, glacial and intractable.

"Okay! I'll try."

"That's all I'm asking you to do."

"Doesn't sound like asking to me," said Teepee.

"YO, HAN, is that one of them pineapple palms over there?"

The spotface soldier was pointing at something, but Han could not tell at what, or what he was saying.

"That one over there. With the vine hanging from it."

Han smiled and nodded and pondered Tiger some more. He was trying to recall all the tales he had heard about Ghostiger. Could they go a long time without rest?

"Yo, Han. You wanna pineapple? I do."

Han smiled and nodded.

"How about I shinny up that vine and pick us some? Like the rope at boot camp. Piece of cake."

Han smiled and nodded. He wished the spotface soldier would stop talking so he could think, think of some way to bring Tiger to bay—if it wasn't Ghost.

"Okay, Han. I'll get us two, and then when Teepee comes back with the machete, we'll crack 'em open."

The spotface soldier stood and walked into the forest. Good. Now Han could think.

IT'S ALL FALLING into place, thought Teepee as he looked through the rattan blinds in Father's Pascal's room toward a cemetery and the jungle frowning beyond it. This colony must have had ten times as many people as it does now. Maybe more. Lepers all over the place, stuck out here at the ass end of the known world, working in those plantations to feed themselves. Most of them are dead now, but this place must still have a reputation. The bad guys probably have standing orders to give this valley a wide berth. And you'd have to pass through this valley and through that gap in the mountains we went through a couple of days ago to get to the places we were before. This whole area is one big isolation ward. The spy planes and the spy satellites never spotted any enemy activity around here because there's been none to spot and so no reason to bomb it or spray it. So he had solved one of the mysteries of the Big Green— a great swath of jungle saved from bombs and herbicides by leprosy.

He turned toward Father Pascal, who sat by the defunct radio, his almost colorless eyes fixed on a gecko clinging to the wall above him.

"*Merde! Pas du réponse. Merde!*" the priest said, in the voice that somehow whispered and boomed at the same time.

Teepee held him in his peripheral vision; he could not bring himself to look directly into that destroyed face; nor, Coombes' assurances notwithstanding, could he bring himself to draw closer than ten feet from the priest, to touch anything in this room. He kept his hands in his pockets.

"*Toujours. La même chose.*" He shook his head. "*Ah, pourquoi?*"

Struggling again to recall the patois heard long ago, Teepee answered, "*Non ici. L'armée française, tout française* . . . uh . . . *partir* . . . Y'know what I'm saying? Gone? Left. *Partir. L'armée française . . . pas . . . non ici . . . c'est loin . . .*"

"*Comment?*"

Teepee raised his hands wide apart.

"Like this, okay? *Ici, quel pays* . . ." He balled his right hand into a fist. "*Et ici, France . . .*" He made a fist with his left. "*L'armée française . . .*" And he described an arc, right to left. "*Vous comprehend?*"

"*Non!*" Father Pascal attempted to rise but only half succeeded, then he tried again, tottering, his hands with their rotting fingers laid on the table for balance. He was trembling, from the effort of standing or from agitation, and Teepee could almost hear the man's bones rattling.

"*C'est vrai.*"

Words flew from the priest's mouth, dozens of them, it seemed, and listening to that hissing, whispering sound they made, Teepee imagined them as bats flushing from a cave, dozens of bat words winging past and over him and he struggling to capture just enough to make sense of them. He caught one, two, four, and thought he got the gist: They could not have left without us. . . . They were to relocate us. . . . They could not have abandoned us. . . .

"*Du calme, Père Pascal. Du calme . . .*"

More bats slapped out of that red, decaying cavern, and Teepee's mental net captured a few: *Vous . . . la Légion Étrangère . . . ici . . . pourquoi . . .* and he forced them to yield their meaning: If the French army left, then what are you and the other legionnaire doing here?

"*Je suis américain, Père Pascal. Non Sénégalaise. Mon ami—américain. Soldat américain. La guerre est finie pour France . . . La guerre . . . La guerre américaine . . .*"

The priest only stared, uncomprehending, and then collapsed back into his seat. He sat staring through the blinds at the cemetery. A long time passed, or what seemed a long time in the heat and in the silence broken only by the whine of flies. It's all psychological, isn't it? thought Teepee. How we perceive time. Maybe it doesn't really move. Maybe we only seem to see its arrow flying forward, present becoming past as it pierces the future. Yeah, maybe. But its flight's real to us, so how do I tell this decaying man of God that the arrow shot right past him? A leprous Rip Van Winkle in the jungle, stuck in the past. How do I tell him he's lost nearly twenty years?

"*L'armée américaine?*" Father Pascal muttered.

"*Oui.*" Teepee grasped a piece of his uniform, but the priest wasn't looking at him. He was looking at the graveyard. For sure there's got to be some dim recognition in the back of his mind. All those people dying, year after year. Got to be some sense, even in the compression and crunching of the years in his mind, that a lot of time's gone by.

"*Et la guerre . . .*" His voice faltered, fell off.

"*Finie. Pour France.*"

And now the priest turned to him, folding his hands on the table, his blanched eyes seemingly without pupils, like a statue's eyes.

"*Quelle année?*" he asked, his voice tremulous.

Teepee could not recall how to say it in French, so drawing his survival knife, he knelt on one knee at Father Pascal's ruined feet and, holding his breath against their reek, carved the year into the dirt floor. Then he stood and backed away and watched the priest's glance fall on the numerals. He frowned, tilted his head slightly to one side, slightly to the other, as if he were contemplating some astonishing riddle.

"*C'est vrai?*" he asked, without looking up.

"*C'est vrai.*"

And again a long time passed or seemed to pass.

"*Père Pascal?*"

The priest didn't move.

"*Père Pascal?*"

Teepee's heart went out to the man, and he turned and left him sitting in the fierce hash marks of light, his gaze arrested by the immutable fact written at his feet.

Outside, the lepers sat crammed into the high-wheeled carts, the buffalo stood with brute patience in their yokes, and the ambulatory people squatted beside them, whisking at flies with their hands or with bamboo switches. They were waiting for the priest to emerge and tell them it was time to leave, waiting for the foreign legionnnaires to lead them out. To where? What refuge had they been promised so long ago? All the history that had been made since, and they knew nothing of it, here in this isolated valley of suspended time.

Teepee had to take a shit. Like time, which waits for no man, he thought, moving off to squat behind a grove of banana trees. Afterward, he rummaged in his rucksack for his toilet paper and discovered he'd used it up. Getting sick of this, squatting in the bushes like some savage, sleeping with not even tent canvas overhead, drenched one day, baked the next. Home. Indoor plumbing . . . Hell, even the outhouse back of Uncle Elmond's bayou hunting camp would be a luxury right now. He pictured his short-timer's calendar and the magic date centered on the mons veneris, pictured the silver Freedom Bird carrying him on mythic wings across the ocean to . . . *home.* Yeah, it'll be beautiful, but meantime I've got to wipe my black ass. He used a fallen banana leaf and was buckling his belt when some bird shrieked in the jungle not too far off. A hideous shriek. He jogged back into the compound, and the cry came once more, only not as loud or shrill—a long, wild, quavering scream in diminuendo. Couldn't have been a bird, or if it was, the damn thing was as big as a condor. It sounded almost human, some monkey or ape maybe. In the broiling, brooding silence that followed, the lepers stood up in the carts—those who could stand. The noise didn't seem to be one they were used to hearing; they turned with frightened looks toward Father Pascal's mud-brick bungalow, but he, deaf in his grief for his lost decades, still sat rigid, staring at the evidence of his loss. *Poor guy. I guess that's what's called catatonic shock,* thought Teepee, and then: *There you go again, playing shrink.* He approached the lepers, aware that they were looking toward him, looking to see what he would do, or how protect them, he the warrior armed, he one of their supposed deliverers. The realization came to him suddenly—no, not suddenly: it had been in his mind for a while, perhaps since he'd recognized what afflicted these people, only he'd been unaware of it until this second; so what came suddenly was not the realization but his consciousness of it. *We're responsible for them. Like it or not, they've been thrown into our laps.*

There was a rifle shot, clean and succinct, and then another, the twin reports and their echoes merging into a seconds-long crackle. At high port, Teepee sprinted across the compound and up the trace of the road. In half a minute, he came upon two rucksacks, Jimmy Neville's and Coombes', Neville's with a rifle propped against it.

"Coombes! Coombes!" He fell silent and fought the panic rising in him. A sniper? He had almost forgotten that there were human enemies out here.

Then an answer came from not far away, his voice flat but not exactly matter-of-fact; a tone of weary irritation, rather.

"Over here, Bledsoe. And . . . bring the machete."

He thrashed through the undergrowth for ten or fifteen yards, coming to a clump of pineapple palm that, he figured, had sprouted from seeds blown into the jungle from the plantations farther off. That was all his mind could absorb of what his eyes saw: Jimmy Neville on his back, his shape transformed into that of a giant beehive—narrow at the top and bottom, bulging hugely in the middle. Han and Coombes, legs spread, were tugging at the greenish mass coiled around Jimmy Neville from his neck nearly to his knees. His face was a gray blue, his eyes were open and still; blood trickled from his nostrils and ears and mouth, and his tongue stuck out. Off to one side lay a head shaped a little like a gator's head and half as big, a head with gaping jaws and twin fangs.

"Give me the machete," said Coombes in that same tired and irritated tone.

Teepee reached over his shoulder and drew the machete from the scabbard strapped to his ruck. Coombes took it, moved Han aside, and struck with a swift but measured stroke. Teepee saw a flash of white meat as Coombes struck again, segmenting the coils that made the bulge around Jimmy Neville's middle; then he and Han began to tug again.

"Bledsoe, give us a hand."

But he couldn't. The thing with its color and thickness—thicker than a man's calf—and the head Coombes had blown off looked like something that had slithered into this century out of the Cretaceous period.

"Can't . . . Can't . . ."

"Another goddamned Dolores . . . " Coombes dug in his heels and pulled backward. "Son of a bitch . . . like cable . . . son of a bitch is dead and won't let go."

He left off and swung again with the machete, and again, the last swipe severing some central nerve; the coils lost their rigidity, and the two men unraveled the snake and flung its limp pieces aside.

"Son of a bitch must've been twenty feet," Coombes said, breathing hard. "Python."

Jimmy Neville looked all caved in, rib cage and breastbone probably like broken china.

"What . . . ? What . . . ?"

"Hell if I know," Coombes answered. "Came back, found Han by himself. He said Neville had gone off into the bushes. Figured he was taking a dump. Next thing . . . You must've heard it."

"Who didn't?" Teepee looked toward the palms, leaning out away from one another, as still as trees in a greenhouse. "He was going to pick those. Must've thought the snake was a vine. Grabbed it. That's what he said back a ways. He wanted to shinny up a vine like the rope at boot camp and pick some pineapples."

"A rope with one mean defense mechanism. The stupid little shit."

"For Christ's sake, he was only a kid. He was eighteen years old."

"Old as he'll get." Coombes moved off a couple of yards and with one heel marked a rectangle in the ground, then stuck the machete in the middle of it. "Got another one to dig. Get to it."

"CIGARETTE ME, *trung-si,*" said Han after he'd heard what probably had happened.

Resting against his rucksack, Coombes gave the montagnard a smoke.

"The *My* soldiers are clumsy and foolish! They are making this too difficult! First the one with the talkingbox falls from the bridge, then the redface goes away by himself into the forest, now the spotface grabs a big snake. Among my people, a small child knows not to do that."

"Han, listen: here, in these forests, these soldiers are like small children, and—"

"I know, and listen to me, *trung-si:* you do not take small children to hunt Tiger."

"This other one, he isn't clumsy, isn't foolish, isn't like a child."

"The blackface?"

"Yes."

"What should we do now?"

"Kill the tiger."

"I don't like this. Too many bad things happening, and Tiger . . ." Han looked toward the ground. "I have been thinking. Tiger very very big, eats a lot, maybe that's why he is so strong and can keep walking walking without rest. But how does Tiger eat so much? I think I know. The fighting, *trung-si.* So many dead people. I think that's what he's been eating, and . . . and those killed in fighting, they have no burial, no ceremonies to quiet their souls. That's bad luck! Many, many unquiet souls, and if Tiger has eaten those souls . . ."

"Not that ghost bullshit again," muttered Coombes in English.

"Trung-si?"

"Go on."

"I wish to see Tiger, then I would know."

"The ghost tiger looks different?"

"It's the color of the moon."

Coombes sensed that he was losing control of the situation, and of Han, but now he saw a way to begin reclaiming it, saw a way to overcome the montagnard's superstitious fears. He wouldn't tell him the whole truth, only enough.

After he did, Han sat without talking, rubbing the stock of his crossbow with its inlaid rings of mother-of-pearl.

"It's true? You saw him?"

"And I spoke to the man who shot at him that night. The tiger is not moon-colored, and it does not eat souls. It's the color of fire, and it eats flesh, like all tigers."

The anxious frown vanished from the montagnard's face.

"Now tell me, tell me, Han. Have you made a new plan?"

He shook a cigarette from his pack and watched its smoke and the smoke from Han's commingling in a spear of sunlight that thrust through the canopy.

"No more tracking. Tiger knows we are tracking, knows we have guns, and keeps walking walking. . . . I don't know. . . . If I were with my own people, in my own country, I would know what to do."

"What?"

"We would draw Tiger from the mountains. We would find a clear place in the forest and make a platform there in a tree for the hunters. Inside the clear place, we would tie Deer or Pig to a stake for bait. Then beaters would find a fast way to circle around behind Tiger and drive him toward the bait. When he is close enough to smell bait, hear it, the beaters stop, let Tiger think he has found prey. When he comes into the clear place, the hunters shoot their crossbows. That is what I would do among my own people in my own country."

The cigarette smoke curled and drew forms in midair, like skywriting. Whole and entire, a plan presented itself to Coombes. He'd always been good at this—adapting to changed circumstances, finding the advantages in disadvantage.

"We can do that here," he said. "In this country, with these people. We can use some of these people as beaters. Can you talk their talk?"

"Yes, but I'm afraid of them."

"What did you promise me?" Coombes jackknifed himself, bending his torso toward the montagnard. "Do you see my nose? Is it not there on my face? And these . . ." He raised his hands, thumbtip joined to thumbtip, and fanned his fingers. "Do I not have all I left with?"

"But you are *My!*"

"Not because I am *My.*" He crushed and field-stripped his cigarette, slowly tearing paper and filter to give himself time to formulate an explanation of concepts like contagiousness and immunity that Han would understand. "Touch my nose, Han. Touch it, then touch my fingers, and then touch your own nose and your own fingers."

Han hesitated.

"Go ahead."

The montagnard reached out and ran his forefinger down the bridge of Coombes' nose, drew back to touch his own; then the two men sat for a split second, palm to palm, as if playing patty-cake.

"You see, there are people in that village who have lived there all their lives and have their noses, fingers, feet, because they have a magic."

"That cannot be!"

"But it is. I can show them to you. You won't have to get near them, just look from afar. You will see. They have a magic, and they gave their magic to me, which I have given to you."

"Powers against the curse?"

"Yes." He thought for a few moments. "You and the blackface soldier will go with the beaters. I'll be in the platform. The tiger's mine to kill."

"As you wish. As long as you pay me."

"I'll pay you twice, but he's mine to kill. . . . With the crossbow."

Han stared as if he hadn't heard right.

"You take my rifle, I take the crossbow."

"But, *trung-si!* This was my father's."

"I will care for it. And, when I'm through, give it back."

"I don't know the rifle."

"You pull this," said Coombes, tapping the trigger. "You have seen the soldiers do it. You only pull it. It's easy."

Han did not say anything, one finger tracing the pearl concentric rings.

"You said he can smell the guns. I don't want any gun smell on me or near me," said Coombes, but he thought: *And I have to marry myself to all this, become part of it, get inside it, no maps, compasses, radios, watches, and no rifle, either. He'll come if I don't have a rifle; I'll be worthy to kill him . . . .*

Shirtless, sweating, Bledsoe returned from his grave-digging detail, threw down the machete, and hoisted Neville's rucksack and rifle.

"What're you going to do with those?" Coombes asked.

Bledsoe said nothing and turned to walk away.

"I get it. You'll bury him with his sword and shield. A warrior of old."

Bledsoe paused: a half-turn of his head, a sliver of oyster shell under the lowering eyelid. Nothing more sullen than a sullen spade, thought Coombes, rising. Now I've got to get him back, get everything back on track. He pulled the rucksack off Bledsoe's shoulder, gripped the rifle but didn't take it from his hand.

"I'll finish up. Take five."

"That's what you think I need?"

"What do you need?"

"Nothing. I'm thinking that you're racking up a lot of dead and missing you'll have to account for."

"Seems to me I didn't push Gauthier off the bridge, seems I didn't tell Neville to try climbing up a python to pick pineapples, seems that it was Red who had me at gunpoint." He snatched Neville's rifle, crisply, like a sergeant at an inspection. "And don't forget, when it comes to accounting for, it's going to be we. *We,* Bledsoe."

The grave was shallow, two feet deep. That was good—it wouldn't take a lot of time to fill in. Kneeling, Coombes searched Neville's rucksack for anything that might prove useful, pulled out a packet of freeze-dried onion soup and a rope with a snap-link attached, then tossed the ruck and rifle into the grave. He pocketed the freeze-dried, tied Neville's ankles with the rope, passed it through his crotch and around his waist for extra security, and ran the bitter end through the snap-link. With the rope coiled around his shoulder, he dragged the body several yards into a dense thicket. Twenty feet above, a teak branch spread its leaves. Not too big a branch, but enough to hold a skinny guy like Neville, Coombes thought. But before he got on with that, he went back to the grave and covered the rucksack and rifle under a nice, neat mound to make it look as if a body lay underneath. A precaution, just in case Bledsoe stopped by to pay his last respects. Bledsoe didn't need to know; no one needed to know.

HAZY FINGERS of light curled over a nearby ridge, as if the sun were clinging to it, reluctant to let go of the earth and slip into darkness. The lepers had climbed down from the carts and, by the glimmer of small oil lamps, sat on the ground eating some indescribable white mush wrapped in banana leaves. Father Pascal sat near them, but he was not eating, only sitting with his impossibly thin legs drawn into his sunken chest. His statue's eyes were turned toward the ridge, beseeching—or so Teepee imagined—the sun to stay its fall and give him just one more day as token recompense for all the days that had slipped through his fingers.

Han was speaking to the montagnards, the ones who hadn't been touched by the disease, and they spoke back to him with tongue clicks and short, high-pitched ejaculations. The conversation went on for some time, staccato bursts of talking, long intermissions of silence, during which the montagnards, their leathery faces impassive in the flickering oil lamps, would scratch in the dust with fingers or sticks or woodcutters' scythes. Then they would start talking again. Teepee noticed a change in them or, rather, in his perception of them; they didn't appear so frail and helpless as they had this afternoon. Like Han, they had youthful bodies, striated with muscle, reminding him of bantamweight fighters. Made sense. They probably had to do most of the work for the colony, had to hew and draw, cultivate as much of the plantations as six men could, thatch the roofs, gather firewood and hunt small game for the pot.

The light lost its hold, and night came down. Now the notched ridge in the near distance looked two-dimensional. Han and the montagnards had fallen silent again. One of them, wearing a kind of sarong tucked up into his crotch, a sheathed machete belted to his waist, went over to Father Pascal and began speaking to him. If the priest was saying anything, it was in a voice too soft to be heard. Teepee had begun to feel uneasy, for the other montagnards were staring as one at him and Coombes, with expressions as impenetrable as the jungle. He looked away from them and watched the first strange stars of these equatorial skies coming out. He knew none of the constellations in this hemisphere except the Southern Cross, which now showed low on the horizon, leaning sharply.

Beside him, Coombes was practicing dry mounts with the crossbow, snapping the stock into his shoulder, sighting. Maybe it was Coombes making him uneasy.

"Tell me you're just screwing around. Tell me you're not really going to try and kill him with that."

"No 'try.' Will."

"If he's as big as we think, it oughta be me and you in the platform, with M-16s. Full auto crossfire. Rock 'n' roll, and cut the son of a bitch in half."

"You want that, don't you?" Coombes asked, with a sly, sidelong look. "Sure. It's what we're all about."

"Who?"

"Us. Americans. We subdue the wild. We overcome. It's what we've been all about since Plymouth Rock."

"My people didn't come over on any goddamned *Mayflower.*"

"It's in you too. Don't bullshit me. But sorry. He'll smell the guns and won't come. Besides, you'd be surprised what these little mothers can do. They were outlawed for a while in the Middle Ages because they could go right through chain mail, fuck up some Sir Lancelot's whole morning. Watch this." Straightening one leg, he stuck his foot through what looked like a stirrup at the bow end, bent double at the waist, grabbed the bowstring, then leaned far back and locked the string in a hook set in the groove of the stock. He drew one of the short arrows from the quiver, placed it in the groove, and shouldered the weapon. "See that?" A flashlight's beam drew a circle on a tree stump ten or twelve yards away. "The one compromise I had to make," Coombes said, as if apologizing for the flashlight taped to the side of the stock. "In case he comes at night."

"Compromise?"

"To this, Bledsoe. All this. Now watch."

The bowstring snapped and the arrow struck, centered in the bright circle as in a target and buried halfway to its feathers.

"That's solid wood. It'll drive through that tiger like he was made of pudding."

"Yeah. And that little mother takes about a month to reload. You're gonna have one shot."

"That's all I'll need." He pulled a leather pouch from his shirt pocket. "The arrows'll be dipped in this. Krait poison. Even if I hit him in the ass, he'll be dead in twenty minutes."

Han walked back to them, squatted, and laid down the rifle, which was too long for him. He and Coombes fell into one of their palavers. After three or four minutes, Coombes shouted something, got to his feet, and kicked the ground.

"Goddamn it!" he said. God . . . damn . . . it!" He looked down at Teepee. "All right, it's your turn to talk some talk to the sky pilot. Seems the Yards are afraid of the tiger. Seems they've seen him before, carrying the bodies of dead soldiers in his jaws. That's his diet. The war's his fast-food franchise. So the Yards are scared of him. He's too big, too used to eating people. They won't go unless the padre tells them to and gives them his blessing, but the sky pilot isn't talking."

"No, he's—"

"Talk to him, Bledsoe. Talk the talk. That coon-ass French—shit, you said you know Latin; then talk to him in Latin like he's some fuck-ing Roman emperor, but tell him we need these people."

"Coombes . . ."

"What now? What, goddamn it!"

"Shouldn't we . . . Know what I'm saying? Don't we owe it to them?"

What is it with these guys? Coombes asked himself. They couldn't stay focused. Swenson obsessing on clock-puncher Hightower's schedule; Neville deciding he had to pick a pineapple and grabbing onto twenty feet of python instead; now Bledsoe wanted to play Red Cross.

"There's no debt," he declared, fighting to keep himself under control.

"Then maybe we owe it to ourselves."

"How about I give you that? That leaves a practical problem—most of 'em can't walk to the latrine. So they've got the oxcart. Any ideas on how we'll get *that* through the Big Green?"

"Not right now, but we could put our heads together."

"Neville spooked you, that's all."

"Sure I'm spooked. I'm not used to seeing guys I know get strangled by pythons. But I'm getting there."

This was all too much: Han and his folktales, and now a sullen do-gooder spade.

"Here it is, Bledsoe. If these people go to work for us, then we'll owe 'em and I'll see to it we do what we can. All right? I'll charter them a medevac to the Mayo Clinic. All right? But not till that son of a bitch's stripes are nailed to the wall. You tell that to the priest."

He's lying, but I'll do it because I'm afraid of him, Teepee thought. *And because . . .*

"Talk your talk to the sky pilot. Get to it."

And because I'm afraid of myself and what I'll think of myself if I don't see this through and the son of a bitch's stripes nailed to the wall.

He approached the gaunt ruin and said, because he didn't know what else to say, *"Bonsoir, Père Pascal. Ça va? Va bien?"*

Jesus, what a ridiculous question! Of course it wasn't going well. It was a million miles from going well.

The priest didn't speak or move. Teepee tried to tell him what was wanted. He spoke in his bad French, made signs and extravagant gestures, mimed the actions of someone cutting poles for a platform, and made something of a fool of himself, falling onto all fours and growling through bared teeth. The moon had risen by the time he finished. And still Father Pascal didn't move or speak. Teepee sat down, exhausted by his efforts, by thirst and hunger and all that had happened since he'd crossed the bridge. Then he saw in the twilight made by the moon and the lamps that the gray pupilless eyes were on him. And then, with the rattling sibilance of a last breath, the priest spoke two words.

Teepee stood and went back to where Coombes waited with Han.

"No good," he said. "Can't get through to him."

"You're not coming through for me. You're not coming through, Greek-speaking, Latin-speaking, coon-ass French-speaking Thomas Bledsoe."

"Goddamn it! The whole French Academy couldn't get through to him. All he can think, all he can understand, all he can say, is 'Twenty years.' Got it? He's Rip Van Winkle and gone in the brain. Shit, I should have let it be. Let him think it's 1954 and that we're foreign legionnaires, come to the rescue."

"Got no time, no patience, for any more bullshit." Coombes strode across the compound to where the montagnards sat and, dropping the crossbow, grabbed two, one in each hand, jerking them to their feet with no more difficulty than it would take a father to pick up two small children.

"Bledsoe! Here," he hollered over his shoulder; then, as Teepee hesitated, "I said here! Now!"

All six were standing when Teepee got there. They were in a kind of shock, having been assaulted so unexpectedly by a man they'd thought their deliverer. Behind them, the lepers sat, just as stunned and confused. A stirring passed through them; they seemed to want to run from the towering, angry figure; but all they could do was watch with helpless tension as Coombes pulled a bight of rappelling rope from his rucksack and shook the coils loose.

"One of these Yards tries to break, blow him away," he said to Teepee, then spun the first montagnard around by the shoulder, pulled his hands behind his back, and tied them.

"What the hell are you doing? Coombes, you can't—"

"Shut up. Just cover these people till I'm done."

He cinched the rope around the waist of a second man, bound his hands, and went on to the third.

"They're going to learn what to be afraid of," he was saying. "We've got a full moon to work by tonight. We're going to take 'em into the bush and find a spot for the platform and put 'em to work building it. Come morning, you and Han'll take 'em out and beat the bushes, and if you've got to do it with them tied up like this, then that's how it'll be."

The montagnards were looking not at him but at Teepee. Could they see that he didn't want to hold them at riflepoint while Coombes tied them up? Could they tell that he thought this all a sudden madness and that he had no heart, no belly, for it?

"Listen to me," he said in the tone with which you'd address a mad dog. "It's been one helluva day, and you're . . . you've—" But before he could say that Coombes had snapped, the voice of Father Pascal came across the compound, with a sound like rustling leaves.

"*Arrêtez vous! Arrêtez!*" He swung toward them on his crutches, shaking his wintry head. "*Arrêtez!*"

"He's telling you to stop," Teepee translated.

"Yeah? Well, he's been relieved of command." Coombes poked the first montagnard with the crossbow and commanded, "*Chung ta hay di! Di mau!*"

The men didn't move. Their eyes locked onto the priest, who now stood unsteadily on one crutch while he held out a chancred hand, seemingly freezing all movement with that gesture.

"*Arrêtez!*" he said.

His agitation made him lose his balance. He swayed for a moment on his crutches, toppled sideways, and rolled over face first in the dirt.

Teepee started to go to help him up, but stopped when he saw the stain spreading across the back of his patched shirt and the stubby arrow stuck in the ground a few yards behind him. A spasm passed through his body, and then he stiffened and lay still.

Everyone, arrested by the suddenness of the evil just witnessed, sat or stood like a figure in a frieze. Coombes knew it was in the nature of people to obey and even in a way to admire the man who proves himself capable of anything. He will be their master, so long as he shows no signs of faltering and gives them no time to recover from their shock. He didn't waste a second. He kicked the first montagnard and barked, "*Di-di!*" and sure enough, the train of bound men began to shamble forward.

"*Maulen, maulen,*" he commanded to keep them moving, then to Han, "*Di! Chung ta hay di.*" And Han, too, started to follow. Then to Bledsoe, "C'mon, let's get to it!"

T. P. Bledsoe was surprised to find himself moving right along, for he no less than everyone else was too stunned by the swiftness and ruthlessness of what had happened to do anything but comply. If Coombes could kill a sick priest without a second's hesitation, he'd kill me even quicker, he thought, but then a woman broke the spell with an awful shriek. It stopped Teepee cold, stopped the montagnards in their tracks. They turned as one to look at her, kneeling beside the body, making the sign of the cross with one bent hand while she howled some pagan lamentation.

Teepee recognized her as the woman who had shooed him and Coombes from her vegetable garden that afternoon; and feeling that he'd been shaken out of a trance, he cried, "You murdered a priest!" as if he had just recognized that fact. He drew his survival knife, meaning to cut the montagnards free, but they misunderstood his intentions and panicked. Like a line of kids playing crack-the-whip, they surged forward and flung themselves at Coombes, wrapping him in the rope and their bodies. He fell heavily beneath them, yelling, "Bledsoe! Bledsoe!"

Teepee piled on and cut two of the men free; then the rest, piled atop Coombes, tumbled sideways as he thrust himself onto all fours, heaving their bodies off his. He stood for a moment, wobbling, until his left leg crumpled and he dropped into a sitting position. One of the freed men—the one in the tucked sarong—drew his machete and rushed him. Teepee shouted, *"Lai-dai!"* and fired a burst into the air. The man with the machete flung himself down, then rolled to his feet, looking surprised to find himself still alive. Coombes was trying to reload the crossbow when Teepee grabbed him under the arm and pulled him up.

"No! No, goddamn it!"

"Waste him, Bledsoe, waste the little—"

"No!"

Thin and quavering, Han's voice reached them: *"Trung-si, trung-si!"* They couldn't see him. *"Trung-si! Trung-si!"* he called again. His voice was coming from a grove of pineapple palm less than fifty yards away, across a swath of furrowed gardens.

"There!" Teepee said, and sprinted into the trees.

He called for Han, practically tripping over the hillman as he crouched behind a trunk, and then realized that he'd made the dash alone. Hopping on one leg, dragging the other, Coombes wasn't yet halfway across the furrowed ground. Behind him was a sight that Teepee knew would give him nightmares in the future—if he had a future: the montagnards, all cut loose now, and ten or twelve lepers were coming after Coombes, the montagnards with severed rope trailing from their wrists, scythes and machetes in their hands, some of the lepers holding up oil lamps and some striking their walking sticks together to make an arrhythmic, osteal clacking, and all moving across those mooncalcimined fields, slowly, haltingly, and yet with an implacable purpose.

Teepee fired a long burst into the air, a shorter one over their heads, stopping the advance of that appalling army. They stopped, but didn't fall back, as if they sensed he didn't have the heart, didn't have the belly. He ran out into the field, put his arm around Coombes' waist, and together the two men stumbled toward the grove. From behind them came that clattering of walking sticks again, hollow as old bones, the percussion for death's dance band, the zombie jamboree. Coombes muttered, "It's only my knee; just popped my knee when I fell," as if the minor nature of the injury mattered somehow, and Teepee thought, *I'm rescuing a murderer, a killer of priests, and it's not because I'm afraid of him—no, that's not why, because I'm not afraid of him anymore, so I don't know why. . . .*

In the trees, Coombes sat spread-legged, rubbing the wrenched knee. Teepee loaded a fresh magazine. This was a humbling experience—retreating before an army of lepers and tribesmen armed with scythes and machetes. They were still coming, at that deliberate, almost leisurely pace. There was a burst of rifle fire. Bullets passed overhead with a sound like someone sucking in rapid breaths through clenched teeth. They had an automatic rifle! Teepee fired another five rounds over their heads. Again they didn't run, didn't hit the ground, just stopped and stood, waiting.

"Where the hell did they get a weapon?"

"It's my piece," Coombes said, then grabbed Han by the hair and shook him. "This stupid little shit took off and left it. Waste 'em, Bledsoe. I want that piece back."

"No."

"Damn you!"

Coombes grabbed the barrel of Teepee's M-16, but the hot steel seared his hand, and he let go.

"Nobody else dies—got that, you crazy motherfucker! We're getting out!"

Teepee's point was underscored by a second rifle burst and the chunking of bullets striking tree trunks.

And so they fled through the pineapple grove, down a straight path between the trees. Han was in the lead, Teepee in the rear, and Coombes between them, moving now with none of his old fluid animal grace but stumbling on his hurt leg, one shoulder rising as the other dipped, that rising and the other dipping. He looked like a spastic figure in an ancient film, or like a mechanical man that wasn't functioning right.

They climbed the scrub-choked ridge that rose on the far side of the grove. Coombes made it up, through the ferocity of his will, and sat down on a bald, rocky spot. His first act was to thrust his good leg into the crossbow's stirrup and reload the weapon, his second to roll up his trousers and examine his knee—it was swollen, but nothing more—then wrap it tightly in an Ace bandage from his first-aid kit, and his third was to light a cigarette. He didn't bother to hide the flare of his Zippo.

Bledsoe looked at him, scowling to say that the light would give their position away.

"They're not going to charge up this ridge. They're packing it in. They just wanted us out of town."

He gestured below. The pinpricks of light made by the oil lamps were moving back across the field toward the compound. Amazing how close it was—half a mile at farthest. Coombes felt as if he'd run ten miles.

He smoked the cigarette down to the filter, giving his emotions time to settle, his mind time to regain its suppleness and agility. He needed to figure out what to do next.

Han moved off and lay down, and looking up at the stars, he thought about his wife and children and wondered how he would buy them rice. He would not be paid for leading the *trung-si* to Tiger, because he wasn't going to lead him to Tiger. The *trung-si* had done a wrong thing; now Tiger would kill him and anyone who was with him.

Teepee sat against a boulder, his legs drawn up, hands clasped around them, his forehead on his knees. His belly was so empty it seemed to be digesting itself, yet he wasn't hungry. His mouth felt like dust. He straightened up, pulled out one of the canteens on his belt, and drained it. Then he rested his head once again on his knees.

"You sulling up on me again?" Coombes asked, nudging him.

"You murdered a priest."

"He's as dead as Moses, but listen up: this isn't a part of the world where the word 'murder' has a whole lot of meaning."

Teepee turned to him and looked into the face with its intransigent eyes like metal disks, its mustache the color of iron shavings. Still had the mojo working, but at low power now.

"You murdered a priest."

"That any different than murdering anyone else? Anyway, he's only dead in the here and now. In the there and then, which is the same thing as the will be, he's still alive. Look up there," he said, pointing at the vast fleets of stars. "All that's the past. Light from some of those stars started toward us when there wasn't a living thing on earth but some slimy bacteria. They might not even exist anymore, in their time, but they do in our time. We see 'em, right? So they exist and don't exist at the same time. And so does the past. The past doesn't disappear—it goes somewhere. Now, take that star, that real bright one. Sirius. Don't know how far it is, but let's say it's fifty thousand light-years. Want you to imagine something, Bledsoe, so you don't get too outraged about the dead sky pilot. Imagine there's a planet orbiting that star, inhabited by a highly advanced race of beings. Imagine they've got a telescope ten million times more powerful than anything we've got, and that scope is pointed toward the earth. It's so powerful it not only can see the earth, it can see what's going on here, take pictures of it, like the satellite cameras we've got. Well, what are those little green astronomers gonna see? Keep in mind now that nothing can travel faster than light."

Teepee could only stare with his mouth ajar. If Coombes had started singing Italian arias, he could not have sounded crazier.

"What they're gonna see is the earth like it was fifty thousand years ago," he rambled on. "They'll see a mastodon or two, Neanderthals slouching around with clubs on their shoulders, humping their old ladies dog style. Now, to us, those Neanderthals are dead; to the green men, they're alive. Just like the stars, they exist and don't exist. Same with your priest. His electrons or whatever are flying out there somewhere, and fifty thousand years from now, those green astronomers will see him, walking around, playing king of the lepers. Got it, Bledsoe? Past, present, future . . . those are all inventions. Don't mean nothin'. Tick-tock, bong-bong. Same thing with life and death. Don't mean nothin', don't mean a thing."

"Y'know, Coombes, you're so fucking nuts you almost make sense."

"Sure. And we've still got a tiger to kill. That *does* mean something."

"Yeah, for you. You're afraid of him, just like us. And you can't stand that, being just like us. You can't stand knowing that there's something out there that scares the piss out of you. Got you figured out, *Lincoln*. You're afraid to be afraid, and that's the worst kind of coward there is."

"You listen up, you black-ass shrink, you listen up. We'll see who's the coward come tomorrow—"

"We're going back," Teepee interrupted.

"You're spooked again."

"Goddamned right I am. This jungle spooks me, that tiger spooks me. Difference between me and you is that I'm not afraid to admit it."

"That makes you better, Bledsoe?"

Teepee did not say it. *Maybe I am, maybe not, but courage is the ability to overcome your fear of fear.*

"Listen up," Coombes said. "What happened tonight was a little setback, that's all, and he's still out there and I've got a pretty good idea of where he's going to go. You and Han will—"

Teepee stood, with his rifle aimed from the hip. *Not spooked by you anymore.*

"We're heading back, and when we get there, I'm reporting you in for murder. There it is."

Coombes looked at the gun barrel and said placidly, "Hate to break your heart, but you know, I've gotten used to having rifles pointed at me by people who don't mean to use them."

Teepee lunged forward with his right foot, swinging the rifle butt as he had thrown hooks in the Golden Gloves, and caught Coombes flush on the jaw. He fell backward, out cold. Straddling him, Teepee gave him two short, hard rights between the eyes for good measure as well as for the pure satisfaction of it. The second punch broke a knuckle. It hurt like hell, but the pain was a dollar well spent. Then he took his own rappelling rope from his rucksack, cut off a six-foot length, and tied Coombes' hands in front, then, running the rope down to his ankles, tied them there. *Big boss man, don't you hear me when I call? Well, you ain't so big, you're tall, that's all.*

"*Trung-si? Trung-si . . . ?*" asked Han, squatting close by.

"He's all right. Don't you worry about your *trung-si.* Tsetse Fly just put him to sleep for a little while." He dropped to his haunches and looked Han in the face. "Hey, listen: Tomorrow? *Di-di.* Me, you, him," he said, pointing at himself and each of them. "Get it? *Di-di* for home." He pointed in the direction they'd come from. "Understand?"

Han nodded, and whether he did because he understood or simply wanted to be accommodating made no difference to Teepee. He moved his ruck off the rocky spot, spread his poncho, and lay down and watched the stars in their slow and stately sail across the heavens. . . .

His chest seemed to be caving in under a crushing weight. A warm, fetid breeze touched his face. Something that felt like wet sandpaper scraped his cheek. His eyes popped open and looked straight into a single, almond-shaped eye, huge and glowing with a color like fire reflected in polished brass. His scream rose from the deepest part of himself, and the great weight was off him. He leaped to his feet, a numbness in his knees and arms, a feeling that all blood had drained from his skull.

"Coombes! It's him! Jesus Christ, it was him! Jesus! Jesus! He was right on top of me! Coombes!"

He caught his breath, snatched his rifle.

"Jee-sus? Jee-sus?"

It was Han, down in his squat, rubbing sleep from his face.

"Jee-sus?"

"No, not Jesus, you goddamned little savage!"

Han stood suddenly, his eyes widening. He uttered a single word, which Teepee did not understand yet understood.

"That's right. Tiger! He was right on top of me!"

He reached into his ruck for his flashlight and shone it on the ground, the beam trembling with the trembling of his hand. Han bent low, studying the earth for prints. He circled around and around for several minutes, following the light, but he found nothing—not a pawprint, not a broken twig. Then he looked up and shook his head.

Teepee touched his cheek, felt his sweat but no other kind of dampness, smelled his shirt for cat stink but caught only his own.

Han solemnly shook his head once more and said something, which Teepee again understood and did not understand. Above, the Southern Cross had passed well beyond the celestial meridian; the moon had set.

"Okay, right, Han. Dream. Bad dream. Goddamn, but it was real. . . ."

He paused, spotting in the beam, beside the boulder where he had left Coombes, a rope roughly sawed in half.

"Coombes?" he said, softly at first, then louder. "Coombes! Damn you, Coombes!"

Big boss man . . . Tall, that's all . . .

He circled the boulder, finding a sharp protrusion on the back. He ran his fingers along the edge. It was perhaps a foot long, and sharp enough to cut through a rope if you put the effort into it. Dammit! Teepee thought. Why didn't I see that before? How the hell did he do it? Had him trussed up like a Christmas turkey. Must've rolled himself around the boulder and then lay on his back and swung his legs side to side, sawing through the long part of the rope. Then he would have stood with his back to the rock and freed his hands. Crazy priest-killing white boy, but you had to hand it to him, yeah, you had to do that.

He swept the flashlight across the ground. It fell on a bootprint perhaps ten feet away, and on a second, deeper on one side than on the other—Coombes' bad leg.

Han, his eyes on the ground, was meanwhile scurrying back and forth with the desperation of a miser looking for a lost nickel. He looked up, his seamed little face creased with worry, and said something that Teepee didn't understand at all. Then he spotted the bootprints.

"Trung-si? Di-di?"

"Yeah, he's gone, all right."

Han began to speak in sign language, raising one hand in front of the other, hunching his shoulders as if aiming, then pressing his palms to his chest.

"Your crossbow?" said Teepee. "Yeah, it's gone too."

Han gestured at the prints, made a sweeping motion, then clenched his fists and drew them sharply back into his chest.

"And you want it back. Yeah, got you. You need the crossbow, I need you to get me the hell out of this motherfucking jungle." He walked back to his gear, rolled up his poncho, and rucked up. "All right, Han, *chung ta hay di*. Let's go find him."

THE RAIN HAD let up but hadn't stopped. It had drizzled all night, and Eric the Red had slept fitfully. Maybe he hadn't slept at all. Now, in the gray dawn, the rain had turned to a chilling mist, through which he walked among the bomb craters, walked and walked to keep himself warm. It did no good. He shivered uncontrollably. Sometimes he could not see where he was walking—not because of the fine, foglike rain but because he saw other things: the congregation in the Lutheran church in Spokane, all singing "How Great Thou Art"; halftime shows and the band marching downfield in clear autumn sunshine; the face of the devil in the tunnel, in whose rank darkness he'd vanished from the sight of God.

He didn't know that what he had seen in the tunnel was a hallucination. The face belonged to an enemy soldier killed by the grenade someone had tossed into the tunnel, but it had looked Satanic when Eric the Red shone his flashlight on it. He didn't know that he was hallucinating now, walking among the craters, thinking one minute that he was in church, the next that he was playing his tuba at halftime.

There were a lot of things he didn't know, big things and little things and things in between.

One of the big things was that being in God's sight does not necessarily mean one is in God's grace. No sparrow falls without His seeing it, true, and yet it *does* fall.

Another big thing was that in following his ears instead of the stream, as Teepee had told him to do, he had walked in the wrong direction, a direction one hundred eighty degrees opposite from the one he'd thought. No, he had not mistaken the rolling thunder of a storm for the rolling thunder of the war. It really was the rumble of bombs that had guided him through the jungle—the very bombs that had made these craters. They had fallen across the border, onto the soil of a neighboring country, which the enemy used as a sanctuary and a staging area. Because this country was, technically, not involved in the war, American troops were prohibited from pursuing the enemy into it, and the bombing of it was a military secret kept at the highest level. Being at the lowest level, Private First Class Eric Swenson did not know about the secret bombing. Nor did he know that he had crossed the border. He was where no American soldier was supposed to be.

He also did not know that he was going into hypothermia. His body temperature was already more than two degrees below normal; he was losing body heat rapidly, and his mind was being lost with it. His mind was playing tricks on him, sleights of hand performed by a sleep-starved, blood-deprived brain; and one of its feats of prestidigitation was to create the sound he so desperately wanted to hear—the throb of rotor blades—and then the sight he wanted to see: an armada of helicopters, dropping like technological angels out of the clouds, their rotors whipping up miniature typhoons, their skids flared for landing.

He ran toward them, waving and yelling: "Here, over here, I'm over here!" He ran blindly down a narrow, muddy bridge between two craters. The mud gave way under his weight, and he tumbled down the steep slope of a crater into three feet of water. His pith helmet fell off. It floated a few feet from him, on its brim. He thought it looked like a bulging lily pad, a lily pad with a tumor. That image made him giggle—a tumorous lily pad. He waded to it and jammed it back on his head and stopped giggling. The fall and the cold shock of the water restored him to his senses: he realized that he'd only imagined the helicopters. Like a mirage, he thought, and cautioned himself to keep his grip on reality, not to be fooled again by his trickster brain. It had landed him in a serious fix. The crater looked to be twenty feet deep and was almost sheer-sided. If the rain kept up and he didn't get out, he could drown.

He looked up, noticing that the crater was funnel-shaped—steepest at its bottom half, flattening and widening out toward the top. If he could climb out of the stem of the funnel, the rest would be easy. He reached for a handhold and dug one foot deep into the crater wall and pulled himself up out of the water, but the mud gave way again and he fell. He tried again, and a third time. On the fourth try, he made it into the mouth of the funnel. But the slope, though gentler, was very slick. Trying to climb it was like trying to climb a playground slide coated in motor oil. If he moved even an inch, he started to skid back down. He could only cling, his belly pressed to the greasy incline, and move up by fractions of inches.

It was then that he heard again the beating of rotor blades. Don't listen to 'em, he warned himself. Only in your imagination. He kept crawling, but the throbbing grew louder. Ever so carefully, he raised his head and saw them overhead—two gunships. Had to be real—he'd caught the U.S. markings, the stubby gun barrels bristling in the noses. The throb grew fainter, and his heart fell. If they were real, they hadn't seen him. Real or not, it was all the same: he was stuck here, in a bomb crater. . . . No . . . wait. The noise was getting louder again. Circling? Were they circling to have another look? He had four or five more feet to go. He reached with both hands, dug his fingers into the mud, and hauled himself farther toward the crater's lip. All he had to do was get there, and then he could wave them in to pick him up. *Hey, guys, what took you so long?* He reached once more and clawed his way out.

On flat ground again, he stood and turned toward the sound. There they were, almost at ground level, coming toward him, growing larger and larger. He signaled with both arms, not knowing that the gunship pilots did not see him, Eric Swenson, American soldier, but saw an armed man in a zone where no American soldier was supposed to be, an armed man clad in green and wearing an enemy helmet.

The stubby gun barrels flashed.

LINCOLN, LINCOLN . . .

Forehead bruised, knee throbbing, a cold ache in his jaw. Pain. The pain was not distracting in any way; on the contrary, it kept his senses on the keenest of edges and helped him concentrate. The pain was good, a mortification of the flesh that purified the warrior-hunter. In the morning twilight, he moved toward the thicket where he'd hidden Neville's body, stalking as he had stalked deer in the woods by the Cedar River. The toe first, planted firmly, then the heel, brought down carefully so nothing would crack or rustle underfoot. Move ten or fifteen paces. Stop, listen, look, eyes sweeping outward in widening half-circles, left to right, right to left. Move again. He couldn't be sure that the tiger hadn't gotten to Neville ahead of him, guided through the forest darkness by the radar of its nose. It could be in the thicket now, eating. And so he crept with all the stealth he had learned hunting deer along the Cedar, sneaking up on prairie puddles to jump-shoot ducks, hunting human beings here.

. . . What's that stuff that you've been drinkin' . . . ?

He stopped, stood motionless, and listened. Han had told him that the alarm cries of birds were a sign of a tiger on its kill. He heard nothing, moved a few yards, listened again, and looked, first in the near distance, then as far out as he could. He rubbed his jaw. It was swollen and tender. Probably broken. Didn't think Bledsoe had it in him. Bledsoe had potential, the most he'd seen so far in the clowns they sent over here, clumsy numskulls who fell from bridges and grabbed onto twenty-foot pythons. He admired Bledsoe enough to hope he wouldn't have to kill him. And I won't have to if he realizes that I could have killed him in his sleep last night, or left him and Han without a weapon. Realizes it and appreciates it and forgets this nonsense about reporting me for murder. Murder! Here! Okay, stop thinking about that. There's a very big cat out here.

. . . Is it whiskey, is it wine . . . ?

Better this way. To be after it alone, no one beating, no gun smell on me, and only a crossbow. This was meeting it on as equal terms as possible; it was earning the right to see and kill it. This was purity. He had the tiger figured out now. He'd got inside its cat brain. Han was right—the war must have driven out or destroyed the beast's natural prey, but the war provided it with an endless supply of human flesh, for which it had acquired a taste. The war taketh away and the war giveth, and the cat knew where the war was and where it wasn't. It listened for the sound of gunfire, waited till it stopped, and then walked in, snatched what it could get, and retreated to its sanctuary to eat and rest. Why had it come after a living man? Maybe because it had grown tired of being a scavenger, wanted to be what nature meant it to be, a predator that stalked and killed.

Coombes went on and, after a while, wondered if he'd somehow bypassed the thicket. He doubted it. How many times had he amazed officers by his ability to navigate simply by guiding on the sun and the contours of the land, leading a patrol to the exact place where it was supposed to be? Learned that from the old man. Hunting was the old man's only release from the Rath meat-packing plant and the world of tick-tock, bong-bong. On bird-hunting trips up north, in the Minnesota woods, he would park the car on a logging road, disappear into the boonies for five or six hours, and come out within, at most, a hundred yards from where he'd started.

. . . *Oh, my God, it's turpentine!*

That damned song! Couldn't get it out of his head. Girls in junior high school used to tease him with it, following him home, he five or six inches too tall for his age, a star on the junior high basketball team but otherwise gawky and awkward. *Lincoln, Lincoln* . . .

He stopped again, listened, looked, eyes ranging outward, left-right, right-left, and then he saw the rope tied to the tree and the rest of it lying on the ground and Neville's body gone. *So it got here ahead of me.* Coombes stood for a full minute, hardly breathing, sniffing the air for the stench he knew so well. There was no sound, the jungle so silent it was as if no man or beast were in it, only the mute life of vegetation. No smell, either.

He moved up and searched the ground, finding Neville's blood-caked dog tags, shreds of clothing, and a drag mark and those awesomely huge tracks. He stood beneath the teak and wondered how the tiger had done it. Couldn't have climbed and walked out onto the branch—tigers didn't climb trees, so far as he knew. It must have jumped up and grabbed onto Neville. A twenty-foot spring from a standing start, straight up? Maybe. But I had that rope taut as a tightwire. The body would not have come down, unless . . . He looked more carefully, into the tree and then on the ground, and found the branch, broken unevenly. That was it. The tiger figured out that the rope was holding Neville up there, and it figured out that the branch would break under its weight, and then it had leaped, and the two of them, man and beast, had dropped down together. Which would make it not only big but smart. Five or six hundred pounds with a brain.

Worst kind of coward there is.

Coombes looked ahead, into the jungle dappled in green-and-yellow sunlight.

To master your deepest dread is to master all dread.

He followed the pawprints, and now his knee was becoming a distraction, making him wince with its little electric jolts of pain, making him feel vulnerable. He could sense the big cat's nearness and fought to erase the memory of its calm yellow eyes.

The track led into a swale of saw grass almost as high as Coombes' head—a perfect spot for an ambush. He had no choice. He plunged in. The prints were clear and distinct on the trail the tiger had cut through the grass. His heart was beating faster now, his head turning left to right, right to left, but he couldn't see six feet into the matted tangle. In a few moments, he came to a shallow stream, crossed it, but found no tracks on the other side. Moving back, he stalked downstream for twenty or thirty yards, studying the muddy banks, then returned to his starting point and tracked upstream until he came to a wide, deep pool encircled by boulders. Still no sign. This damn thing was a genius when it came to using rivers and streams. He took out one of his canteens and squatted to fill it in the pool, while he tried to put himself in the tiger's place and figure where it had gone.

I must have missed something, he thought, staring at his reflection wavering in the ripples made by the air escaping from the canteen. It must have turned off somewhere in that saw grass.

The ripples vanished as Coombes capped his canteen, and then he saw its head mirrored so clearly in the pool it seemed to be staring up at him from underwater instead of down from the boulder behind him. He whirled, shouldering the crossbow in the same instant the tiger roared, and that and the sight of its fangs and its luminous eyes, not serene now but narrowed in rage, unnerved him and he shot hastily, the arrow cracking off the rock beneath the tiger's paws. The beast crouched. It was going to spring! Coombes, staggering backward into the shallow part of the stream below the pool, pulled the crossbow's trigger again and again, and he was puzzled that no noise was coming from the weapon, for in his panic he'd forgotten it was a crossbow and not a rifle in his hands. He slipped on a mossy rock, his injured leg folding at the knee. As he crashed down, his thigh was jabbed by something sharp, a pointed rock or a honed piece of shale. He scrambled on all fours up the opposite bank, got to his feet, and ran as best he could, ran into the jungle, no thought in his head, no awareness that the tiger wasn't chasing him. He ran, quite simply, in blind animal fear, thrashing at branches and underbrush until, at last, his consciousness of himself returned and he stopped to regain his wind. He burned with shame. No one had seen him run, but no one had seen him freeze in Valesquez's tent, either. No one but himself, and that was one witness too many.

The jungle was still again, though the roar echoed in his inner ear. Like the roar the tiger had made on Black Grandfather Mountain. Warning. He realized then that the cat had intended not to kill him but only to drive him off, like a landowner evicting a trespasser. He cursed aloud the fate or power that had caused the tiger to come upon him when he was least prepared, to surprise him while he was filling a canteen, his back turned. If it had showed up half a minute earlier, he would have been ready. It seemed an injustice, for he had gone in pursuit of it stripped down to the barest essentials, practically weaponless, and alone and full of pain. He had earned the right, goddamn it, he had earned it. He felt terribly cheated.

And this sense of having suffered a grave wrong heightened when he reached into the belt quiver to draw another arrow and reload. All but one had spilled out when he'd tripped, and that one, under the force of his fall, had pierced the hide case and cracked above the barb. The others would be floating downstream now, lost, lost . . . He didn't deserve this . . . Hold on. He recalled that the stream was sluggish, practically no current. The arrows could not have floated far. He could go back and retrieve them, or at least one, just one; and if he didn't find any and that beast came back to snarl and roar in warning again, he would not run, he would stand his ground with his knife drawn . . . No. Got a better idea . . .

He drew the knife, took the roll of camouflage tape from his ruck, and bound the knife tightly to the fore end of the crossbow's stock. Got a few tricks left, you magnificent son of a bitch. As he worked, he felt a tingling in his fingertips, almost like frostbite. He rubbed them together to get the circulation going and finished up by smearing the blade with the venom in the leather pouch. He would stand his ground and force the tiger to spring on him. It would impale itself on the poisoned knife. He would die, but so would it, and slowly.

He started back toward the stream, hobbling, his outrage now replaced by the courage of despair.

He had gone only a short distance when he became aware of a new difficulty—he was having a hard time breathing. He paused, lowered his chin, and tried to suck air in, then threw his head back and spread his arms to expand his lungs. Far overhead, in the triple canopy, a bird called with a low hooting, like an owl's, only there were no owls in the jungle.

His breath was growing shorter, and his arms felt heavy. His legs as well—not heavy, but oddly stiff, as if he had a charley horse. And the tingling in his fingers had become a numbness. The canopy seemed to whirl, so he dropped his chin again, clutching for air. The ground whirled . . . *Lincoln, Lincoln . . .* No, *he* was spinning, not the ground, not the canopy . . . *What's that stuff that you've been drinkin' . . . ?* He dropped to his knees, then lay on his back and gagged. His hands ran down his trouser legs, and he felt, just barely felt with his numbed fingers, a tear in the left one, blood trickling down his thigh from where it had been punctured by the pointed rock. *Whiskey . . . wine . . . Oh, my God, it's . . .* Oh, my God . . . It wasn't a rock, or a piece of shale. *Turpentine.* He wanted to cry out a protest against this last joke fate had played on him, but he hadn't the breath for it—no, none. The canopy vanished and everything went black for an instant, the canopy reappeared but grew gradually dimmer, the myriad leaves and branches first, then the sunlight shining through them in dazzling pinpoints, growing fainter and fainter, like tiny electric lights on a dimmer switch.

Lincoln . . . Lincoln . . .

THEY HAD BEEN THREE, and now they were two. They moved along the stream bank, trying to assemble a narrative out of the tracks printed in the mud, the arrows they'd found floating slowly downcurrent. Teepee had put part of the story together after Han had followed Coombes' trail to the thicket where they discovered Jimmy Neville's dog tags, pieces of his uniform, a length of frayed rope, and—Han's most amazing feat of reading signs—a hank of the tiger's fur in a splintered branch lying on the ground. With much gesturing, he'd explained that the tiger had jumped onto the branch and clung to it, then fallen when it broke in two; and with frowns and shrugs, he declared that he could not understand why the tiger would do such a thing.

It was a mystery to Teepee as well, and so were the dog tags, the bloodied shreds of clothing. Remembering what Coombes had told him about the cat's diet, he figured it had dug up Neville's body, but when he and Han went to the grave, they found it undisturbed and no pawprints around it. For a while, they remained there in baffled silence, Han nervous about their nearness to the leper colony and signing for a cigarette, Teepee signing in response that he didn't smoke.

He decided to open the grave, and when he uncovered the rucksack and rifle only, tumblers in his mind fell into place and he unlocked the mystery, its solution leading him to ponder the greater mystery, eternal and insoluble, of the human mind and its capacities for evil. Sure, in the hierarchies of the wrongs man did to man, the killing of Father Pascal would have to be judged the greater, but when he thought of the men he had known who had risked and sometimes lost their lives to pull dead comrades from the battlefield, what Coombes had done with Neville's body seemed the worse outrage.

He took Han back to the thicket and said, "See what happened? He hung Jimmy up there for safekeeping until he was ready for him. He was going to use him as bait, but the tiger got here first. How do you figure a son of a bitch who'd do something like that?"

He didn't expect an answer and didn't get one. He picked up the dog tags, scraped them clean with his knife, and put them in his pocket, picturing as he did these things the tiger springing to clasp Jimmy in a brutal embrace. Gruesome, but not nearly as cruel as what Coombes had done. After all, the tiger didn't know it was devouring Jimmy Neville, son of Mr. and Mrs. Whoever Neville of Pensacola, Florida, who would grieve for him. It didn't know it had left Angel Valesquez's wife a widow, his children fatherless. It would have killed and eaten Albert Einstein, the Pope, the President, the Queen of England, Miss America, not out of malice, not because it had something against the theory of relativity or Roman Catholic doctrine or British policies in Northern Ireland, but simply because it was hungry. Did the President in his oval office know that there were creatures in the world who would see him as nothing more than a slice of baloney? Did the Queen in her royal palace? Did they know that no matter how brilliant or beautiful or important you are, sometimes you're just lunch?

Teepee had been musing on these matters when he and Han heard the tiger roar, from somewhere not very far off. That sound, no less terrifying for his having heard it before, had brought a sudden reversal in his new and kindlier feelings toward the tiger. He did not see himself as lunch, did not want to die, and so it was still an adversary; yet he did not hate it as he had before.

Han, rearmed with Neville's rifle, had taken the lead, studying every leaf and bent blade of grass. Covering him as he made his examinations, Teepee heard noises that because of their distance or softness had been beyond the range of his ears earlier—a single flap of a bird's wings, the scratching of an insect as it scuttled on the ground. He saw details to which he'd been blind; a leaf that would have looked a single shade of green showed subtle variations of color. He spotted an almost perfectly camouflaged lizard when it made the slightest movement of its tail. He thought that if he stayed at this long enough, he would be able to hear the trees growing and count the cells in their bark, and this amplification of his senses strangely exhilarated him, strangely because he knew it would not have been possible without the presence of the great cat.

The tracks had led them to a thicket of elephant grass, which they approached with the tensed curiosity of an ordnance disposal team approaching an armed booby trap. Teepee would have felt a lot more confident if his trigger finger and right hand hadn't been so sore. Shouldn't have punched him, he thought.

It had taken them a long time to creep through the grass. Afterward, they came upon the stream and found the bootprints and pawprints, the dropped arrows that spoke of some disaster but did not reveal its nature.

Han was now making a study of something he'd found across the stream. He pointed at a rock, then at another, up on the sloped bank. Teepee squinted and shook his head. Han took his wrist and pressed his finger against one of the rocks. He felt something damp and sticky, then licked his fingertip. He squinted at the rocks again and saw beads of blood, each bead no bigger than a pinhead.

"Jesus," he whispered to Han, "you've got microscopes for eyes."

Han continued his investigation and pointed at some marks in the mud, which revealed themselves to be handprints. Then he got down on all fours.

"Gotcha," said Teepee, still in an undertone. "He crawled up the bank."

Coombes' trail led into the bush, Han signing that he had been running. The tracks were distinct enough for Teepee to follow without help and to read their history: some fifty yards farther on, Coombes had stopped, then turned and backtracked toward the stream.

"Walking," Han said with his hands.

They found him a few minutes later, lying on his side between two enormous trees through which the sunlight fell in streaks slender as rain. Seeing no blood, nor any mark on him, Teepee at first thought he was unconscious, that he had collapsed from exhaustion.

"Coombes?" he said quietly, and nudged him with his foot. The body rolled over, as dead bodies do. Teepee looked down into the blue, still-staring eyes, their cold light extinguished, and at the partly open mouth, the lips curled back, and the ants crawling over his face.

"*Trung-si . . . ?*" asked Han.

"Like he'd say, dead as Moses," Teepee answered. "Look at this," he said, prying the crossbow from the rigored fingers. "Gave it a bayonet. He was going to take that thing on with a bayonet, the crazy—"

But he stopped, for he knew it had been not madness but pride. *Pride drove him,* he thought. *Me too. It was all for pride.*

Han bent low, cut the knife from the crossbow, removed the leather bag from Coombes' shirt pocket and then the quiver from his belt, the quiver torn at the bottom, a broken arrow sticking through it.

Teepee couldn't figure it out. Not a claw or tooth mark on him, not even a scratch. Like he'd died of natural causes, which, in these jungles, was the rarest death of all. He knelt down and felt Coombes' forehead. Hadn't been dead for long. Then he noticed a rip in one trouser leg, the cloth around it wet with blood. He widened the rip, exposing a puncture the diameter of a small finger and not even half an inch deep. Hardly a mortal wound.

He looked at Han and shrugged. The hillman drew the splintered arrow from the quiver and stuck its tip in the puncture wound. It fit perfectly. Then he performed an elaborate pantomime: Coombes running . . . Coombes falling . . . falling on the quiver . . . the arrow pricking him . . . Teepee watched the demonstration with bewilderment until Han held up the leather bag.

"I'll be goddamned, I'll be twice goddamned," he said, remembering what it contained and thinking: *Toxophile. Toxon (bow) + philos (love) = lover of the bow. Toxic, from the Latin, toxicus.* He reached down and pulled Coombes' dog tags from around his neck. "Snakebit, only he bit himself. I'll be goddamned."

EVEN WITH HAN'S HELP, it took a while to dig a grave so big. Teepee felt that he'd dug so many on this journey that he now qualified for a direct commission as a grave registration officer. When it was done, they rested for a while, ate the little that remained in Teepee's rucksack, then started back to search for whatever remained of Jimmy Neville. He would bury that if he could, then they would begin the long trek to base camp. He had worked out a sensible plan for the lepers. When he returned—and he was confident that he would, despite the odds—he would tell Captain Hightower about them and suggest that they be medevaced by helicopter to a leprosarium. He was fairly sure he could find the colony's location on a map. On the return journey, he would make careful notes of the terrain, the directions, the distances traveled.

This was what he was thinking of when he and Han came to the stream and saw the tiger drinking in the pool, drinking with its eyes raised so that it saw them as they stood arrested in midstride. It went right on lapping, as if it wasn't about to have its drink disturbed by two creatures as petty as they. Teepee was astonished by its size. With its forelegs bent as it drank, it looked as wide across the shoulders as Han was tall, the muscles defined with the sharpness of an anatomical drawing, and then its back arching toward its raised haunches, its spine hugged by two symmetrical ridges of muscle, each the thickness of a strong man's legs and twice the length—all in all, an assembly of power that was truly breathtaking: that is, Teepee could not breathe. And yet it was its beauty that captured and mesmerized him. The white whiskers, the white patches around the eyes, the texture of the fiery coat, the clean articulation of its stripes, bolting across its back. His first thought was: *It can kill me,* his second an amazed: *My God, it's beautiful!*—as if anything so obviously lethal could not possess beauty. Then, its thirst slaked, it raised its head almost languorously and glared at the two men with eyes so like those Teepee had seen in his nightmare—flame reflected in polished brass—that he wasn't entirely sure he had seen them in a dream. Its lips drew back, unsheathing its fangs, and it began to make a noise that was neither growl nor snarl and was certainly not a purr: a low, threatening rumble.

Teepee very slowly wriggled his right shoulder, to unsling his rifle, but Han tugged at his sleeve and shook his head emphatically: Don't try it. He'll be on you before you can aim and fire.

Now the tiger stepped into the stream and began to cross it with leisurely grace, making that baleful rumble. Han turned his head slightly to the side, bending at the waist in a kind of bow, and started to back away.

Teepee didn't move. Halting in midstream, its whole great length reflected in the jade waters, the tiger seemed affronted by his motionlessness and let out a snarl. Han hissed, gesturing to Teepee to do as he was: Don't look him in the eye; he'll think you're challenging him. But don't turn your back; he'll charge.

And so he dropped his gaze and bowed and walked slowly backward alongside Han, the tiger following them, never closing or widening the distance between them; and it came to him that they looked like two subjects leaving the presence of an emperor, humbled yet not humiliated in their acknowledgment of his sovereignty. At last, satisfied that it had established who was who, the cat gave a final hiss, wheeled, and was gone.

Teepee did not sit down; he fell. Han collapsed beside him, signing with a palm fluttered over his chest that his heart was pounding. Teepee wanted to say that his was too, but he wasn't yet capable of speech. He reached for one of his canteens, then remembered that both were empty, so he pulled a leaf from a bush, rolled it up, and chewed it until he worked up enough saliva to spit.

The two men sat for a while, allowing their terror to dissipate. Han was the first to stand. He made a jerky movement with one arm.

"Yeah, yeah," Teepee answered, rising. "We'd best get started."

He slung his rifle, shouldered his ruck. They weighed on him as heavily as before, yet he felt within himself the same lightness that had buoyed him as a kid when he exited the confessional, his sins acknowledged and absolved.

"Wasn't that something, Han? Weren't we lucky to see him like that? Up so close?" he asked, knowing, again, that he wouldn't receive an answer, knowing that they had been touched by more than mere luck. "Man, wasn't that just something?"

"Chung ta hay di," said Han, and, with his crossbow braced across the back of his neck, started off, T. P. Bledsoe following. Teepee couldn't wait to get back to camp and his friends. He had something to tell them.

A NOTE ABOUT THE AUTHOR

Philip Caputo was raised on the outskirts of Chicago.
After college he served with the Marines for three
years, including sixteen months in Vietnam, and then
spent six years as a foreign correspondent for the
Chicago *Tribune*. He was held hostage in Beirut in
1973, learning only upon release of his shored 1972
Pulitzer Prize for reporting on election fraud in
Chicago. Two years later he was wounded in Beirut
and, during his convalescence, completed the manu-
script for *A Rumor of War,* a Vietnam memoir that was
published while Caputo was in Moscow, back on as-
signment for the *Tribune*. In 1977 he left the paper and
turned to novels, of which he has written four, plus another memoir (*Means of Escape*). He lives in Connecticut with his wife, Leslie Blanchard Ware.